A Bard on the Pampas

A Story of Irish Migration to Argentina

by John Anthony Clancy

First published in 2025 by Immortalise
in Hackham, South Australia.
info@immortalise.com.au

ISBN: 978-1-7638310-2-5

Cover layout, editing and typesetting by Ben Morton

To the memory of the original Richard, 1854 to date and place of death unknown, who, I have been told, did make it to Australia.

A Word on Languages Used.

This novel includes words in Irish, Yola dialect, Spanish, and Guarani Indian. It also includes various incorrect spellings for some common words spoken by the Irish characters in Part I. As a boy during the 1950s, I remember some of the very old neighbours pronouncing words like those. The characters Malcolm and David Sutton intersperse their English with some Yola words, probably to add some colour. Richard and Malcolm use Spanish words at times, while they become familiar with the new language. Xiemen uses some Guarani words at times. It is possible that the original Charrúa Indian language was similar to Guarani. On my first use of a foreign word, I provide the meaning in italics, but not on subsequent use.

Acknowledgements

To Seamus Foley for his imaginative and lyrical poetic setting of certain prose passages.

To members of my family and my friends who provided suggestions and, where necessary, criticisms of early drafts of the novel.

To La Trobe University Library. Sincere thanks to La Trobe University Library, Bendigo Campus, for providing access to a public computer and for creating a peaceful, quiet, and inspiring environment that enable me to work on this novel. To the staff of Bendigo Library for the use of their computers. Also, for their being always ready and willing, with a smile, to assist me in matters of technology.

To Writers Victoria Service.

Contents

Part III. The Odyssey To Patagonia

Author's Note

This novel is based upon events which happened on the various sides of my Irish forebears during the past four hundred years. On the Clancy side during the later 1800s, a boy born out of wedlock and reared by my great grandparents, possible trouble with landlords and their agents, and resultant forced emigration of individuals. On my maternal side, the Mullallys, their staunch Jacobite loyalties, resultant dispossession, and forced departure from Ireland as Wild Geese. And the Barrons, once lords of Burnchurch Castle, County Kilkenny, were dispossessed by Oliver Cromwell. I have striven to weave together the various strands in this story.

PROLOGUE.

August 1852.

Castledown, County Kilkenny, Ireland.

The doctor turned his horse and trap into the lane. He led the horse into the lower haggard, tethering it to the sycamore tree. He looked at the pond at the bottom of the lane. No sign of infection there, normal in colour. His gaze fell on the small farmhouse in the field, about twenty yards behind the pond, bushes separating field and pond. The original builders had had the foresight to build the house on a level patch of ground. The slight slope leading down to the fence could prevent it from flooding. The doctor walked into the field, halting to inspect the house, a solid building, about fifty years of age, typical of small farmers.

The walls were made of mud, with a foundation of stone, the roof thatched with straw. A fresh coat of whitewash had been applied to its exterior, a precaution against famine fever. A single chimney adorned the roof. The doctor's knock was answered by footsteps. A woman slowly opened the door. She was of medium stature, probably in her early thirties, of pretty countenance, but marred by worry. She wore a paisley frock, complemented by a lace cap on her shoulder-length brown hair, a linen apron, and rawhide slippers on her feet.

"Come in, doctor," she said, ushering him into the kitchen. Her own personal care and cleanliness were reflected by the state of that room. The two windows, though small, had plain linen curtains. The clay floor was clean, aided by a couple of rush mats. The presence of the chimney resulted in a relatively bright and airy habitat. All of this could be advantageous to a sick patient.

With trepidation, she recounted the recent event, "Sure, and didn't the illness come on the boy last night, when he began to suffer from terrible stomach pains and mess himself. This became worse as the night went by. My husband kept giving him cups of water. He stayed up until the boy fell asleep. When I was up early lighting the fire, I heard him vomiting onto the floor. Then he kept trying to be sick, but was not able. Sure, I cleaned up all that, while he lay withered away with his head on the pillow. He found it difficult to keep down any water. What really puts the fear in me, doctor, was that as the morning went by his eyes sank deeper. His last attack of vomiting happened about half an hour ago. At least, he is sleeping now."

The doctor queried. "Mrs. Barron, you say that you and your husband held water to him. Did either of you at any time touch his skin?"

Fearfully rubbing her face, the woman replied. "No, doctor. We were both that much feared of catching a fever that we wore linen gloves, and covered our faces with scarves. Did we do wrong?"

"No. You did the correct thing. I will do the same. We will wake him gently. Can you then go and fetch your husband, if he is out working close by."

Both doctor and woman went into the bedroom situated to the right of the kitchen. The only furnishings were a chair and a small bed, on which lay a small boy with a deep white pallor. Having woken him, the doctor indicated that the woman could leave. Mairead Barron bolted from the house, returning a few minutes later with her husband, Andrew. Taller than his wife, and probably in his late thirties, he had brown hair, and was clean shaven except for some stubble on his chin. His somewhat cumbersome movements, and his garb of striped cotton shirt, wide and shabby trousers, and muddied boots, typified the small farmer class. The husband collapsed into the upright chair, the wife into the wicker chair. Neither exchanged words nor glances.

The doctor's reappearance interrupted their troubled thoughts. He remained standing, like an Old Testament messenger bearing devastating news. "I cannot be sure, but I think it could be cholera." A look of sheer terror spread across husband's and wife's faces. Cholera! that deadly pandemic had invaded Ireland during the black year of 1849, mowing down in death up to half of those stricken, like the clusters of corn before the scythe of the reaper. Its course from infection to death could be terrifyingly rapid, often as little from one to three days.

The doctor sensed their terror, "I repeat that I cannot be certain. Am I correct in thinking that so far there has not been any bad watery diarrhoea. You know what I mean by that?"

Husband and wife nodded. They were both thinking not just about the possible death of the boy, but the risk of contagion to themselves and their other two children. The doctor continued, "I did see what could turn into some blue patches on the boy's skin, but as yet no wrinkling of skin, often a sign of bad cholera.."

Andrew Barron, speaking for the first time, almost whispered. "But what can we or you do to stop the sickness getting worse?"

The doctor answered. "I have brought with me some laudanum, and some whiskey. These I will mix with water and give them to the boy, leaving you enough for the next few days. Do you have clean, pure water?"

Andrew replied. "Since the beginning of all these terrible fevers, we have got all our drinking and cooking water from the pump of our good neighbours the Shanahans up the lane."

"Very good, Mr. Barron. I am also asking you to mix these substances for both the boy and for yourselves. Each hour from now, give him smaller portions of that laudanum and whiskey mixture. I will give him a pill of opium from this bottle for the vomiting. You give him one every hour until it may stop."

The doctor continued, "You, man, can continue your work outside, but one of you must always remain in the house. Do you have any other children?"

Andrew answered. "His older brother Patrick is with the Shanahans, helping them with the harvest. He has been there for the past four days and nights. They are a childless couple, his god parents."

The doctor advised. "One of you must go to them immediately. Tell them, but not your son, what has happened. It could be a Godsend that he has been with them, because I don't think that he has become stricken. Is there another child?"

Mairead answered. "Only our one-year-old daughter. She sleeps in our room. She has not been near the sick boy for two days."

"Good, Mrs. Barron, but before I leave. I will look at her." Mairead led the doctor to the bedroom on the left. A more relaxed look came from the doctor as he examined the child. "There is no sign of cholera with her. Keep her warm, woman, and maybe mix a little whiskey in her milk." The doctor placed his hat on his head. "Who knows what may happen to the boy. Ye should hope and pray for the best, but prepare yourselves for the worst. Please remember to give him his medicine as I instructed." The doctor left the house, untied his horse, and departed.

While he drove back to Kilcolman, he ruminated about how persistent epidemics could be. The worst of the cholera epidemic had passed in Ireland in 1849, but sporadic outbreaks still occurred. The grim reaper was always capable of striking unexpectedly on defenceless prey.

Mairead Barron spoke, "I told Mrs. Shanahan from her gate about the boy's illness. Patrick was out in the corn fields with the men. She said that they would be only too happy to *kape* (keep) him as long as needed, and, if we are not careful, they will kape him forever. The *spailpin* (itinerant workman) from Tipperary joins with them during the evenings. Herself and her husband, and especially our boy, love to hear his tales of the old times. She said that Patrick sings to them, and hasn't God blessed him with a beautiful voice for a seven-year-old." Husband and wife were sitting by the fire. The sick boy was asleep, following the doses of laudanum and whiskey. The wife's voice and mood underwent a sudden and rather angry change. "How did that boy end up getting cholera?"

The husband replied. "Maybe not having his brother with him might have led to it. He looks after him, kapes an eye on him. Richard, a friendly boy, might have ended up talking to some of the people of the roads. One of them could have given it to him."

Mairead scowled. "Being a friendly boy could get him into bad trouble, if he survives. His skin is turning to blue in places. God preserve us all if we have been struck by this killer plague."

Andrew replied. "I will lock the gate leading into the roadside. No neighbours, passers-by, evicted people, tinkers, or beggars must enter our yard. We can only wait and see what God brings us."

Silence.

Mairead Barron slowly expressed her thoughts. "You know, if God were to take him, mightn't it be for the better. He is only five years of age. He will go straight to the angels."

"How can you say that, *A Bhean* (wife)?"

"Listen, *A Fhear* (husband), What kind of life lies ahead for him? He will always carry the mark of his birth. Our eldest son will take over this farm and carry your name. What future now lies in this country for second and other sons? Labourers in Ireland or England or America, become a traitor policeman in Ireland. America, coffin ships, emigrants dying in their thousands, in agony and among strangers." Mairead stood up, opened the door, cautiously looked into the bedroom, and returned. "He is sound asleep. His breathing seems to be better. Yet, if he passes away, doesn't he go surrounded by his family, with all love and care. What more could we have given him?"

Her husband ventured to suggest. "Then let us pray a turn of the rosary, the joyful mysteries. Pray for his recovery or, if it be God's will, for his painless passing."

They had reached the middle of the fourth decade when the clip-clop sound of a horse's hoofs echoed from the lane. Andrew waited until the footsteps paused. On opening the door, his eyes took a couple of moments to focus on the sight which confronted him.

Standing at the front door was a handsome young man in about his early thirties, with dark brown hair and of medium height and build. His healthy features, tweed jacket, shirt, tie and trousers to match suggested that he was of the 'strong' (land owning) farmer or even minor gentry class. The young man removed his hat and his leather gloves, in order to shake the hand of the husband. He silently accepted the chair offered to him to kneel for the rosary. On reaching the fifth decade, Andrew indicated to him that he should lead it.

Seated on his chair, half looking at the visitor, Andrew asked,

"Master Drummond. Why have you come? What did you find out?"

The visitor answered nervously. "I had been to Kilcolman. When I had reached the outskirts, I met the doctor, who told me about the boy's illness. We discussed a few ways in which we would be able to help him – food, drink, care, nursing, I immediately, returned to the town, and bought some things. They are outside in my trap. Please do not think of these things as charity, but instead as medicines for the boy, and for your use as well, as the doctor advised."

Mairead spoke, "Sure, haven't we talked about this terrible situation. We feel that, if the good Lord so wills it, the boy may peacefully pass to him. I will kape giving him the doctor's medicine. However, I cannot work miracles. Besides, we have to think of our two, I mean our other two children. God protect us that we should lose them or that they be left as orphans."

A short silence.

Gaining some courage, the visitor declared, "I feel a natural responsibility towards the sick boy. I cannot watch or hear of him slipping away without doing all I can to save him."

Mairead queried, "How can you do that, Sir?"

"I have considered all your worries and fears, good woman. On the doctor's recommendation, I drove to the house of a nurse who lives on the other side of Kilcolman, Mrs. Alicia Marshall. She has nursed children in the workhouse suffering from cholera, and has saved most of them from death. The doctor and Mrs. Marshall hope that caring for a child in this clean and airy house could well save the boy's life."

"So. this woman works in the workhouse," Mairead interjected.

The visitor replied, "No, not just there, but wherever her healing hands are needed. She has saved children in the cabins, the farmhouses, even in the mansions of the gentry."

Pausing a moment to let his words sink in, and to win over the sceptical wife, the young man pressed his argument further. "Mrs.

Marshall has on occasions used herbal medicines to treat cholera, as well as treatments advised by Dr. Collis, Ireland's leading surgeon during the cholera epidemics of twenty years ago. Her husband tenants a farm of forty acres. They are a childless couple. That might explain why she feels her calling is to nurse sick children."

Encouraged by his argument, Andrew spoke. "We are blest to have such a skilled doctor, and now an able nurse, to help us. How could we say no to your offer?" His wife moved from her chair to stroke the fire, speaking. "Yes, sure we must do all we can to save him."

The visitor suddenly seemed on edge. He coughed twice, as if struggling to release his next words.

"Are you alright, sir?" Andrew enquired. Reassured, the visitor succeeded in speaking again.

"Yes, Thank you. There is one more thing which I must tell you now. Mrs. Marshall, is not of our faith. She is a Protestant, a member of the Church of Ireland."

Mairead declared, "A Protestant woman nursing our boy in our own house!"

Looking at her directly for the first time, the visitor continued. "I have heard from reliable people that this nurse's own faith does not interfere with her work or care. She treats every child equally, Catholic, Protestant, even one or two Jews whom she has cured. She shows great respect for Catholic children, their families, and their religious objects."

Mairead persisted. "But she is still a Protestant."

Andrew Barron, asserting himself as the master of the house, stood up, "While we argue about all this, a boy lies maybe dying in that room. During the past five years, we all have witnessed acts of goodness, charity, and real Christianity performed by Catholic and Protestant alike. Our own landlord, the Protestant Marquis of Ormond, has been a great example of this. It is decided. Mrs. Alicia Marshall will nurse the boy back to health, or, if it be the will of God, to a peaceful end."

Rising from her chair, Mairead enquired, "Where would this nursing woman be now?"

The visitor replied, "She is outside in the trap." Finally accepting the inevitable, she slowly spoke,

"Please bring her inside."

The visitor exited, and walked to the trap. He explained to the nurse Mairead Barron's fatalistic attitude. The nurse was puzzled.

"But why? He is their son. Surely, she does not want to see him die an agonising and slow death."

"Mrs. Marshall, I need to tell you that since the Great Famine a certain fatalism has come to dominate Irish Catholicism. They regard it as the hand of God at work, as the inevitable." The nurse paused to consider.

"Well, Walter, should I go in?"

"You must, Mrs. Marshall. Young Richard is a beautiful child. We cannot just let him suffer and die. And, believe me, Andrew

Barron is the master of this house. He loves his son dearly. If Richard dies, he will be absolutely devastated."

"Then, Walter, we are going in."

The arrival of the nurse imbued a new atmosphere into the kitchen. Mrs. Marshall's face presented a fresh and somewhat glowing pallor, a friendly and optimistic smile, complemented by her apparel. She wore an ankle length blue and white dress, a hand knitted light cardigan and an apron. Her leather shoes and woollen stockings were not atypical of members of her religion and social class. Her flaxen hair was bound by a headscarf. On entering the kitchen, she removed her woollen gloves, offering her right hand to husband and wife. Andrew then led the three adults to chairs.

With typical Protestant efficiency Alicia Marshall took charge of the situation. "As you have been told, I have been recommended by your doctor. I have saved the lives of many of the children stricken with cholera in the workhouse and in their own homes, and before that a number who were struck down with famine fever. Now, I have succeeded in this only when my nursing was not interfered with. In this house, if I am to save your boy, I must be free to do as I see fit, and to ask you to help me in my work where necessary. Also, I will ask you to keep certain rules for your own health and safety and those of your other children. Is all that alright to you both?"

Andrew immediately responded. "Yes, of course. You are the only nurse in this house."

His wife, momentarily delaying, stated, "Well, if it has to be so, so be it. I will not get in the way of your good work."

Satisfied, the nurse continued, "Firstly, I must look at this boy." She placed a netted face mask on her face, and two linen gloves on her hands.

The trio of adults remained seated in silence in the kitchen. After about five minutes, the nurse re-emerged and sat down. "The boy has been looked after well since the doctor's visit. There are signs of diarrhoea, but that may slow as he continues with his medicine. The skin shows blue patches, but no signs of wrinkling. The eyes are sunken in. I feel that we are at the point where this illness could go either way. Swift action by us now may help to better things. Now, this is my final condition. I see that ye have a second bedroom where, I understand, you and your baby sleep. I have to request that, for your own safety, ye live there for the next few days. Ye can of course leave the house to continue your tasks outside. I will live in the kitchen, and I can sleep in the settle bed. I will call for your help when and only when I need it, or if his condition worsens and it looks as if death is near."

"And where are we to have our meals?" interjected Mairead.

"I will cook all meals for the boy and for yourselves. I will use this fresh food, and I will serve them to ye in your room. Now, do I have your word that this is alright with you both?"

Andrew replied, "Yes, indeed it is."

Mairead nodded.

The nurse now addressed the visitor, "Walter, you are now free to leave. Thank you for bringing me here. We will now begin our tasks to try and save the life of this lovely child."

The visitor requested, "Before I leave, can I please see the boy? I would like to spend a couple of minutes in his room. I can sit by the window, away from him."

"It would not be for the best," replied the nurse.

Andrew Barron intervened. "We would like him to do this. God only knows what may happen to the child during the next few days, or even hours."

"Very well, sir," said the nurse, "but please put on your leather gloves, and open the window. We three will now begin our preparations."

The sick room with its small window was quite dark, although its whitewashed walls granted it a little light. A couple of religious objects adorned its sparse walls. The two bed sheets betrayed evidence of vomiting and excrement. The sparseness of the room had its counterpart in the spectacle of the sick boy, lying on the bed, clinging on to life. His pallor matched the colour of the whitewashed walls. The sweat on his hair and face reflected the dampness of the bedroom. Patches of blue were noticeable on the exposed parts of his body, his arms, his lower legs, his neck. On his awakening, his sunken eyes displayed a fear and pain. It was if his upper torso was held in a vice. He leaned over to the left of his bed, retching once, twice, a third time.

Within seconds, the strange woman with a netting over her face was at the boy's side. Holding his left arm, her other hand pressed against his stomach. Her firm but yet gentle pressure began to force up the contents. She lifted the basin to his mouth, into which he vomited three times. The boy followed this with retching twice again, after which he sank his head back to the pillow. One hand brought a glass of pure water to his lips, the other hand bringing his head forward to drink. The boy emptied the glass, feeling a sense of relief in his stomach. The woman left the room. Sleep began to descend upon him. But wait! Who was sitting by the window? A handsome young man with dark brown hair. His hands were joined, as if praying. Was he a priest? The boy moved his upper body up and down, looking around him, frantically gripping the sheets. Where was he? In the fever hospital? In the workhouse? In a stranger's house? Where were his parents and his brother? He tried to sit up. He felt the hands of the strange man gently touching his upper arms and easing him back onto his pillow, followed by a gentle pat on his head. But the boy could hold his eyes open no longer. He drifted away to an exhausted slumber. Shortly afterwards the solace of sleep had enveloped him.

The various ministrations were underway. The visiting gentleman had departed silently. On emerging from the bedroom, he had bowed slightly to the wife and the nurse. However, the wife could swear that she had noticed tears in his eyes. Well did she understand the reason why. If he had spoken to her husband before he boarded his trap, the latter had not said anything to her.

Meanwhile, nurse and woman continued their ministrations. Initially the nurse had stuped the boy's body with flannels wrung out in a mixture of hot water and whiskey. She had dressed him in a fresh night shirt, and fresh linen had been laid on his bed, together with a blanket. The wife had, upon the nurse's instructions, poured hot water into a few bottles, which were placed on the boy's body, together with a hot brick wrapped in brown paper, and placed upon his stomach. Finally, both women prepared a poultice consisting of flour, moistened with whiskey, which the nurse placed on the pit of his stomach. All of these might help in the battle against the potentially fatal disease.

On the nurse's advice, the man and his wife had taken a walk up the lane to their neighbours' field. The wife's initial sullen mood and petulance had improved somewhat, aided by her husband's reminder that they could look forward to some nutritious meals of meat, vegetables and potatoes cooked and served by the nurse.

Man and wife were met at the door of their house by the nurse, her expression optimistic. "He is sleeping now and is not vomiting as much. He is also holding down the water better, and has started taking some food. I have given him some small pieces of apple, mixed with water and sugar. There has been no more diarrhoea. I feel that all that we did for him is helping. However, it is too early yet to say how things will turn out. You may now go to your work outside the house or inside your room. I will prepare dinner now for all of us and I will join you for it."

The following day, the second full day of the boy's illness, his condition showed some improvement. If he was still in some danger or succumbing to death, the nurse did not reveal it. Mairead Barron worked on knitting a warm garment for the boy, while Andrew absorbed himself in tasks on the farm and in the yard and haggard. As far as he could make out, there was no sign of blight on his potatoes. However, he had learned during the recent years, that it could swoop down like an eagle, and devastate all that lay in its path. Nonetheless, this fine and warm summer promised a good yield of wheat, barley, and oats. Their cows were yielding good supplies of milk from the farmers' rich and green pastures.

On the morning of the next day, husband and wife were met by the nurse in the kitchen. Her face was tired and drawn, betraying a troubled night. "The child did not have a good night. The signs of cholera are decreasing, but he developed a fever during the night. This is not uncommon among children suffering from cholera, famine fever, and other epidemics. Such fevers are caused usually by dehydration, and he did vomit a few times around midnight. He indicated to me, by his touching the sweat on his forehead and head and by whining, that he was in severe pain. So, I prepared one of my herbal mixtures to help with it. I also bathed his head and forehead with cold water." The nurse touched Mairead gently on the arm. "After a couple of hours of this treatment, his fever broke. I think he must have also had a bad nightmare. He woke in terror, trying to speak words which sound like 'the man with the spear.' But now he's sleeping peacefully. I am pleased to say that his eyes are returning to their normal position. You may both go and have a quick look at him, but please do not wake him. As for myself, I am very tired after the night. Would you allow me, please, to take my ease in your bed for an hour or two?" To Mairead, "You can move back into your kitchen again. But please do wake me if the boy wakes up and sounds as if he needs anything. I do not think that we are out of the dark forest yet."

Taking the nurse's hand in her own, the wife consented.

It had begun like a beautiful vision. Richard was walking towards his family's small orchard, only to behold its wooden gate replaced by two gates of gleaming crystal. On entering, he became aware that it was magnified and transformed into an exquisite garden. Flowers of beautiful colours provided a carpet, bluebells, carnations, red and pink roses with no thorns, and other lovely unknown flowers, all interspersed with paths of verdant green grass. A few cuddly bunny rabbits played with some equally cuddly lambs and puppies. He collected a rabbit in his arms, stroking his silky brown and white fur. A couple of small trees provided shade from the summer sun. The multi-coloured birds of blue, yellow, ochre, pink, sang melodies which floated up to heaven. A small fountain gurgled with crystal-clear water. In the middle of the garden stood a tree, from whose branches juicy apples and apple blossoms hung. By its side was a very handsome bronze skinned young man clad in a loin cloth. He indicated a hammock tied to the apple tree. Feeling tired, Richard climbed into it and, inhaling the scent of the flowers and the trees, drifted away to sleep.

Still in his dream, Richard woke shivering. The sun was hidden by some dark clouds. No bird sang. The rabbits, lambs and puppies crouched in the grass as if in fear of an enemy. He felt a throbbing pain in his head and a parched throat. On reaching the fountain, he found that its water had turned into blood. Attempting to take an apple from the tree, the bronze skinned man, whose face had now become dark, cruel and terrifying, spear in his hand, and now clad in a tunic and headdress, raised his hand in a forbidding gesture. "This is the tree of life. No one can eat its fruit. If you eat it, you will die." He raised his spear. Terrified, Richard ran towards the gate. He must escape.

The bronze-skinned man chased him. But he could not find the gate. Maybe the spear held poison, which would kill him. Richard tried to scream, but his voice made only a whine.

He woke up, his face and body dripping with sweat. The candle by his bed was lighted. The netted woman began to wash his face. Her gloved hands were soft. "*Ashtore,* (my dear), it was only a dream, but a bad one. You are safe in this house, in your own room, and your parents are here too. Drink this now."

Richard took the long draught of the apple flavoured water, his voice still murmuring the word "man with the spear." The netted woman continued to comfort him, assuring him that there were no such men in the house, nor in Ireland. She changed his pillow, and sleep enfolded his young body.

As the morning progressed, the wife began to assume her role as mistress of her own kitchen. On occasions she was relieved to hear that the boy was taking long regular breaths, the sign of deep and untroubled slumber. By mid-morning the nurse awoke. Both women worked together as partners preparing the usual ministrations for the boy. Over the previous couple of days, the nurse's efficient but cheerful manner had had a positive effect on the wife. She explained. "Cholera is a disease which ravages our and other lands every few years. Although it invaded Ireland four years ago, it had little to do with the Famine." Nonetheless the nurse continued her embargo on husband or wife entering the sick room. Andrew Barron regarded this as a good sign, because it indicated that the boy was not approaching death's door, soothing his wife with this belief.

From the afternoon of the day following, the boy appeared to be on the road to recovery. There was still some diarrhoea, and he was still weak and lethargic. However, the medicines, the nutritious meals, the constant drinks mixed by the nurse, her care of the patient, and the ministrations prepared by both women, all seemed to have warded off a possible death. Mrs. Marshall informed the parents that this path to recovery was fairly typical of child patients. On the fourth day she explained further. "Cholera usually runs its course within two to seven days. We are now on the fourth full day of the boy's illness, and I do feel that he is recovering. If it is alright with you, I will remain here for three more days, in case things change. Would you have something in which to drive me home then, please?"

"Only a humble horse and cart, but quite comfortable."

"That will be fine. You will also find out where I live. But please promise me that, if the boy should become ill again, you will return for me. In a couple of days time, it will be safe for one of us to go and collect your eldest son. I would like to meet him and hear him sing."

"That is provided his godparents agree to let him go."

The sixth day since the cholera had struck was met with an increasing sense of relief in the household. Mairead, now reinstated in her kitchen was knitting by the fire. The balmy warmth of the late summer afternoon had caused her to nod off. She heard Richard's bedroom door opening. Mairead sat up with a start. Emerging from that room was the boy, bleary eyed, his steps slow and tentative like a sleep walker. Mairead called gently "Richard, *Ashtore*, I am here." His pace quickened slightly as he walked towards her. She arose from her chair, swept down, collected the boy in her arms, placed him on her lap, whispering endearments in Irish. Richard felt safe, but somewhat amazed. As far back as his young memory would allow, he could not recall his mother every having shown him such deep affection. The sight of this five-year-old helpless child, his clinging to her, his rescue from the jaws of death, had brought about a form of metamorphosis in Mairead. Irrespective of his flawed and scandalous birth, he was a beautiful child who desperately needed maternal love. From now on she would try to fulfil the role as a mother, and not just as a foster mother, and to treat him the same as she treated her own two beloved children.

The nurse had been persuaded to remain for one extra day. Andrew Barron had decided that a small evening celebratory gathering should take place, at which she would be the guest of honour. Mrs. Marshall had agreed to this on the strict understanding that she would decide how much of the gathering Richard could attend. The Shanahans were invited, as well as the *spailpin* James

Gleeson of Tipperary. Mairead, now fully reinstated as queen of her kitchen, prepared an appetising meal of meat, potatoes, and vegetables, while the nurse's offer to prepare a dessert of apple baked in pastry and served with cream from the cow had been graciously accepted.

In deference to the nurse's religion, the dinner was preceded only by saying of the Lord's Prayer. But Andrew Barron thanked God for the miracle worked by the good nurse, for the good man who had found her and had brought the provisions which had aided the boy's recovery. Andrew's words of thanks then moved to the Great Famine which had finally passed.

Richard ate heartily. When the meal ended and tea was being served, Mrs. Marshall suggested that a sleep would do him good.

It had been decided by the Barrons that the small celebration would be a low-key affair, to be held in front of the house, and not a loud *seisiún* (musical session). A few other neighbours had also been invited. Andrew served whiskey to the menfolk, while the nurse and Mairead deigned to accept one glass of sherry each. There was still about an hour of daylight left for some quiet singing, story-telling, and camaraderie.

Mr. Thomas Shanahan played a few tunes on his tin whistle. James Gleeson related a couple of stories from the better days. However, it was young Patrick, Andrew's and Mairead's pride and joy, who entranced the audience with his pure boy soprano voice. One of the neighbours remarked that even the birds in the neighbouring trees had lapsed into silence, unable to compete with it. Mairead

Barron, practical as ever, pointed out that since the advent of the terrible time the birds had ceased to inhabit or sing in those trees anyway. Nonetheless, Patrick's rendition of two songs learned from the *spailpin*, partly in the old disappearing Irish language, evoked among the adults a profound nostalgia for their old world which was vanishing before their very eyes. The disappearing Gaelic Ireland, despite its poverty, privations, and persecution, had bound families and communities together. The Great Famine had partly sounded its death knell.

Richard woke to the sounds of beautiful singing and a flute playing. Maybe he had died and was in heaven. He was not afraid. The singer, probably an angel, was singing in a strange language. He had heard once that the angels sang in Latin, but it did not sound like the Latin of the Mass. Gradually his eyes took in his surroundings. No, he was not in heaven, but in his room and comfortable bed. That was his brother Patrick singing outside the house. He would ask Patrick later about the language, although Patrick would call him a real *amadán* (idiot) for mistaking him for an angel. For now, he wished to sleep some more. He said his prayers and drifted once more into oblivion.

Andrew Barron drove Mrs. Marshall the four miles to Kilcolman town. For some of the journey they talked about their lives on their respective farms. The nurse was puzzled, however, by Walter Drummond's deep concern for the boy. Also, why had he not been invited to the dinner and celebration held the previous evening? The likely reason was that the Barrons had felt that Drummond, a 'strong' farmer with ninety acres of prime land, would have felt somewhat uncomfortable in their relatively humble surroundings.

"Andrew, for how long has your family lived in Castledown?"

He replied, "We are of Norman stock. My branch was originally lords of Burnchurch castle. We supported King Charles I in the English Civil War. The result was that we were dispossessed by Oliver Cromwell. We pinned our hopes to regain our castle and lands by fighting for King James II at the Boyne, Aughrim, and during the terrible Siege of Limerick. After that two Barron brothers crossed over from Limerick to east Tipperary. The Barron name made it easier for them to lease land there. I believe that around 1750 my great grandfather headed down from there to Castledown and leased our present farm from the Marquis of Ormond. He is an excellent landlord, so we always strive to remain on good terms with him and with his agents."

Mrs. Marshall now carefully asked,

"And the Drummond family, Andrew. What is your connection with them?"

Andrew seemed to hesitate, "Yes, the Drummonds. The horses are the connection. My father Patrick Barron had dealings with Walter's father."

"What is or was his name, Andrew?"

"His name was... R.. R.. Robert Drummond, I am sure." There was a sudden shift in Andrew's countenance. It was as if a shadow suddenly disappeared from his face. "Isn't the day turning out glorious now, Mrs. Marshall?"

By now they had almost reached her home. Andrew, ever the gentleman, assisted her down from the cart. His sincere and profuse thanks for what he described as the miracle cure echoed through Alice Marshall's mind for the remainder of the day.

Andrew spoke to his horse on the way home.

"Pooka, I see a promising harvest of cereal and grain crops. But, think back to the Famine years. The battering rams at the cabin doors. The clearances of the cottiers, thrown to the mercy of famine, fever, freezing winter cold, forced emigration on coffin ships. The recovery of my beloved boy Richard fills me with hope. He was saved by the miracle-working nurse. We too must nurse our beloved land back from almost certain death to a brighter future. But, we must learn from our mistakes. The Famine, *buiochas le Dia* (Thanks to God) is past. But, Ireland can no longer depend upon only one crop. Division and sub-letting of farms, early marriages, and abundance of children which follow. All these must become things of the past, Pooka. The consequences of the Great Famine will last for generations."

PART I.

THE DISPOSSESSED

Chapter 1.

Cortes Leads the Expedition.

A spring day in 1855.

Two boys aged eight and ten were availing of the benevolent sunshine to walk through the wet grass, clad in rough shirts, home-knitted jumpers, home-crafted trousers, and broken boots a couple of sizes too big for them. There would be none of the summer's abundance of nature which could appease their periodic attacks of hunger, such as crab apples, damsons, vetches, and sometimes mushrooms. But that was a minor consideration. The long, dreary, harsh winter had passed, and spring promised more wanderings and explorations.

Patrick and Richard had left their own farm and crossed into the fields of Mr. Kennedy, the new tenant. The previous tenant, the 'strong' farmer Mr. Townsend of Townsend Hall, had terminated his lease on his 150 acres the previous year. Various reasons were given, mainly his generosity to his neighbours during the Famine, some resultant debts, and his own wish to retire due to failing health. Of his three sons, the eldest had been ordained a priest, the second son had become a solicitor, and the third son a policeman. During Mr. Townsend's tenancy, the Barron boys had always been welcome to wander in his fields. The Kennedys were less welcoming. Accordingly, Patrick and Richard were advised by their parents to keep close to hedges and ditches. However, both boys were in an adventurous mood, and today they wished to explore further afield.

The two explorers reached a thick and rather high ditch, the boundary between the Kennedy farm and the estate of Captain Henry Saunders. The latter leased around a third of his lands to small farmers and cottiers, utilising the rest for mixed farming and the breeding of horses. Patrick and Richard looked at each other. Their father had always forbidden them to cross over to the Saunders' lands, but the spirit of adventure was taking hold.

"Pretend that we are Herman Cortes and his Spanish *conquistadores* (conquerors)," exclaimed Patrick. "We have reached the walls of the Aztec capital city of Mexico and we have to get through to it. You are going to be my lieutenant, Gonzalo de Sandoval. There must be some opening somewhere in this great wall."

Walking in front of the fence, Richard spotted a hole ascending upwards at an angle. Cortes declared, "I, Cortes, will lead the way. Soldiers, place your hand just above your eyes, to protect them from Aztec arrows."

The two boys were paying heed to their mother's advice to be especially careful of thorns and briar bushes. Having reached the top of the fortification, the *conquistadores* carefully made their way down to the bottom.

Cortes and his band moved cautiously towards an oval shaped grove of furze bushes. Inside this grove they discovered ten bases about six yards apart. Each base consisted of stones, gravel, clay and wood, measuring about four yards by four yards. What could they be? Sandoval began to feel a growing unease. "Patrick. Is this an ancient fairy *ráth* (fort)? I am scared of fairies. They might come out, attack and even kidnap us."

"I am not Patrick, remember. *Conquistadores* do not become scared. Besides, fairies only come out at night. Sandoval, look, some things are scattered on the ground. We might even find some Aztec gold." The *conquistadores'* search revealed a small piece of earthenware plate, a wooden comb, and a fragment of a clay pipe. But look! Cortes had found some gold, a half penny showing the young Queen's head. "This is no fairy *ráth*, lieutenant. It is a place where people have lived years ago. Soldiers, we must explore further."

About fifty yards beyond the furze bush grove the *conquistadores* could see a large field of grass, enclosed by a wooden railing. In the field was a pastoral scene of sheep grazing peacefully, some cows, and a few horses. The Spanish soldiers' eyes scanned the plains for Aztec soldiers, or a procession bearing Montezuma, the emperor. To the right side of the railing Cortes identified a grove of trees about two hundred yards away.

"Men, look, there is a forest. There may be treasures there." Approaching it tentatively, he and his lieutenant came across about twenty mounds of clay, roughly a yard apart. The majority were simple clay mounds, most of them grassed over. However, six of them contained crosses on their surfaces formed out of small stones, while three of them had slabs of stone. Cortes's gaze moved towards the sun. "You know, my men, I think we could be in a graveyard."

His lieutenant looked at him in horror, "How do you know?" Patrick replied, "All these mounds face the same direction, to the rising sun." Richard, discarding his identity as Lieutenant de Sandoval, pleaded, "Then let us get out of here. I am scared of graveyards."

"We play handball against the gable end of Castledown's *auld* (old) chapel, beside the graveyard." Patrick laughed.

"That is different," Richard pleaded. "There are headstones in it and our grandparents are buried there. Please, let us go."

A sobbing sound emanated from the grove of trees. Richard, turning a deadly white, cried out in terror, "It's one the dead people crying." As if in answer to the sobbing, a distant wail followed.

Patrick cried, "That is the wail of the *banshee* (fairy woman). Quick! Let's run." Holding hands, the two terrified boys galloped like young Spanish steeds out through the furze grove. They scaled the fence, not worrying about thorns and briars, and jumped to the other side.

Without pausing for breath, the two intrepid *conquistadores* continued their gallop through the middle of two of Mr. Kennedy's fields, stopping only when exhaustion had overtaken them. It was then that Richard became aware of blood dripping from his face, and scratches on Patrick's face. Patrick plucked some wet grass, applied it to his brother's face, and stemmed the flow. "Come on, let's get home quickly." Resuming their run, although less frantically, they slowed their pace only when they had reached their own fields. Patrick noticed that his jumper was torn. His mother would murder him.

Andrew and Mairead Barron and Philip Keating were enjoying an after-dinner cup of tea. Philip's wife had died three years previously. His daughter Alice was Richard's godmother. She had been a great friend of his mother Catherine Barron, and had stood by her friend during all the scandal and denouncements prior to and after Richard's birth. Alice had married a small farmer and had moved some miles away. She had requested of her father that he should act as a new god-parent to Richard, a task which he took on willingly. Philip Keating had worked for Mr. Townsend for all of his life, and the latter had bequeathed him a small cabin and one acre on his land for life. Thus, he had a reasonably secure future.

The three adults were interrupted by the entry of two boys, panting, gasping for breath, faces terrified and wounded, one of them with his jumper torn, looking as if they had both been in the wars.

"*In ainm an athair* (in the name of the father), what has happened to the two of ye? Have ye been attacked by Mr. Kennedy's bull?" Andrew Barron queried. He was answered by both boys gabbling a babel of words about Captain Saunders' land, strange bases, graves with crosses of stones, the wail of a dead person, and the cry of the banshee.

Both men gave way to laughter, but Mairead Barron declared, "Look at the cut of the two of them. One of them has his face all scratched. The other has his good jumper, which I knitted, torn. Didn't I always tell ye to be careful of briars and thorns."

Andrew Barron sat upright in this chair. His face had darkened, as he pointed a finger at Patrick. "Patrick, I tould you boys never to cross over or bring your friends into Captain Saunders' lands. Only five years ago, during the hungry years, two starving boys little older than you, Patrick, stealed on to his lands. Brophy, the captain's agent tied them both to the gate and gave them the thrashing of their lives with a big stick. The agent got away with it all, and the poor boys could not walk properly for days."

Philip Keating was more sympathetic. "Boys will be boys. These two boys like to explore. Were the two of ye playing one of your pretending games?"

Richard answered. "We were pretending to be Spanish conquerors attacking the Aztec Indians' fortress in Mexico. Mr. Ford has been reading the story to us. They went to Mexico to bring civilisation and Christianity to them pagan Indians."

"And will ye look at where their pretending games has landed them," cried their mother. "Can you two men make yourselves useful. Each of you put each of those *grabijes* (young scoundrels) across your knee and give them a few good wallops on the backside. Sure, isn't it the only way they will learn."

"But Mairead, come on," laughed Philip, "These two soldiers of Christ have been wounded bringing civilisation and Christianity to them pagan Aztec savages. Haven't they been doing God's work?"

"God's work, my foot! Isn't it us women are the ones who will have to mend their clothes and *trate* (treat) their wounds. You men are too soft on them boys. Well, you can still make yourselves useful. Each of ye can hold each boy while I put some herbal stuff to their scratches. This is going to sting them mighty awful."

Philip put his arms around Richard. Patrick stood proud, "I am the conquistador Herman Cortes. I will suffer the pain on my own. No one needs to hold me."

His mother in answer ripped the torn jumper off him, followed by her applying the balm to both of their faces. Both boys sustained the pain without protest. After that she flung their dinners on tin plates in front of the two of them.

As it had begun raining, Andrew decided to postpone his work outside. He turned to Phil Keating, "Phil, I wonder if you could tell these two lads about some things that happened here during the past few years."

"Aye, that I can," Philip replied. Both boys sat on the floor, for they loved Philip's stories. "Now lads, the crying sound ye heard, was it a wail or a sound on more than one note?"

"It was more than one note," Richard replied hesitantly. "At least I think so."

"Right," said Philip, "it was probably a curlew that you heard. They can sound like they're sobbing. Because ye were in a graveyard, I'd say yer imagination got the better of ye." A visible look of relief passed across the boys' faces.

"What about the banshee wail that we heard?" Patrick asked. "That's what put the heart up us."

Philip continued, "Ah yes, the wailing sound. Sure, don't I remember the first time I heard that meself. It was many years ago now. I was a young lad, a few years older than yerselves now. I was coming back late from the river after some fishing. I was walking past the old castle when I heard that screech. Well, didn't the hair stand on the back of my head and I thought I was going to wet my britches." The boys gasped in amazement. A giggle snorted from Richard first, and then both boys had to cover their mouths with their hands to keep the laughter in. "Oh yes." Philip continued, "I ran like a hare on coursing day and I didn't stop until I was at the other side of the church. When I got home, I poured my story out to my father who was still sitting up. He laughed so much. 'That was a vixen you heard, you silly boy. They screech like that when they want the company of another fox."

"Oh." The boys said together. It sounded like a sigh of relief.

The atmosphere in the kitchen now lightened, Philip Keating continued his explanations. "Yes, I am sure that the bases ye had seen were the remains of houses. It had been an old Irish and Celtic custom to build small cabins in a group very close together, and some tenants of Captain Saunders had lived in those. Over the years those tenants when they died had been buried in the nearby graveyard, known as the *relig*. Most of the tenants had died during the bad years. However, about five years ago Captain Saunders and Brophy had decided to *clare* (clear) all the tenants left over out of their cabins, so they had evicted all of them. Now the people who used to live in them cabins had had their patches of potatoes or 'gardens' in a field right in front of the grove of trees. What had ye seen there, boys?"

"We saw sheep, a few horses, and cattle," answered Patrick.

"Exactly," Philip continued. "The captain and his agent had decided that they could make much more money by getting rid of people and putting animals in their places. This happened all over Ireland, and, I believe, in Scotland, which is also ruled by the English. So, all the people in those cabins, working men, women, children, old people, were evicted, and their potato patches were changed to grassland. Their cabins were knocked down by the constabulary, and what you boys saw today are the remains, the bases, of those same cabins."

Richard in his distress asked, "But, uncle Philip, where did all those people go to?" Philip Keating looked to Andrew Barron for approval to explain, who answered by a nod. "Mr Townsend gave some of them shelter in his barn. However, on hearing this, Brophy informed on him to the constabulary. This could have brought Mr. Townsend a great deal of trouble. So, the people departed during the night, secretly and silently."

"But where did they go?" persisted Richard.

Philip answered. "Some of them may have been lucky to find other cabins with a better landlord. More of them died of hunger or cold during a harsh winter. Some more of them could have died of the fever. A few lucky ones would have emigrated to England or to America. Who knows?" At this point, Richard stood up, his eyes betraying tears.

"But, uncle Philip, you cannot just turn people out of their houses and replace them with animals. Think of those poor children dying of hunger and those old people freezing to death."

Philip Keating placed his hands on the boy's shoulders. "We live in a country which can be very cruel, *Ashtore*. Over the centuries the English have persecuted us, but since around 1825 they have begun to trate us a little better. Our real persecutors are the landlords, many of whom are now Irish and some even Catholics."

"I should say now, Philip," Andrew Barron spoke, "that the Marquis of Ormonde has never trated his tenants like Captain Saunders has done. He is a very good landlord, and I want you two boys to remember that. In a few days time, when ye have recovered from yer battle with the Aztecs and yer terrible frights, I am going to tell ye about the bad years that happened ten years ago. Do you agree that I should do this, Mairead?"

"Yes, you should, *A Fhear.* It is about time they heard about those years and how lucky we were to survive on this small farm. Thanks be to God, and to generous neighbours. And God save, bless, and kape the Marquis and the Marchioness."

A few nights later Andrew Barron related to the two boys the broad outline of the terrible years of famine. He did not go into too many details, because he did not want to frighten them too much, because its spectre still hung over Ireland. It was also because, as with so many people who have survived famines, plagues, genocide, and brutal wars, the memories of the terrible time still haunted him. Memory can sometimes be almost as cruel and terrifying as the actual experience itself.

CHAPTER 2.

'If Music be the Food of Love, Play On'[1]

A Day in June, 1855.

Two brothers walk across their own and their neighbours' fields on the way to the national school. They carry their couple of copy books and pencils in their cotton cloth bags. The older boy aged ten does not really enjoy the tedium of lessons, especially those in spellings, writing, some arithmetic, and grammar. More to his liking are the classes in geography, reading, and gardening. His best days are those when his father tells him that he must take a day off school to help him on the farm. By contrast the younger boy, aged eight, seldom volunteers, for he enjoys his learning at school. Yet he too is happy to miss some school when the annual rural rituals of sowing or digging potatoes or saving the hay or corn come around. Nonetheless, neither of these boys 'is creeping like snail unwillingly to school.'

The young Quaker master Mr. Ford has proved himself to be a progressive primary educator in this small corner of rural Ireland. Seldom does he have to resort to corporal punishment, except for serious breaches of discipline. Master Ford also maintains excellent relations with both Catholic parish priest and Protestant minister. Religious instruction classes are held twice weekly after school hours for each denomination by their respective ministers.

---

1 (William Shakespeare)

Late afternoon – that same day in June. Patrick and Richard are seated in the Shanahans' kitchen, enjoying their tea and freshly baked scones, having completed their usual Friday after-school chores for their generous neighbours. Patrick's eyes have alighted on a small man walking up the lane. He is bearded, clad in a rather long flowing overcoat, boots on his feet, and carrying in his hands two small bags.

"Mrs. Shanahan, look, there's a man coming up the lane. Do you think he is a beggar?"

She moves to the window, gazes out intensely, and exclaims, "*Dia linn* (God with us), why, isn't it Colum O'Leary himself. Colum O'Leary, the great fiddler. We have not seen him since … for at least ten years. Patrick, please go and tell Mr. Shanahan to come in at once. He will be mighty glad to see Mr. O'Leary and to hear him play again."

The itinerant fiddler is greeted at the front door by Mr. and Mrs. Shanahan and both Barron boys. Richard is rather apprehensive of the old man with the beard and the long flowing coat, but he longs to hear his music. The Shanahans silently give praise to God for sparing the life of this great musician during the black years. They take both his hands in theirs, and then instruct each boy to shake his hand too.

Seated by the fire and partaking of his tea and scones, Colum O'Leary recounts his itineraries during the past decade. He had confined his travels to the midland and eastern counties, as far west as Longford, as far north as Meath, and as far south as Wexford town. People in those regions were usually generous.

Colum O'Leary removes his fiddle and bow from his bag. He plays a slow air, a more martial tune, a jig and then a hornpipe. His audience is entranced to hear these lovely old Irish airs again. Young Richard is mesmerised not only by the melodies but also by the dexterity of the artist. He has heard the fiddle played before, but this fiddle player is a virtual magician. Andrew Barron has already told the fiddler that Patrick has a beautiful singing voice. The Shanahans persuade him to render *Shule Aroon*, and Mr. O'Leary will accompany him. The fiddler then turns to Richard asking him to sing a song. The latter explains that his voice in no way matches that of his brother, but that he would love to play a few notes on the fiddle, having taught himself to play the tin whistle. The fiddler offers to teach him a scale. The Shanahans suggest that they will carry on with their work inside and outside the house. Patrick declares that he needs to get home to do his chores, but he will tell their parents that Richard has been delayed. Richard draws his chair closer to Colum O'Leary, convinced that this is a dream.

Colum O'Leary speaks, "Now, my lad, as you can see, the fiddle has four strings. Their names are E, A, D and G, but don't you be worrying about them names yet. For many of our Irish songs and airs, you need only the second and third strings, with sometimes the first string added as an open string." He explains the meaning of an open string. The master places the instrument and the bow in the boy's hands, adjusts his posture, and directs him how to play the open strings. He then places the boy's first three fingers over the three positions on the third string, instructing that the gap between second and third frets should be narrower. He gently guides the boy's right hand as he draws the bow right and left to each of the three notes, preceded by the third string open. The master fiddler now moves the boy's hand to the second string and to do the exact same thing there. He now asks the boy to repeat that whole process. "Tell me what you have played, my lad."

"I do not know, Sir."

"*A Mhic* (Son), you have played the scale of D major. Wonderful. Can you come up here tomorrow morning. I will teach you your first tune, *The Dawning of the Day* or *Fainne Geal An Lae.*"

"Sir, My brother sings that song in English."

"Great, *Ashtore*, I will see you tomorrow morning."

"*Gura maith agat* (Thank you), Mr. O'Leary." Richard runs down most of the lane. He almost bursts into the kitchen. "*A mháthair* (Mother), I can play the scale of D major on the fiddle."

She looks at him in bewilderment. "What in *ainm an aithair* is a scale of D major?" Richard suddenly realises that he does not really know. "Go and chop the wood, boy. A scale of D major will not kape the fire going to cook our supper, but wood might."

Richard feels hurt. Why can his mother not share in his excitement? He is sure his father will support him better.

Over their supper of oatmeal porridge Richard excitedly recounted to his father his achievement that day. "And Mr. O'Leary has promised to teach me my first song tomorrow."

His mother remained dismissive. "Do you want to become a travelling fiddler, homeless, probably half starved, maybe even teased by children? Besides, where are we going to get the money to buy you a fiddle?"

Richard's father intervened. "Think of how it might brighten our long dreary winter evenings to have Richard play some lovely old Irish airs when our neighbours call around, sometimes with Patrick singing."

"I do not want to sing to the sound of a cat being strangled," Patrick exclaimed.

"Will you hush, boy," Andrew commanded. "Mairead, I have at times told you that one of my direct ancestors was a famous piper. He might even have played for the Barron battalion just before they marched or rode into battle at the Boyne and Aughrim. Who knows, Richard might be gifted with that musical gift. Richard will have his lesson tomorrow with Master O'Leary, and we will see how he goes. If he becomes good at the fiddle and likes it, I may be able to trade in something for an old fiddle with a tinker at the fair."Richard rewarded his father with a beaming and loving smile.

The next day – Saturday. Richard Barron stood in the Shanahan kitchen, observed benevolently by master fiddler Colum O'Leary. The latter looked more presentable today. He had had a good wash. His hair and beard had been trimmed, and he was clad in a fresh clean shirt. "Now, my lad, look at this sheet of paper with its four lines of numbers. Each number stands for a finger of the left hand on positions of the second or third string." Richard played each note of the first line tentatively, repeating it a few times as requested, followed by the fourth line repeated. The master teacher asked. "What do you notice about the first and the fourth lines of numbers, *A Mhic*?"

"Sir, they are the same."

"And the tunes you played?"

"They too are the same too, sir." Already the master was surmising that the boy was intelligent and that he possessed a good musical ear. "Now, lad, play me the second and third lines, each a few times." Richard complied. "What do you notice about the numbers and the tunes of those two lines?"

"Sir, they too are the same as each other."

"Well done, my lad."

The teacher elaborated further, "Now, *Mo Bhuachaill* (my boy), we will give each line its own letter. Lines which have the same tune will have the same letter. Line number 1 we will call A. Line number 2 is B, because it has a different tune. Tell me the letters we should give to lines 3 and 4."

"That is easy, sir," Richard responded, "B and A of course. They have the same numbers as lines 2 and 1."

"What else, *Mo Bhuachaill*? This time use your ears rather than your eyes."

"Sir, they sound the same as lines 2 and 1."

"*Go ana-mhaith* (very good)," exclaimed the teacher, giving the boy's arm a light squeeze. "You have worked out that this lovely old melody has the design of ABBA. Many of our old Irish airs have that same design. You have a good musical ear, *A Mhic*. Many of our great Irish fiddle players, harpists, and pipers played mainly by ear. Now play me the whole four lines. Let your ear guide you as much as the written numbers." Richard did as bidden.

The master left him for a while to practise the air, the former taking a walk around the fields to talk with Mr. Shanahan and the workmen. As Richard became more competent with the tune, he felt that the beauty of the simple melody of *Fainne Geal an Lae* was carrying him along as if on a column of air. On his return the master was effusive in his praise. He had found a student of talent.

Master O'Leary remained at the Shanahan house for six days, sleeping in their sleep house. Richard was presented with a new tune each day. Confining him initially to the second and third strings, the master taught him how to play *Eileen Aroon* followed the next day by Thomas Moore's *The Meeting of the Waters*. Having introduced the boy to the first string open on his next lesson, Richard was now learning the lovely old Jacobite song *Mo Ghile Mear* (My Gallant Hero), a lament for Prince Charles Edward Stuart. During his fourth lesson Richard noticed that Colum O'Leary sometimes had to sit down. Was he feeling weak? He mentioned this to his father, who remained silent.

On his departure Colum O'Leary confided to Andrew Barron that from now on he would confine his itineraries to his native county Kilkenny, but he might travel a little into counties Waterford and Wexford. He was getting old now, weaker and lacking the energies of his younger days. He promised Richard that he would return in two months, at harvest time.

The master fiddler proved as good as his word. His second visit occurred at the end of August, followed by another at the beginning of November, the time of potato picking. On his return again early in February, the Shanahans persuaded him to remain at least for a week. His features were becoming more haggard, showing a pain, although he did not complain. His appetite was declining. His step was less sprightly. Nonetheless he continued to imbue young Richard with his love of music. The boy's dexterity on the fiddle improved from one course of lessons to the other. By February he was playing competently on all four strings.

"If he possessed an instrument of his own his progress would move in leaps and bounds," the master told the boy and his parents. Even Richard's mother was being won over. But how, in their straitened position as small farmers, could they overcome that seemingly insurmountable hurdle?

Late April of 1856.

Richard and Patrick were helping their father to sow the potatoes. Patrick saw two strange boys walking up their road, aged about thirteen and eleven, carrying a small bag. They reached the Barron fence. The older boy called out, "Is this Barron's?"

"Yes" Andrew replied. "Who are ye?"

"We are Edward and Gerard Egan from Dromana."

"Dromana," replied Andrew. "Isn't that five miles away? What brings ye here?"

The younger boy answered, "A dead man in our house asked us to bring this bag to you."

Patrick laughed, "A dead man?"

Edward interrupted, "Don't listen to that *amadán*. Let me explain. Colum O'Leary the fiddler was staying in our house. He began to feel weak and sick on his third day, so we called the priest and the doctor. After that he went down quickly. Two days later he passed away peacefully. Our parents and ourselves and some of our neighbours were with him. That was three days ago. We buried him yesterday in Dromana graveyard to a mighty big crowd. A day before he died, he asked that we bring his fiddle to you. It is for Richard. Which of you boys is Richard? I am to hand it to you."

Richard, incredulous of the reality, sprang forward to receive the treasured gift. He was about to open the bag, when his father reprimanded him, "Richard, these two boys have walked all the way from Dromana. Bring them into the house and you serve them some tea and some of your mother's scones. If you two boys would like to stay the night, I will drive you home tomorrow after our Sunday Mass. Richard will come with me. We will visit Colum O'Leary's grave, and pray for the great fiddler."

While the two guests were avidly eating their scones Richard withdrew the instrument from the bag. He took time to run his fingers over its beautiful yew woodwork, delighting in its craftsmanship. His mother had told him to delay playing it until after supper. Meanwhile Richard must accompany the two Egan boys up to the Shanahan's to pass on the sad news and tell them of the generous gift bequeathed to

Richard. After that Richard should give the boys a tour of the Shanahans' farm, and show them the Mass rock.

Following supper Richard was finally able to draw the bow lovingly over the strings of his newly acquired instrument. The evening witnessed the Barron household resounding with some ancient Irish airs and a few songs in English rendered by Patrick.

The following morning, Sunday, Andrew Barron drove the four boys to Dromana graveyard after Mass. The Egan boys guided father and sons to the spot were lay the renowned fiddler, indicated by a mound of fresh clay. Silently all five prayed for his soul, Richard striving to hold back tears. However, he also felt honoured and privileged that he had been entrusted to perpetuate O'Leary's ancient legacy. On their arrival at the Egan farmhouse, they were entertained to Sunday dinner, followed by a toast of *uisce beatha* by Andrew Barron and John Egan to the departed master fiddler. Richard then tentatively raised his question.

"Mr. Egan, I have given your sons sixpence each for safely bringing the fiddle, but I still have almost four shillings left. Would that be enough to pay for a Mass for Mr. O Leary?"

John Egan considered. "Yes, it would certainly be enough, *Ashtore*, but I have another idea. Should the name of Colum O'Leary be forgotten? A small headstone over the musician will help to preserve his memory, and I am starting a collection for that."

Richard immediately requested. "Can I be the first one to pay to it?" followed by his father who pledged five shillings.

John Egan was euphoric, "The name of Colum O'Leary, master fiddler and a preserver of Ireland's ancient air and song tradition, will not die."

The penultimate stone in the edifice of O'Leary's legacy was added shortly afterwards. Andrew had taken Richard to Mr. Daniel O'Sullivan, a fiddler and music teacher who lived about a mile from their home. Andrew, with Richard's help, had made a small wooden case for the precious instrument. Impressed with the boy's playing, Daniel O'Sullivan immediately offered to teach him. Aware that the Barrons were small tenant farmers, and needing some help around his own cottage, it was agreed that in payment Richard would chop O'Sullivan's wood and milk his cow on the day of his weekly lesson. The old Celtic system of interchange of skills would live on in this part of Ireland.

The middle and late childhood years of Richard Barron passed in a manner similar to that of so many other sons of small farmers in post-Famine Ireland. It was a time when both large and small farmers began to experience a level of prosperity marginally higher than their pre-Famine forebears. Yet over all the rural community towered the spectre of possible potato blight and famine again, rack rents, insecurity of tenure, eviction and likely emigration. Nonetheless, the Barron family and their neighbours were relatively secure as tenants of the benevolent Marquis of Ormonde.

During the years after the Famine, the Barron household had been blessed with two more children, a daughter christened Ellen born in 1851, and a second daughter named Anne born in 1854, valuable additions to the family labour force. However, Andrew Barron did not confine his children to the drudgery of school and farming. Possibly due to his own Norman-Irish background, he aimed to foster their obvious talents and abilities. His wife Mairead took it upon herself to teach Patrick the old songs and the more recent ballads of Thomas Moore, and he was always encouraged to sing at gatherings of neighbours. Andrew also insisted, although unnecessarily, that Richard practise his fiddle most days of the week.

Richard also demonstrated a great love and ability with horses, the Barron horse tradition having been initiated by his grandfather. Richard had displayed his equine skills when, aged only seven, he had learned to ride the small family pony which he named Oisin. The Barron family mare served the more mundane tasks of pulling the cart, the plough, and other implements of farm work.

Meanwhile, Richard's lessons on the fiddle with Mr. Sullivan progressed at a rapid pace. After a year of tuition, he was playing reels, jigs, hornpipes, slow airs and ballads. His teacher then introduced the boy to music notation, a separate discipline. Richard' s high level of intelligence ensured that this presented few obstacles to him. Soon he was playing from notation melodies by composers from the Baroque, Classical, and Romantic eras. Around the time of his eleventh birthday Mr. Sullivan explained that Ireland too had produced a few renowned composers whose works had become even more celebrated than their English contemporaries. Subsequently the Barron household resounded with melodies from William Vincent

Wallace's evergreen opera *Maritana* and Michael Balfe's *The Bohemian Girl*. Meanwhile, Patrick had eschewed his earlier reluctance to being accompanied by "a cat being strangled," and he and Richard would practise and perform together the ballads of Thomas Moore. The tedium of the daily grind, the concerns for the future, all could be alleviated by the solace of live music, especially during the long and dreary winter evenings. Exactly as Andrew Barron had predicted.

CHAPTER 3.

'Up With the Kettle and Down with the Pan'

Patrick Barron's glorious singing, accompanied by his brother Richard's playing on the fiddle at the special Mass in Castledown chapel for the feast of the Assumption on 15th August 1858, had become the talk of the district for a while. It was Patrick who conceived of the idea that they should make some money out of their talents and go 'on the wren.' Their parents approved of the idea.

They looked an unusual sight as they wandered along the byroads on St. Stephen's Day in 1858 – four young boys dressed in hessian sacks, white masks with holes for the mouth, nose, and eyes, and hats or caps. Ellen, the eight-year-old sister of Patrick Barron, now thirteen, and Richard, now eleven, had begged to be allowed to join them. But the four boys had been adamant. How would anyone regard them as true wren boys if a girl had joined their ranks? They would be laughed at, jeered, and thrown out of every house they visited. No, the boys would not allow it.

Patrick and Richard were joined by their school friends, Michael Nolan and William O'Neill, both aged ten years. Patrick's famed boy-soprano voice showed no sign of breaking or changing yet. Michael displayed a passable ability on the tin whistle, while William could handle basic beats on his drum. They reckoned that, with such talent, and their repertoire of eight songs they had an advantage over other groups of young wren boys. However, Andrew and Mairead Barron had advised the boys that they should begin their serenading no less than one mile from the Barron home. This might assist in their preserving the sacred wren boy code of anonymity, leaving their own immediate area to other visiting wren boys. Patrick carried the money box. Michael, with only his tin whistle to carry, had been entrusted with the honour of carrying the live wren, tied to a small holly bush decorated with ribbons. Therefore, everything about this group proved that they were true wren boys, minstrels and guardians of that ancient Celtic tradition.

By mid-afternoon the four boys had covered about three miles on their musical odyssey. Having sung outside a few poor cabin doors, with the reward of a penny in only two of them, they had decided to concentrate on the better-looking cabins and the houses of farmers. This had proved to be a profitable strategy. Patrick found that the money box was getting heavier with many pennies, some threepenny bits, and even a few sixpenny pieces. He had felt hurt when occupants of a couple of the cabins had questioned his gender, declaring that they were convinced that his lovely voice was that of a girl. As all four boys adhered strictly to the sacred wrenboy code, Patrick was unable to reveal his face to one of the cabins' male occupants who had made lewd suggestions. Still, the total money collected compensated him, and his companions had not taunted him. However, Michael came in for some teasing from the other boys due to his mishap with the wren.

The boys had been fortunate that nature had conferred on them a fine winter's day. However, by mid-afternoon, with the clouds gathering, William suggested that they make one final call, namely to the large farmhouse of the Heffernans, situated up a short drive, reputed to be generous people and lovers of music. Richard supported the idea, because Colum O'Leary had told him that the Heffernans had always given him a great welcome.

The four young wren boys positioned themselves in front of the closed door of the Heffernan farmhouse. Their first rendition was of *Shule Aroon*, that haunting old Irish ballad which bemoaned the exile of the Wild Geese around 1700. This was followed by *Eamonn An Cnoic* (Ned of the Hill). Patrick sang the first verse in Irish and the remaining verses in English. Their recital concluded with the song of the wren.

That evening Patrick would recount to his mother what happened next. "Sure, didn't a girl dressed in an ironed frock, a clean apron, and a lace cap open the front door. She bade us to wipe our shoes on the mat. We could not believe our luck when she led us into the parlour. And we all thought we were dreaming by what we saw there."

"Tell me more about the parlour and the furniture, *a mhic*," his mother asked.

"Well, *a mháthair*, it was a powerful large parlour. The walls were painted blue, and the ceiling painted white. There were some paintings on the walls. There was a large wooden dresser, full of beautiful *delph* and some ornaments. And such a welcoming fireplace with a warm blazing fire. Two armchairs in front of it. A lovely large mahogany table. Oh, I nearly forgot. There was a piano in the corner.

There were people sitting around the table on comfortable wicker chairs."

"How were they dressed, Patrick?"

"The four men were dressed in their better than Sunday clothes. The men wore well ironed shirts, suits, waistcoats, and ties. The lady wore a long flowing white gown."

"What was on the table, Patrick?"

"Knives, forks, spoons, plates, wine glasses, almost empty wine bottles. The men were drinking whiskey in small glasses. Oh, and the nicest thing on the table was a lovely iced Christmas cake, with about a quarter of it already eaten."

"Did ye feel a little frightened?" Patrick's mother asked.

"Well, we all did. We thought that they were going to give out to us for spoiling their dinner." Patrick concluded.

For the remainder of his life, Richard would recall what happened next. Mr. Heffernan spoke. "You boys are the fourth group of wrenboys who have visited us today."

Patrick summoned up his courage, "Sure, aren't we sorry, sir, for interrupting you again." The farmer stretched his body along his chair in a relaxed manner, speaking in a welcoming tone, "What do you mean by 'again,' my boy? Ye are the best wren boys that we have heard today, the only group which I have invited inside. We have just finished an excellent dinner, and are enjoying the best *uisce beatha* (whiskey) in Ireland. All we need now is some good music and singing. You are most welcome. Any suggestions, gentlemen?"

The man beside him spoke. He was dressed similarly to his companions, and sported a pocket watch and a folded breast handkerchief. Perhaps he was a solicitor. "Would you boys know any of the songs of our own great bard Thomas Moore?"

Patrick answered. "Sir, we know *The Minstrel Boy.*"

Their audience expressed immediate approval. Patrick's soulful singing of this song, with skilful accompaniment by his friends, ensured a grateful ovation from the audience.

The end of the table nearest the fire was occupied by a smiling man with a twinkle in his eye, who spoke, "That was a great performance. However, how can you boys call yourselves true wrenboys?"

"Why not?" Mr. Heffernan queried. "These are the best young wrenboys Honora and I have heard in a few years."

"I agree, but where is their wren?," the smiling man queried. None of the boys answered. Richard ventured a response. "We did have a wren, sir."

"So, what happened to it?" The boys began to giggle, each prodding the other to tell. Patrick assumed the position of spokesman. "Sure, sir, weren't we only walking up Mr. Harvey's drive. Four mighty fierce greyhounds charged down on us, so we turned and ran. Mi-, our wren carrier and tin whistle player, dropped the holly bush with the wren tied to it. The wren must have become loose because it flew away. We ran powerfully fast and escaped with our lives."

The five adults and the boys themselves erupted into good-hearted laughter, but the smiling man was not finished. "So, you will have to kill your tin whistle player this evening, instead of the wren."

For the first time the dark brown-haired man at the other end of the table spoke, "But did you boys intend to kill and bury the wren?"

Richard answered, "No sir. I told them that I would not come with them if they were going to kill the bird."

"Good work, boys. Killing a little wren is a savage act," exclaimed the man. "I am glad that it is dying out in our country at long last." The smiling man had to have his final quip. "Well, gentlemen, we now know whose greyhounds to back at the hare coursing next month. Be sure to put your money on Harvey's greyhounds."

The dark brown-haired man countered this, "That too is a barbaric sport. Greyhounds tearing apart a little defenceless hare. You will not find me attending that coursing."

Mr. Heffernan assumed position as host of the occasion. "Enough discussion, gentlemen. We are ready for another song."

The professional man spoke. "As you boys cannot tell us your names, I will christen our fine young singer. Gentlemen, we will call him Master Kelly. Michael Kelly was a great singer from Dublin. He sang in the opera houses of Italy, Vienna, and London in the last century. Now, master Kelly, would you know, *Believe me, if all those Endearing Young Charms?*"

"Indeed, we do, sir."

An even more appreciative ovation followed their performance. The smiling man then addressed the professional man. "Thomas, do you have a name for our young fiddle player?"

"Yes, I do. We will christen him Master Wallace. William Vincent Wallace, a great violinist and composer of *Maritana*, came from Waterford. He performed in countries as far away as Australia." He addressed Richard. "Have you heard of him?"

"Yes Sir, I can play a few of his melodies, and some of the ones by Mr. Balfe as well."

"Excellent." Mr. Heffernan addressed his guests, "We may hear some of them later."

"Honora, do you have a request for the last song from these talented boys?"

She answered, "I would love to hear *The Last Rose of Summer*."

The boys performed it, finishing at the end of the second verse. Honora now addressed Patrick, "Master Kelly, do you know that there is a third verse to that song?"

"No, ma'am."

"I will speak the words for you," she offered.

This was replaced by calls from the men for her to sing the verse herself. Following some reluctance, she agreed, remaining seated. Her mezzo soprano voice filled the kitchen, while Richard, elated and honoured, accompanied her. *So soon shall I follow when friendships decay, and from love's shining circle the gems drop away.* More applause followed.

Honora spoke, "Now, boys, I am sure you all have mouths on ye for some good food and drink. Brigid, bring them a jug of lemonade with four glasses, four slices of Christmas cake, and a few mince pies each to that small table. Boys, as you cannot eat and drink while wearing your masks, you will need to sit facing the fire and with your backs to us. Master Kelly, can you and those two boys please bring in the *furrum* (bench) outside the door."

Richard, somewhat uncertain, asked, "Can I do anything?"

"Yes, you can, Master Wallace," Mr. Heffernan replied, "You will entertain us with some of the melodies from *Maritana*. Which ones do you know?"

"Sir, I know *The Harp in the Air, Scenes that are Brightest, In Happy Moments.*"

Mr. Heffernan turned to his wife, "Honora, you sing those first two songs beautifully. Won't you honour us with them." The lady again expressed some more reluctance, but the party mood was by now established.

Brigid was carrying the lemonade and food to the small table. Mr. Heffernan poured generous portions of whiskey for his guests. Honora gracefully left the table. Her initial reluctance banished, she walked up to join Richard, her bearing and long gown displaying the elegance and confidence of a diva singing on the stage of Kilkenny Theatre. For *The Harp in the Air*, singer and violinist now stood and faced their audience. Honora had indicated to Brigid that she should sit at the big table. Even the three boys sat in silence, enjoying their repast, while the mezzo soprano transported her audience to the old

Moorish halls of Granada. Honora was gaining in confidence. Richard was enchanted at accompanying for his first time a lady singing a ballad from an opera. Appreciative words from the gentlemen were followed by requests for *Scenes that are Brightest*. Now enjoying her rare moment to perform, Honora seemed even more at home with this beautiful ballad, for she sang it with some real artistry.

Honora was about to move back to the table. However, her husband asked Richard, "Master Wallace, would you know *When Other Lips* from *The Bohemian Girl* by Michael Balfe?"

"Yes, I do, sir. My father tells me that my aunt Catherine used to play it on the piano and sing it. So, I had to learn it." Nobody in the room noticed the slight start made by the dark-haired man. Mr. Heffernan spoke, "Honora, can you and Master Wallace give us this as an encore. Truly it is your best song."

Not one sound, even that of a glass being placed on the table was heard during the rendition. Richard allowed his eyes to wander. They rested upon the dark-haired man, whose countenance had assumed a sad and mournful expression. As Honora sang the final lines, "*When hollow hearts shall wear a mask, 'twill break your own to see, in such a moment I but ask that you'll remember me,* Richard was convinced that he could see tears in the man's eyes. He was not disturbed by this. Mr. O'Sullivan had told him that great performances can move people to tears. Richard had believed that this only applied to women. After all, men were not meant to cry.

The loudest ovation from the gentlemen followed, with Mr. Heffernan replenishing his guests' glasses. Honora bestowed on young Richard the honour of leading him to the *furrum* for of his repast. Only one bare mince pie remained on the plate. She queried, "So what has happened to Master Wallace's cake and mince pies, and his drink?"

Once again, the re-masked boys indicated that the other one should tell. At last, Michael chimed up, "The wren came to visit us. We had to give them to it, because it was *quare* (queer) hungry, and *divil* (devil) a lie in that."

The smiling man quipped. "The wren? More like a trio of scavenging birds!"

Honora laughed. "Never mind, Master Wallace, Brigid will bring you two slices of cake and some mince pie, as well as a drink. You had better sit on this arm chair, away from these scavengers. Sit sideways, so that we cannot see your face."

Patrick now mentioned to Honora that it was almost time for them to leave. Mr. Heffernan placed a large silver half crown in the money box. He instructed the three boys to move the *furrum* outside the door again and to sit on it, adding that Richard would not keep them long. The three boys left the farm house with sincere expressions of thanks and appreciation from the full company, followed by an invitation to return next St. Stephen's Day.

Honora sat on the armchair opposite Richard, her face averted. She praised his fiddle playing, encouraging him to develop his talent, and to practise hard. Honora suggested that he and his teacher might consider more classical music. She mentioned composers Mendelsohn, Schumann, and even melodies from operas by Verdi,

Donizetti, and Bellini. Honora promised Richard that she would send a book containing melodies by these composers to Mr. Sullivan's cottage. Mrs. Heffernan then stood up, and moved into the scullery to supervise the work there.

During Honora's and Richard's conversation the men had been discussing farm matters, prices, landlords and their agents. The smiling man now queried, "Does anyone know where did Wallace travel to after his sojourn in Australia?"

The professional man stated, "He sailed to Chile in South America. Few people know that Wallace actually crossed the great Andes mountains on horseback into Argentina with a friend. However, on his arrival he found that the great city of Buenos Aires was being blockaded by, I think, the French navy. So, he had to turn back and return to Chile."

The other three men reacted with statements condemning the French and especially the British for their usual interfering actions against other countries. Richard had never heard of Chile and Argentina. Yet his imagination had been awakened by the thought of a man riding on horseback across a great range of mountains. He must look them up on the school map.

Mr. Heffernan now queried "But why did Wallace travel to Argentina?" The professional man answered, "I cannot answer that question, Michael. That was around 1840. The Irish settlements in Argentina did not begin until 1845." Mr. Heffernan was puzzled. "Irish settlements in Argentina, what are you talking about, Thomas?"

The professional man expounded further, "Many people do not know that the Irish have set up successful settlements in the pampas, the prairies of Argentina. Sure, was not the whole scheme established by Father Anthony Fahy, a Galway priest who spent some years in the Black Abbey in Kilkenny? By all accounts, the settlements have been very successful, and some of the Irish have made great fortunes through cattle and sheep farming out there."

"Any of them from Kilkenny?" Mr. Heffernan enquired.

"Not many. Most of the settlers went to the Argentine from counties Offaly, Westmeath, and Longford, and, rather unusually, Wexford. I do not know the reasons why, but I have read some articles about all this."

Richard was only half listening to this conversation. Snatches of the men's discussion entered his reverie: Argentina, a Catholic country which welcomed the Irish, unlike England, Canada, America, and even Australia; some of the best farm land there in the world; an emerging great city there called something like Bwainos Aires; savage Indians. But the dark-haired man was moving uncomfortably in his chair, not participating. Maybe he needed to go to the lavatory after all that wine and whiskey. The man excused himself, and went into another room. When he returned Richard was ready to leave the house, donning his mask again. Mr. Heffernan, the smiling man, and the professional man all extended their hands to say goodbye and thanks again. By now, Richard had reached the dark-haired man. The latter shook the boy's hand. Speaking in almost a whisper, he asked him if he could tell him just his Christian name. The boy obliged. To his surprise, the man placed both hands on the boy's upper arms, and gave him a light squeeze, followed by a pat on his head. A coin was then placed into his hand. Being well mannered, the boy could not look at it. He rewarded the man with a beaming smile from behind his mask, turned, placed the coin in his pocket, and left the house. The man was overcome by feelings of deep affection and profound sorrow. He was reminded of the words from that lovely English folk song *The Foggy Foggy Dew. And every time I look into his eyes it reminds me of that fair young maid.*

Richard rejoined his companions, walking on a cloud. However, on his surreptitiously glancing in his pocket, he was brought back to earth. William cried out, "Boy, what are you looking at? Boys, he has a coin, a silver coin." Richard found himself surrounded. "It is a whole shilling," William announced. "Who gave you that?"

"That man with dark hair who did not speak much gave me it. I suppose he enjoyed my playing. I don't know."

"Is it wanting to break the code you are?" William accused. "You have to divide that shilling between us all."

"And didn't you scavenging birds break the code when you ate all my cake and mince pies."

"You ended up getting two slices of cake and loads of mince pies."

Patrick intervened, "Look, boys, we have had a great day and have made powerful money. Our parents have tould us that we must reach Castledown chapel by darkness. We don't want to meet the people of the roads."

"But sure, they *nivir* (never) would rob wren boys," stated Michael.

"Boys," Patrick declared, "hunger can drive people to do terrible things, even robbing boys. We will start walking quickly now. When we reach the chapel, we will be safe. Let our father decide on what we should do with the shilling."

On arrival at the Barron home, all the boys told Patrick's and Richard's parents about their various adventures and the great welcome they had received at Heffernan's. Andrew Barron decided that they could discuss it all and decide on the shilling during dinner time. Meanwhile, Patrick and Richard had to do their chores, helped by Michael and William.

After dinner Patrick produced the collection box. All the money was divided equally between the four boys. On the great matter of the shilling, Andrew Barron had decided that Richard should keep sixpence. Obviously, the man who gave it to him had been really impressed especially with his performance of the songs from *Maritana,* and each of the other boys should have two pence each. Michael and William left the Barron home, well pleased with their first experience of being wrenboys. They would look forward to an even bigger and better St. Stephen's Day the following year.

Richard was still puzzled about the dark-haired man. He was absolutely certain that he had seen him before somewhere. No doubt the man had enjoyed the music and was generous. But he had behaved in an unusual way. Why had he shed some tears during their last song? It was strange that he had asked Richard for his Christian name, and even stranger that he had gently squeezed his upper arms. Then suddenly he remembered. Lying on his bed, near death, the strange, handsome young man at the window. His two hands easing Richard back into his pillow. Actions almost identical. The same man!

Richard told his parents about the dark-haired man, not mentioning the action. He added that he had heard the other men address the man as Walter, not noticing the glance that passed between his parents.

Richard persisted, "But, *a mháthair,* I am sure that I saw that man before and that I saw him in this house."

"When?" she asked nervously. "Do you remember that time I was really sick with cholera, I am sure I saw him sitting on a chair in my room?"

"Child, it was all a dream. Isn't it rambling in your head you were. Say a prayer of thanks to God that He and that good nurse saved your life and stop talking such *ráiméis* (rubbish). A man sitting on the chair in your room! Did you ever hare such *auld* nonsense, Andrew? Richard, go and *rade* (read) your book that you got for Christmas. You four children were lucky to get any presents. And you be sure to tell me whether King Arthur marries Guinevere."

During this interchange Andrew Barron had not said a word. He had sat silently by the fire, smoking his pipe. But then, he usually did that after his hard day's work.

CHAPTER 4.

The Search for El Dorado

"It is said that he was a famous *raparee* (highwayman) around here." Patrick Barron, now fourteen, told his brother Richard, now twelve. "His name was Matthew Doran. A well-off farmer from the east of County Tipperary, he had fought for King James against William of Orange. When his lands were taken from him, he became a wild *raparee*."

"What happened to him in the end? Did he die a natural death?" Richard enquired.

Patrick continued, "Old Tom Holden told me that Matthew Doran was captured by the English soldiers outside Urlingford. He was put on trial, condemned to death, and hanged in Kilkenny in 1720."

"That was terrible," Richard exclaimed, "but what is the big secret you are going to tell me?"

Patrick replied, "Cross your heart, and promise me that you will keep it a secret." Richard had to consider, but then Patrick was his brother and really his best friend.

Richard crossed his heart with "The divil of one will I tell."

Patrick spoke quietly. "It is said that Matthew Doran hid a casket, a box full of gold and silver coins in a quarry somewhere around here."

Richard interrupted. "There are plenty quarries, many with lime kilns around here. Why would he bury a casket in a quarry where people were burning lime?"

"I will tell you if you stop butting in. Matthew Doran had a number of hideouts in different places. The best ones for him would have been quarries with caves. And," Patrick bent down and whispered in Richard's ear, "Old Tom Holden says that one of them is *nare* (near) here."

"Where?" Richard asked, his excitement rising. "Mind you, if it is on Captain Saunders' land, I am not going nare it."

"Don't worry," Patrick assured him. "It is not. It is on Mr. Mahony's land, and they allow us to wander in their fields."

Richard considered again. His parents got along well with the Mahonys due to their mutual interest in horses. "So, what is your great plan for us to find this treasure?" Richard asked.

"On Saturday afternoon we will take two spades. We will walk through Slatterys' farm, and cross over into Mr. Mahony's farm. This natural quarry is near the boundary of the Mahonys' farm and Captain Saunders' lands. Don't look so worried, I've told you it is not on the captain's lands."

"But," Richard objected, "don't we have to tell the Mahonys about the treasure and *ax* (ask) for their permission to look for it?"

"I don't think we should. Remember it is only a story which may not be true. This quarry may not be the one with the treasure. If we do find it, we will bring it straight to the Mahonys. They are our friends, and I am sure they will share it with us. Think of all the toys and books that we can buy."

Now convinced, Richard agreed to go along with the plan. Some of the books he had read were about boys hunting for buried treasure. This would be a safe adventure. Patrick did warn him with "Say nothing about this to our parents, especially to our sister, and certainly not to our friends at school. This, Richard, is our secret and our plan."

On the following Saturday afternoon, the omens looked promising. The two brothers had finished their chores by dinner time. After dinner they informed their parents that they were going on a ramble. Patrick discretely obtained two spades. When walking through Slatterys' and Mahonys' fields, the two treasure hunters kept close to the ditches. The fact that they were carrying spades might have resulted in some awkward questions.

Patrick and Richard silently followed their course almost to the boundary of Captain Saunder's lands. As they entered the Mahonys' third field their gaze fell upon a number of trees roughly in an oval shape close to the captain's fence. Excitement grew as they approached them. Walking between two trees the boys stopped in their tracks. The surface of the land dipped sharply. Had they found a natural quarry?

The quarry was not big in area, probably no more than sixteen yards long by ten yards wide. "Come on," Patrick said, "This must be the quarry. Now we must find the cave." They wended their way cautiously through the ground overgrown with grass and weeds. Placing their spades in front of them to check for cavities, the two intrepid explorers continued their search. About halfway through the quarry, Richard pointed to what looked like a natural wall of rock behind a thick clump of furze bushes. Their hearts beating faster, they ploughed through the jungle-like furze. On their emerging, staring them in the face at a distance of about two metres was a natural cave within the rock. What a perfect hiding place for a *raparee*! The cave itself was not big, probably four yards long, three yards wide, and six feet high. Yet it could provide a modicum of shelter. The floor was of clay. Digging into it should be relatively easy.

Patrick's excitement mounted. "This is definitely it, Matthew Doran's cave. The treasure could be here." Indicating the inner-most point of the cave, he instructed Richard, "We will start digging from up there. You dig on the right side, and I will take the left side."

Both boys dug their spades into the earth, sinking them to a depth of about eight inches. They worked their way backwards towards its mouth. For about the first two feet only earth and small stones emerged. *Zing.* A sharp note resounded from Richard's spade.

"I've struck something. It sounded a note. I must have hit iron or metal."

Patrick punched him lightly, "Dig more, but be careful. You don't want to damage it."

Richard dug as bidden, moving backwards. "It's long, but it seems to have changed its shape." Turning his spade to the right, the zings continued for about another foot. He then reversed his course, digging to the left and finding the zings extended for about eight inches. "I've found something about four feet long so far and nearly two feet wide. It might be the casket." he cried exuberantly. "We will dig it out together," Patrick's voice rose excitedly. "You dig along its length. I will dig on its width."

They both dug as meticulously as archaeologists would have dug at Tara. Slowly the object revealed itself. Not a casket. A strange shape, brown in colour, rather like a normal farm implement. What a terrible disappointment. The thing was about six feet long and about one inch thick, all made of metal. The head of the implement became narrower in thickness. The thing to the left side of the horizontal section was in the shape of a hook; the thing to the right side broadened out to a width of about three inches.

"I think I know what it is. It's a pike." Richard declared, "It's the kind of weapon they fought with in 1798. Let's dig it all out." Both boys dug feverishly, removing the weapon carefully. It was rather heavy for Richard, but he felt exuberant. What a joy it was to hold in his hands a weapon which some brave United Irishmen might have fought the English with, possibly at Vinegar Hill. Moving backwards out of the cave, he manoeuvred the head of the pike to a fighting position. The furze bushes became his enemies.

"What are you doing?" Patrick demanded.

"I'm fighting them bloody yeomen and redcoat bastards at Vinegar Hill."

"Watch your language. You know that our father hates that word."

"Don't you see," Richard declared, "that this is the kind of weapon which the Barron battalion may have fought with at the Boyne and Aughrim."

"Well, if they fought like you are doing, no wonder they lost both battles. You can hardly hold the thing. What are you doing now? You are not even aiming it at the yeoman."

"I am aiming to stick its hook under the bridle of the redcoat cavalry man, and to pull the horse and the rider down on to the ground. That is what the rebels at Wexford did."

"You would injure the poor horse more than you would harm the redcoat."

"So, I am not a pikeman, am I? Let me show you then. *Attention. Charge. Front. Point. Advance, cried Rory of the Hill.*"

Richard charged at Patrick who was standing in the mouth of the cave. The latter stepped backwards too quickly, tripped over a root plant, and landed on his backside, shouting. "Will you put that thing down, you *amadán*. You could have taken my eye out."

Richard, who had halted a few inches from him, laughed. "That would have been your own fault. You should have resisted me with your own weapon. But don't worry. The point of this is so blunt I could not have even drawn blood from you."

Richard ran his hand lovingly along the pike. "What are we going to do with this?"

"What do you think we will do with it? We will bury it where we found it."

"Can't we bring it home?"

"Bring it home! Where on Earth would we hide it?"

"I know," Richard answered, "We could hide it in the rafters. That is what Rory of the Hill did with a pike. Don't you know the poem by Mr. Kickham?" Richard recited the first verse, but Patrick was adamant, "Enough of your poetry. Hiding a weapon is against the law. What if the peelers discovered it? We could all be jailed and we would lose our farm. And the Mahonys could be in trouble too. Will you learn some common sense, boy."

Accepting his brother's verdict, Richard reluctantly agreed. "All right. We will bury it again, but we will leave *nairn* a trace that we found it. But maybe we should test the rest of the ground in the cave to see if any other pikes are buried there."

"Why?" Patrick laughed, "are you going to use them for the next rebellion?" Richard became serious, "Can't you see. If other pikes have been buried here, wouldn't them who buried them have found the casket and kept it? So, why dig up the whole cave? We should dig at certain points parallel to where we found this pike." Patrick had to agree that this made perfect sense.

The boys' testing of the earth revealed that Richard was correct. They found five other pikes, buried at different depths. However, they just scraped the earth around each 'zing' point to make sure each one was a pike and not the casket. In the end the boys had to accept that this possible hideout of Matthew Doran did not contain the casket. It was probable, Richard conceded, that a couple of United Irishmen could have hidden there, and might have found anything of value. So further digging by the boys in that cave was pointless. Before leaving the cave, they covered their excavations with branches, long grass, and weeds.

On the journey home Richard was unusually buoyant. Alright, they had not found the casket, but they had found part of Ireland's and Castledown's history, a kind of treasure. He was sure that the pikes belonged to the rebellions of 1798, for they were old and blunt. Richard told Patrick a couple of stories about the '98 rebellion which Philip Keating had told him, including some of the less commendable actions of the rebels. A silence followed. Rebellions often led to atrocities on both sides. As the boys walked into their own lane, Patrick gave his brother a light punch on the back, adding, "You know, boy, I sometimes tell you that you are mad, that your head is full of fancy ideas, that you are an *amadán*. But, you know, with all that we have done together, no lad could ask for a better brother than you."

Richard replied, "That is my real treasure."

1. CHAPTER 5.

'The Pikes Must be Together'[2]

Richard Barron proved himself to be one of the most able students at Burrane National School, developing a particular ability in Latin and Mathematics. Patrick left school at fourteen years, remaining at home to work on the farm. Had the family's finances been better, Richard might have graduated to the Christian Brothers' secondary school in Kilcolman. But extra income was needed by his family, so he too said goodbye to school shortly after turning fourteen.

Master Ford greeted this not unexpected news with sadness. However, he impressed upon Richard's parents that he would continue to coach the boy in Latin at no cost, if the latter were free on Saturdays. Andrew Barron intimated to the master that this could be possible, as a position was becoming available which could suit him.

The Poe family owned a farm of about two hundred acres of prime land situated two miles from the Barrons. Descendants of 'planters' granted the land by Oliver Cromwell, they were Protestants who maintained good relations with their Catholic neighbours. Through their mutual dealings with horses, Andrew Barron was friendly with Henry Poe. It was agreed that Richard, now an able young horseman, would assume employment with the Poes. His duties combined those of stable boy, groom, and exerciser of the

---

2   (John Keegan Casey)

horses, as well as some additional works with the horses on the farm. The Poes provided Richard with a horse to ride home on every evening and back to their farm early every morning, although some nights he stayed over in one of their sleep houses. Importantly, Richard had every second Saturday free in order to pursue his Latin studies with Mr. Ford, as well as his lessons on the fiddle with Mr. O'Sullivan. Like many of their religion and social class, the Poes valued music, culture, and literature. A cultured and talented boy like Richard Barron could well be an asset to their workforce.

About a year after his leaving school, Master Ford had introduced Richard to the classics of Roman literature, especially Julius Caesar's *Gallic Wars* and Virgil's *Aeneid.* These were followed by Livy's *History of Rome.* By the time he reached seventeen, Richard's classical studies were crowned by a study of Horace's immortal *Odes.*

By age eighteen, Richard Barron was a reasonably quiet, rather religious, fairly sensitive, and cultured young man. He possessed dark brown hair, a good brow, a rather lean jaw, and a somewhat serious aura. Although he could not be described as handsome, he possessed an engaging smile, which people loved. Richard was fond of a drink, a dance, and a flirtation with a girl. His social conscience had further developed, especially in relation to the evils of the landlord system and the treatment of the cottiers. However, he was conscious of his own position of employment with the Poes, and the relative security of tenure of his own family with their landlord. As his father often reminded him, "In Ireland, land is the only thing that matters, for land is the only thing that lasts."

Lacking a formal secondary education, Richard began to realise that the emigrant ship represented the only means for him to achieve his ambitions as a farmer, a teacher, or a musician. He yearned for a country with wide open spaces, where such land might be available to a hard-working lad like him, a country where he could foster his talents and scholastic ability. Did such a country exist anywhere?

August 1870.

Kevin O'Meara launched his tirade, "I tell you it is true. Robert Fraser, that new young agent of Captain Saunders is going to do it. All the rest of the cabin dwellers of the Saunders estate will be cleared out in a month's time. Eight families will be evicted to walk the roads in all weathers, to fight off starvation by begging their bread, them and their children to die of cold and exposure when winter comes. We all thought that Brophy was bad, but Fraser is a young Orange bastard from the North who thinks he can get away with this. And he will get away with it if people down here sit on their arses and do nothing."

Richard Barron, Kevin O'Meara, and the two Gorman boys, seated on the grass bank, had just finished their Sunday afternoon games of handball in 'the alley' in Castledown. Kevin was two years older than Richard, a farm labourer, hard-working.

"Well,"enquired Richard tentatively, "what should they do?"

Kevin answered, "They can do what the Whiteboys and Ribbonmen did, burn the hay in Fraser's barn, uproot his orchard, maim his cattle and horses."

Richard protested, "We cannot return to them dark and evil days. Life in the country has become better since then. Tenant leagues have been established. And I would never support actions which harm defenceless animals."

Kevin spat, "Tenant Leagues! It will take more than those to stop Fraser. This needs real action by lads like us."

"What do you mean by action?" asked Gerard Gorman. "We threaten Fraser not to evict those people? How? With a letter?"

"A letter!" snorted Kevin, "Why don't we send him a Christmas card with it? No, boys, we will act like true sons of Ireland. We will waylay him, ambush him, teach him a lesson."

"If we are going to kill him or injure him, I will not have anything to do with it," declared Richard. "That will lead only to more violence, and we will put our families in danger."

James, the older Gorman boy, spoke, "What if we just frighten him, threaten him?"

"I think I could be part of that action," Richard said, "but how would we do that?"

"I will tell you my plan," Kevin stated, "but I need you all to cross your hearts and promise to kape it all a secret." Kevin expounded, "Every Friday evening Fraser meets Slavin, the head of the Kilcolman constabulary. They drink and have a meal in McDermot's pub. Fraser rides home alone around 8.30 when it is dark. We can waylay him on that isolated stretch of road called 'the common.' We hide in the ditches, two of us on each side of the road, wearing masks like the Whiteboys did. We pull him off his horse, threaten him and warn him not to evict those families. Richard, you know horses, so you can send his horse galloping off. Fraser then has to walk the rest of the way home. We might partly strip him. We do not injure him."

"But won't we need weapons to frighten him?" enquired Gerard, intrigued. "What do we use? Pitchforks?"

Richard's memory went on a journey ten years past. Pitchforks could be dangerous. "I know," he exclaimed, "the pikes."

"Pikes!" said Gerard, "Are we going to poison him? How are we going to do that?"

James looked at him, uncomprehending, "Poison him with a pike?"

"Yes, people eat pikes, don't they?"

James laughed. "Richard is not talking about fish. He's talking about weapons, you *amadán*. Aren't you, Richard?"

"Yes, I am, James. Some years ago, Patrick and I discovered some old pikes in Mahony's quarry, and they are probably still there. They are blunt, so we cannot injure Fraser. Still, the sight of masked men armed with pikes should frighten the hell out of him. Kevin, should we use those pikes? He might think we are ghosts from '98."

Kevin was slow to reply. "Yes, boys, those pikes, even blunt ones, should do the job fine. All I want to see is Fraser shitting in his under trousers. Nothing more."

James Gorman winced.

Gerard spoke. "This is going to be one mighty *craic* altogether."

James reprimanded him. "Gerard, this is not a *craic*. It is serious business."

Kevin concluded. "We now agree on a date, and remember, boys, no word to anyone. Breathe a word of it, and I will rip your arse open with a pike." Kevin's blazing eyes suggested that he meant every word.

The pikes were buried in the cave, apparently undisturbed. Richard dug out four of them, hiding them in the furze bushes. However, his memory floated back to some words of advice of Master Ford fourteen years back, warning him about other people's plans. Nonetheless, Richard's doubts and reservations about the planned action were resolved by his conviction that something had to be done to try and prevent mass evictions. His godfather Philip's stories had affected him profoundly. Besides, after their action all four lads would melt back into their homes and their community. Fraser, new to the region, would not recognise their voices. He would probably be too ashamed to tell anyone about the incident. Hopefully he would see sense and stay his hand from the planned evictions.

Richard considered about Kevin O'Meara. While not really regarding him as a friend, he did trust him. Kevin was a bit too fond of the drink and of using profane language. Richard also disliked his attitude to girls, just there to be used. Still, Kevin had nothing to gain by the action, and Richard admired his spirit and his sympathy for the underdog. Lads like Kevin, not prepared to accept a lifetime of serfdom, were needed in Ireland. Richard made up his mind. He would join the other lads on the designated Friday.

Richard and Kevin had collected the pikes. "What are you doing with that stone, Kevin?" asked Richard.

"I'm sharpening it of course. All pikes must be sharpened. Otherwise, how do I draw blood?"

Richard, horrified, drew himself to his full height, stuck his pike vertical in the ground, and stared at Kevin. "No blood is to be drawn. We are using these pikes only to frighten him, nothing more."

Kevin taunted, "Come on, Barron, are you afraid of drawing a little Orange blood? That will frighten the shite out of him."

Richard would not yield. "The agreement between us and the Gorman boys is that we are using these pikes only to threaten. That is why I revealed where they were. If you are not going to stand by that agreement, I am going to bury my pike and go home. And there will be no point in your carrying the two pikes to James and Gerard. If I am not there, they too will not be part of your plan. Throw away that stone now. You decide. That is my final word."

"Do you really mean that?"

"Yes, I do, Kevin. I have told you all that I will not see people or animals injured."

"Well, Barron, if you fellows are so bloody yella,' I have no choice." Throwing the stone into the bush with a snarl, he said, "Let us go to strike our blow for Ireland without spilling blood."

The four young Whiteboys had donned their masks. James had provided them with an old white sheet each, a hole cut in its middle, which they placed over their torsos. Armed with the pikes, they had assumed their positions about one hundred and fifty yards beyond the bend in the narrow and lonely road of 'the common.' The half-moon had raised its lamp above. Richard and Gerard were positioned in the right-hand ditch, Kevin and James in the left hand one.

Kevin spoke, "Fraser wears a dark suit. He rides a white horse at a moderate pace, and the turn in the road will slow him down." All four lads' hearts beat faster. The fifteen minutes of waiting seemed like endless time. The occasional bird called. A small animal scurried through the undergrowth. The tension grew, the lads silent. A sound some distance away became louder. Horse steps. A canter. It slowed down, nearing the bend. The young would-be ambushers held up their pikes. The figure came into view. A white horse, a rider dressed in dark clothes. Kevin whispered loudly, "It's him."

"Are you sure?" the boys queried, Kevin answered, "Yes, it's him. To action, boys."

When years later in his retirement cottage in Kingstown, the rider on the white horse reflected on what happened. It was difficult for him to remember the sequence of events, on that memorable night.

The rider was tired after the events of the evening, but a couple of more miles and he would be home. Having rounded the bend, he patted his horse to resume a canter. Four spectres sprang from the two ditches, each holding an implement. The rider's natural impulse was to plough through them, but the horse ground to a halt. It neighed, reared on its hind-legs, at which point the four figures jumped back. Resuming its position on its four legs, the horse looked as if it would charge the assailants. A figure on the right moved to the horse, bravely grabbed the bridle, calming the animal with soothing words. A figure on the left side advanced in a threatening manner with his implement, which the rider perceived to be a pike. Another horse charged up on the rider's left-hand side.

"What is happening, doctor?" its rider called. Two of the assailants dropped back further. Another continued to hold the first rider's bridle, and the fourth one maintained his position.

"Doctor?" the bridle holder called.

"Yes, I am doctor Bradley," answered the first rider.

"And I am Father Aylward," the second rider called. "What is the meaning of this outrage? Are ye highway robbers or what? In the name of God, I command you to put down those weapons, take off your masks, and show your faces."

The four assailants did not move from their positions, but doctor and priest could see that their postures had become more nervous and that two of them were probably not much more than boys. "You heard what I said," the priest shouted. "Do as I say."

The two boys looked as if they would obey, but the threatening assailant turned to them in a fury. "Do not drop your weapons, boys, nor show our faces. The clergy are hand in hand with the peelers and the landlords. Hold fast." Turning back to the first rider he found himself staring into the barrel of a pistol.

Doctor Bradley's voice was calm, "Young man, you see this pistol. It is loaded. All I have to do is prime it and shoot. You are threatening me with a weapon. If I fire, it will be in self-defence. Father Aylward is a witness to that. I may accidentally maim you or even kill you. No judge or jury will convict me even of manslaughter. And the Catholic Church teaches that self-defence is justified."

The horse holder spoke. "Lads, do as the priest and doctor tell you. Neither of these men are our man. Remember that we cannot have any bloodshed."

James Gorman was the first to drop his pike and take off his mask, followed immediately by his brother. Richard threw his pike back into the ditch for fear of disturbing the horse, followed by the removal of his mask. Kevin O'Meara, furiously and slowly dropped his pike in the ground, and removed his mask. Both riders dismounted. They walked in front of their horses and faced their would-be assailants.

"I know all of your lads," the doctor said. "What on Earth are you doing? Are you pretending to be *raparees*? Are you trying to rob innocent travellers? Or-," looking now at Richard, "were you planning to attack someone else? We demand the truth."

Father Aylward now spoke up. "Whatever you were planning, you could not have picked a worse night."

"Why, father?" the boys asked.

"Have you not heard the terrible news?"

"News, what news?"

"Mr. Michael O'Keefe, agent of the Earl of Stanbrook, has been murdered a few hours ago. Shot by two men in cold blood in his own field. Doctor Bradley and I have just come from where he lay. The doctor tried to save him, but his wounds were deadly. I managed to give him the last rites, so he is now with the Lord, *requiescat en pace* (may he rest in peace)."

After a stunned silence, Doctor Bradley spoke. "We all need to get off this road immediately. Otherwise, you four boys could be facing the full force of the law for your insane actions this evening. And for God's sake, please remove those sheets."

The four would-be heroes, Dr. Bradley and Father Aylward sat on some rocks in a field, about 200 yards from the scene of the abortive ambush. The doctor had detailed the assassination of Mr. O'Keefe. It had occurred around six pm that evening. O'Keefe's workmen had finished stacking his corn around 5.30 pm. He had paid off those men and went to inspect their work. Two masked men had jumped out from behind a stack and had shot the agent point blank in cold blood. The shots had alerted two of his cowhands and his wife, who had rushed to the scene. Mr. O'Keefe had lingered in the agony of death for around two hours. His wife had sent her son William by horse to Kilcolman to inform the constabulary. The doctor, the priest, and the constable sped to the crime scene. The constable remained there for only about twenty minutes to observe the victim, get his statement, and give the doctor a pistol in self-defence.

"It was by the hand of God that the constable stayed only for that short time." Fr. Aylward said. "If he had travelled back with us, you four freedom fighters would now be on your way to Kilcolman police station for severe questioning."

Kevin O'Meara asked nervously. "So, Father, are you two men going to inform the constabulary about our actions? I wish to apologise about what I said about the clergy. I did not mean it. It just came out in the heat of the moment."

The doctor spoke calmly, "That depends on what you lads tell us about your actions and your intentions. It may well be that the whole story does not need to go beyond the four sides of this field. Do you agree, Father Michael?" The priest agreed.

Father Michael queried. "Now, James, you and your brother are students at St. Kieran's College, are you not? And, James, I believe that you are intending to enter the seminary next year."

"Yes, Father. I think that I may have a vocation."

"Then, James, do not concern yourself that your actions tonight will be an impediment. Young hot-headed boys sometimes commit actions without thinking of the consequences. So, can I ask you, James, to tell us honestly what led to you lads' action. You have Doctor Bradley's word and mine that we will not go running to the constabulary." James looked at Richard and Kevin, both of them nodding their assent.

"Firstly," Father Michael stated, "we need to know where each of you lads were around six pm this evening. Many people could well be questioned by the constabulary." Each of the four lads had a convincing alibi. Richard had been having his tea with the farm hands at Poe's, and had spoken to Henry Poe before he left for home. Kevin had been stacking corn with co-workers at the Hughes' farm. James and Gerard had been milking their family's cows. Whereupon Father Michael asked James to begin the story.

James recounted the events in a composed manner. He told both men about how Kevin had informed them about Fraser's planned evictions and their resultant deep anger; how they had devised the plan to warn and frighten Fraser, but not to injure him in any way; how Richard had suggested the use of pikes, subject to that condition.

Dr. Bradley picked up a pike, "I don't see how any enemy could have been injured by this ancient replica. They are so blunt that I would believe you, James. Now we need to know, for your own safety, whether any of you lads gave the slightest indication to anyone else about this plan."

Gerard Gorman now burst out with, "No, doctor, none of us would have. You see, Kevin told us that if-"

A light punch and a "Hush boy" from James silenced him.

James did not wish that any of them should hear the cited profanity, so he explained. "Each of us made a promise not to breathe a word to anyone."

Dr. Bradley took charge of the situation, declaring that the priority now was to get rid of the evidence, namely the pikes. He led the four lads to the next field and indicated a large pond, instructing each lad them to wrap his pike in his own white sheet and throw it towards the middle of the pond. On seeing each weapon sink immediately, Gerard quipped that he expected a hand to come up from the water and take his pike. A look from his brother prevented him from elaborating further.

All were seated again on the rocks, Father Aylward resumed his role as counsellor. "Each of us must promise and vow on the bible to God to keep absolute secrecy. This is so that you boys will protect each other, as well as protecting Doctor Bradley and myself. If this story ever gets out, the authorities may view it as part of a wider plot to intimidate, injure, or even murder landlords and their agents, because it has happened on the same night as the O'Keefe murder. So, which of you will be first to take this vow?" James Gorman raised his hand.

All six people in turns placed their right hands on the bible, and solemnly vowed that they would never reveal to anyone in Ireland the planned action. The story would now remain within the four sides of the field. In answer to Father Aylward's questions to what they would tell their parents about their whereabouts that evening, each pair of lads came up with reasonably convincing alibis. Fr. Aylward declared that a potentially dangerous and even tragic situation had thankfully been prevented. After the Gorman boys had left, having shaken priest's and doctor's hands, the priest mentioned to Kevin and Richard that, in the light of the O'Keefe murder, he hoped that Fraser would now reconsider his own plan to carry out the evictions. He himself would visit Captain Saunders and hopefully persuade him to stay his agent's hand. So, it might well transpire that the boys' intentions would be achieved in a peaceful manner.

The doctor, however, did not trust Kevin O'Meara to keep his mouth shut, especially if under the influence of drink. Better for all concerned if he could be moved from the district.

The doctor spoke, "Kevin, my brother Peter owns a foundry in Dublin. Two days ago, he sent me a telegram. He is urgently looking for a new worker, a hard-working young country lad. The pay is 15 shillings a week, which will increase as he gains more skills. Peter's business is thriving, so it offers good security. Would you consider accepting this job?"

"Can I let you know tomorrow or Sunday, doctor?"

"I am afraid not. I have a couple of other local lads in mind, but I am now offering the job to you. My brother needs to know by telegram tomorrow. You will lodge with the family of one of his workers, good people. You can travel to Dublin by train on Tuesday or Wednesday, and start work on Thursday, and I will advance you the fare. This is an opportunity which may never come again."

Father Aylward voiced his support. "Dublin is not England or America, so, Kevin, you will not be breaking ties with your family."

Kevin decided immediately, "Yes, doctor, I accept the position. It will be best for my future. I thank you and your brother for this offer."

While the doctor discussed the final arrangements with Kevin, Richard had to go and answer the call of nature. On returning he encountered Kevin heading home. Richard extended his hand to wish him farewell and good luck, but Kevin looked at him with vehemence, "I do not shake hands with turncoats. You and them two Gorman boys are yella' cowards, bastards. And you, Barron, are the biggest bastard of all, in every sense of the word."

With those words, Kevin was gone from Richard's life. As if pierced by an icicle, Richard stumbled back to join the two men. Dr. Bradley silently handed him a small flask of whiskey, advising him to take a couple of swigs. The drink warmed his inner body, but nothing could warm the pain in his heart unleashed by the cruel and vehement words.

As Doctor Bradley and Father Aylward needed to commence their homeward journey soon, they outlined their proposal to Richard. Even to a hard-working, intelligent, and talented young man like him, Ireland in its present state offered few opportunities. Had he considered migrating? Richard replied that he had, but was unsure of his destination. Both priest and doctor presented him with a vista of a far-away country. Land and possible land grants were available there for farming. Gold had been found there in abundance. Cities were being built which required hard working young lads. Educational institutions could well enable him to complete his education, and his musical talents could be cultivated there. Thousands of Irish had settled in that far away land, especially since the Great Famine. Richard would be welcome there, especially with his talents as a horseman and a musician. And what was the name of that promised land? Its name was Australia.

Richard answered, "Gentlemen, I have considered going to Australia, but have been put off by the passage money of around 15 pounds. Are not assisted passages available?"

"Richard, applying for one could be a long process," Father Aylward replied. "The diocese of Ossary has some funds which could help talented lads to migrate to Australia. Between assistance from this fund, some money contributed by your father, and your own savings, the passage money can be reached. Can I speak to your father on Sunday?"

"Of course, you can, Father."

Patrick Barron was surprised and rather perplexed by Mr. Mahony's news two days after the O'Keefe murder. "Yes, Patrick, sure wasn't it a terrible murder. But you know, and maybe I should not tell you this, I saw two young lads walking across my far field that same evening, each of them carrying what looked like two forks." Patrick gave a nervous start. "Who were they?"

"Well, Patrick, I have to say that I am sure one of them was your brother Richard. Would you have been the other one? He did not look like you, though."

"No, it was not me."

"Sure, I never mind people walking across my fields. But where would they have been going as dusk was falling? Look, lad, don't worry about it. I won't breathe a word about it to divil a one. Sure, aren't you, Richard and your two sisters almost family to us."

Meanwhile the whole district was on tenterhooks. Many people had been questioned by constabulary. Richard told his family that, if questioned, he had a perfect alibi. He had been having his tea with the farm workers at Poe's. But, Patrick remembered, Richard had disappeared for around two hours after arriving home. His answer to his family next morning was that he and Kevin O'Meara had arranged to go to O'Riordan's pub that evening. On arriving there they had found it closed. They did not know the reason, but decided to go back to their homes. That, Patrick mused, would not have taken two hours, but maybe the lads had met up with some girls. Neither Patrick nor his parents really liked Kevin, but his sister Ellen said that they were just being snobs. Kevin was a good lad, a hard worker, and he made her laugh. It was with some relief when the Barron family heard the following Wednesday that Kevin O'Meara had departed for Dublin. Nobody thought any more of it, because the doctor quite often found work for local lads and girls in the surrounding towns, and even in Dublin. Richard felt even more secure when the two Gorman boys returned to Saint Kieran's College the next day. However, he was still hit by worry, now that his announced plans to emigrate to Australia were taking shape. But the one who was the most worried was Patrick.

Forks, sprongs, scythes. These implements had been used by tenants against landlords and their agents in the past. Sometimes they had used actual weapons like pikes and guns. *Pikes*. The recollection struck Patrick like a bolt from the sky. The discovery in the cave ten years prior. Two days after O'Meara had departed, Patrick was in that same cave. The first thing which struck him was that fresh grass, weeds, and shrubs had been placed recently over the cave's floor. Patrick's foreboding grew as he removed them and began digging. No zings in the original areas where he and Richard had found four of the six pikes. But what about nearer to the cave wall? Could Patrick bring himself to see if the two remained? His initial feeling was no, it was too much to bear. But a feeling of anger was pervading his being. For all their sakes, Patrick had to discover the truth. He dug furiously in that space. *Zing.* The familiar sound resounded. Within ten minutes, Patrick found the remaining two pikes. He did not need to dig them out. Four of the original pikes had been removed, probably no further back than two weeks. He covered up the remaining two.

Patrick sat on a rock, his face in his hands. Richard must have removed the pikes, either on the Friday evening itself or a few days prior. Kevin O'Meara and two other accomplices must have been involved. When Patrick's anger and grief had subsided, he began to apply a logical framework to the events. He became convinced that it was sheer coincidence that Richard and Kevin had carried the pikes on the same night as the O'Keefe murder. However, they could have been planning some action against a different landlord or agent, possibly Fraser, because of his planned evictions. Patrick remembered that, when his family and neighbours had talked about the O'Keefe murder, Richard, unusual for him, was silent. Had Richard and his accomplices heard about the murder and had decided there and then to postpone or even abandon whatever plans they had hatched? Alternatively, they could have removed the pikes from the cave for a future planned action. Whatever was the case, with the murder, O'Meara gone to Dublin, and Richard's impending emigration, it was extremely unlikely that any such future action would eventuate.

Still, Patrick could not remove himself from the rock. He spoke to Richard as if the latter were standing before him. "My brother, you have betrayed me. Even if you are not my brother, like some people have hinted, I loved you as if you were. I sang to your lovely fiddle playing. We went to school together, went on adventures together, did everything together." Patrick's anger rose. He picked up two stones and squeezed them hard as if he were strangling his brother. "You betrayed our parents, our sisters. You let, I am sure, that O'Meara bastard talk you into a terrible and dangerous action. Yes, we made a secret pact as children about those pikes. But you broke it. You put us all in danger. I warned you back then about how bringing a pike home could have meant us losing our farm. The farm which we have lived on for over a century. My farm. The farm I love. The farm I want to pass on to my children and grandchildren, I hope as owner. How could you have done such a stupid and dangerous action? I am trying not to hate you, God forgive me." Patrick's anger subsided. He began to think of the logical solution. Richard had to depart for Australia as soon as possible, because it was unsafe for him or for his family that he should remain at home. Patrick would make every effort not to betray any of his suspicions to Richard before he departed, but he would keep a close eye on him. Nothing, even former close fraternal feelings, would deprive the Barron family of their land.

For Richard, the plans for his migration moved at marathon speed. Within less than four weeks after the fiasco, everything had been finalised. Father Aylward had secured eight pounds from the diocesan fund, Andrew Barron adding five more, and Richard another two. Dr Bradley and Father Aylward had given him glowing character references. His father and brother, while displaying regret at his imminent departure, betrayed a slight uneasiness in his presence, impressing on him that on no account should he change his mind. Richard's sisters were openly distressed at the prospect of never seeing him again. By contrast his mother was her usual pragmatic self, displaying few extra tokens of affection, and repeating that it was all for the better. Richard had given his notice to the Poes, who also gave him an excellent reference and a parting bonus of five pounds. Two days before departure Richard had bid goodbye to Master Ford and Mr. O'Sullivan, both men moved to tears. On his final day Richard had bade his farewell to the Shanahans, the Mahoneys, and a few other close neighbours.

Even though two men had been arrested on suspicion of the O'Keefe murder and would appear in court in Kilkenny the following week, the district was still tense. Accordingly, Andrew and Mairead Barron had decided against holding the traditional wake for Richard. It might draw undue attention from the authorities.

Richard had packed his bag. The family had partaken of a special dinner. The mood had been sombre. Richard had then walked the fields of their farm with his two sisters, the green fields which he loved so much. Next morning everyone had risen early. They had just drunk a cup of tea, for Richard and his father would breakfast in Kilkenny. The horse was tackled to the cart. Richard announced that he was ready to go. There was no point in waiting around. His family assembled on the roadside outside the gate. Richard hugged his sisters, and kissed each of them on the cheek. He held Patrick's hand for a couple of seconds before shaking it, followed by a quick embrace. His mother gave him a quick handshake and hug, but no kiss. Richard jumped on to the cart. Standing up, he took one last look at the family home behind the pond, the green and verdant fields, the unique home sky above.

Richard Barron's gaze fell on the family tableau group. Years later he would regret that he had not borrowed one of those new things called cameras, for a photo as an eternal memento. Half -way down the road Richard turned. The group was still there. His wave was returned. Just before the turn in the road Richard turned one last time. His mother and Patrick had left. He waved to his two sisters, who responded. As the horse turned the corner, Richard knew in his heart that that chapter of his life had closed forever. He would never again see the home of his childhood in Kilkenny.

Richard and his father had finished a good breakfast in the Club House hotel. All through the journey Richard had debated in his mind whether to ask the ultimate question, but was resolute in his decision. "*Mo'Athair*, there is one question I feel I have to ask you before I head to Australia. Will you promise not to be angry with me?"

His father shifted uneasily in his chair. "How could I be angry with you, *Mo Mhic*, before you depart for the ends of the Earth?"

Richard's courage rose, "My question is this. Am I actually your son?" A silence ensued. Richard repeated his question, his eyes and voice pleading.

The blood drained from his father's face. "What makes you think you are not my son?"

"I don't look like any of my sisters or my brother. Over the years some people have made comments, some by accident, a few in malice. Also, more importantly, at times I have sensed that I did not really belong to my family."

His father countered. "And did you feel that we treated you differently? Oh, sure I know that your mother favoured Patrick over you, but that is not unusual with the eldest son. Yes, she was a little harsher on you, but she was harsh on all four of you and only as circumstances demanded. If you do not think we are your parents, who do you think is?"

Richard responded, "I have heard that during the Great Famine good people like ye sometimes adopted children of parents on the brink of death. I was born in June 1847, the height of the Famine. Children were sometimes adopted from the Kilcolman workhouse, weren't they? There are two years between myself and Patrick and four years between me and Ellen. Maybe you and my mother felt that ye would be limited to one child and-"

"*A Mhic*, listen to me. You were not adopted in that manner. Nor were you adopted from any workhouse. You are going to Australia. I will most likely never see you again. You cannot deny that you were always my favourite child, can you?"

Richard touched his father's hand, "No, *Mo Athair,* I cannot."

Andrew Barron continued, "Look at yourself and at all the gifts the Almighty has given you. You are a lad of very high intelligence. I have always regretted that we could not afford to have sent you to secondary school. God gave you great talents, as a violinist and musician. And I love to see it too that you are a great hand with the horses. From where in your family did all those gifts come?"

"I am sure, *Mo Athair,* from the Barrons."

"Exactly, *A Mhic.* Your mother's family, the Kinehans, were good people, but they did not possess the brains nor the music of the Barrons. And I know for a fact that my grandfather trained and worked horses. Your aunt Catherine was a fine pianist, trained by the Presentation nuns in Waterford, to where she won a scholarship. I remember my grandmother and her glorious singing voice. It was from them that you and Patrick got yer musical gifts."

Richard spoke slowly. "My aunt Catherine, was she the aunt who went to New York?"

"Yes, *A Mhic,* she left our home in September of the black'47. She went out to our brother Michael. Catherine, an intelligent young woman, saw that there was no future for her in this ravaged land."

Richard mused, September'47, three months after he was born. "Did she keep in touch with ye?" he asked.

"She did for a while. She got a very good position as a governess out there. Later on, she married well, but over the years we have lost touch, like I have lost touch with my brother Michael. So, have I answered all your questions, *Ashtore mo chroi* (dearest of my heart)?"

Richard smiled. "Yes, you have. So, *M'athair,* I have your word of truth that I am a Barron through and through?"

Andrew Barron joined his right hand with Richard's. "*A Mhic,* as the Almighty God is my witness, and as you depart for that faraway land, you have my absolute word of truth that you are a true Barron, of proud Norman-Irish lineage, the same as my son Patrick and my daughters Ellen and Anne. Wherever you go, you shall carry the Barron name with utmost pride, for that is the proud Norman Irish name which is yours by blood and heritage."

For his final act of assurance, Andrew Barron placed his hand inside his pocket and took out an envelope and his pocket watch. Handing the envelope to Richard, he said, "This is from another of those unknown persons who loved your violin playing. He requested that you put it towards buying a new violin."

Richard opened the envelope to reveal a five-pound note. His amazement was stretched to incredulity when his father placed the pocket watch in his hand. "This watch belonged to my grandfather Andrew Barron. You have seen me wear it on special occasions. It is a family heirloom, but I want you to have it as you go to Australia."

"But, *M'athair,* I cannot accept that. You must give it to Patrick, your eldest son."

"No, *A Mhic.* Patrick will inherit the farm. That is his birthright. My giving this watch to you is proof that you are a true Barron, our own flesh and blood. Only promise me that you will never part with it, whatever your circumstances. Maybe one day you will pass it on to your own son in Australia."

Fighting back his tears, Richard managed to say. "*M'athair,* I will honour this pocket watch with the same reverence as I do the crucifix given to me by the bishop and blessed by his Holiness the Pope. You remember that it was presented to me at that special Mass on Assumption Day all those years ago, when I accompanied the choir on my fiddle, and when Patrick sang solo so beautifully."

The journey to Kilkenny railway station passed with pleasant conversation. The embrace given to Richard by his father was an expression of true paternal love. Both men smiled to each other with their final wave as the train moved off. Richard felt an overwhelming sense of relief. He was pretty convinced that he knew the identity of his natural mother, and he had a suspicion too of who his real father was. But, whatever his actual parentage, he could rest assured that he was a true Barron of Castledown, a descendent of the Barrons, lords of Burnchurch Castle, County Kilkenny.

CHAPTER 6.

The Force of Destiny

September 1870.

The streets of Wexford town. Unlike Kilkenny and Waterford, Wexford bore an air of relative prosperity. Its occupants walked with a certain confidence, their faces presenting a qualified level of happiness with their lot in life. This contrasted with the growing melancholy of this young exile. On reaching the infamous bullring, Richard Barron recalled the story of that barbarian Oliver Cromwell herding old men, women, and children into it, and unleashing his ironsides to butcher them like cattle. Their blood had flowed down the streets to mingle with the waters of St. George's channel.

Richard's own mood darkened as he wandered aimlessly down towards those same waters. An exile from his own home, his farm, his family, his homeland. But were they his family? Their attitude towards him had definitely changed since the fiasco. He felt that he had become a black sheep exiled to Australia, reputedly a favourite destination for such species. No farewell wake, the hurried goodbyes from his family members. Richard felt as if the sword of one of the ironsides had carved his heart into two pieces. The wind was rising from St. George's channel. The owners of the boarding house had told him that a bad storm was imminent, and that his voyage to Liverpool would most likely be delayed for a couple of days. Could anything possibly get worse?

The Selskar Arms, a medium sized public house during early evening. A welcoming open fire; some marine artefacts adorning the walls; a cheery landlord attending to his few customers. Richard sat with his back to the bar, sipping his ale, his head drooped. "Feeling a little low in spirit, are you?"

Richard raised his head. "Sorry, what did you say?"

The voice responded. "I said, are you feeling a little low?"

"And if I am, what is it to you?"

The voice became a person. "It is something to me. I never like to see a young lad being sad. Would you mind if I sat down with you a moment?"

Indicating his assent, Richard was immediately struck by the stranger's physique. Square shoulders, a straight back, strong bodied, rather muscular. Richard could not recall ever having seen a more handsome young man in his life. He guessed that the stranger was probably about two years older than him, two inches taller, clear skinned and healthy looking, with black hair. He was clad with a clean shirt, a cravat around his neck, a tweed jacket, and cotton trousers.

But it was the magnetic pull of the stranger's eyes which impressed him most. Richard's guard immediately arose. This young man could be a spy, an informer, even a peeler. He extended his hand. "Malcolm Sutton is my name. Maybe you would like to tell me yours, if you please."

"Richard B….Butler."

"Ah, derived from the princely family of the Butlers. So, you are from County Kilkenny."

Richard gave a slight start, "No, from County Waterford."

Sutton replied. "Still, either way you are from the ranks of the Norman aristocracy. I regret to tell you that I think the Suttons were only your foot soldiers. Still, we all did quite well down here, being treated fairly by our own aristocracy."

"So, you are from Wexford town," Richard asked.

"Not at all," Sutton answered. "I am from Kilrane in the barony of Forth. I am proud to say that I am a true Yole."

Richard was puzzled. "And what on Earth is a Yole?"

Sutton gave a short laugh. "So, you have never heard of the Yoles. Well, I would not have expected one of the Waterford Butlers to have heard of us." He gave Richard's arm a friendly squeeze. "Would you like me to tell you a few things about the Yoles?"

Richard nodded. There was no harm in listening to a yarn spun by a handsome and affable stranger.

Sutton indicated Richard's almost empty glass. "Can I get you another glass of ale? Or maybe you would prefer a pint, even a whiskey?"

Richard's guard arose again. Maybe Sutton, if that were indeed his name, wanted him to drink too much, become loose tongued, and careless with his wallet. He indicated that a glass would be fine.

"Very good. You are a temperate man. We Yoles are famous for our temperance too."

While Sutton was obtaining the drinks, Richard discretely moved his wallet from his trousers pocket to inside his under trousers.

"Well, my friend, you are ready for a new story?"

"Sure," thought Richard. A good story from a potential trickster. "And where is that Yola region of yours, Malcolm?"

"Right at the bottom of county Wexford, in the two baronies of Forth and Bargy. I think that most of us came from Wales or the west of England as foot soldiers with the Norman invasion. The baronies of Forth and Bargy are separated from the rest of this county, and indeed from the rest of Ireland, by the Forth mountains. So, we Yoles developed a way of life rather different to the native Irish. The great majority of us, peasants, small farmers, and most of the landlords, remained Catholic after the Reformation. This led to some of the old Norman landlords having their estates confiscated by that tyrant Oliver Cromwell. Can I ask you, my lad, if you yourself are a Catholic?"

"I am."

"Good for you. So am I," said Sutton, smiling a mesmerising smile which drew the listener closer. "Oh yes. Relations between the Yoles and even their Protestant landlords have always been good. You did not find in Forth and Bargy any of those Whiteboys or Ribbonmen killing, injuring or threatening a landlord, his agent, or his cattle, like you did in other parts of Ireland." This nonchalant statement caused a sudden start from Richard, resulting in Sutton momentarily looking into his eyes. "Should I continue with my story?"

"Y… Y… yes. I find it very interesting."

Sutton squeezed Richard's arm again. "Relax, my friend," he said. "My story gets better."

Yes, thought Richard. Whatever he felt about Sutton, he certainly was good at spinning a yarn. Richard made sure to discretely check on his wallet.

Sutton continued, "The Yoles were a very peaceful and industrious people. We lived quietly in our cabins, law abiding, clean, with few beggars. One of the reasons for our relative prosperity was that we did not rely on the potato. No, we grew our own peas, and especially beans, eggs, fowl, and honey."

Absolutely convinced now that Sutton was a trickster, Richard enquired. "So how did your Yola land fare during the Great Famine twenty years ago?"

"Do you remember the Famine, Richard?"

"Yes, but only toward the end of it."

Richard suddenly realised that he had effectively given away his age to a potential informer or peeler. What an idiot he was! But Sutton continued regardless.

"I remember it from about 1850 onwards, but it did not affect us much in our two baronies. In fact, there was no serious hunger, deaths from starvation or fever in Forth and Bargy. The population barely changed, upwards or downwards, and the lower population was caused by emigration."

Richard was growing tired of Sutton's yarn. However, there was something about Sutton which simply mesmerised him. Richard felt that he was almost being drawn under a spell. He enquired, "Which language, Irish or English, did you Yoles speak?"

"Neither. We had our own language for centuries." Richard stared at him.

"What? Are you serious?"

"Exactly as I said. We had our own language since the Norman invasion, known as Yola. As with your Irish language, it has almost died out now. It is said to have been a mixture of Old English, some Saxon speech with a little Flemish thrown in. I can teach you a few phrases. Can you speak any Irish?"

"Only a few phrases, learnt from my parents and friends."

Sutton smiled. "Good, you can teach them to me. So English is your only language?"

"I have learned a certain amount of Latin. We learned it at national school, and my teacher continued to teach me it for some years afterwards. He declared that it was a beautiful language which every Irish scholar should know, as well as being the foundation language for French, Italian, Portuguese, and Spanish."

Sutton beamed. "So you would have little trouble learning Spanish."

"Why on Earth would I need or want to learn Spanish?"

Sutton replied. "Oh, nothing, no reason. I just thought-."

Richard, observing that both their glasses were almost empty, offered to buy two more glasses of ale. He would leave the public house after drinking his. This cock and bull story about the Yola language was the last straw.

Sutton flashed his winning smile on Richard's return. "So," he asked, "I am presuming that you are feeling low because you might be about to emigrate to England or America."

Richard paused, "I am on my way to Australia, to the ends of the Earth."

Sutton whistled, "Yes, indeed a long, long way. Probably no chance of coming back from there. Have you some family members, relatives, or friends there?"

"No, no one there. I am the second son. My older brother will inherit our farm. I have to take the emigrant ship. I have been told that I may be able to get a land grant there."

"So, Richard, you have worked on a farm?"

"Yes, on our own and on other farms. I am good with horses. I worked on the farm of one of the minor gentry, grooming the horses, exercising them, even riding them to round up sheep. Maybe in Australia-"

Sutton glowed, "Richard, you would be worth your weight in gold in any country." A pause. "You see, my friend, I am emigrating too."

Yes, thought Richard, to Australia I'm sure, where he can wheedle his way into my confidence and rob me of my money when we are in Liverpool. "And where to? Not to Australia, I'm sure."

"No, my friend. Actually, I am emigrating to the Republic of Argentina."

Richard stared at Sutton. This statement was beyond belief. "Argentina! I've never heard of any Irish person emigrating there. Why in God's name are you going there?"

Sutton stretched out his body in a relaxed position. "Because my uncle David, a bachelor who migrated there from Kilrane 25 years ago needs me. He owns an *estancia*, that is a ranch, of 12,000 acres, a *morcal* (huge) amount of land, on which he farms mainly sheep and some cattle. He would be in his mid-50s now. So, he needs preferably a family member to help him run that vast enterprise. I too am a second son who will not inherit our Yola farm. So, you see, we have some things in common."

"Yes," Richard stated, "but Argentina. You will find no Irish there, only savage Indians. Who runs the country? What language do they speak? Not English or Irish I bet, or even Yola."

Sutton chuckled, "No, they certainly don't speak Yola there, although some of the old migrants from Forth and Bargy might a little. Spanish is the language of the Argentine Republic. But in the Irish settlements, which stretch across the pampas, English is their spoken language." Sutton moved his hands and arms like a conjurer casting a spell. "The pampas, like the prairies of North America, are vast open spaces of grasslands, fertile plains containing some of the richest land in the world, and excellent for sheep and cattle."

Richard was completely lost. 'But how come I have never heard of Irish settlements there?"

"Probably because few people from rural Waterford ever migrated to Argentina. Can I tell you a little about Irish migration to

Argentina, Richard?" Richard, although not in the mood for another fairy story, assented. The Argentina yarn might even be better than the Yola nonsense. Yet, Richard could not deny that since meeting Sutton his previous depressed mood had lifted considerably.

For his Argentine yarn Sutton fixed his magnetic eyes and gaze upon Richard. "The Irish migration to Argentina began around 1845. It was established by a Dominican priest, Father Anthony Fahy from County Galway, working with a couple of successful Irish businessmen in Argentina. Most Irish migrants to Argentina hailed from counties Longford, Westmeath and Wexford. The Wexford migrants hailed mainly from Forth and Bargy."

Richard could not avoid another quip "So, Yola land was transplanted to Argentina."

Sutton laughed. "Well, that is one way of putting it. Now, Father Fahy insisted that the Irish migrants should not stay in the cities, but get out to the pampas, and stick to what they were good at, namely sheep and cattle raising. A system known as 'halves and thirds' entitled a young Irish migrant to obtain from the *estancia* owner a half or third share of the flock's annual produce of wool and lambs. So, the Irish shepherd could build up his own flock of sheep, and eventually was able to purchase his own land. A pretty good way of getting to own your own land, don't you think?"

Richard considered, "Maybe, but why wait all them years? In Australia you could get to own your own land through a land grant." Sutton countered with. "Possibly. but I reckon it would take some time. And you still need money to stock it with sheep, cattle, or horses. Alright, a young migrant like you might get a bank loan, but you are still putting yourself into debt. I have been told that the land in Australia varies in quality, unlike the pampas. Also, that they have terrible droughts, bushfires, flooding rains, sand-storms, even plagues. I don't deny that they have these in Argentina too, but remember, that the pampas are among the most lush and fertile lands in the world. Fortunes have been made there by many of the Wexford men who have migrated, including my uncle."

Sutton spoke as if inspired, "Richard, have you booked and paid for your passage to Australia yet?"

Richard's guard rose again. "No, I have not, should I have?" Sutton relaxed. "Then take my advice, and don't book it yet. This gathering storm will give us a couple of precious bad days. It would not be a good idea to book your ship for Australia until the storm passes. Can I ask you a small favour, please?"

Richard mused. This is it. A request for a loan of money. "Depends on what it is."

"Richard, it is not for money. My request is can you please wait right here for me. I am going to run back to my relatives' house to get a newspaper article for you about Irish migration to Argentina. I can also bring back an article about Yolaland."

Richard smiled. "Yes, please, I would like to read both."

Sutton's countenance was radiant. "So, you will wait here. I will be no more than twenty minutes. I promise."

Richard answered, "I promise too." Another squeeze on Richard's arm, slightly harder this time.

"That wind would cut the *ber* (cheek) off you. Now, Richard, the two articles are in this large envelope. I have another favour to ask, and again it is not for money. Can you please meet me in this public house tomorrow at 1 pm? You will be my guest for dinner."

Richard considered. Why not accept? Sutton was very good company, and he could look forward to another fairy story. Both sealed the promises with a handshake.

Sutton, holding Richard's hand for rather longer than normal, declared. "And now let each of us head for our places of abode, for the skies will open with the *downgurry* (downpour) in the next few minutes. Good *nicht,* Richard."

"*Oiche mhaith,* Malcolm."

Richard Barron relaxed in the short metal bath. Now he felt cleansed in body, and his earlier depression had largely lifted, partly due to Sutton's handsome looks, his stories, and his camaraderie. But what a load of poppycock! A small corner of Ireland whose inhabitants lived an idyllic existence, free of blatant poverty, famine, and crime. If Yola land was only about fifty miles from his place of birth, why had he never heard of it? Absolute nonsense! And better still, Yola land had been transplanted to another faraway country of which he had barely and rarely heard. Richard had no intention of reading the articles given to him by that trickster, most likely not genuine anyway. He soaked his body thoroughly in the warm waters. Having reluctantly stepped out of the bath, he could see the reflection of his naked body in the full-length mirror. Although only five feet eight inches in height, his body looked full and strong, with muscular arms. His hips and lower legs were well formed. Why, he might even pass for a Yole!

Richard awoke suddenly from a bizarre dream. It was early morning, but still dark. His brother Patrick, their two friends, and he himself had been performing as wrenboys in the house of the 'strong' farmers, the Heffernans. All four boys were now enjoying their repast of Christmas cake and lemonade. This was interrupted by the entry of a handsome young man, who spoke in a strange language. Mr. Heffernan requested that he speak in English. The visitor told them that he was leaving that day for Argentina, and asked if any of the boys were coming with him. At their refusal, the young man grabbed Patrick. Richard dashed to rescue him, clinging to him, but the young man gave him a violent push, at which point Richard woke up.

Slowly the realisation dawned on Richard. That remarkable day ten years prior at the Heffernans. The discussion about Wallace riding over the mountains, the Irish settlements on the pampas, the counties they came from. So, Malcolm Sutton was not lying. Richard sat up in bed, his hand reaching for the oil lamp and the matchbox. He looked at his pocket watch. It read 6.20 am. He opened the envelope, removing an article titled *Argentina, Land of Promise for the Irish*, dated April 1865 and published in *The Wexford People* by Father Antonio Fahy himself. He wrote of the opportunities and the good life which awaited Irish migrants in the Argentine, but did not ignore the vicissitudes – the upheavals caused by nature's destructive force, the Indian attacks, the lack of entertainment, and especially the isolation, with the nearest other homestead often being dozens of miles away.

One particular quotation, caught Richard's attention. *Would to God that Irish emigrants would come to this country instead of the United States. Here they would feel at home, they would have plenty employment, and would experience a sympathy from the natives very different from what they receive in the 'States. There is not a finer country in the world for a poor man to come to, especially with a family.* But could not this article be a fake? Unlikely, but possible. Well, there was one way of finding out.

Within twenty minutes the young man at *The Wexford People* office had presented Richard with the required April 1865 edition of the newspaper, as well as the edition dated May 1868, which featured the article on the Yoles and their language. Richard, his hands shaking a little, found page fourteen for the former article. It was exactly the same as the article in his possession. Why should he have doubted that handsome and engaging young man? As he walked back to his boarding house in the pouring rain, he decided that he would accept the dinner invitation. However, he arranged with the boarding house's owner and his wife to leave most of his money in their secure safe.

Malcolm Sutton greeted Richard Barron with a glowing smile, "I never doubted that you would come. I am so glad that you have."

Richard responded. "I never refuse the offer of hospitality. It was most generous of you."

Both seated, Sutton suggested that they both might avail of the beef and vegetable soup, followed by the good steak, complemented by a glass of good Spanish red wine. During their main course their discussion was polite but friendly, talking about the two articles on Argentina and the Yoles.

The main course finished, Sutton had ordered apple pie and cream for both of them. Smiling, he said, "You seem to be in better spirits today. Why?"

Richard replied. "When a young lad leaves his home, his family, and is about to depart his country to sail to the ends of the Earth, I suppose that it is natural that he feels that way. Meeting you has raised my spirits a good deal."

"I am very happy it has. But, was there anything else? I could sense yesterday that you were suffering badly."

Richard spoke slowly. He recounted his doubts about his paternity in a manner similar to his conversation with his father, and the latter's words of assurance. His companion considered, "It is possible. Your parents might have considered Australia as a good destination for a foster child. It was or is a place to where families used to send their black sheep, but you are not one of those, are you, Richard? Can I ask you, did your family's attitude to you change somewhat during the weeks or days before you departed?" Richard felt emboldened to confide to Malcolm some aspects of his mother's and brother's change of attitude, the lack of a departing wake, no overwhelming signs of affection to the child they would never see again. Sutton flashed his mesmerising smile.

"Well, my friend, I think that another glass of red wine will do us both good." Standing up, he gave Richard's cheek a light squeeze. Meanwhile, their apple pie and tea had arrived.

Malcolm produced two letters from the inside pocket of his jacket. Handing one of these to Richard, he explained, "My first cousin Eamonn was meant to come with me. My uncle David sent passage money for both of us, but Eamonn has got cold feet. His excuse was that his mother has become ill recently. Fear of the unknown. David has given us a fair description of life on the pampas. You can read the letter, Richard. It will also prove that I am heading for Argentina. Actually, I do believe you that you are going to Australia, although I do not have any proof. However, I know now that you do not have relatives there who would write you a letter."

Richard considered this. Malcolm was right. In a way, their positions had been reversed. With no evidence of his destination, not even a ticket, Malcolm might even believe that Richard was a possible trickster.

Malcolm Sutton assumed a relaxed position, enjoying a cigar. The letter was dated May 6th 1870, with an address of *Estancia Kilrane, San Antonio de Areco. Republica de Argentina*, and addressed to Malcolm Sutton Esq, Kilrane, County Wexford. Richard was immediately impressed by the honesty of David Sutton. He stated that his average profit for the previous two years was around one thousand pounds per annum; how after a year or two most migrants became happy with their lot and their rich and varied diet, summing up by saying that Argentina was the best country on Earth. Yet David Sutton did not flinch from presenting the other side of the coin. Many Irish migrants had succumbed to the demon drink, probably due to the rural isolation, sometimes with deadly consequences for themselves and their families. Fortunes would not be made in just a few years. David Sutton described the droughts and the floods which could devastate flocks of sheep, the dust storms which could annihilate all before them like a biblical plague. But, he added, they were fairly rare occurrences. The letter concluded with David Sutton requesting that Malcolm bring out some seeds, implements, and a plough. Malcolm had ordered these from traders in Wexford, and, as he and Richard would take the same ship to Liverpool, he would be grateful if Richard would help him to carry them to the ship. Richard consented, convinced that Malcolm was genuine.

Sutton handed Richard a second envelope. A photograph fell out. Malcolm explained that it was a photograph of his uncle's house on the pampas. He asked Richard to read especially carefully the lines which he, Malcolm, had underlined.

The letter was headed 'David Sutton to his Nephew Malcolm Sutton, June 29th, 1870.

Dear Nephew Malcolm,

I am sorry to hear that your first cousin Eamonn, my sister's son, has decided not to accompany you to our country, but I respect his reasons. His mother's health must be a worry, and he is after all her favourite child. However, it may be for the better. As I have told you before, life here is not easy. As Eamonn does not have much experience of farm work, he might find it all too difficult, might move to one of the cities and leave me wanting badly for help. However, we should not give up, and you may succeed in finding someone to replace him during the weeks before you sail.

Nephew, please be guided by my advice in your selection. Ideally a young man reared at home rather than in an orphanage or workhouse would be the best choice. If he is the second, third, or other son of a farmer he will have acquired sufficient farming experience. Furthermore, if he has experience of and competence with horses, he will be perfect for life on this estancia. The young man you select should be of good upbringing and character, of sober habits, and treats women with courtesy. We Irish on the pampas try to treat our womenfolk well, and this part of Argentina is one of the best places in the world to bring up children. A young man who enjoys a drink in moderation is perfectly acceptable and even welcome.

Richard glanced at Malcolm, who was now seated upright. He was gazing into Richard's face with those magnetic eyes. Richard felt that the spell was becoming deeper. He continued reading.

'As for my share of the bargain, nephew, you are free to use your cousin Eamonn's passage money to bring this suitable young man from Wexford to Buenos Aires, second class travel in a two-berth cabin. The young man should agree to work on my estancia for six days each week for the wage of two pounds and ten shillings a week as well as his own room and board in my house. (I enclose a photograph of my new house built only four years ago). He must agree to work with me for at least one year from the date of his arrival in Buenos Aires. After that date he is, if he wishes, free to leave my employ. On the other hand, if he chooses to remain, I shall

give him a third share in my new flock of sheep. My Indian servant women will prepare good, ample, and nutritious meals. My dear Malcolm, it is also best if at all possible you choose a young man of about your own age and somewhat similar temperament, someone whom you find is convivial to live and work with in this, the best country on Earth.

Please remember to extend my deep affection to your parents, your brothers and sisters, and to your aunt Catherine for her improved health, as well as to your cousin Eamonn. May God bless you all and keep you safe and well.'

Your affectionate uncle, David Sutton'

The inner voice spoke to Richard. "Pull yourself back, mate. Do not lose control of yourself." He managed to speak. "He sounds like a good and generous gentleman."

Malcolm replied. "That he is. I have met him when he visited us eight years ago. He showed great affection for me, my brothers and sisters. He regards us like the children he never had. I suppose it would have been hard for him to find a suitable Irish wife on the pampas then. Things are easier now that more Irish women have emigrated there. So, a handsome lad like me should have no problem finding a wife, although I might fall for a dark eyed Argentine beauty."

Richard queried. "That is all in the future. I take it that you have found a suitable man."

Malcolm's face fell, "Sadly, no. It is only two weeks since I received that letter. None of my friends is willing to accompany me. Tied to home and hearth, I suppose."

Richard shook his head, "It is a very generous offer." A brief silence followed.

Malcolm's response was to stretch out his right hand, this time placing it gently under Richard's chin, forcing the latter to look him straight in the face, and saying. "You know, I think I might have found my ideal mate for the pampas."

"Who? Where?" Richard nervously asked. The right hand remained in position.

"I think he is right here in front of me." Richard's automatic response was to turn around and back again. "You mean …. me?" Richard asked.

Malcolm stroked Richard's chin. "Yes, you. You fit almost perfectly my uncle's request and advice. Can I lay my cards on the table?"

Richard nodded.

"Richard Butler, let us be honest. You are planning to go to Australia, a *fur* (far)-away country where you have no kinsfolk, relatives, or friends. You are leaving behind a family to which you are not even sure you ever belonged. I do not know how much money you have for your passage there and for settling in and, to be honest, I am not interested. I have known you for less than twenty-four hours, but already I like you and trust you. I am not too concerned about whether you like me or not. However, trust is the most important thing. Do you trust me as a genuine fellow?"

Richard decided that honesty was the best course. "I was not sure about that last night. But the newspaper articles, the letters from your uncle, and your conversation and good company have all convinced me to trust you. And ... I think I like you as well." Richard's face reddened a little, causing another light squeeze on his arm from Malcolm.

"Great, Richard. I think we will get on *amain* (fine). "

Richard Barron's inner voice spoke, "Break the spell. Do not let him possess you. Leave." Although he wished it to happen, he seemed to be tied to his chair. "But I am meant to go to Australia. My father and the diocese of Ossory raised most of the passage money. I cannot trick them."

"Richard, that shows your integrity which we will value greatly. You will not be using that money for your passage to Argentina. You would be binding yourself to my uncle for only one year. Keep all your money. If after a year you decide to travel on to Australia, we will not forbid or detain you. You can cross the Andes mountains by horse or even by a vehicle, and take a ship from Santiago in Chile to Australia. The decision to remain in or leave Argentina will be completely yours. You have my word and that of my uncle on that, the word of two Yoles of integrity. We will obtain our own two berth cabin, so our money will be safe."

Clashing thoughts and sentiments in Richard's mind. Do I go with him? Surely not. Best to ask for some time to think. "When do I need to let you know my decision?"

Malcolm replied. "The port authorities tell me that this storm will most likely last until tomorrow, so sailings to Liverpool should resume the day after. Take the rest of today to think it over. Hey, why don't we let God have a hand in your decision? We could both go to ten o'clock Mass tomorrow morning at the Church of the Assumption. I can arrange for you to have a talk with the priest Father Rossiter. He knows my family and my uncle David. Then you can decide. If your answer is yes, we will go straight to the shipping agent and book your passage to Buenos Aires. So, you will join me for ten o'clock Mass tomorrow morning, Richard?"

"You have my word that I will."

That night Richard Barron could not sleep. He tossed and turned, weighing up the pros and cons of accepting Malcolm Sutton's offer. After an hour of this, he drifted into slumber. He woke early, the answer clear in his mind. He would be guided by the advice of Father Rossiter. Richard was convinced that destiny had led him to the Selskar Arms and to that chance meeting. The force of destiny might be leading him to Argentina.

Richard entered Father Rossiter's parlour. Its walls were painted a light blue, adorned with a few paintings. The housekeeper had invited Richard to sit in the comfortable armchair by the warm blazing fire.

Other pieces of furniture included a bookcase, a drinks cabinet, and a carpet of a dark blue hue.

The grey-haired Father Rossiter's bearing and countenance matched the pleasant atmosphere of the parlour. Seating himself on the opposite armchair, he exuded a mood of kindliness, benevolence, and ease. He informed Richard that Malcolm Sutton had explained to him Richard's dilemma, and that he would do his upmost to provide fair and realistic counsel. However, he talked initially about other migration destinations.

"Richard, England, the United States, Canada, and Australia, are the distant lands to which our people have traditionally migrated. Since the Fenian rebellion and activity in the US and Canada, those two countries have taken a harder attitude against the Irish. I am in touch with some Irish priests in Australia, and its inhabitants are more welcoming. However, even there some prejudice exists. Is it not your good fortune that you have been invited to live and work in a Catholic country, with little British influence, and have been offered a home there?"

Father Rossiter continued, "The Suttons are respectable and honest people. I have known them since my childhood, spent near Kilrane. So, I knew Malcolm's father and his uncle David quite well. Indeed, the latter visited me here eight years prior. I am convinced that Malcolm and you will be treated well on the pampas. You have been given an honest and realistic picture of life there. The provisions of a free passage to Argentina and only a one-year initial commitment are very fair, and you can then travel on to Australia if you choose.

Richard, you are being offered a new home and a new family in a prosperous welcoming country."

On Richard's expressing his concern about his ignorance of Spanish, but that he had learned Latin, the good priest confirmed that the Irish community on the pampas lived their lives quite separate from the Argentine community. Their language was English, not Spanish. However, moving to the bookcase, he took down a book titled *Spanish Grammar for Beginners* and gave it to his young client.

Father Rossiter became thoughtful. "The only matter that now remains, Richard, is our complete trust in you. Malcolm knows certain things about you, but you might have something else to tell me. Let me assure you, my son, that even though you are not in confession, anything you confide in me will be in complete confidence. I will not inform Malcolm without your clear permission."

Richard, a little taken aback, considered. He felt that he should reveal a little more to this good priest. "Father Rossiter, the first thing I must reveal is that my name is not Richard Butler, but Richard Barron, and I am from County Kilkenny and not Waterford. Malcolm will need my correct name when he books my passage."

"Richard, it is often a good idea not to reveal your personal information to a stranger, especially in a public house. I am sure that Malcolm will not have a problem with that."

"And is there one more thing you feel you might tell me, Richard?"

Richard looked his confidante in the face. He explained that he could give the outline but not the details of a certain fiasco he had been talked into. He and his comrades had taken a vow on the bible that none of them would ever reveal to anyone in Ireland the planned action or the names of his comrades. Richard added that the plan involved only frightening or threatening the landlord's agent, but that two professional men had talked the boys out of their insane plan.

Father Rossiter was reassuring. "Some agents and landlords deserve to be frightened. As no blood has been spilt, I do not see the need for you to inform Malcolm about it. You are in my opinion a good young lad of great integrity and honesty, with a concern for those who were suffering oppression. You will be an asset to any country, and your whole life is before you." Glancing at the clock. "Malcolm should be here shortly. Have you made your final decision, my son?"

Richard Barron took out his wallet. He removed eight pounds. He handed it to the priest. "Father Rossiter, can you please send this money to the diocese of Ossary in twelve months' time. Do not tell them of my whereabouts."

"And where will your whereabouts be?"

"Argentina. I am going there with Malcolm Sutton. God through you, Father Rossiter, has led me to that decision. And, although you may consider this reason to be foolish, I feel that my true destiny awaits me in that great land."

Richard had made a visit to the lavatory. On his return, Malcolm asked. "Father Rossiter tells me that I have to get one important detail from you. What is it?"

"It is my name. It is not Richard Butler, but Richard Barron, and I am from county Kilkenny." Malcolm laughed,

"So you are not of Norman aristocratic stock, just a common foot-soldier like me."

Father Rossiter intervened. "Ah, I believe the Barrons were a branch of the Butlers, so he is still of higher rank."

"Well, I will claim the choice of bunk in our cabin, that is if this lower gentry lad is coming with me. So, my lad, are you coming to Argentina?"

"Yes, Malcolm Sutton, I am coming to Argentina with you." With that Malcolm jumped from his chair, his smile radiating through the entire parlour. "*Viva. Somos amigos para vida. (*We are friends for life)." He bestowed on Richard a quick embrace. His apology to Father Rossiter was followed by the priest moving to the cabinet, removing three glasses and a bottle of Bushmills whiskey. Pouring moderate amounts, he handed each young man a glass, raising his own in a toast. They agreed that both young lads had decided correctly to venture to that vast land, and how good it would be for them and for Malcolm's uncle. The discussion ended with the priest giving them the final blessing.

The Selskar Arms, that night. Richard's passage to Buenos Aires was booked. They would sail next morning to Liverpool, and three days later direct to Buenos Aires. Malcolm had decided that they should have a small farewell session in the Selskar Arms. On hearing for the first time that Richard played the fiddle, he was entranced. Live music on the pampas was always a godsend. Richard felt redeemed, for he would now enjoy a form of Irish wake.

Both young emigrants, the centre of attention in the public house that Friday evening, confined themselves to ale. Richard's playing on the fiddle brought about some dancing and singing of traditional Irish songs. About halfway during the session the revellers were visited by Father Rossiter. Having accepted a glass of whiskey from Malcolm, he offered to sing a short song in Yola. A hush fell upon the full company as the priest held his audience spellbound with his rendition of *The Wedeen of Ballymork*. As the song contained some words in English, Yola words similar to English, and even a few in Irish, Richard was able to follow the trend of the story, captivated as he was by the fifth verse in particular:

A peepeare struck ap; wough dansthe aul in a ring;

Eearch myde was a queen and earch bye was a kin.

Zoo wough aul veil a-danceen; earch bye gae a poage

To his sweetheart, and smack lick a dab of a grough.

The priest bade his final farewell to the two young emigrants, his eyes betraying a few tears. He had advised Richard that Malcolm must sing *The Boys of Kilrane*.

By the third verse Richard was tentatively joining in on the fiddle. The melody was in the Dorian mode. Again, a hushed silence pervaded the Selskar Arms.

From Ballyhire, Nicholas Leary, a most superior man.

*James Pender, Patrick Howlin, and John Murphy from
    Hayesland.*

And Laurence Murphy from Kilrane, joins them in unity.

They are bound for Buenos Aires and the land of liberty.

The poignant farewells, handshakes, hugs, and some tears were over. Malcolm and Richard had left the public house at a relatively early hour. Both felt an encompassing contentment, as each knew that he had made the correct decision. As they neared Richard's boarding house,

Malcolm placed his arm around the younger man's shoulder, reciting, "*Amigo,* we are bound for Buenos Aires and the land of liberty." Giving the latter a light squeeze, he turned and proceeded to his own lodging.

Richard gazed out at the sea on this star-studded night. This would be his last night in Ireland, most likely forever. Yet he no longer felt a fugitive, or even an exile. He would be welcomed to a land which had opened its arms to his countrymen. No, he had not been cast under a mysterious spell. Rather did he sense that his destiny lay in the great land of Argentina.

2. CHAPTER 7.

The Voyages of Azucena and Manrico.

Wexford Town, September 1847.

The woman alighted from the Bianconi car. The driver hailed a young boy to help her carry her trunk for two pence to her boarding house. Its owner was a pleasant and helpful woman. She led the woman to a bright room on the ground floor. Yes, she was travelling to Liverpool. She did not offer any further information, and her host did not pry. She suspected, however, that the well-dressed woman's ultimate destination was much further, possibly America, Canada, or Australia. She gave her name as Catherine Barron.

Next morning the same boy arrived promptly at ten am, excited at the prospect of helping the woman carry her purchases and earning a further threepence. The woman entered the dining room for lunch. Seated there were a man and his wife. They revealed that they were Quakers from England on route to Waterford, conveying money and seeds to alleviate the terrible distress in Ireland. The seeds were for the sowing of vegetables other than the potato, as the Quaker Central Relief Committee was convinced that Irish farmers had to diversify their crops. They asked the woman about the terrible distress in County Kilkenny. She informed them that many of her neighbouring small farmers and cottiers were on the verge of starvation, also mentioning the wholesale clearances of cottiers.

Catherine did not flinch when describing the horrific scenes which she had witnessed the previous day when passing through Thomastown – the dead and decomposing bodies in the ditches on the town's outskirts, people the shapes of skeletons, children with the visages of old men and women, a small crowd of such desperate people surrounding their Bianconi car and begging for alms or food. She had witnessed the harrowing scenes of those same spectres clamouring and begging to be admitted to the overcrowded workhouse, the wailing of women, the searing cries of children racked with starvation. While Catherine spoke, the man took down notes for his report to the Quaker Relief committee in Waterford. Catherine explained that the notorious Gregory clause, together with the closure or winding down of the public works, had represented the death knell for the poor and destitute of Ireland.

Later that afternoon Catherine Barron sat with her cup of coffee on the verandah of a nearby hotel. She reflected that she too was a victim of the devastating famine, driven from her homeland, her family, her friends, and above all her child by a number of circumstances all converging during the past year: the deadly escalation of the famine; its representation by clergy and some eminent people as a punishment from God; the attitude of society towards the birth of a child out of wedlock; the blaming of the woman as the chief protagonist; her own abandonment by her lover; the arrangements made by her own family with him, partly to help them survive the grim pestilence. The terrifying gap of hunger a famine victim must feel within his or her body had its counterpart in the void which Catherine experienced in her heart and soul. This was the eternal void a mother must feel at being separated from her beautiful and beloved baby. She knew in her heart that she would never see or hold her son again. "Richard, my beautiful and beloved son. You will always be the greatest love of my life."

Catherine walked through the streets of Wexford. It was refreshing to see that this town displayed few manifestations of the devastation and starvation sweeping the rest of the country. Yes, there were some beggars and tinkers in the streets, but that was the limit. Shops were open, selling meat, vegetables, some potatoes, bread, clothes, shoes. She would spend about a week in Liverpool awaiting her ship, but would do so in comfortable lodgings, largely removed from the depressing scenes there of the Irish fleeing their homeland, bound mainly for New York or Quebec. Still, the city to which she was voyaging offered promise of new hopes, achievements, a new life. For that city was none other than the emerging metropolis of Buenos Aires.

It had been Catherine's own decision that Buenos Aires would be the site of her new life. When it had become obvious to her and to her own family that continued life in their house and indeed in their region was untenable, New York had been their choice for her exile. Her brother Michael, his wife, and their child had migrated there the previous year. But Catherine had not relished the thought of landing on their doorstep, a fallen woman from Ireland. She would manifest her independence and choose her own future. It was their neighbour, the 'strong' farmer Mr. Townsend who had informed her of the new migration scheme to Argentina. The scheme was gaining momentum. Prospects for single women were very promising in that faraway land, especially for English speaking governesses. Catherine made enquiries. The question of the high fare was resolved by her brother approaching the father of her child. The latter promised that he was willing to provide Catherine with a second-class fare to Buenos Aires. He would also honour his promise to provide her with a trunk, money for clothes, and more money to help her settle in on her arrival at her destination.

The one condition stipulated by the father of her child was that Catherine's new destination be kept an absolute secret. Let the neighbours and everyone else believe that she was going to New York. Her two former employers gave her glowing references. The procedures for her migration to the Argentine were organised in the space of six weeks. Catherine Barron reflected on all of this as she meandered through the streets of Wexford. It was exactly three months to the day since her son had been born.

The Voyage. September 1847.

Catherine Barron surveyed her second-class accommodation on board *The Filomena*, docked in Liverpool port. It consisted of a bed in a four-bunk cabin, two chairs, a washstand with a basin, and a few small items of furnishings. Second class passengers would be provided food and water superior to that of third class. They would, however, have to cook their food in the third-class communal area of the ship. From Liverpool to Spain, Catherine would be the only occupant of the cabin. There she would be joined by a lady and her two daughters, travelling to the Argentine to join her husband. The avuncular captain had assured her that *The Filomena* was a new ship, built in England by experienced dock workers. He further elaborated about how the journey through the Bay of Biscay would almost certainly be rough, even frightening, but after that it should settle down as they crossed the ocean. The whole journey from Liverpool to Buenos Aires would take from two to three months, and boredom would be the chief enemy.

Catherine, however, had formulated plans to counteract the boredom. She would write a journal about the voyage. More importantly, she would immerse herself in her books on Spanish grammar. Her plan was to find a female Spanish speaker on the ship anxious to learn or improve her own English. Catherine's knowledge of both Latin and French would provide an excellent foundation for learning Spanish, and place her in a prime position for gaining good employment. Finally, she would have ample time on the voyage to reflect on the events of the past year which had so profoundly changed her life forever.

September 1870.

Richard Barron and Malcolm Sutton were pleasantly surprised by the quality of their second-class cabin. Two beds positioned on the floor, a small table with two chairs, two small arm chairs, a wash-stand with a basin, two oil lamps positioned above each bed, a safe for their money, and a few other small furnishings. A curtain suspended from a pole across the ceiling divided the cabin in two. "This is a good deal better than I expected, Richard," Malcolm said, "and, *Amigo*, we don't have to choose between the beds."

"Yes, we are back to equal status here." was the reply, which resulted in Richard receiving another light punch.

The two friends had to spend only two nights in Liverpool. Their ship was a steamer, one of the new style vessels which would complete the journey to Buenos Aires in about a month. The shipping agent in Wexford had given them accurate and reliable information. For their meals they had the choice of obtaining their food daily and cooking it themselves in third class. The alternative was to pay an extra five pounds for both of them for the full voyage, and a waiter would bring their cooked meals to their cabin every day. Malcolm's response had been, "Why not, we may as well travel in style." Richard had agreed, but only on condition that he, Richard, would pay for this luxury. Now, having seen their cabin, Richard thanked God for his good fortune in meeting Malcolm, convinced that a good life awaited him on the pampas.

As both lads took a stroll on the deck shortly after departure, Malcolm confided to Richard that he hoped that, after they had docked in Corunna or Vigo in Spain, he would be able to meet some lovely and charming Spanish ladies. His face fell somewhat when Richard responded with the information that he would be lucky because neither of them spoke a word of Spanish. He suggested that they should study Spanish together for two hours each morning.

September 1847.

Catherine Barron was delighted to meet the new occupants of her cabin. Doña Amelia de Sanchez, a lady in early middle age, and her two teenage daughters Luisa and Anna Matilda. Their ultimate destination was the Argentine city of Santa Fe, north of Buenos Aires. Her husband was a doctor, who had assumed his position there two months prior. She conveyed this news to Catherine through a mixture of broken English, some basic Spanish which Catherine understood, some sign language, and a map. Both Doña Amelia and Catherine agreed that they would commence Spanish lessons and English lessons next day, the two daughters joining them for the English lessons. Doña Amelia was surprised that Catherine was travelling alone to Argentina and not to America. However, on Catherine's relating to her of the horrific situation in Ireland, the coffin ships to New York, and the unwelcome reception in America for Famine migrants, she expressed great sympathy. Catherine as a governess would be a great asset to Argentina.

September 1870.

Richard and Malcolm commenced their Spanish lessons the day after their ship left Vigo. Richard, with his advanced knowledge of Latin, found the new language easy, but Malcolm was the problem. His enthusiasm for the classes was less than Richard's, although he did put in a good effort. However, the main problem was, because they had chosen a table on the deck for their lessons, Malcolm's attention was being distracted by the pretty Spanish and Latin American girls promenading with their parents, siblings, and chaperones on the deck. Richard could not help but notice the admiring glances which many of those beauties and even their mothers cast in his friend's direction. Well, he could not blame them for that. Malcolm's very handsome features were what had captivated Richard on their first meeting. Finally, Richard decided that it was best that all future lessons take place on the table in their cabin. Meanwhile he had become friendly with a young Spanish man named Abdias. The latter had agreed to join the two Irish lads to help them with their Spanish conversation, followed by a session of English conversation with Richard. The more private setting of the lessons and the Spanish conversation sessions resulted in Malcolm becoming more settled, and he made better progress.

October 1847.

While on her lengthy voyage to the Argentine, Catherine had ample time to review the events which had completely transformed her life. The vastness of the ocean made her reflect on the minuscule importance of our individual lives, although her own life until then had been rather unique for a woman during the pre-Famine era, even in Ireland.

Catherine Barron had been born in 1825 to Patrick and Ellen Barron. The third child of that union, her brother Andrew and her other brother Michael were four years and two years respectively older than her. The two boys had attended a local 'hedge' school, while Catherine was one of the first pupils to attend Castledown

National School on its opening in 1832. She had quickly demonstrated an active intelligence and an enquiring mind. Her father had always impressed upon his children the need for education, prized by his distant Barron forebears. To his delight, Catherine's teacher had recommended that they enter her for a secondary school scholarship being offered by the Presentation Sisters in Waterford. Her parents and neighbours were exuberant when Catherine won the scholarship, which included board and lodgings in the Presentation convent. The result was that the young Catherine received an education advanced by the standards of the day, covering Latin, French, Mathematics, Irish, History, Geography, English grammar and literature, and Music. Indeed, her musical leanings had been spotted early on by one of the nuns, leading to tuition on the piano at which she became quite accomplished.

Catherine Barron left the Presentation secondary school at age seventeen. Almost immediately she accepted the position as governess to the children of the Sherwood family, 'strong' Catholic farmers who lived two miles from her home. Her fame as a teacher spread. In 1844 she secured a post as tutor to the three children of the Maxwells, a minor Protestant gentry family. As their rather grand house and large farm was situated five miles from Catherine's home, the position included room and board, although she was free to return home every second weekend.

It was at the Maxwells' house that Catherine Barron first met Walter Drummond, on his visit in the spring of 1845 to purchase a horse. Catherine could not be described as beautiful, but she had a naturalness, a grace and an elegance which captured the young man's attention. Four years older than her, Walter was quite handsome, with a gentlemanly bearing and an athletic body. The natural attraction between them was characterised by easy conversation, a common interest in farming, love of scenery, nature, and history. A friendship developed between Catherine and Walter. He lived only two miles from the Maxwell home. Initially they would meet every second Sunday after Mass in Kilcolman. When this evolved into the stage of 'walking out together,' Catherine felt it was her duty to inform Mr. and Mrs. Maxwell and her own father, her mother having died three years earlier. None of these adults raised any objection. Walter was a respectable young man, the eldest son who was due to inherit the tenancy of his father's ninety-acre farm. Catherine, whose family tenanted only twenty-four acres, was, however, an educated and cultured young woman.

The storm clouds, however, were gathering. The first partial failure of the potato crop occurred in the summer of 1845. For various reasons this did not affect the Barron or Drummond families to any great degree, although for many cottiers in the Kilcolman region the winter months of '45 to '46 proved to be lean and hungry ones. Walter's father, Richard Drummond, became a member of and a contributor to the Kilcolman Relief Committee. Meanwhile Walter's and Catherine's relationship had developed into a full courtship, with them now discussing the prospect of marriage. When the blight, the resultant starvation and fever intensified in the summer of '46, Catherine's brother Michael Barron decided that he would flee Ireland with his wife and young son and head for New York. He foresaw a tsunami of emigration on the horizon, and had decided to avoid it. So, he signed over his tenancy of five acres of the Barron land to his brother Andrew, who in turn provided Michael with the passage money for his family to New York. Michael and his family had lived in a cabin half way up the lane, which old Patrick Barron now moved into.

Catherine had on a few occasions met her prospective parents-in-law, Richard and Eleanor Drummond, and their other son Stephen. Aware of her lower social status, but also of her convent secondary education, they had been welcoming and even gracious, although Catherine could detect a certain condescension in Eleanor's attitude. The latter even displayed a disdain and even at times a lack of sympathy for the starving cottiers. Stephen, however, seemed entranced by Catherine. He shared her love of books and music, and demonstrated a knowledge of culture superior to that of Walter.

By the summer of 1846, Walter Drummond felt that the time was ripe for him to officially call on Patrick Barron. Arriving in his trap with Catherine on an August Sunday after Mass in Kilcolman, the young man formally asked the father for the hand of his daughter in marriage, witnessed by the visitor Philip Keating. Patrick Barron immediately consented, sealing the prospective marriage with glasses of *uisce beatha*. Walter and Catherine's next call was to Andrew and Mairead Barron, in their small farmhouse down the lane. Following the usual congratulations and well wishes, Walter assured Andrew that no dowry would be necessary. The young prospective married couple left the house in a joyful mood, although Catherine had observed a slight jealousy on the part of her sister-in-law.

Two weeks later, Catherine's joy had been replaced by disbelief, anger, and defiance. Having driven to a clearing near a bridge over the river, they paused their journey, allowing the horse to graze. Walter revealed to Catherine the reason for his silence during the journey. "Catherine, my dearest, I have to tell you that my parents are objecting to our marriage, at least for now."

"For what reason, Walter? Sure, isn't it because I am the daughter of a small farmer?"

"Catherine, you know that that is not the reason. My father is not really against our marriage. However, he feels that, with the terrifying prospect of the famine getting far worse, a wedding is not the right thing yet."

"And what about your mother? What does she advise?"

"Well, my mother has said little about it, but she will support my father."

"Actually, Walter, I think it is the other way round. She has never been as warm to me as your father and especially Stephen have been. Isn't that the real reason?" Walter tried to calm the situation. "Catherine, Stephen gives us his full support. He says that he will be the best man whenever the marriage takes place." When Catherine had dried her eyes, they discussed alternatives – postpone their marriage, postpone their courtship, elopement and a clandestine marriage. Dismissing the first two possibilities, they considered the second two and the likely consequences. Walter was concerned that a clandestine marriage might well result in his being disinherited by his parents. Catherine's concern was that the Catholic church had condemned clandestine marriages some years prior.

It was Walter who came up with a possible solution to the intractable problem. "Catherine, if I were to put you with child, how could my parents continue to object to our marriage? The church would support it. Our child would be legitimate if we married before its birth. Neither of us would be taking advantage of the other, because we love each other so deeply. You are a woman of very good character."

Catherine, struck dumb, eventually found her tongue. "Walter, how can you even think of such an irresponsible act, let alone suggest it? That would be a mortal sin, deserving of hell for all eternity. Think of my reputation, my family's good name. The priests would condemn me from the pulpit. My neighbours would turn their heads away from me. And it is even worse that you have suggested this when Ireland is in the grip of such terrible famine and disease." And, she considered, how could she be certain that Walter would marry her in the end?

Walter took both her hands in his. "Catherine, my dearest. My parents would not wish to see you dishonoured. I know that they would agree to our wedding. Trust me, all will be right. Now, dry your eyes, and I will drive you home."

They drove back to the Maxwell house in virtual silence. Still, as she gazed into Walter's eyes during their long farewell kiss, she realised how strong and lasting was their mutual love. She promised to meet him as usual two Sundays from then.

Catherine and Walter drove along a quiet by-road. The few words they exchanged were words of endearment. Both were conscious of what lay ahead. On reaching a wood, Walter turned the horse on to a wide track. After ten minutes they stopped. Taking Catherine's hand, her other hand holding the rug, he helped her down. Silently Walter led her through the trees. After fifteen minutes they reached a bower, surrounded by ferns. He led her inside, speaking tenderly. "This is our place. Here we will consummate our love. Are you frightened, my dearest?"

"A little, but my undying love for you overcomes any fear." Walter placed the rug on the ground. They lay in each others' arms, caressing, kissing. Walter ran his fingers through Catherine's hair. He whispered endearments into her ear. He sensed that she was ready. He promised to be gentle. Catherine lay on her back at his bidding. She sensed his excitement as he prepared to enter her. Although Walter thrust gently, she still felt that stabbing pain. Some blood flowed. Catherine felt his manhood within her as he thrust more assertively. Relaxing more, Catherine began to feel that she was floating on air. She wished the feeling to prolong, but then suddenly he exploded. He released his seed inside her, the seed from which their child would begin its life. Walter lingered inside her a little longer, then gently he withdrew. For a while they lay in each others' arms. Silently they returned to the trap, Catherine still feeling ecstatic, banishing the sense of guilt and the misgivings she had initially felt. Walter loved her and she loved him absolutely. He would move Heaven and Earth to secure their union in marriage.

For the next two Sundays, two weeks apart, Walter and Catherine consummated their love in the same bower, the experience becoming for her easier and even more uplifting. The week following, Catherine missed her monthly. On her informing Walter, he was overjoyed, but somewhat put out when she insisted that they halt any further intercourse until she had visited the doctor. Catherine surmised that he had enjoyed the experience even more than she had done. Her visit to the doctor confirmed their hopes. Catherine was pregnant. They decided, however, not to inform their parents for some weeks in case of a miscarriage. They continued to meet every second Sunday, to which Walter's parents did not raise much objection, as there was no further talk of marriage for now.

The cruel winter of 1846 / 47 had arrived, with hundreds of people in Kilcolman and surrounds staring into the face of death from starvation and fever. Mrs. Maxwell had initiated the benevolent act of having a large stew cooked in her kitchen every Saturday. Her foreman, assisted by Catherine, conveyed it to all the hungry colliers on their estate each Saturday afternoon. By the end of January, Catherine's pregnancy had advanced to four months and was beginning to show. The young couple felt that they must inform their respective parents soon. Walter begged for more time. Catherine reluctantly agreed, but insisted that they inform them at the latest by Ash Wednesday in mid-February.

On the Sunday morning preceding Ash Wednesday Catherine informed her father of her condition. To her surprise he took the news rather calmly, although expressing his gratitude that his wife had passed on to God. Assured by Catherine that Walter would not desert her, Patrick expressed his hope that the wedding would take place during Easter Week.

That afternoon Walter collected her from her house. Catherine knew from one look at his ashen face that something was amiss. Having stopped the trap at Castledown chapel he broke out weeping, "Catherine, I have to tell you that yesterday I told my parents about your condition. A horrible scene followed in our parlour. My mother began to shriek, calling you every name under the sun. She refused to believe that the idea was mine, and that you were so reluctant to be part of it. She walked into her bedroom, and I have not seen her since. She did not come to Mass this morning, telling us that she is badly ill. If she really is, and if she dies, I will feel that I have killed her."

Catherine remained calm. "And your father, what did he say?"

"I have to tell you that he threatened to disinherit me. I cannot let that happen."

"And Stephen. Did he say anything?"

"No, he did not. But I think he blames me for it all. I am sure his opinion of you has not changed." Walter now broke down completely, bringing his hands up to his eyes. "I cannot go against my parents' wishes. I am torn apart, but you know that my love for you has not changed one jot. Believe me, we will find a way to be together."

"Please let me know, Walter, when you have found that way. I will walk home alone." With that Catherine Barron stepped out of the trap. She did not look back once at that shell of a man. She should have realised ages ago that he was made of clay.

Catherine Barron approached her changed predicament with much fortitude. Two weeks after this incident, she informed Mrs. Maxwell. Her Protestant employer did not condemn her. Catherine was welcome to remain in their employ and in their house until Easter. Mrs. Maxwell gave her some clothes to conceal her state from servants and labourers. Another two weeks passed. No word from Walter. Catherine could wait no longer. One of the labourers drove her home, where she quietly informed her father and brother that there would be no marriage. Their anger was directed towards the man who had abandoned her, and more so towards his parents with their high notions. Andrew Barron swore that the Drummond family would not be let free of their responsibilities, but his father calmed him, advising that they wait until after the birth.

On Holy Thursday, in late March, Catherine bade farewell to the Maxwell family and to their three children aged eight, ten, and twelve, all of whom she had grown to love. Mrs. Maxwell's parting gift consisted of some more clothes suitable for her condition and for the forthcoming birth, as well as a bonus of two pounds. The baby was due in about three months' time. Catherine returned to live in her father's cabin. Attitudes in the district varied. Some of the farming families and especially the cottiers had little sympathy for her. She had aimed above her station, broken the moral and Church code, and deserved her fate. Why, she had even left her good Catholic employers and gone to work for the Protestant gentry. However, old established friends like the Shanahans and the Mahonys supported her. It was, however, from her long-established friend Alice Keating that Catherine received most support. She proved to be the stalwart rock, the lighthouse in the storm. Assuring Catherine that she would find a good midwife, she herself would assist at the birth. Furthermore, she would be most happy to be the child's godmother, and her father Philip would be the godfather, if invited.

Richard Barron gazed down at his audience, a hundred or so strong, from the small stage in the first-class dining hall of the ship. The diners had finished their main course and were awaiting dessert and coffee. The captain introduced the talented young Irish violinist.

"Esteemed ladies and gentlemen. Three evenings ago, I was fortunate to hear this young man play to a gathering on the ship's deck. There he had played for singalongs, dances, and a few individual solos. However, ladies and gentlemen, his repertoire extends far beyond that. It includes the composers of the classical and romantic eras, and especially melodies from some of the great operas. Be prepared to be moved to tears. And please remain silent during the fifteen minutes recital."

Richard felt a little nervous as he looked down on this exclusive gathering. After a couple of pieces by Schumann and Mendelssohn, he launched into the melodies of Bellini, Donizetti, and Verdi. His audience gave him full attention and enthusiastic applause. Following his encore and final bow, some gentlemen approached the stage and threw coins and American dollar notes at his feet. What a debut experience!

The young violinist sat as a guest at the table of Don Enrique Alguilo and his daughter Catalina. The rest of the family were taking an after-dinner stroll on the deck. The family was returning home after a business trip to Spain. Catalina, aged seventeen, displayed all the manifestations of becoming a beautiful Latin lady, dark haired, with an ever-winning smile lighting up her whole face. Richard recounted to them some of his life story. Don Enrique recommended that he must aim to see operas and concerts at the newly opened great Colon Theatre. He extended his hospitality further by inviting Richard to join him and his family for dinner next evening. "Are you travelling alone?"

"No, my friend Malcolm is travelling with me."

"Excellent. Then he must join us as well," Don Enrique declared. As they parted company, Richard received a glorious smile from Catalina.

Richard found a rather disconsolate Malcolm lying on his bed. "Well, I suppose you conquered your audience as usual. Did any of the ladies swoon or faint like they used to do for Liszt and Paganini?"

"No, but they listened to me, applauded me, and some men threw coins and dollars at my feet. More importantly, I was invited for coffee and brandy by Don Enrique Alguilo, an Argentine businessman, and his beautiful daughter Catalina."

Malcolm sat up excitedly, "Tell me more. Are you seeing her again?"

"I certainly am, tomorrow evening for dinner with the whole family."

Malcolm slumped, "What! So, I am going to have another long evening alone, stuck in this damn cabin."

"No, *Amigo*. You have been invited too. I explained that you are my close friend. That will make up the table of eight. There are two young boys as well."

"Richard, are there any other daughters?"

"Yes, there is one other, named Isabella, two years older than Catalina." Richard did not have the heart to tell his friend that the other daughter was homely looking and best described as rather plain.

The two young men walked into the first-class dining room, dressed in their best and exuding confidence. Richard noticed that quite a few ladies, young and not so young, turned their heads in their direction as they moved through the tables. Don Enrique stood up to greet them. The formalities were extended in proper Argentine fashion. Don Enrique welcomed them with a formal handshake, introducing first his wife Doña Alejandra and then his two daughters. Both young men shook the hand of each lady and gave a slight bow. Don Enrique then introduced his two young sons, Sergio and Francisco aged thirteen and eleven years, handshakes following between them. Doña Alejandra sat to the left of her husband. Don Enrique seated Malcolm between his wife and his daughter Isabella, with Catalina to her left. Richard was placed on Catalina's left, with the two boys on his left.

The level of the family's English varied between its members, Don Enrique, Catalina, and Sergio displaying the highest level. Richard found the two young boys to be excellent company. They asked him many questions about Ireland and especially about his work with horses. Don Enrique gave a more detailed account of his import-export business, while Malcolm outlined his uncle David's *estancia* work on the pampas. If Malcolm was a little disappointed by the lack of beauty of his dinner companion Isabella, he did not reveal it. Rather did he fully turn on the charm, producing a vitality in the young lady. Richard noticed that Doña Alejandra beamed with happiness. Obviously, Isabella lived somewhat in the shadow of her prettier sister.

For his part Richard was captivated by Catalina. Her interests covered music, literature, history, and art, among others. She diplomatically asked Richard about his plans for his new life in the Argentine, suggesting that in some years time he might move to Buenos Aires, Cordoba, Montevideo, or one of the other emerging cities which would offer good society and culture.

On only two occasions did the table conversation drift into deeper waters. Catalina informed Richard of how she had loved his playing of the duet *Home to our Mountains* from Verdi's opera *Il Trovatore*. "Do you know the story of the opera, Richard?"

"Not really, Catalina. All I know is that it is about gypsies in Spain during a civil war and that Manrico sings the duet with his mother Azucena while they both await execution."

Catalina began to narrate. "An old gypsy woman, believed to be a witch, casts a spell on the child of the Count de Luna. The old woman is condemned to death by burning."

"And was she burned?" called out the excited Francisco.

Doña Alejandra sat up straight, speaking sharply in Spanish. "Catalina, what are you telling those boys?"

"Just the story of the opera *Il Trovatore*, mother. Richard does not know it."

"Catalina, I forbid to tell the boys that story. You know that Francisco suffers from bad nightmares. No more of it, please."

Don Enrique intervened, speaking English. "I agree that it is not the most suitable story for young children. However, Malcolm and Richard, if the opera is ever performed at the Colon Theatre, you must come and see it as our guests."

Richard experienced a twinge of sudden sadness, as he would have loved to hear the story from Catalina. His sadness was immediately banished by the touch of her fingers on the back of his wrist, she apologising for having brought up the subject.

While the table was being served coffee, brandy, and sherry for the ladies, Francisco came up with his question, in Spanish, "Father, might not Malcolm and Richard be attacked or even killed by those savage Indians on their *estancia*?"

Don Enrique looked at him. "Why do you ask, my son?"

"Richard and Malcolm are our new friends. We would hate to see them being killed."

Don Enrique queried. "Malcolm, what has your uncle David told you about the Indian situation?"

"*Señor,* on his visit home some years ago he told us about earlier attacks by the Indians. However, he assured us that since the Irish had pushed into the interior of the pampas the threat had lessened considerably."

"Was that because the Irish killed all the Indians?" asked Sergio.

His father answered. "I do not think that the Irish or any other settlers deliberately set out to kill the Indians. They may have done so when defending their homes, *estancia*s, and families. I am not aware of great massacres of the Indians of Argentina as occurred in the United States, Australia, and elsewhere."

Don Enrique Álvarez addressed the whole table. "We must remember that the Indian and aboriginal populations of all these countries is small. Argentina especially possesses vast stretches of some of the most fertile lands in the world, sufficient land for settlers and native peoples. I believe that the population of the province of Buenos Aires alone is about 400,000, but it could support around six million. Why should there be conflict? Our country represents a beacon of light to the people of poor and devastated lands of Europe, people fleeing poverty, tyranny, and persecution."

The captain swept on to the dining room stage, "Ladies and gentlemen, the watch has called out 'land ahoy.' We are in sight of the coast of Brazil. Our voyage is nearing its end."

Francisco jumped up from his chair with a whoop. A reprimand from Doña Alejandra stopped him in his tracks. "I, my daughters and my sons will leave this dining room together in a civilised manner." Don Enrique, however, invited Malcolm and Richard to remain and partake of a brandy nightcap. Both young men then went through the protocols of farewell to the departing family.

No further discussion ensued between Malcolm, Richard, and their host about the Indian situation. However, Richard could not help but compare Sergio's and Francisco's questions about the Indians to the questions he had asked Philip Keating in his own kitchen all those years ago about the clearances of impoverished cottiers.

About half an hour later, when he and Malcolm were gazing at the coast of Brazil, he felt the latter's hand on his shoulder, and heard the words, "You know, Richard, I often thank my lucky stars and God that we both went to the Selskar Arms that evening."

"And I feel exactly the same, Malcolm."

During her extremely long voyage Catherine Barron at times recalled the confrontation between her father, brother, and herself against Father Dunphy, parish priest of Kilcolman. It had been noted by the Armstrongs and even by the Drummonds that, since the onset of famine, the Catholic Church was gaining in power and influence in Ireland. This was seeping into the national school system, the political life of Ireland, and even the private lives of individuals. Catherine had always considered herself a religious person, and her greatest regret at her becoming pregnant was that she had grievously sinned against God's commandments.

The altercation had occurred in mid-April, about ten weeks before the birth. Preparing the meagre dinner for her father and herself, Catherine heard a horse and vehicle halt at the gate. She moved to the door. Alighting from the trap, whip in hand, Father Dunphy stared at her with a furious visage. Catherine retained her composure, "*Dia leat, a athair* (God be with you, father), do you wish to speak to my father?"

"No, woman, I wish to speak to you. You, brazen woman, have brought shame and dishonour to your kin and to our parish. As if we are not suffering enough with the blight, famine, and now devastating fever." His voice had risen to a crescendo.

The voice of Patrick Barron emanated from the cabin. "Father Dunphy, would you please step inside our humble cabin if you wish to speak to us."

"I refuse to step inside an abode which bears the mark of a grievous sin against God."

"Then, Father Dunphy, I suggest that you be on your way. Catherine, can you please come back inside. The pain is on me again, and I need my medicine."

Catherine did as bidden.

The priest, somewhat deflated, entered the cabin, refusing a chair. "Mr. Barron, this daughter of yours, this wanton, has brought disgrace to our parish by her licentious behaviour. She has led an upright and Godly young man to heinous acts forbidden by God and the church, acts which without true and sincere remorse can lead to eternal damnation. Well, don't either of you have anything to say?"

Patrick answered. "Father Dunphy, what evidence do you have that my daughter was to blame for those same acts? After all, it takes"-

The priest interrupted him with his tirade, "You may or may not know the Old Testament, Mr. Barron. It is always the woman who leads the upright man astray. Eve persuaded Adam to eat the forbidden fruit. The Philistine Delilah got Samson to reveal the secret of his strength. The prostitute Jezebel married King Ahab of Israel to introduce the worship of Baal, and to kill the prophets of Yahweh. You, woman, are in their company. You have fallen to the utmost depths of sin."

Patrick replied. "That may be true, Father Dunphy. But we need to look to the forgiveness of Jesus. He forgave the Magdalene for her sins, as he did to the woman taken in adultery with the words, 'Sin no more.' Is my daughter permitted to tell you her version of the story?"

The priest reluctantly agreed.

Catherine maintained her dignity by remaining standing.

In a composed manner Catherine Barron recounted Walter's courtship, their mutual love, their engagement and intention to marry, his parents' opposition, his suggestion about the only way he and Catherine could get them to change their minds. She described her deep reluctance to partake of intercourse before marriage, her becoming pregnant, and his abandonment of her, again due to parental opposition and threats.

Her defence was answered by a typical outburst from the priest. "I don't believe a word of what you say, woman. It is all lies. You tried to ensnare the son of a wealthy farmer. You led him to this vile act when you saw how all the potatoes had rotted last year. It is because of wanton women like you that God has sent this scourge on Ireland, his vengeance for the licentious behaviour of Ireland's people, especially the women."

Her anger rising, Catherine was compelled to defend the women of Ireland. "Father Dunphy, it is not only our land which has suffered from the blight. France, Scotland, Flanders, Cornwall, parts of Germany and Scandinavia have also been victims. Ireland has suffered the most because we are ruled by England and because our farmers do not own their land, although our own landlord, the Marquis of Ormonde has been very benevolent."

The priest's fury had reached its peak. "Silence, woman! You can contemplate your sins in the workhouse, a fit place for you and your kind."

Patrick Barron sat upright. "What do you mean by the workhouse, father?"

"That is where she will give birth to her bastard child. And that is where she and that child of sin will remain."

Catherine moved to her father. With the help of her arm and his stick, the old man stood up to his full length.

He spoke quietly. "Father Dunphy, for the past one hundred years, every child born of us Barrons has been born either in this cabin or in our small farm house down the lane. My daughter will give birth to her child in one of those two houses. Do I make myself clear?"

"So, you defy your parish priest, Barron."

"I defend the life of my daughter and of my grandchild. You know as well as I do, Father, that the Kilcolman workhouse has been devastated by famine fever since January, for you have bravely ministered to the dying there. My daughter will not be sent there by anyone. It would be a death sentence for mother and baby, and the fifth commandment clearly states, 'thou shalt not kill.'"

The priest, now livid with rage, raised his horsewhip, "Barron, how dare you quote scriptures to support the actions of this woman."

Catherine screamed. "Oh, no!"

"Father Dunphy, please put down that whip," a voice commanded from the doorway. The priest spun round. Framing the doorway was Andrew Barron, holding a thick stick, his visage set in anger. His body was well built, albeit his face now betraying signs of hunger. "Surely you would not strike a weak, sick, and defenceless old man. This may be only a humble cabin, but we who live here are civilised people. Catherine, please draw up a chair for his reverence."

The priest countered with. "I will not spend another minute in this house of shame."

But Andrew Barron did not move. "Father Dunphy, please take a seat. There are matters in this business which we need to discuss."

The priest sat down, albeit reluctantly. Andrew continued. "Can I ask if you have used your priestly authority to try and persuade Master Walter Drummond to do the honourable act and marry my sister, as I believe you have done in similar circumstances?"

"No, I have not, nor will I."

"Can I ask you why not? My sister is an educated and cultured young woman, a fitting wife for any strong farmer."

Catherine interjected with. "It is because we are small farmers, and as his reverence has stated already, the Drummonds are big farmers. That is the reason why they have refused their permission even though Walter and I love each other."

Andrew Barron spoke. "Father Dunphy, there is a legal matter in this case. Walter Drummond became betrothed to my sister Catherine. He called to this house and asked our father for her hand in marriage. Philip Keating, a respectable man, was a witness. Then Master Drummond called into my house with his betrothed and assured me that no dowry would be necessary. Due to pressure from his family, Walter Drummond has broken off the engagement, so he may well be guilty of breach of promise."

Catherine interrupted him with. "Andrew, I have told you enough times that I do not wish to hear about that. I love Walter and will not be part of any such action. I am not out to make money out of all of this."

Andrew moved to her, taking her hand. "Yes, Catherine, but Walter Drummond has a moral obligation to provide for your child. So, Father Dunphy, are you prepared to approach master Drummond about how he intends to provide for the child, his child? Can I ask you, please, to bring our case to him."

"Why cannot you bring it to him yourself?"

Andrew pounded his stick on the floor. "Because none of us have seen nor heard from him since before Ash Wednesday, when he did the disgraceful act of abandoning my sister to her fate."

The priest pondered for a couple of moments. "Yes, I will speak to Walter Drummond and his father, although I cannot promise anything." Standing up from his chair, and without any word of farewell, he walked out of the cabin, and was gone.

Catherine never found out how and when negotiations between Andrew and the Drummond family were initiated. She suspected that Father Dunphy had contacted the Drummonds, for she was informed by Andrew that he, Andrew, and Stephen Drummond had had some meetings. The outcome was that Walter had agreed that, provided Andrew and his wife Mairead were willing to adopt the child, he would provide for its maintenance until it reached the age of fourteen.

Mairead was initially reluctant. However, with the prospect of the famine overwhelming them, and with no sign yet of a second child of her own, she was won round. This would mean extra income during terrifying times.

In the weeks preceding the birth, Richard Drummond, Walter and Stephen, Patrick, Andrew and Mairead Barron moved towards the consensus that the best prospect for Catherine's own future was for her to emigrate. The Drummonds would provide her with a first-class passage to New York, a trunk, money to purchase clothes, and for settling in. Catherine, sadly resigned to the fact that Walter would never marry her, accepted this as the best possible outcome. Her child would be sufficiently cared for. She herself could start a new life, putting behind her the whole unfortunate episode. If she were to remain in Ireland, and especially in her geographical region, it was most unlikely that she would ever find a suitable husband, because in the eyes of Victorian society she was 'tarnished goods.' Who would employ her as a governess with an illegitimate child in tow? And, more importantly, her child would be forever known as 'the bastard Barron.' His being adopted by her brother and his wife might mitigate this. So once again the woman was subject to the verdict of the male jury.

Surprisingly, Walter Drummond conveyed to Andrew the news that he and Stephen wished to attend the baptism. Walter also informed the Barrons that, if a boy, his father had given permission for the child to be christened Richard, after him. If a girl, on no account should she be named after Eleanor. All the conditions which the Drummonds had agreed to were, however, subject to one vital stipulation: the child should never be informed of his or her paternity. They had also conveyed this condition to Father Dunphy who unhesitatingly agreed to abide by it.

On an afternoon in June 1847, Catherine Barron in her father's cabin gave birth to a lovely baby boy. The birth was surprisingly easy, the child being delivered by an able midwife, assisted by Alice Keating and Mairead Barron. The baptism of Richard took place in the family cabin, performed by the curate. Walter and Stephen Drummond arrived, bearing a box of food and some alcohol. Stephen was the godfather, Alice Keating the godmother, and her father Philip also attended. Catherine, still weak, returned to bed shortly after the baptism. Walter remained for a further thirty minutes, partaking of a drink. While Andrew and Stephen took a walk, the latter revealed that Walter in four months' time would marry Johanna O'Loughlin, the daughter of a strong farmer from County Tipperary. It sounded like an arranged marriage, the bride bringing a sizeable dowry. Stephen also intimated that, intensely saddened by the scene of the baptism, he did not think he could bring himself to be the best man.

Both Andrew and Stephen had by now developed a mutual respect for each other. Stephen, handing Andrew the first payment, arranged that every three months he would deliver each payment to Andrew in a certain public house in Kilcolman. Andrew then informed Stephen that Catherine would have departed to New York in three months' time. She would keep young Richard for the next two weeks, after which Andrew and Mairead would assume their role as parents, when Catherine would then begin her preparations for her effective exile.

On 15th December 1847 the *Filomena* finally docked in Buenos Aires. All passengers had had to undergo a period of seven days quarantine in a station a few hours from Montevideo. Small boats conveyed them from the ship to the port. The de Sanchez family had given Catherine the address of their relatives, with whom they would be staying in

Buenos Aires until after Christmas. They were sure that they would be able to put Catherine in contact with a family requiring a governess. Following farewells, Catherine proceeded to find Father Fahy.

Catherine did not have to look far. In a prominent position in the assembly hall stood a young priest holding a large placard which read, *Irish Immigrants assemble here*. Probably Father Fahy's assistant, he was surrounded by about fifty of her co-passengers. After fifteen minutes had passed, the priest welcomed his flock to a new country and a new life.

Father Dempsey apologised to the immigrants that Father Fahy himself had been unable to meet them. "The reason is that only a few days ago a terrible incident has occurred in this city involving a most respectable Irish-Argentine family and the Church. So, Father Fahy's untiring efforts are required elsewhere. However, the good father will visit each group of immigrants in their guest house."

With much efficiency the young priest read out their names in groups of four, for their conveyance by vehicle to their guest house. The drivers were good and respectable men, paid in advance, so the women were in good hands.

Within three days of her arrival, Catherine conveyed a message about her whereabouts to the de Sanchez family. Two days later she was their guest in their relatives' home. There it was arranged that she should travel next day to the home of Don Miguel de Silva and his wife Doña Margarita for an interview as governess to their four children.

Don Miguel was a surgeon, and he and his family lived in a new spacious house in San Telmo, an up-and-coming middle class barrio of Buenos Aires. Catherine secured the position immediately. She would commence work early in January, residing in their house. She would have her meals with the family, for her social position was higher than the domestic servants. The position offered a good salary, most of her evenings free, giving her the opportunity to enrol in some evening classes in Spanish language and literature. As the de Silva home possessed a piano, Catherine could continue her musical studies, for among her duties was the teaching of piano to their two daughters.

The evening of 23rd December. The occupants, all female, were enjoying a small pre-Christmas party hosted by Mrs. Burke, owner of the guest house in Buenos Aires. The mood was jovial, for Catherine Barron was playing some Irish songs and Christmas carols on the piano. While they were singing *The Meeting of the Waters,* the door of the parlour opened. In walked a priest, his countenance unsmiling and austere, rather glaring eyes, hair turning grey, surely Father Fahy. He stood at the left of the piano.

When the song ended, he spoke, "*Ashtore*, you have played that song beautifully. Now, can you please allow me to speak briefly to these good women."

"Of course, Father."

Father Fahy did not remain for long. He welcomed all of them to Argentina, the best country in the world for the Irish. He was sure that they would find good employment here, meet some decent Irish

Catholic men, marry and have Irish children, strong and steadfast in their faith. He would interview them all here after Christmas had passed. Meanwhile, he wished everyone a happy and holy Christmas in this excellent and true Irish home. With those words he departed.

For the remainder of her life, Catherine would not forget her meeting with Father Antonio Fahy on 3rd January, 1848. It was preceded by his giving the assembled Irish women a short talk, when he elaborated further on his previous short welcome. Despite his gruff manner and austere countenance, one could not doubt his concern for and sincerity regarding the Irish in the Argentine.

Father Fahy explained to his audience his three precepts for an emigrant: "Get out of the cities. Stick to what you are good at, which is mainly sheep raising, and keep out of Argentine politics. Good positions await you on the pampas as housemaids, cooks, and governesses. However, your ultimate goal is surely to marry a good Irish Catholic man, to create a stable and loving Catholic home, which will be a beacon of light in this vast and partly untamed land. Which of you women here wish to be the first to be interviewed?" Catherine Barron raised her hand.

Catherine informed the priest that she had been educated to secondary school level by the Presentation Sisters in Waterford, implying that she came from a rather small farm a couple of miles from there.

On hearing that she had worked as a governess for a few years, a flicker of a smile crossed his lips. "I have the ideal post for you. A farmer from County Wexford who owns two thousand acres is desperately seeking a governess for his five children, his wife having died six months ago. The farmer is very enterprising. He built his own house two years ago. His property also includes a cabin, their former home, in which for the sake of propriety, his cook and the governess will reside. Furthermore, as no doubt, Catherine, you are seeking a good Irish man to marry, God will guide this to end in a union between you and him."

Catherine listened to this proposal, not really surprised. The priest's last statement caused her to speak assertively, "Excuse me, Father, but I think I have to speak. I have found a position with a good Argentine Catholic family here in Buenos Aires, with a good salary, my own pleasant room, and the opportunities to further my education. I wish to get to know my adopted country, become competent in Spanish, and develop my skills as a pianist."

After all she had endured in Ireland, Catherine Barron was determined to assert her independence. No longer would her destiny be determined by men. The Catholic Church might provide her with spiritual enrichment, but nothing more. Seeing that further discussion with this stubborn and high-notioned woman was useless, Father Fahy terminated the meeting. Nonetheless, Catherine praised the priest's emigration scheme and handed him a pound towards his Irish famine relief fund.

Catherine Barron's position with the de Silva family exceeded her expectations. The family was generous, cultivated and devoutly Catholic. The four children, two boys and two girls, aged from five to eleven years, were respectful, affectionate, and keen students. Father Fahy made his first visit to the de Silva home in February of 1848. He was graciously received by Doña Margarita and by Catherine. Satisfied with the young Irish woman's situation, he again broached the subject of the farmer from Wexford. Catherine skilfully handled the situation, mentioning how wonderful the de Silva children were, and how she had commenced evening classes in Spanish. A gift of two pounds from her, matched with a similar amount by Doña Margarita towards the famine relief, saw the priest leave the house in a positive manner, although without achieving his objective. As for Catherine, she had decided that this would be her final break with Ireland and Irish priests.

PART II.

IRELAND TRANSPLANTED

Chapter 8.

The Journey

Richard Barron and Malcolm Sutton had bid fond farewell to the Aguilo family. Don Enrique was effusive. "Malcolm and Richard, all of us have enjoyed your company so much on the ship. You have really made our voyage. Both of you with your stories, Richard with his music. Remember that you have our addresses because we want our friendship to blossom. You really must contact us on your very first visit to Buenos Aires. Both Doña Alejandra and I myself are delighted that our daughters have met two such genteel and cultured young men. You are a great example to our two boys as well."

Francisco had to speak. "Malcolm and Richard, do you think you might be able to bring me to the *estanciu* someday soon? We do not have to bring Sergio."

"Why not, Francisco?" Richard queried.

"Richard, he likes the city, books, school."

Malcolm stepped in. "If Sergio wants to come, he will be most welcome. Would you like to come too, Sergio?"

"Of course, I would. Besides, someone has to keep an eye on Francisco and make sure he does not drive you two lads and your uncle David mad."

Don Enrique spoke. "That is all in the future, boys. Malcolm and Richard have to settle into life on the *estancia* first. That may take some time."

Their ship having docked in Buenos Aires at nine am, it had taken them only two hours to clear customs and immigration. Richard and Malcolm spent part of the first afternoon getting the feel of the city centre. They were struck by the preponderance of the Italian style of architecture in the new public buildings. Their hotel owner had told them that Buenos Aires hosted a population of 180,000 souls, and that increased immigration, especially from Italy, would see the city expand much further. For the rest of the afternoon, they rested.

The next morning the two young travellers rose early for Mass at the metropolitan cathedral, recently completed. Following breakfast, they set out on their main assignment, namely to collect a gig from a reputable coach builder in the city, ordered by David Sutton. There they were met by the craftsman himself.

"*Jovenes,* (young men) welcome to Argentina and Buenos Aires. Your vehicle awaits you, all completed. See, as *Señor* Sutton requested, I have built it as a mixture of a gig and an Irish trap. The first seat is elevated like a box seat, for two people. The main body of the vehicle is more comfortable, and will hold four passengers."

Malcolm spoke. "And I understand that my uncle has paid you in advance for the vehicle."

"That he has done. You have the money for the horse with you?"

"No, *Señor.* We do not. My uncle has instructed me that he will forward that money to you after we have arrived with the horse fresh and not showing any injury."

"But is that fair, *Joven*? How do I know how you *jovenes* will drive the horse? You may cause him injury." Malcolm introduced Richard. "*Señor*, my friend Ricardo has worked with horses for much of his life. There is no way he will mistreat or over-work the horse. True, Richard?"

"Yes, but does that mean I have to drive the gig for the entire journey? I thought we would share the driving."

Malcolm whispered to him. "Say that you will be the sole driver. We can share it later on."

Reluctantly Richard spoke. "I will be the only driver, *Señor*. I will treat the horse as if it were my own."

Somewhat reassured, the *señor* spoke. "Well, I fully trust *Señor* Sutton to pay me as soon as you both arrive. You also will have two guides and protectors. They will watch how you handle the horse." With that the two young men left the workshop.

The owner of the music store greeted them with welcoming words and a handshake. "You are Irish. *Irlanda, la tierrra de Tomasio Moore y Guillerme Vincento Wallace.*" (Ireland, the land of Thomas Moore and William Vincento Wallace). Richard spoke. "*Señor*, I am here to buy some music for the fiddle, and to look at some of your violins."

"You would like to buy a violin?"

"Not now, later." Richard replied.

"You have a violin, *Joven*?"

"No, *Señor*, I have a fiddle."

The owner was puzzled. "A fiddle, what is the difference?"

Malcolm intervened. "*Señor,* I do not really know the difference either. All I know is he plays beautifully the music by Bellini, Donizetti, and Verdi on the fiddle, and he is looking for music by composers of around that time. I think he has confused us all."

The *señor* gently took Richard's arm, leading him to a collection of music by the Romantic composers. Having selected twelve individual pieces of music and some small folios, Richard spoke to the owner quietly. "Do you, *Señor,* possess the book of *Il Trovatore*?"

"The book, Ricardo?"

"Yes, *Señor,* I mean the book with all the music."

The store owner smiled. "Ah, I think you mean the score of the opera. It contains the melodies sung by the singers, the words in Italian and English translation, the piano accompaniment."

"Such a thing exists, *Señor,* and you have one of that opera?" Richard was so excited. "Of course, I do, *joven.* After all my shop lies in the shadow of the great Teatro Colon. Please take a seat. Young Eduardo will bring you both a *café* and the score of the opera."

Within five minutes Richard was perusing the score and enquired about the price. "That score will cost 200 Argentine pesos, *joven.*"

Jubilant, Richard's took out his pesos. "I will buy it." Both lads left the music store on most amicable terms.

"So, Ricardo, you now have a score of *Il Trovatore.*"

"Yes, Malcolm. I can now play more melodies from it for Catalina."

Twenty seconds of silence lapsed. Richard then realised that the subject of Catalina must not create division between him and Malcolm. He must be careful in future.

The vehicle had been loaded with the goods purchased in Wexford and Liverpool. Malcolm and Richard would sit on the box seat. Both guides had well-built and strong physiques. Their skin was tanned, and their faces had that dark, grim, and almost fierce look. The older one had his hair in knots, thick with sweat and dust, and sported a tangled dark brown beard.

"Malcolm," Richard asked quietly, "are we putting ourselves into the hands of two desperadoes? I do not like the look of the older one."

The coach builder, sensing their anxiety, assured them. "*Jovenes*, these guides will also protect you. They are very experienced and trustworthy. Your road to San Antonio de Areco is usually safe. Do not be afraid just because they have rifles across their shoulders and long knives in their belts. You two *jovenes* will carry rifles too. God help any scoundrels who try to attack you."

The travelling party drove through the inner suburbs. After four hours of driving, they had reached the fringe of the city and the start of the great plain of the Argentine pampas. Before them lay their new life, thousands of miles from Wexford and Kilkenny.

Their journey on that first day had covered about forty kilometres. Richard had decided to wean the horse in gently, ignoring their guides' occasional urgings to travel faster. Their *posada* (inn) was situated about five kilometres beyond a fledgling town known as El Talar. On arrival there, they surmised the reason for their guides' haste. Seated around a fire in the open was a group of other drivers who greeted their two guides with handshakes and words of welcome. All were drinking from wooden goblets. The *posada* owner advised the two young men to bring all their possessions into their room. Having washed themselves, both lads lay on their beds, and within ten minutes were enjoying a mid afternoon *siesta*.

On awakening, Richard and Malcolm stepped outside the *posada*. Juan their younger guide beckoned them to join the group. He took his own goblet, placed some tea leaf like things in it, and poured hot water on top.

"*Jovenes*, the leaves are called yerba, the drink is called *maté*, the national drink of Argentina." Juan stirred the mixture with a long silver tube, which he named as a *bombilla*, and handed the goblet to Malcolm. The latter tried to drink it through the same side of the tube, causing a gale of laughter from the group. "Drink it through that other side, *Joven.*," Juan laughed. "Take a few swigs of it."

The laughter continued, causing the normally composed Malcolm to blush deeply. With relief he passed it to Richard. The other drinkers watched the two young foreigners. Richard did not really like the taste, but he had to appear courteous. By the time the goblet reached them the second time round, both lads were more relaxed about partaking in what was obviously a form of ritual. Most of the drivers smiled and nodded, indicating that the two *Irlandés* (Irishmen) were to some extent members of their group.

The second day dawned. The travellers would commence their journey an hour after sunrise. Malcolm emerged from their room to find Richard smoking their horse's nostrils with the fumes from a burnt weed.

"What on Earth are you doing?"

Richard replied. "Juan has warned me that we must always watch what the horses eat. On the pampas there is a poisonous weed named *romerillo*. To stop them eating it, we should burn it and smoke the horse's nostrils with the fumes. Don't forget that you are driving today."

"Richard, I think it is best if you continue driving. You have proved yourself to be a master with the horse."

"But, Malcolm, I want to be able to view the pampas, their vegetation, their wildlife."

Malcolm smiled, "And I want to present my uncle with the treasure that I found."

"Malcolm, it was the coach builder who found us this horse." Malcolm laughed. "I am not talking abut the horse, you *gam* (clown). I am talking about you. You are the gem I found, right from the Emerald Isle. The horse will arrive fresh under your command."

After about twelve miles they had reached the town of Pilar, stopping there briefly for some refreshments. A further ten kilometres of travel began to reveal the pampas in their total vastness. Trees, bushes, shrubs, and even rocks gave way to vast stretches of light green grass, seemingly stretching to infinity. The rough road between Buenos Aires and Pilar had deteriorated into a wide track. As they progressed it seemed to Richard that he was steering a craft on a never-ending ocean of grass.

Juan proved to be an excellent guide, pointing out the few landmarks, the even fewer animals and birds, and some risky or dangerous plants. "Look, *Jovenes*, there is the pampas fox, mainly a nocturnal animal." Further on he stopped the travellers. "Look into the grasses. What can you see?"

"Only grass and more grass," answered Malcolm.

"I see something. It is moving," said Richard.

"Well done, Ricardo. It is the pampas cat. It has learned to hide itself within the grasses, being of a similar colour."

"Ah,,"Malcolm declared, "Like humans, some birds and animals have a hidden side. Do you have a hidden side, Richard?"

Richard was somewhat taken aback. "What a question! If I have, would you expect me to tell you?"

"I'm sorry, *Amigo*. I am probing again. Something which I promised you in the Selskar Arms I would not do again. Nothing will ever come between us."

Richard ventured with, "Not even *Il Trovatore*?"

A brief pause. Then, "Not even *Il Trovatore*," Malcolm replied.

Shortly after midday the travelling party rested. Juan had pre-informed them that they would take their *siesta* under the shade of the ombú tree. Its silhouette came into view miles before they reached it, standing in its lonely posture, surrounded by the sea of grass. As they approached, they were struck by its impressive size, its enormous trunk reaching a height of about thirty-five feet. Its branches, twisted and gnarled, spread in all directions like a sinister ogre. However, those same branches provided a welcoming and benevolent canopy which would protect weary travellers from the unforgiving and sweltering sun. Furthermore, the overground roots of the tree formed alcoves where *siesta* sleepers could curl up as if occupying a large cradle. The party alighted, tied their horses to the tree, lunched on their bread and beef, and within a few minutes were enjoying their sleep. Miguel, the older guide, insisted on remaining awake and keeping guard.

Two hours later the travellers resumed their journey for the final eight miles. The landscape remained unchanged, but signs of habitation protruded. From their high box seat Malcolm and Richard spied domesticated herds of cattle in the distance as well as an increased use of wire fences and even barbed wire. Some birds sitting on the fence posts were identified by Juan as *lechuzas* or burrowing owls. They greeted the travellers with their hideous screeches. Eventually the second *posada* came into view. Less prepossessing than the first one, it still presented a welcome haven.

Following their wash and rest, the two friends joined their two guides and a few other drivers for *maté*. The atmosphere was friendlier than that of the previous evening, in this oasis in the desert. Richard's gaze moved up to dwell on the sun starting its decline in a cloudless sky.

Richard's and Malcolm's attention was captured by a distant slow-moving figure. At first, they wondered if it might even be an illusion, a mirage, but both of them could identify its outline as it approached. A horse, a rider. They could make him out more clearly. His build was stocky, his skin so sunburnt it was almost black, his face blistered, his hair long and tangled. He wore *bombachas*, (wide trousers). A poncho, threadbare and displaying some holes, covered his upper body. On one side of his horse were a whip, his gourd for his *maté*, and a large knife known as a *facon*. On the opposite side of his horse were his blanket, a small guitar, and a small wallet-style bag. The rider rode into the yard of the *posada*, dismounted, and strode inside.

Juan whispered, "A *gaucho*."

"Will we be inviting that *gaucho* to join us for *maté*?" Malcolm enquired.

Juan replied, "If he chooses to join us, we will make him welcome, but we will not invite him. You see, *joven*, the true *gaucho* looks down on working men like me. We have settled down, living in our homes with our wives and children, part of communities. The *gaucho* despises that."

"But, Juan," Malcolm asked, "do they still lead their old life, riding freely over the pampas?"

"I'm afraid, Malcolm, their life has changed too. You have observed that much of these lands have been fenced in with wire. *Estancia* owners are taming the wild cattle and breeding them. The *gaucho* can no longer ride over the pampas as he has done for centuries. Some do. More of them are finally settling down, abandoning their old life and becoming just workers on the *estancia*. Your uncle may even employ them at times."

The door of the *posada* opened. Out strode the *gaucho*, his head held high. Without bestowing even one glance at the *maté* drinkers, like a medieval knight he slowly threw his right leg over his horse and resumed his journey. First the horse disappeared, then the rider's torso, and finally his head and hat. Don Quixote, riding across the plains of Spain to resurrect once again the old code of chivalry. This *gaucho*, one of the last remnants of a lost race sailing through the ocean of the Argentine pampas.

The third day, the final day of the journey, dawned. Richard observed that Malcolm's mood was exuberant. "I cannot believe that in a few hours I will meet my uncle again."

"Malcolm, I am rather nervous. He does not know about my arrival. What if he thinks I am not suitable?"

"Richard, he will welcome you almost like a long-lost son. A master of horses, a fiddle player, a lover of books. You will be his emerald."

The gig, together with Juan on his horse, had reached the top of a small hillock. Looking down, the travellers observed about half a mile away a habitation surrounded by trees. Malcolm's face broke into a look bordering on ecstasy. Grabbing Richard's arm, "Richard, this is it. I recognise it from the photos. We have arrived. We are home at last. We have made it. The Sutton homestead."

A middle-aged man emerged, followed by a woman, a young girl, and two men. They stood in a tableau, their faces revealing smiles as the gig bore down on them. The man, obviously David

Sutton, was of tall and upright bearing and of solid build. He presented a rather patrician aura, and, although grey haired, looked somewhat younger than his mid fifty years of age. Malcolm jumped from the moving gig, and ran to embrace his uncle, both of them teary eyed.

"Welcome, nephew Malcolm. *Bienvenidos a Argentina y a tu hogar nuevo*" (Welcome to Argentina and to your new home).

David looked at Richard with approval. "And who is this fine young man you have brought? Come down, *Joven*, and meet me." Richard alighted, whereupon Malcolm grabbed his forearm and led him.

"Uncle David, this is Richard Barron, my great, new, and true friend, educated, master of languages, a fine horseman, and brilliant violinist. Richard, meet my uncle David himself."

David took Richard's hand, slightly bowing with old world courtesy. "Richard Barron, welcome to Argentina. I welcome you as a member of my own family."

Richard replied, "Thank you, *Señor* Sutton. *Mucho gusto de encontrarle, agus gura maith agat*" (Great pleasure to meet you, and thank you).

David Sutton's face lit up. "So, Ricardo, you are from Wexford too? From Forth and Bargy? But, Barron is not a Wexford name."

"No, *Señor* Sutton, I am from Kilkenny."

"Ah, but I could not have found a better man anywhere in Wexford," Malcolm said.

David spoke. "Whatever his county, he is most welcome to my *estancia*. Both of you please come into my house. Marita, bring some cool lemonade and three glasses of cool white wine to the courtyard. Tomas and Santiago, please unload the gig. Bring the young mens' trunks to the lounge. I must examine the gig first, but already I feel it is in excellent shape and displays great workmanship."

Rosa, Marita's daughter had let the young men into the courtyard, where they could observe the nature of the homestead. Instead of constructing one house, David Sutton had built four single storey apartment style buildings. The walls were made of concrete, and the floors of each apartment were tiled. The trees surrounding them provided vital shade from the sun. Seated in the courtyard, Malcolm and Richard enjoyed their lemonade. After ten minutes, David joined them.

"Richard. you took extra care with the gig and the horse, for the animal shows no real sign of over tiredness. Wasn't Malcolm lucky to find a young expert on horses."

The conversation flowed in an easy manner, covering their voyage, the Alguilo family, the quarantine, Buenos Aires, their journey here. David expressed his pleasure also on their induction into *maté* and their seeing a *gaucho*, and the ombú tree. He could sense that they were embracing the uniqueness of their surroundings.

Malcolm enquired, "Uncle David, why did you choose an unusual style of homestead?"

"The idea of four departments and the courtyard appealed to me. Up to about ten years ago attacks on homesteads by Indians, some nefarious *gauchos*, and even bandits were relatively common. This design made the homestead easier to defend from various positions. Also, incidents of homesteads burning down by accident had occurred on the pampas. So, this design was part of my overall strategy of not putting all one's eggs in one basket. Besides, when it had become obvious to me that I would need to bring out from Ireland one or two lads, I felt that the young men would value a modicum of privacy and freedom."

On their guided tour of the property, Richard and Malcolm were first of all taken to their respective rooms in one apartment and separated by a corridor. Each room consisted of a three-quarter size bed, a desk with a mirror, a wardrobe, and a couple of small pieces of furniture. A trough for their daily ablutions was sited outside the apartment. The second apartment comprised David's own bedroom, a guest room, and a bathroom. The third apartment consisted of the kitchen, the scullery, the laundry, and Marita and Rosa's room. The fourth room was the most comfortable, consisting of the carpeted lounge and dining room. Tasteful furniture included a couch, armchairs, drinks cabinet, book cases, a desk and chair, a grandfather clock. The lounge also contained an outside verandah.

That evening's dinner was to be a special occasion. On their entering the dining room, dressed for the occasion, the two lads found the table arrayed with a Spanish style table cloth, Dutch delft, and some fine Waterford crystal glasses. The quality of the meal was excellent. The menu comprised beef soup with bread, a main course of mutton and chicken served with potatoes, cabbage, onions and corn. The desserts consisted of melons and pineapples served with cream. Two bottles of Spanish wine heightened the sense of occasion.

David advised them that they should not expect this fare every evening, although he strove to make Sunday evening dinners the highlight of the week. He impressed on the two men the importance of a varied diet with plenty of vegetables. During the meal fourteen-year-old Rosa, clad in a light blue dress interspersed by yellow floral patterns, and overlaid with a white apron, served their courses with gentleness and a touch of elegance. Richard imagined that the scene would not be too different from that at the mansion of Captain Saunders back in Ireland.

The dinner conversation flowed easily. During the main course David had to hear how both young men had initially met. Between them they related their own parts of the saga, Richard not hiding the fact that he had been meant to go to Australia. However, the uncertainty of his prospects there, Malcolm's persuasive charm, his offer to join him in Argentina on a trial basis, and David's letters especially had convinced him that Providence was leading him to this great land. Malcolm added his usual brand of humour to the story, mentioning how initially Richard thought he was a trickster, while he himself suspected that Richard might be running from the law. An amused David Sutton relaxed in his dining chair, giving Richard his word that the contract would be initially for only one year.

"But, Richard, we have had some Irish immigrants who have arrived here with intentions similar to yours. But after some months they abandon those. You see, *Hijo,* (son), the pampas slowly weave a magical spell on you, drawing you in. Rather like a woman does, you may feel at first that you are not drawn to her. Slowly, and without your even realising it, you wake up one morning to find that her beauty, her charm and uniqueness, her magic have taken possession of you. She has enveloped your being, and you give your body, your heart, and your soul to her. That is how I feel about the pampas of Argentina after thirty years. I am not just talking about the good life we enjoy here. No, it is far more profound than that."

Over breakfast David Sutton gave his two initiates the run down on his stock and *estancia*. "The total number of horseflesh in my stables amounts to fourteen, which includes mares, colts, cobs, geldings, and a couple of ponies. These horses are used for working on his *estancia* and for riding. But my principal output is sheep, which currently number around 20,000, together with some cattle. I have expanded the area of my *estancia* over the years. New acreage often includes coarse grass unsuitable for sheep. On such grass I placed the wild cattle, who eat it, and in turn make the pasture attractive and nutritious for sheep. I use my dozen cows for domestic reasons only, namely to supply the *estancia* with milk, cream, butter, and cheese. Cattle, horses, and cows are an adjunct to the *estancia*. It is the sheep which represent wealth and success for so many Irish on the pampas."

Richard proudly led his chosen mare out of the stable. David had informed them that he had commenced his program of constructing good solid outbuildings in the early 1860s. His first priority had been the shearing shed, followed by the wool room and two stables. All of these buildings had been constructed from mud bricks, natural insulation for the animals during extremes of weather. Other outbuildings included quarters for some of the *estancia* workers and sheds. A constructed circular shaped well, known as a cistern, provided water. The shearing season had commenced that year on the first of October, lasting for a full three weeks. Because it was now approaching mid-November, both lads would have to wait for some months for their induction to that task.

That first morning on the pampas made a lasting imprint on Richard's mind. He decided there and then to write down his impressions of the pampas at the end of that day, a practice which he would continue. Some time later, he would try turning them into simple poetry. His first prose and poetic attempts read:

'The starlight night began to yield to the emerging semblance of dawn, the first manifestation of the rising sun spreading a golden light over the landscape. The morning dew revived the thirsty pampas for another early summer day. I felt an intense peace and happiness. The radiance of dawn was welcoming me to my new homeland. The cries of some unknown birds, in call and response format, broke the stillness of the departing night. I had no idea of their names, but that did not matter. The bleating of some distant sheep added to the awakening chorus of nature. The new day had been welcomed by God's creatures on the pampa.'

The dawn seeps slowly from the east. The starlight pales and
   yields

The scattered songs of morning birds in boundless dew-wet
  fields
Their voices strange upon my ears, their unfamiliar throng,
No robin, thrush nor blackbird here with their familiar song.
A bounty on the glistening dew to slake the thirsty land,
Gives hope to distant bleating sheep on ground as bare as
  sand.
And then the first rays of the sun burst forth in radiant joy
And bids fair welcome to this place a lonesome Irish boy.'

David Sutton was observing how the two young lads were handling their mounts. Malcolm was capable, showing no fear on his medium sized horse. Richard's mare was a little smaller, but how at home that young lad looked in the saddle. He patted his steed, calmed it when one bird flew unexpectedly out from the undergrowth, and soothed it when needed. Richard informed David that horses had been bred and worked by his father, grandfather, and very likely further back.

Nonetheless, Richard could not help observing how the once vast cloak of the pampas was, nonetheless, betraying the encroaching hand of the human. Clusters of trees had been planted to provide sanctuary and shade for the animals from the unmerciful and all engrossing sun. The three riders were grateful, at times sharing the shade with the sheep. It was, however, the hundreds of yards of fencing which symbolised the end of an era for the vast grasslands over which for centuries the indigenous tribes and *gaucho*s had ridden free and unhindered.

The next day, Sunday, provided the two young arrivals with a glimpse of the nature of the Irish community on the pampas. Richard drove the gig, seated beside David. Malcolm, Rosa, and Marita the housekeeper and cook occupied the other seats on the mile and a half journey. Marita's and Rosa's apparel reflected their change from their working clothes to that of members of the Catholic church community. They wore stylish colourful dresses which ran below their knees, elegant shawls, and hats. David pointed to the shearing shed.

"Until four years ago sometimes we attended Mass there, read by an Argentine priest from San Antonio de Areco. He continued to do so even after our own chapel was completed four years ago. However, a young priest from Saint Peter's Seminary in Wexford, Father Andrew Cullen, arrived in 1867. He lives in San Antonio but ministers to the Irish churches and community within a radius of twenty miles. On occasions he has stayed at my *estancia*."

On arrival at the chapel, Malcolm and Richard noted another building. "That," explained David, "is our school for the Irish children, which also serves as a community centre. It was built in 1862. Normally in some Irish communities here, the church is built first, followed by the school. I suppose we just wanted to be different."

The chapel was well furnished, with sufficient pews for the whole congregation, a well-crafted wooden altar, and even a small harmonium to the left of the altar space. As Father Cullen entered the chapel from the front, accompanied by four altar boys, Mrs. Barry the organist struck up the entrance hymn, *Soul of my Saviour* the congregation joining in with gusto. The same enthusiastic fervour was evident in the singing of the other hymns for the Mass. Richard could tell that the majority of the older attendees were Irish, while some children showed signs of mixed-race parentage. Father Cullen in his sermon used a theological language and moral dictates almost identical to that of the priests of Kilcolman. An Irish community transplanted!

After Mass, numerous people came up to Malcolm and Richard to shake their hands, introduce themselves, welcome them to their community, and offer any assistance they might require. The genuine welcomes convinced both lads that they were regarded as a valuable addition to life on the pampas. Some humour also had its place.

A Yola man asked, "Malcolm, you say that this young lad is not from Forth and Bargy, or even from Wexford. How can he stay here?"

Malcolm responded. "Well, you had better not hold that against him if you are trying to race him on his horse or dancing a reel to his fiddle."

The Yola man answered. "Sure, haven't we only been *clammin* (joking) him. We can make him an honorary Forth and Bargy man. Better to have a Kilkenny man than a man from Westmeath."

While driving back to the *estancia*, the names of Furlong, Cardiff, Osborne, Boggan, Devereux, Kehoe, Redmond, Sinnott, and half a dozen other Wexford surnames continued to ring in Richard's ears from the myriad of people who had sincerely welcomed them.

Two Sundays later David Sutton had invited a few guests for dinner, the schoolteachers Robert and Patricia Barry and Father

Andrew Cullen. David had learned that Richard had continued his classical education after leaving school, so both priest and teachers would enjoy conversing with him. They would also relish getting to know Malcolm, a recent arrival from their county. Following a pre-dinner glass of wine, all sat down to table.

Richard opened the conversation, "I feel that I have been transported to a unique Irish colony in the southern hemisphere. There is nothing wrong with that, but are there similar unofficial Irish colonies in, say, North America or Australia?"

"Give me some examples of our Irishness, Richard," Robert Barry requested.

"Well, we have the Irish style Mass and sermon, and the Irish library in the school, which I investigated last Sunday. There I found a collection of books about Ireland or by Irish authors, all written in English, but hardly any books in Irish."

Robert Barry gave his reasons. "The three counties supplying the bulk of emigrants to Argentina, Longford, Westmeath, and Wexford, were all English speaking well before the 1840s. The Irish community on the pampas had effectively isolated itself from the larger Argentine community. The studies at our local primary school are similar to those at an Irish national school, and they are essentially English centred studies."

A lively discussion followed. This culminated in Father Cullen providing a background to the scheme of Irish migration to the Argentine. He outlined Father Fahy's aims for his community, stressing that the latter believed that it was Irish Catholicism which had preserved Irish culture against Engish oppression, and how this same culture and religion had been transplanted to the pampas of Argentina.

Father Cullen elaborated further. "Much as we love our Irish language, we must accept that, with the growth and spread of the British Empire, English is becoming an international language. The Irish who migrated to English speaking countries such as the USA, Canada, Australia and New Zealand suffered enough discrimination because they were Catholics. What would it have been like for them if they had arrived with no English? Here in this great country the Irish were welcomed mainly because they were Catholics and because they spoke English."

Richard interjected. "And if you people in Forth and Bargy had stayed speaking Yola, you would have had even less of a chance when arriving in any English-speaking country."

Laughter all round.

Father Cullen had not quite finished, "One final thing I need to say is that Father Fahy held the Irish on the pampas to a strict moral code, despising drunkenness, gambling, fighting. I must say that we Wexford immigrants are regarded as sober, peaceful, and law-abiding citizens, and we aim to keep that reputation. Father Fahy also insisted on very high moral standards for our young people. Births out of wedlock are almost unknown among our Irish communities here, and I insist that our menfolk treat their wives with respect."

Richard could not help but notice that the priest had glanced at Malcolm. He must have observed the admiring glances in Malcolm's direction at Mass. The priest concluded with, "That is all I have to say, David, on these matters."

David offered a calming reply. "Don't worry, Father Cullen, I have also mentioned such matters to our two new immigrants. They will have *maws* (lots) of work for six days each week. Saturday nights, and, as far as possible, Sundays will be their own time to rest and to enjoy in moderation life's innocent pleasures. Malcolm is my heir, so he cannot stray too far, and by mutual agreement, Richard is on probation here for a year. Now, shall we retire to the parlour for whiskey, and for you, Mrs Barry, a sherry? For the past two weeks these two good lads have been working as shepherds on the *estancia*. They are learning very quickly, and, even though working separately, are coping with the isolation. I have thrown them in at the deep end."

The rest of the evening passed in amicable discussion. Patricia Barry arranged with Richard that he would play the fiddle at morning Mass on Christmas Day, she playing the harmonium. Robert Barry turned out to have some knowledge of the Yola language and Yola traditions. He and Richard agreed to spend some time together on Sundays in their mutual pursuit of that almost dead language. It was early to bed for all, because the two lads had to be up before dawn to resume their duties as shepherds.

Chapter 9.

'Go, For They Call You, Shepherd, From the Hill.'[3]

Richard's and Malcolm's lives as shepherds had commenced two weeks prior to the above-mentioned dinner party. On the Monday, three days after their arrival, each lad had mounted his horse, carried provisions for the next six days, and were led by a Creole *peon* to their respective pastures. Richard's pasture was situated about two miles from the *estancia*, Malcolm's a further two miles beyond. Each lad had been given a well-trained sheep dog. David had explained that the isolation felt by the shepherd often had presented the greatest challenge to life here. However, he had aimed to minimise it. Each lad would return to the *estancia* late on the Saturday, twelve days afterwards. Provided that they were willing to return to their duties at their shepherds' huts for a couple of hours early on Sunday mornings, they could return to the *estancia* for that night's stay.

Both Richard and Malcolm were each charged with the care of around a thousand sheep, taking up much of each day. Being December, night would be limited to around ten hours of darkness. David assured them that attacks by Indians, recalcitrant *gaucho*s, or bandits had by now become rare. Nevertheless, both lads had been issued with rifles.

The two young initiates gazed at the outside of the *rancho*, the shepherd's hut. It consisted of a one room mud cabin, its roof constructed from rushes and durable pampas grass. Neither a chimney

---

3 (Matthew Arnold).

nor a hole in the roof were visible, but the *peon* pointed out a small brick construction at one gable end which would be used for cooking. The walls of the *rancho* were built with mud bricks, supported on the inside by a frame of vertical posts secured with wire. The mud bricks were plastered with a substance made with grass and other products of nature. David Sutton had had the foresight to plant a few trees to provide shade near the cabin.

The *peon* informed them that cabins on the *estancia* had been improved about ten years prior. "A single bed, a table with a chair, are quite new things. Nonetheless, the old iron bar still runs from one gable wall to the opposite wall. Hang your cooking implements from it as well as your weekly amount of mutton."

Richard placed his other food, bread, fruit and vegetables, tea leaves and *maté* leaves, and sugar in the chest. A *peon* would bring supplies of food for the second week. A few rough mats adorned the cabin floor, having replaced the traditional trampled grass. On their journey to the cabin, Malcolm had confided to him that David had initiated these improvements with the aim of minimising the isolation in order to induce shepherds to remain in his employ. The two friends parted, reassured by the knowledge that they would see each other again in twelve days' time.

As Malcolm disappeared, Richard experienced a momentary nostalgia. He suddenly realised that they had been virtually inseparable for the previous six weeks, since their first meeting at the Selskar Arms. Each of them must now build up his own individual relationship with his new master, the pampas of Argentina. David had explained to them that in his early years there he had bred Saxon, Negete, and Rambouillet Merino flocks, aiming for better meat and finer wool. By selecting within the resulting genetic pool, he had succeeded in breeding the Argentine merino. Richard was familiar with some of the diseases to which sheep were prone, especially footrot, catarrh, and scabby mouth. The fencing installed by David meant that his flocks could be less open to infection from wandering sheep belonging to other owners. Still, Richard and Malcolm would need to be vigilant for such diseases.

One of the shepherd's most important tasks was, with the advent of summer, to ensure that the flocks were well watered. He had to lower a large water container into the well, with one end of the rope attached to the container, the other end attached to the horse's saddle. Moving away from the well, the horse would raise the filled container. The shepherd would then pour it into a constructed channel, from which groups of sheep would drink. This process, which lasted for some hours would be repeated over and over until all the sheep were watered. If any sheep had died during the day, the shepherd had to skin it for the value of its hide and wool. Following his evening meal each day, Richard might have some time to meditate on the uniqueness of his surroundings.

Richard would from that moment onwards always inform people that his love affair with the pampas began on that first night. During his four-week initiation as a shepherd he felt that they were slowly and subtly seducing him. There is something about the life of a shepherd which may well bring those who follow it into a closer relationship with the universe, with nature, with the spirit world, and even with God. Richard began to identify sights, sounds, and even smells related to the passing of each day and each night. The bleating of sheep would fade during evening, only to reassert itself again at the advent of dawn. He could also smell the aroma of wildflowers best during sunset. He was inspired to write a few more verses of prose, later converting it to poetry. His early prose commenced with the words:

'I took the time to observe and revel in the sheer beauty of the sunsets and sunrises. I came to regard the former as "the golden hour." The far horizon assumed the persona of a ribbon of gold, over which hues of different colours emerged, the contrasts of these colours gradually becoming more pronounced. Above these colours clouds of various colours formed, one like a small tree, another like the wing of a bird, yet another one the form of an angel. All clouds were rather dark in colour, a beautiful contrast to the sun's light, which by now had assumed an orange or amber hue. On a different part of the horizon, I observed some longer strips of darker clouds. However, the rest of the pampas sky remained absolutely clear. Gradually faint stars would make their appearance, followed by numerous others. A vast canopy of stars.'

'I would rise early to observe the sunrise. A sheen of gold from the east, interspersed with tiny ribbons of dark clouds, longer and shorter ones, broken and unbroken ones, heralded the advent of day. On other parts of the horizon small pockets and clusters of clouds, some snow like, some darker, made their appearance. The sheen of gold was gradually replaced by an emerging brightness. As if welcoming the sun, the master, a long ribbon of light blue was to be observed on the western horizon.'

1.   The rise and fall of the sun, the metronome of my days
The sacred hour of evening drapes the sky
With ribbons of gold and the red and orange of sunset.
The sinking orb darkens the clouds,
Tracing shapes of rocks and trees and angels' wings across the
*   heavens.*
And the stars like a shy child come faintly at first,
Then crowd the sky in a rich palette of twinkling light.

2.   I stood to watch the rising sun, a sheen of gold in eastern
*   skies,*
With scattering trails of darkened clouds, and cotton puffs of
*   snowy white.*
And then his majesty the sun, with gilded beams for bugle call,
Ascended to the lightening sky, and spread benevolence over
*   all.*

'But the pampas did not remain static, for impressions of it could alter as the rhythm of the day progressed. The welcoming early morning sun, as I washed myself outside the cabin, would by early afternoon force me to seek the protective and comforting shade of the trees. The chorus of pampas birds, teros, chajas, chamangas which had announced the dawn could by midday have relinquished their pre-eminence to clouds of gulls darkening the sky, and to the screams of vultures fighting over the carcass of a dead sheep. Even early during the summer, the fresh morning odour of the pampas grass provided me with an uplift for the day ahead. But by midday this same smell could well have been eroded by the tyrannical hot air. My favourite time of day was dusk when the heat had subsided. As the sun set, small clouds might gather to herald the momentary defeat of that same tyrant.'

'No, the pampas did not remain static, for it could change its mood dramatically even in the space of one day. One of the *peon*s had declared that it was like a woman. I disliked that comparison, partly because my experience and understanding of women were somewhat limited. I preferred to compare the pampas to a piece of music, the movement of a sonata, the aria from an opera. An opening in the major key could modulate to a development in the minor key as the mood changed. After other modulations, the original key would usually return triumphant and, like the pampas, enfold the listener in its embrace.'

Christmas Eve witnessed the end of Malcolm's and Richard's introduction to shepherding. David Sutton joyfully welcomed them back to the *estancia*.

"Both you lads have acquitted your apprenticeship to shepherding in flying colours. However, change is on the way. With much of my twelve thousand acres wired off, shepherds for large flocks of my sheep are now less necessary. The shepherd, like the *gaucho*, is becoming a vanishing breed."

"So why, then, uncle did we have to shepherd?"

"Malcolm, because it was an excellent introduction to the trials and rewards of life on the pampas?"

Richard queried, "How will the sheep be watered in the future?"

David explained. "Richard, new methods of watering sheep are being developed, including the creation of dams. Under such a system, a boundary rider can supervise most of the flocks. Thanks to my nephew's initiative at the Selskar Arms, maybe such a rider is now sitting with us right here. But, we will consider all this in the New Year?"

The courtyard of the *estancia* was laid out with four tables laden with a large variety of foods. David Sutton had invited all his *peon*s, *Indio* and Creole workers, to celebrate a late afternoon Christmas dinner. David had stipulated to Rosa and Marita that any individual traveller or *gaucho* must be welcomed to dine with them. Accordingly, Malcolm had instructed some guests that one space must remain free at their table.

David, Malcolm and Richard would serve all the workers from the central buffet table. The Christmas dinner fare consisted of a prime turkey, hams, beef steaks, mutton, other meats, potatoes, a plethora of vegetables, gravy, sauces. Richard gazed in awe at the buffet table, casting his memory back to the goose enjoyed by his family on Christmas Day. Its source had always been a secret, but he now had a strong suspicion as to who its donor was. At this moment he doubted whether the table of the Poes or that even of Captain

Saunders would this day provide such rich and varied fare as here arrayed.

Richard's ruminations were interrupted by a nudge from Malcolm. Standing in a corner of the courtyard was a figure, a lone man. "Richard, it is the *gaucho*. Remember him, at the *posada*. Uncle David, look there."

"Why, Malcolm," David replied, "that is none other than Don Sacando, one of the few authentic remaining *gaucho*s. Richard. bring him to that table over there, and sit with him as his host. He plays the guitar, so you will have something in common."

Richard approached Don Sacando, observing him now in more detail than he did at the *posada*. His chest was full and firm, his stomach somewhat deflated, his hips and legs rather narrow from constant riding, his hands strong and bulky from never ending labour. Rather slanted and small eyes suggested some Indian blood, but their most noticeable feature was a sadness, a sense of loss or yearning. His clothes were those of the traditional *gaucho*, a leather belt, under which was secured a basic and crude whip, a well-worn shirt reaching just below his waist. His trousers and *chiripá* (overtrousers) looked as if they belonged to another age. His boots, probably crafted by himself, were made from cattle hide.

Richard smiled at the *gaucho*, who just nodded in reply. Then, taking his arm, he led him to the end of the nominated table. Richard could not help but notice the look of disdain cast by some of the invited company towards the visitor. Two children snuggled up to their parents. Richard took his place to the right of the old man, requesting another man to pass up the half jug of sangria. To the amazement of everyone, the *gaucho* picked up the jug and drank from it. When his plate of food was placed in front of him, he proceeded to eat it with his fingers. Richard enjoyed a quiet chuckle. It was good to show so called civilised people the old ways.

While Richard conversed easily with the other guests at his table, the *gaucho* ate mainly in silence. But Richard did not want to lose the opportunity of finding out more about this vanishing breed of man. Having finished their meal, he asked David's permission to bring the *gaucho* into the shade of one of the trees outside the house. David and Malcolm assumed Richard's and Don Sacando's places at the table.

The first twenty minutes passed easily, as Richard and the *gaucho* sipped their sangria, discussing how Richard had ended up on this *estancia*. Don Sacando did not interrupt or question much. When Richard had finished, he took a long drink, then looked intensely at the young man, "Ricardo, you were guided by the hand of fate. It was your destiny to come to Argentina, and not to Australia. You were fated to meet a good and decent young lad like Malcolm and his uncle David, a kind, generous, and Christian man. Fate had treated you kindly this time. But we *gaucho*s believe that fate will also deliver us blows, trials, difficulties, and even tragedy, and we must accept them without complaint, as the other side of fate. I will leave you soon, to ride away again."

David Sutton approached, bearing a jug of sangria and half a bottle of brandy.

It was now seven pm. The majority of the guests had left, but some had joined David, Malcolm, Richard, and the *gaucho* in the shade. Richard played a few Irish airs on the violin, Malcolm rendering a couple of Wexford songs, including *The Boys of Kilrane*. David had also sung two songs, one in English and another in Yola. Now, it was Don Sacando's turn. Armed with his guitar, he announced that he would relate in Spanish the story of the Argentine *gaucho*, using a mixture of rhyme, prose, chant and song.

"Our forebears were the children of Spanish soldiers and settlers and Indian women, *mezitos*. I am very proud of my Indian blood, for it was we who walked a millennia ago from that ice cold land of Canada all the way down to these pampas. The settled people called us *vagos,* because we would not remain in one place. My father was a *vago,* but he possessed his own horse. For that reason, he was known as a *gaucho*. When I was fourteen, he took me from my cabin and from my mother, his *china* (wife/girlfriend). He became my *padrino* (godfather, patron), teaching me all he knew about life as a *gaucho*.

"The Spanish had brought the horses, but multitudes of them ran wild. We *gauchos* broke them in. The pampas were our kingdom, our wide-open spaces. We followed the seasons. We castrated the cattle, and then herded and drove them on our infinitely long drives. We sheared and branded the sheep. The grass of the pampas was the floor of our house; the star-studded sky our roof. A team of horses was our only wealth. Our poncho was our raincoat, our warm coat, our blanket. Our saddle was our pillow. Look at the stars, you settled people. The sun, moon, and stars were our clock. They were the compass which guided us on the eternal sea of the pampas. The meat of the animal, cattle or sheep, was our food, the *maté* our drink of life."

Richard, as he listened to the old *gaucho*'s narrative in words and song was drawn into the magic of the moment. Here on the Irish settlements of the pampas, he was spellbound by this old man, a story teller, a poet, a composer of songs, a musician. This *gaucho* was truly a bard, like the bards of ancient Ireland.

"The Argentine army recruited me to fight when I was younger. Yes, I fought with Rosas, and I did some bad things. Yet I have never been subject to a master. My only master is fate, more so than God. No woman has been able to tame me or keep me in her house. Some of the *gaucho*s took women as their *chinas*, and had children like my father did, but that was not for me. Yes, of course I have used women for my pleasure on occasions. But my horse has been my real *china*. My guitar has been my solace on my countless nights on these plains. The songs and the poems I have composed are the children which I will bequeath to posterity. I have sung them in the *pulperia* (local store) to the tears of my listeners. We *gaucho*s have kept alive the songs and poems of our forebears."

This statement resulted in a lump in Richard's throat. He could not but remember the songs and airs learned from Colum O'Leary in the Shanahan kitchen. He looked down at his fiddle.

"Yes, we *gaucho*s were for centuries lords of our own domain. Our horses carried us wherever theirs and our moods converged. But, alas, things changed over time. *Estancia* owners, Irish, English, Basque, arrived and bought the lands on which we had roamed since time immemorial. Some owners were bad and cruel; some indifferent to us; some, like *Señor* Sutton, were generous and hospitable gentlemen. Over time, the sheep have been placed in wired pastures and within corralled fences. The cattle no longer freely wander the vast plains. Yet, whenever I arrive at the Sutton *estancia*, my horse and I are free to ride all over it. Long life to *Señor* Sutton, to young Malcolm and young Ricardo. May the god of the pampas guide you, preserve you and help you all to prosper."

The *gaucho* bard had put down his guitar and lapsed into silence, terminating his beautiful but poignant narrative. Like the Irish bards, Don Sacando had praised his host for his hospitality and for his respect of the traditional rights of the *gaucho*. The audience remained silent, because the bard was now silently praying to or meditating on his own god. When he raised his glass of sangria, quiet conversation resumed.

Richard had heard the *gaucho*'s full story. A couple of guests departed. Rosa brought the remaining group some sangria. Don Sacando once again picked up his guitar, and sang a few *gaucho* songs. Then silently he collected his gourd and guitar, and ambled towards his sleep-out. David Sutton spoke, "Before retiring for the night, the *gaucho* always tends to his horse. He will depart well before day break, but he will return. When? Maybe in weeks, months, or even years."

Don Sacando's exposition of the *gaucho* enshrined a lament also, a lament for another vanishing race of people. His knowledge, his stories, his experience, his songs were, like those of the Irish bards, passed on orally. They represented a vanishing world, but a world of immeasurable richness. The Irish on the pampas had found a richness of a mainly material kind. But had they usurped an earlier and deeper richness, a richness of ancient traditions, spirituality, deep communion with a noble understanding of nature?

Chapter 10.

Life on the Pampas

The year 1871 dawned, a year of decision for Richard Barron. He agreed with Don Sacando that fate had dealt him a benevolent hand. He would immerse himself in the rhythms of work and of the seasons. Furthermore, he would bestow on his new life and work all his dedication, all his energies. Richard's work followed a pattern of sheep rearing common to North America, Europe, Australia, and New Zealand during the late nineteenth century. This pattern did not alter a great deal for much of the 1870s. Each year had its major and minor events, its transitions, its challenges, its vicissitudes, its recapitulations. Indeed, the year could be compared to the movement of a sonata.

At the advent of the new year, David Sutton had decreed that their first priority was to harvest the corn. He had twenty acres of wheat and fifty acres of Indian corn. The reasons for growing Indian corn were twofold.

"It serves to cool the land, preparing it well for wheat, and it is good feed for pigs. I give the Indian corn to the Malones. Originally from Taghmon, they live on a small farm six miles away, and they breed pigs. In return they supply us with cured bacon."

A fleet of ten reapers, Malcolm and Richard included, armed with heavily toothed reaping implements, launched into the acreage of wheat. They commenced their work at 7 am, reaping until noon, when they broke for lunch, followed by their *siesta*. The heat was still intense when they resumed, but it diminished as the day waned. Both lads had had experience of reaping corn in Ireland, and they revelled in their membership of a large team. Gradually the large field of golden wheat had been transformed, its former regiment of stalks now lying on the pampas floor. Once the team of reapers had cut down an acre of wheat, they exchanged their toothed *regiers* for *loghter* hooks, which drew the stalks into sheaves, both implements of Irish origin. David pointed out, "Unlike in Ireland, we do not place the sheaves immediately into stooks. Here we leave them lying on the ground for a couple of days."

Subsequently David demonstrated a stook by arranging eight sheaves into an upside-down cone shape, with the ears of corn joining at the top of the cone, the straw bases touching the ground. "Is that the way you built them in Kilkenny, Richard?"

"Not quite. My father used to arrange them like a tent. Three sheaves on each side, one on the front, and one on the back. He said that the ears of corn would benefit from the breeze blowing through on all sides."

David Sutton considered. "Let me think about this, because it does make sense. We might try it for a few acres. I grow corn for our own use only, so we can afford to experiment."

A week after the sheaves had been stooked, they arranged them into stacks. The method followed was similar to that used in Ireland. About twenty stooks made up a large stack.

Meanwhile, Malcolm had thought of one innovation. "The infamous Pamplona wind can sweep down with fury. Why not secure each stack with a rope or *sugan* around its middle, which would help to alleviate that threat." His uncle readily agreed, being something of an innovator on the pampas.

The sheaves of wheat had been drawn in a week before, and big ricks had been built. On threshing day the sheaves were carried by some men into the *estancia*'s big barn, where a large threshing board lay on the floor. Malcolm and Richard joined the flailers, regarded as the upper echelon. As their work progressed, they fell into a rhythm, removing the grain from the ears of corn. The grain was loaded into sacks. The straw was now carried out of the barn, and two new ricks were built. The light straw could be used for thatching outbuildings and even placed within their walls, the heavier straw as bedding for the cows and horses, and for cattle feeding.

The final part of the threshing consisted of a few boys shovelling the chaff into a large pit placed near the barn, where it probably would be burned. With such an efficient team working, it was no surprise that the threshing was completed in two days. A special celebratory dinner in the courtyard followed. The fare excelled by far anything Richard had experienced in Ireland at a threshing, but alcohol was not served in excess.

Malcolm and Richard drove their cart through the outskirts of San Antonio de Areco, part of a convoy of four carts carrying the grains of wheat from the Sutton *estancia* to the town's mill. David Sutton's arrangement with the miller was that he would grind the wheat into flour, helped by the drivers of the Sutton carts. Three quarters of this flour they would bring back to the *estancia*. The remaining quarter would remain with the miller as payment.

Their bags of flour loaded, Malcolm and Richard strode through the town in the relative cool of evening, admiring its features. Dating back a couple of centuries, it boasted some impressive buildings. The two most memorable structures were the municipal building, with its beautifully crafted double doors and intricate sculpture adorning its roof, and the almost basilica style church of Saint Anthony of Padua, completed the previous year. The two friends continued their walk to a somewhat less prepossessing part of the town containing a *pulperia*.

"Should we go in for a drink?" Malcolm asked. Before Richard could answer, the doors were flung open. Out came a trio of rough looking Creole men, the one in the middle falling to the ground in a drunken stupor. His left cheek displayed an ugly scar. Malcolm spoke quietly. "It looks as if he has had too much. As we say in Yola, he is in the *bacus ditch*."

"What did you say?" snarled one of the men.

"I meant no harm. I was only speaking to my friend."

"You have insulted my friend, you bastard *Irlandés*. You will pay for this." The man lunged forward, albeit unsteadily.

"Malcolm, let us run. They won't be able to follow us."

"Richard, no one calls me a bastard *Irlandés*. I can handle him."

The flash of steel from the belligerent creole. "I will cut your throat, *Irlandés!*"

"Come on, Malcolm. Run!"

The man lunged forward.

"Put down that knife, you cur," a voice commanded from the door. The assailant turned to see a *gaucho*, his hand on his own *farcon*.

The man tending to the drunkard called, "Raimondo, leave them. You cannot defeat that *gaucho*. He will cut you to ribbons. We need to carry Jorge back to our gig."

Raimondo looked at the two friends, spat at them and turned away. Don Sacando had reached them. Richard and Malcolm embraced him, effusive in their thanks.

"*Jovenes*, this is not a good part of the town. Avoid it and never enter that *pulperia*. Go get your cart, and follow me to a nicer *pulperia*. Good people and some *gaucho*s go there. Maybe we will sing you some of our songs." He looked intensely at Richard. "*Joven Irlandés*, it was not your destiny to die at the hands of a drunken Creole."

Richard and Malcolm drove to the *pulperia*. "Richard, why did you tell me to run?"

"Malcolm, you were confronting a drunkard, armed with a knife. We would have outrun him. However, if you had stood and fought, you could have been seriously injured, even killed. He was not worth it."

"Does that mean, Richard, that you would always run from a fight?"

"No, Malcolm, at times I would stand and fight. If our *estancia* home were attacked. If it were for a cause I believed in. If I were defending the evicted, the down trodden, the persecuted, then I am sure I would fight. But not to give one of the dregs of society the satisfaction of killing me, or killing you."

"Richard, I don't think I need a guardian angel when I have you with me. Oh, this must be the *pulperia*. Let us join Don Sacando."

Following the task of changing wooden posts to concrete posts, completed in April, David Sutton had one more innovation to add to the *estancia* before the spring shearing. "It is something I have considered doing for some years now. For the past few years, *estancia*s have been plagued by sheep scab. It seems to strike every two years, causing deaths of thousands of sheep to some *estancieros* (ranchers). Two years ago, I lost about two thousand sheep. News has come through from the Carmen de Areco region that it is happening again. I am proposing to build a large sheep dip made of concrete, four yards long by four yards wide. My usual builder has agreed to build it, at an estimated cost of 500,000 pesos."

Malcolm whistled. "That is an amazing amount of money, uncle. How can you be sure that it will cure the scab? What mixture will you use?"

"Malcolm, let me explain further. The two thousand sheep which I lost two years ago would have fetched sixty pesos each that year. How much did I lose, Richard?"

"One hundred and twenty thousand pesos, *Señor.*"

"Very good. The builder says that, provided you two lads can help him with the labour, he can probably reduce that sum by up to one hundred thousand pesos. So, not losing at least two thousand sheep every two years, after six years we should have covered the cost of construction."

"What about the cost of the dip itself?" Malcolm asked.

David replied. "Again, I am going to go by another article which I have read. It recommends the use of tobacco, some lime, salt, and a couple of other minor substances. This would work out at around one peso per head of sheep. Now, lads, as you have seen, I believe in progress being made slowly and carefully. On the pampas we Irish farmers have led the way with improvements. We will initially dip only a couple of the flocks. I have heard that some Argentine *estancieros* rush the dipping of their sheep, and that they have not mixed the ingredients to the correct proportions. So, my lads, are you both in favour of our constructing a concrete sheep dip? The spring rains will fill it with water."

Malcolm voiced his approval, with Richard supporting him. After all, Malcolm would inherit the *estancia*, and who knew where Richard would be when that would occur.

Within two weeks, work was under way on the construction of the sheep dip, at a height of two and a half feet. The builder proved himself competent, and, with Malcolm and Richard mixing the concrete, progress was rapid. Richard had used an aluminium gallon measuring can to work out how many gallons the structure would hold. Arriving at the capacity for the sheep dip, he and David worked out the proportions of the ingredients required, as recommended by the article. A week after its completion, the pampas were blessed with refreshing rains for three days.

The invitation to Malcolm and Richard to attend the opera had arrived in mid August 1871. Don Enrique wrote about the calibre of the singers, the production, and the quality of the chorus and orchestra. Malcolm and Richard would be their guests. David Sutton insisted that the two lads accept the generous invitation. "The opera is ten days away, on 4th September. We will have finished the sheep dip by then. Shearing may well begin around 1st October. But you need to sample the life and culture of the big city and, from what you have told me, Don Enrique has two cultured and eligible daughters. By the way, Richard, who is Francisco?"

Richard explained to him how young Francisco had taken something of a liking to him on board the ship, loved Richard's stories, and how, at the boy's insistence, he and Malcolm promised to bring him to the *estancia*.

David enthused, "Francisco and Sergio sound like fine young lads. It would be wonderful to have a couple of young boys here for a while. You must tell them that they are most welcome. The summer heat would not be the best time. Autumn or spring would be perfect."

Richard sat in the middle of the Alguilo opera party, seated in the front row of the balcony. Francisco was to his left and Catalina to his right. Malcolm sat on Catalina's right, with Doña Alejandra on his right, her husband on the extreme right. Isabella had taken up a position on the extreme left where, in her own words, she could clip either or both boys' ears if they dared to talk. Francisco had promised that he would not do so, provided he could sit beside Richard.

Awaiting the conductor's entry, Richard marvelled at the wonders of this magnificent temple. The horseshoe shaped balcony seats represented a feat of engineering. The beautiful engraved proscenium arch promised some elaborate sets on stage, while the private opera boxes exuded luxury and comfort for their wealthy occupants. The dome shaped centre of the ceiling displayed painted classical scenes. A chandelier crafted from some world-famous crystal hung from the centre of the dome. What an introduction for a young lad from rural Kilkenny to the world of civilisation, outstanding architecture, and now world class music and opera.

The gas lights of *El Teatro Colon* had been dimmed. The Italian conductor made his grand entry to applause. The leader of the orchestra sounded the tuning note. A hush fell on the audience as the conductor raised his baton. The dire mood of *Il Trovatore* was established by the short but dark and sombre prologue.

The curtain lifted on Act I. Ferrando, the captain of the guard of the Count da Luna, the role sung by a Chilean bass, entered and roused his soldiers. He recounted the story of the old gypsy casting a spell on the count's youngest child. As Italian and Spanish are similar languages, Richard and the Alguilo family could largely follow the story. Richard glanced at Francisco, but could detect no sign of fear, even when Ferrando related how the bones of another baby, presumably the count's other son, had been found at the site of the burning of the old gypsy woman.

The curtain lifted on the second scene, the palace gardens. The beautiful lady Leonora, the cruel and scheming young Count de Luna, and the brave and dashing Manrico the Troubadour, brought alive this tale of love, chivalry and betrayal. The roles of Leonora and Manrico, soprano and tenor, were being sung by two Spanish singers, while the role of the count was being sung by an up-and-coming young Argentine baritone. When the curtain closed at the end of the scene, with Manrico and the count drawing their swords for their duel, and Leonora falling senseless, Richard heard to his left.

"Richard, has she died?"

"No, Francisco, she has just fainted. Ladies often do that."

"Who wins the duel?"

"Manrico does, but he is wounded."

"Does he kill the count?"

"No, Francisco, he could have, but a voice from heaven bade him not to."

"That is stupid. He should have killed him when he had the chance. Then the opera would end happily, and we could all go to that nice restaurant for supper."

Sergio explained. "Francisco, most operas end sadly. Otherwise, they would not be real grand operas. They are rather like the tragedies of the great Spanish playwrights and of Shakespeare."

"But, Richard-" Francisco began.

"Francisco, stop annoying Richard," Catalina ordered, "The second act is about to begin."

"It is alright, Catalina, he is just trying to follow the story. Now, Francisco and Sergio, I want to see if you both can work out in the next scene whether the gypsy Azucena is truly Manrico's mother. I will give you both a sign when she sings the aria which holds the clue."

The curtain rose. The wounded Manrico lay on a mattress. Richard was overwhelmed by the great Anvil Chorus. Never before had he heard such choral singing. Now the Brazilian mezzo soprano in the role of Azucena, mesmerised by the campfire flames, relived in her aria the horrifying death of her mother, ending with the words to Manrico, "Avenge thou me."

Azucena's next aria would revive traumatic memories for Richard. He gave the two boys the silent signal. When Azucena had inadvertently indicated to Manrico that he was not her son, and he had asked her then whose son he was, Richard re-lived that scene in the Club House Hotel in Kilkenny. Azucena's reassuring words to Manrico that he was her son almost mirrored Andrew Barron's reassuring reply.

"So, boys, have you worked it out?" Richard enquired.

The Alguilo party sat with their drinks in a lounge room during the interval. Francisco answered. "I do not think that Manrico is her son. Manrico is a knight in shining armour, a troubadour who sings beautifully, brave, and so noble that he does not kill his enemy. If he were a gypsy, he would not be like that. Gypsies are dirty, lazy, smelly. They steal, sometimes stealing children. They even kill. They are like *Indios* (Indians). I hate them."

Isabella countered with, "Francisco, not all gypsies are like that. True gypsies are born in Romania, aren't they, Richard, and they have strict codes of behaviour?"

Richard agreed, adding. "And, Francisco, not all *Indios* are like that either. *Señor* Sutton has some *Indio peon*s on his *estancia* and they are great people. Marita and Rosa are clean, hard-working, and they cook us excellent meals. Now, what do you think, Sergio?"

Sergio, now aged fourteen, and a quieter and less excitable boy than Francisco, aged twelve, answered. "I do not think that he is her son. I think Azucena said something like, *Il figlio mio, mio figlio avea bruciato* which I think means *My son had perished. My son through me had perished.* Did she throw the wrong baby, her own son, into the fire?"

"Exactly. Well done, Sergio," praised his father. "You are a very clever boy. The poor woman. She was so distressed she made that terrible mistake." The bell rang, announcing the commencement shortly of Act III.

The two remaining acts woke a few sentiments in Richard. He could relate to the maternal sentiments of Azucena, when, captured by Ferrando, she lamented the loss of her son with the words *Sola speme un figlio avea, Mi lascio! M'obblia l'in grato.* Richard was unsure as to whether she was referring her own son or to Manrico. The Italian translated to *All my heart's troubled emotion for his loss no words can show. Ah! For him my warm devotion no Earthly mother else can show.* Richard's mind could not help but turn to his actual mother, convinced now that she was Andrew Barron's sister Catherine, exiled to New York. Did she think of him, bewail the loss of him? Did the words of Azucena's lament echo fully the sentiments of Catherine Barron?

In the final act, Leonora promised herself to the count in return for Manrico's life and freedom, taking the poison to free herself from such a fate. When Azucena and Manrico sang their celebrated duet, *Ai Nostri Monti Ritorneremo* (*Home to our Mountains we will Return*), Richard, glanced at Catalina. Whether it was a spontaneous action on the part of both of them, or quasi accidental, the back of each of their hands touched and remained there for about the final twelve bars. After all, it was that music which had first brought them together. Richard could feel the warmth and the slight pressure of her hand, for him and him alone. Even after Catalina had withdrawn her hand at the end of the duet, the feeling of ecstasy remained with him until the end of the opera.

Richard heard the small voice to his left, "Richard, will they burn her? Will we see them burning her?" Annoyed that his ecstatic moments had been temporarily broken, he was about to answer abruptly, "No, Francisco," when that same voice in a louder whisper said, "Oh, ouch. That hurt!" Richard had to stifle a chuckle. Isabella was living up to her threat.

Now the drama was moving to its climax. Leonora begged Manrico to escape while he could. As the poison overwhelmed her, he knew what she had done. The count, on entering and realising her deception, ordered the immediate execution of Manrico. Dragging Azucena to the window to witness it, she finally revealed to him her terrible secret. She had finally avenged her mother after all those years.

The chorus assembled to take its curtain call. The audience clapped, cheered, and called out. Ferrando received a similar ovation. The count, probably because the singer was from Buenos Aires, received even greater acclaim, although with a few boos for the villain. Manrico and Leonora received the applause and cries of exultation from the audience now drunk-like in their enthusiasm. The director had left Azucena, the central character, to take the final bow. The Brazilian mezzo soprano, through her splendid singing, her acting and her characterisation had in some respects transformed this great role. The applause, the cries, and now the stamping of feet were followed by many of the audience rising to give her a standing ovation. The conductor, exultant in his triumph, walked onto the stage, gesturing to the orchestra to take a bow. Placing himself between Manrico and Leonora, he led the full company in five final bows. The curtain closed. The gas lights came up, and the orchestra left the pit. What an unbelievable introduction to the world of grand opera, Richard mused. He walked out of *El Teatro Colon* on a seventh plane.

During the Alguilos' supper Don Enrique asked. "Well, Sergio, did the count ever find out who Manrico was?"

Sergio paused. "*Mi padre*, I think he did. When Azucena saw the axe fall on Manrico, she declared, *Egli era tuo fratello.* Doesn't that mean, *He was your brother?*"

His father beamed "Well done again, *Mi Hijo.* Excellent. But could not Azucena have saved him and possibly herself, if she had revealed it earlier?"

"No, *Mi Padre.* Her final words were *Se vindicate, o madre. Thou are revenged, o mother.* That had become her purpose in life, had it not?"

His father exulted. "Sergio, you are developing the mind of a lawyer. You always base your conclusions on evidence."

Doña Alejandra added. "Sergio, take a bow. You are a brilliant boy."

Francisco, however, had to have his say. "But did they burn her in the end?"

"Are you a bloodthirsty boy?" Richard asked. "Well, no, but she did throw the baby into the fire."

"That was her own baby, you clown," Sergio laughed, "Have I not worked it all out?"

"That is enough, *Mis Hijos.*" Don Enrique commanded "The impression which I favour is that Azucena dies of maybe a heart attack or a stroke, totally overcome by the situation. Now, Malcolm and Richard, you will both remember to join us for lunch tomorrow at *El Restaurante de la Bella Vista.* I have booked a table for one pm. For now, *buenos noches.*"

The Sunday lunch at the restaurant reflected through its cuisine, drinks, conversation, and general atmosphere their first dinner on board ship of almost a year prior. Malcolm to his delight sat beside Catalina. Richard had grown to respect and like Sergio and Isabella. In some ways they were similar to each other, thoughtful, intelligent, studious, lovers of books, art, history.

Much of the conversation centred on Malcolm and Richard recounting their lives on the *estancia*. Richard became more aware of the void that exists between city and rural life in any country.

Sergio queried. "Have you and Malcolm met any *gaucho*s on the pampas?"

Richard replied. "Indeed we have, Sergio, and we have made a good friend of one of them. His name is Don Sacando."

Doña Alejandra spoke. "Then you must tell us all about them. I want my children to learn about what is sadly a vanishing aspect of our own history."

Malcom and Richard told the story of the *gaucho*'s Christmas Day visit. Francisco was fascinated by the *gaucho*'s clothes, his horse, his weapons, his looks. Sergio and Isabella loved how the *gaucho* told his story in prose and poetry, while Catalina was particularly interested in his songs. At the end of the story, Francisco tapped the table, declaring. "That is it! I am going to be a *gaucho*."

"You," retorted Sergio, "You cannot even ride a pony yet, let alone a great horse."

"Well, I am going to learn to ride a pony when-" Francisco stopped. No invitation had yet been given, but Malcolm and Richard saw that Francisco had opened the door.

At the conclusion of the lunch, Malcolm relayed his uncle's formal invitation, causing Francisco to jump up and whoop. "See, I am going to learn how to ride a pony and become a *gaucho*."

"Franciso," reprimanded his mother, "when are you going to learn some manners?"

Franciso apologised.

Sergio politely asked. "Malcolm, when will we be able to go?"

"Sergio, the shearing happens in October. The pampas become extremely hot from November onwards, but they cool down around March. So, my uncle feels that your Easter vacation from school will be the best time. Do you agree, Don Enrique *y Señora*?"

"That time will be perfect. We will bring them part of the way, and you two lads can drive the boys through the pampas for them to savour its mystery and magic."

Richard's final action during this visit to Buenos Aires was to purchase an Italian made violin. Verdi's and other composers' immortal melodies would now be given full justice.

Fate had also bequeathed Catherine Barron a kindly gift, perhaps as a recompense for her misfortunes in her homeland. Her studies of Spanish language and literature had been successful. She had also found herself a Spanish born piano teacher of note, and her skill on that instrument had progressed rapidly. Due to the high opinion in which her employers placed her, she was partly brought into their social circle.

Among the da Silvas' friends was the Álvarez family, their son Eduardo and their daughter Adrianna. Eduardo, a quiet, sensitive, and cultured young man, had for four years trained for the priesthood in a major seminary. Having then decided that such a life was not for him, he had changed his vocation to that of a prospective lawyer, training in his father's business. His parents were, however, concerned that bachelorhood might envelop him in its cloak, and their hopes lifted as Eduardo's and Catherine's friendship blossomed. Catherine, however, trod carefully. She had decided that, for various reasons, her future husband should preferably not have had much experience of women, and Eduardo suited her choice.

After a year of their developing friendship, followed by another year of formal courtship, Eduardo Álvarez and Catherine Barron were married on 7th June 1853, in a small church in Buenos Aires. Only thirty guests attended, including all of the da Silva family on Catherine's behalf, as well as a few of her Argentine friends, and twenty relatives and friends of the Álvarez family. For their honeymoon the newly weds sailed to Montevideo, capital of Uruguay. Their marriage could be described as a happy one.

Eduardo and Catherine had purchased a house in Tigre, an emerging small city about seventeen miles north of Buenos Aires. Having recently qualified as a lawyer, and with his father's influence, professional contacts, and financial backing, Eduardo's legal practice progressed at a steady pace. Meanwhile, Catherine had set up her own private practice as a piano teacher in their house. Catherine's music studio could have thrived further, but domestic duties called. In May 1854 she gave birth to a son whom they named Marcelo. His birth was followed by that of a daughter in 1856, christened Alicia, and by a second son named Paulo in 1858. Catherine Barron's happiness was now complete. Naturally she sometimes reminisced about her life and fate in Ireland, still grieving at times for the loss of her son, Richard, and wondering about his fate. She continued to correspond with her family in Ireland until about 1856, and did inform them of her marriage, but after that she gradually lost contact with them.

Chapter 11.

'Tis the Springtime that Brings on the Shearing.'[4]

It would be the busiest time of year, the highlight at most *estancias*. Shearing at the Sutton *estancia* would commence on 8th October 1871. Two weeks beforehand David Sutton had sent Richard as an outrider to some of the neighbouring Irish farms and *estancias* to reserve some of the most skilled shearers. All eight shearers, two Irish, one English, two Basques, and three Creoles, held a high opinion of David Sutton. Yes, he worked them hard, but paid them well for quality work. His kitchen staff cooked them excellent meals and, rather unique on the pampas, David had built shearers' quarters, small rooms with two bunk beds in each room.

Richard's task also involved asking the Irish farm owners if some of their own workers would be willing to lend a hand at the Sutton shearing for a few days or even a week. Some years prior, the old Irish system of the *meitheal* or communal work party had become a feature of Irish life on the pampas, especially at shearing time. Richard informed the farm owners that David's shearing season would last about four weeks. The shearers would shear about eighteen thousand sheep between them over the course of a month. Most of the Irish farmers agreed to assist the Suttons, as the latter's *peon*s would also assist them in due time. Richard rode back to the Sutton *estancia* happy at having fulfilled his mission.

---

4 (Australian Bush Ballad)

A week before the shearing commenced, David Sutton raised the subject of burrs in the wool. It was a perennial problem, because wool with burrs commanded a lower price from the wool merchants, often as much as twenty percent less. Malcolm felt that the time was right to inform him of his and Richard's experiment.

"Uncle David, we have been thinking about this problem too. A few days ago, we removed burrs together from a few sheep. It took us together an average of just under three minutes for each sheep. They remove easily. Children could do that task."

David asked. "And where, nephew, are we going to find children to come here for four weeks, miss out on school, and me getting into right *dole* (trouble) with priest and teacher?"

"What about *Indio* children?" Richard suggested, "Most don't go to school. They hang around in the square in San Antonio. Would it not be a way of introducing them to honest work? Maybe some of the mothers would come too. We could collect them on the first day of shearing. Could they not stay here overnight in the outbuildings? Then we drive them back home on Saturday evening, and collect them again on Monday morning."

"All right, Richard," David stated, "You work it out mathematically. What say we use a team of ten or twelve *Indio* children and a couple of mothers. We can then compare the cost of that extra labour to the likely increase of twenty per cent in the value of the wool. Then we will decide. We will also consider the advantage we are giving to the *Indio* community."

Malcolm and Richard had a short meeting with Father Mauricio at the basilica in San Antonio. He brought them to a few *Indio* cabins to meet good people who, though living in poverty, could be reliable workers. Their visit to five cabins resulted in their recruiting fourteen workers, two mothers each with three children, and the remaining six children from three other cabins. On Malcolm's arrival at the square early on the first day of the shearing, they awaited him. Aided by Richard's mathematical calculations, David had decided that a profit from the improved wool was highly likely. Even if it proved the reverse, they were helping to improve the lot of the local *Indio*s, the traditional owners of the pampas.

A photographer or painter depicting a shearing session might be forgiven for thinking that the scene exemplified chaos personified: the bleating of sheep, the movement of sheep and people, the din of the pressing machines, and the calling of orders. However, all were hallmarks of a well organised system of labour and of an experienced and capable work party.

The shearers were the aristocrats of the process. David had in the early 1860s introduced the quick New Zealand method of the shearer holding the animal between his knees, cutting off the belly wool, and removing the whole fleece in one piece. That belly wool would be bagged in order to separate it from the baled wool, but it would not be thrown away. The shearer would throw the sheared wool on the wooden slatted floor, from which the nominated picker-uppers would pick it up, throw it in the air so that it would land like a blanket on the sorters' tables, the fleece side up. Thereupon the sorters, the next highest rank in the echelon, would sort out the fleeces into two categories, good and bad, to be baled separately. David had also installed two double boxed wool presses, imported from Australia, one for each category of wool, to compress the wool into bales. Traditionally two workers carried the fleeces from the sorting tables to the pressing machines. Small wonder that the pressers, two to each machine, considered themselves as occupying the third rank in the echelon.

With the innovation of the child *Indio* team removing the burrs, a change in format had to occur. David Sutton had placed that team at the end of the central aisle. Two workers carried the fleeces, both good and bad, to the children's table. When the burrs had been removed, two other workers carried those fleeces to the pressers. Bales of fifteen fleeces were the result, each bale transported to the woolshed by two carriers. So, behind the apparent chaos lay the rhythm of a smooth operation.

On the Thursday of the first week the rhythm of work and the peaceful albeit intense atmosphere were broken by a horrible incident. Elena, a ten-year-old *Indio* child was engrossed in her work of removing the burrs. Feeling a hand on her shoulder, she turned around to face a young scar-faced rough looking Creole, one of the carriers, his hair tangled, and anger in his eyes.

"Water, *Indio,* water, I need water. I need it now." Angered further by Elena's dumbfounded look, he raged. "Don't you know what water is, you stupid *Indio.* You do as I order. Go to the kitchen and get me some water – now!"

Elena, now afraid, answered in broken Spanish. "I cannot leave my work. We must remove the burrs."

Furious, the Creole shouted. "You will do as I tell you, you little *Indio* bitch. Don't try to turn your back on me. I'll teach you what you can and cannot do."

Elena saw the raised fist. She felt the blow across her right eye, the pain, the temporary loss of sight. This was followed by a second blow which pummelled her nose, the ring on her aggressor's finger slicing her upper lip. Elena felt the hot blood streaming from nose and lip, followed by the hand of one of the *Indio* women workers on her shoulder and saying to the Creole.

"Leave her alone. She has done you no harm. All she wants to do is get on with her work."

"You don't tell me what or what not to do, you *Indio puta* (whore) or I will do the same or worse to you. You *Indio*s murdered my father."

Through the mist of her swollen eye and her tears Elena could make out a hand being gripped on her attacker's shoulder from behind, causing him to swing round. Maybe now they would be safe.

Richard Barron faced the child's assailant, who looked familiar. "What are you doing? Why have you attacked that child?"

The creole raged. "I told her to go and get me some water because I am dying of thirst. She refused."

"It is not her task to get you or anyone else water. Our morning break is in fifteen minutes time. Joseph and I are thirsty too from carrying the bales."

The Creole gave Richard a push. "Who are you, *Señor* Sutton's pet boy, to tell me what to do? Those children are only dirty *Indios.*"

Richard answered. "Malcolm Sutton and I, with *Señor* Sutton's permission, brought those children and the two women to work. They will be treated with respect, like all our workers."

The Creole sneered, giving another push to Richard. "Maybe you want to ride the *Indio* women, you Irish bastard. But I doubt that you can ride women as well as you ride your horse. And you don't ride your horse all that well anyway."

The next push, heavier and with two hands, caused Richard to lose his balance, crashing on the wooden slatted floor. Fortunately, his woollen cap prevented a severe impact on his head. His attacker, two inches taller than him and of lean but wiry physique, towered above. Richard's immediate intention was to stand up, brush him aside, and tend to the child. But the next moment the Creole was on top of him with raised fist.

Richard Barron, while working on the Poes' farm in Ireland, had received some lessons in wrestling. Raising his knee to protect against a knee in his groin, he grabbed the Creole's forearms, pitted his own body weight against him and, with a sudden lunge, succeeded in reversing their positions, pinning the Creole to the floor. By now the sorters and the picker-uppers had stopped work, forming a semi circle around them. The count began in various languages. The Creole made a sudden lunge up, but Richard had him well pinned. On the count reaching the number eight, David Sutton flanked by Malcolm framed the doorway near the childrens' table, shouting, "What is going on here? A brawl in the middle of our work. Why is that little girl crying? Both of you young fellows get up and get outside. The rest of you all, back to work."

"So, master Barron, tell me what has caused this brawl. In all my years of shearing, I have never seen anything like it here."

"Let him tell you, *Señor* David. I am not an informer. All I will say is that I came back into the shearing shed with Joseph to collect another bale, and I saw the child's face."

David turned to the Creole. "Did you attack that child, Jorge, and why?"

"I asked her to go and get me some water. She looked at me like a dumb animal. *Indio*s are not much better than animals. I from my hiding place witnessed them murder my father when I was eight years old. Why do we have to have them here? It was Barron who brought them here."

"Richard and my nephew Malcolm did so with my full permission. You can see how well they work removing the burrs. Master Barron, did you then attack Jorge?"

"Jorge, you can tell what happened next." retorted Richard. Jorge replied. "He started telling me that I should treat them with respect. Treat murderers with respect! I gave him one push, then another, and he fell to the floor, probably deliberately. I could see in his eyes that he was going to get up and attack me, so I had to defend myself by jumping on him."

David eyed Richard. "But, master Barron, you managed to reverse positions. How?"

"*Señor* Sutton, I used my wrestling skill because I did not want things to develop into a dangerous fist fight. You saw the rest yourself."

' "Alright, that is the end of it," declared David. "Master Barron, there is some blame on both sides. I feel that you should have gone to find me, Malcolm in the woolshed, or Malachy Curnow, my assistant manager. Jorge, while you are working here there can be no violence, especially against children. I give you a choice. If you wish, you can leave now. I will pay you what you are due and more. I will not breathe a word of it to Mr. Daly, your employer."

The Creole sulkily answered. "There is no need to pay me, *Señor.* Under the work parties, our own employer pays us."

"No, Jorge, I insist on paying you if that is what you decide to do. Go and have a think about it, and let me know after the tea break, when I intend to speak to the whole shearing shed. Now, master Barron, let us go and look at this injured child. From your knowledge of injured horses and sheep, you may be able to offer some advice."

Richard examined Elena, "The child's eye is swollen, but I am sure that that will go down, because the eye is resilient. It should be treated with wild honey. A bandage will probably help. The nose bleed may stop if she leans backwards on a chair, and we put some dressing on the lip. I think the shock of the attack is the worst thing."

Richard saw the *Indio* woman nodding in agreement. David instructed her to bring Elena into the kitchen where the other women would tend to her. He himself would take over their work on the burrs, but Elena should rest until lunchtime. Another Creole approached him, "*Señor* Sutton, I saw it all happen. Richard is in no way to blame. He was just defending an innocent child. That Jorge is an evil and cruel man, and none of us like him. I advise you to get rid of him at once."

"*Gracias*, Pedro, but we will give him one more chance. Mr. Daly has loaned him to us for two weeks, and I hope he has learned his lesson. Richard is a real hero."

David Sutton addressed the assembled shearers and workers. "I know I work you all hard, but I think my reputation is that of a fair employer. During my eighteen years as owner of this property, I have always tried to make it a happy place. An unfortunate incident occurred here this morning, but that is the end of it. Jorge has promised that there will be no repeat of it. I have also reprimanded Richard. Jorge will re-join us in a few minutes time, Elena will do so after lunch. I want no booing nor cheering."

David continued. "Malcolm, can you please show everyone how our fleeces now look. Look at the big improvement with the burrs removed from a good fleece. A new standard for San Antonio de Areco region. This is what our *Indio* children achieved. Doesn't the fleece look beautiful."

A murmur of assent followed.

"Now, Mr. Curnow, please show them what our sorters have regarded as a bad fleece. Even that one, with the burrs removed, is an improvement. All of us here, Irish, English, Basques, Creoles, *Indios*, adults, children, are here to produce the best wool for our region. Yes, there have been differences between our peoples, sometimes terrible conflicts, leading to bloodshed, wars, deaths, dispossession. But while we are in this shearing shed, we will work as one great and united team, to show the world how the Almighty has blessed our abundant land. Whatever your race is, we will treat each other with respect. Is everyone in agreement with what I have said?"

The shearing shed resounded with cries of "*Si, Señor. Ciertamente, Viva* (Certainly, Long live) *Señor* Sutton." Peace was restored.

However, on the Friday work session, when Richard encountered Jorge by chance, he was sure he heard the Creole murmur, "You wait, Barron you bastard. I will get you yet." Suddenly he remembered with a shudder where he had seen him before. The drunkard lying in the dust.

The remaining weeks of the shearing season passed without any other significant incidents. Following Jorge's assault on Elena, Richard noticed that the other Creole workers shunned Jorge, both in the shearing shed and at meal time. True, there was little love lost between the Creoles and the *Indio* races, but the Creoles still believed in a certain code of behaviour, and assaulting a small defenceless child was anathema to them. It was little wonder that Jorge did not return on the following Monday. Six months later they heard that he

227

had left his Irish employer and departed from the region. When Richard collected the *Indio*s from the square on that same Monday, young Taquia introduced his brother named Xiemen, a fourteen-year-old boy, strong and sturdy, with an emerging handsomeness. Richard accepted him immediately, Xiemen assuming Jorge's place, with the Creoles especially welcoming him.

During dinner, a few days before the end of the shearing season, David Sutton came up with a suggestion. "I strive to treat the *Indio*s of the pampas and my *Indio* workers as equals. We always invite the *Indio* workers to our shearing celebration. Richard, why don't we have a short concert as part of it?"

"A concert, *Señor*?"

"Yes, one showing our different cultures, Irish, Creole, Basque. Why, we could have some *Indio* performers this year." Richard considered it. "Yes, *Señor* David, I think it would be a good idea this time."

"Excellent, Richard, you can organise it."

"What should we have in it, *Señor*?"

"Have some songs, instrumental pieces, a few poems. A kaleidoscope of cultures."

Richard addressed the *Indio* boys' and girls' work team. "*Señor* Sutton insists that all you children and you two women attend the *meitheal* celebration. You have done wonderful work, and so should be part of it. There will be plenty food, ample drink, music, dancing.

You two women are allowed to bring your husbands provided they do not, for their own benefit, drink too much alcohol."

Gradually the group warmed to the idea. Ever since Richard had defended Elena, possibly at the risk of his own life, he had become a hero in their eyes.

Richard broached his next query. "Are any of you able to play an *Indio* instrument? *Señor* Sutton would be delighted to have some Indian music and, better still, a song or dance or two."

Lara, Elena's aunt, the woman who had tried to rescue her, pointed to three of the boys. She addressed them in their own language, and, whether it was a result of persuasion, veiled threats, inducements, promises, or the call to duty, the three boys agreed. They would bring their instruments on the following Monday,

Richard surveyed their instruments. Xiemen had brought a wooden instrument, somewhat similar to a recorder, but with ten tone holes. Zamaba, a girl, had brought another wooden instrument, thicker than Xiemen's, with only five tone holes, emitting a deeper sound, which Richard soon deduced could be played as a drone. Taquia presented two percussion instruments, which he named as the *kultrum* and the *mascaea*. The former was fashioned from the skin of an animal over wood. Taquia informed Richard that the *mascaea* belonged to his father, and that it was an instrument from the Banda Oriental. When Xiemen and Zamaba played the tone holes on their instruments, Richard noted that Zamaba's bass instrument was built on the pentatonic scale, Xiemen's instrument on the Aeolian mode. Lara revealed that she and Ada, a young girl, could sing an *Indio* song or chant to the boys' accompaniment. They would display their musical heritage.

The celebration commenced around 7 pm on the Friday in the shearing shed. Beer, wine, sangria, port, rum, gin, and some limited amounts of whiskey and brandy, all under Malcolm's supervision, were available in moderation. Plates of roasted meat were surrounded by smaller plates of sandwiches, rolls, fritters, and small pies. Another table contained sweet pastries, apple pies, slices, and other delicacies. Underneath a tree, close by the shearing shed, Malachy Curnow was supervising the workings of a barbecue. Through the celebratory throng David Sutton wandered, chatting and drinking in moderation with groups of men and women. He did his utmost to make the Indian children and women feel relaxed and comfortable, informing them that they had been booked by Mr. Lynham for the same task on his *estancia*.

The concert program reflected the rich musical diversity of the various cultures. It commenced with some singers, English, Scottish, Irish, Creole, captivating the audience with songs mainly in their respective languages. Then, the *Indio* perfomers, two boys, two girls, and one woman walked on stage. The audience became quiet. Could *Indio*s play instruments? Zamaba commenced by playing the drone, joined then by Xiemen with a melody. Xiemen ceased to play temporarily when the woman and the girl commenced their chant in the *Indio* language, accompanied by Taquia on percussion. Xiemen then re-entered with his original melody, doubled by Richard on the fiddle, Zamaba switching to a different drone. The music gathered pace. Singers and musicians appeared to become possessed. They moved to a climax, concluding their performance with a shout of "Ah! Ah! Ah!" Their audience responded initially with polite applause, giving way on the performers' bow to cheering and some foot stamping. Where had this *Indio* music come from? One did not associate it with a tribe of people identified and reputed as being uncivilised. And those *Indio*s could sing, albeit in a chant. The final item of the concert consisted of two Basque songs, accompanied by two Basque instrumentalists. Again, virtually none of the listeners understood the texts of these songs. Another language facing possible extinction.

Following the concert component, the work party was determined to make the most of the night. A Creole accordion player, two guitarists, and a drummer moved to the stage. They played a couple of dance tunes and a few popular songs. However, the audience, seated in chairs during the concert, was keen to make up for lost time with some further eating and drinking. Malcolm had resumed his post as supervisor of the alcohol, but generally the men waited their turns for standard amounts.

Young Santiago, leader of the Creole ensemble, was master of ceremonies for the dance bracket. For the initial waltzes David Sutton, a skilled dancer, proudly led an Irish widow, to the floor, with a cry of *Vale a dancing*. Other couples followed immediately, including some of the shearers. This was followed by a bracket of polkas, another bracket of waltzes, and then a refreshment break. Hand claps and foot stamps were a feature of the bracket of mazurkas. Another bracket of waltzes completed this section.

Richard Barron stood on the small raised platform to announce the start of the Irish dances. The band consisted of an accordion player, two fiddle players including Richard, three tin whistle players, an *uilleann* piper, two guitar players one of whom was a Creole, and a young drummer. The dances had evolved from crossroads dancing in pre-Famine Ireland to what was now known as ceili dancing.

The band opened with a bracket of reels. By the third set David Sutton and his female companion stepped to the floor. Other couples followed. About twelve couples moving around the shearing shed's perimeter. Steps forward, steps backwards. The lady dancers being swirled around. Reels followed by jigs, followed by quadrilles. The Irish band was joined by two Creole guitar players. Then by young Taquia, with Richard's encouragement, joining young Michael Carey the drummer. Music has a way of breaking down racial barriers.

Two Argentine dances, the *triunfo* (victory) and the *gato,* completed the night. The Creole band moved back to the stage. Two Creole couples in national costume. The singer commenced. Each dancer danced from corner to centre stage and back. Each woman shook her florid dress, to the stomping by the men. Dance sequences were repeated four times, culminating in the bow. For the *gato* two other couples joined them. Driving and pulsating rhythms. Full body turns, half turns, foot stamping, hand clapping. Some improvisation by the dancers. The slatted wooden floor resounded under hard soles. They moved towards the climax. Suddenly, the dance was over. The eight dancers bowed to thunderous applause and cheers. It was as if the enthusiasm, energy, and zest for life which had characterised the Sutton shearing *meitheal* had been transformed into this five-minute capsule of Argentine art and culture. A fitting end to the kaleidoscope of cultures.

Richard Barron relaxed with a glass of sangria. Here on this platform was represented an alliance of races which in the past had been at times rivals if not indeed enemies: Irish versus Creole, Irish versus *Indio*, Creole versus *Indio*. Music was a unifier and indeed a potential healer. He prayed that this spirit symbolised by the music, songs, and general spirit tonight might emanate across the vast stretches of the pampas, joining all races and dwellers therein in one great march towards a peaceful and united region.

"Richard, wait for me." Richard turned around to see a smiling Malcolm.

Malcolm said, "I felt I should escort the *Indios* back to their sleeping quarters as a courtesy to them. Well, *amigo*, we have discovered another gift in you, that of a concert director. I hope you are feeling very proud of yourself."

"Yes, I am overjoyed with how the celebrations have gone. I am especially happy that we had been able to include the *Indio*s, and by how musicians and audience responded to them."

"You know, Richard, we are only a few weeks away from the first anniversary of our arrival here. What are your feelings? I think you know what I mean."

"I have no intention of leaving for Australia, at least not for another year. I feel I am finding my world here." He felt an affectionate hand on his shoulder.

"Ah, maybe Don Sacando was right. The pampas are like a woman, slowly enfolding you in her embrace. This is your true home, *Amigo*."

They had almost reached their respective rooms. Richard felt the hand move up to caress his hair. "You know, Mate, your hair is growing very long. I suggest that you visit the barber. Are you trying to make yourself even less attractive to women than you are already? Did you get 'ere' a *hoult* (hug and kiss) after the dance?"

Richard laughed. "Yes, I did get a few hugs and even a couple of kisses. But, we Irish cannot make ourselves as handsome as certain twenty-six-year-old Yoles."

A light punch on his back was the reply, followed by mutual, *Buenos noches, Amigo.*

David Sutton's and Richard Barron's informal meeting a few weeks later lasted barely a few minutes. The former could not hide his joy at hearing that the young man wished to extend his unwritten contract for another year. He pointed out that Richard could now consider taking ownership of one third of the new lambs born since his arrival, under the pampas system of 'thirds.' Richard replied that he would prefer to remain as a salaried employee for another year, and would consider the offer after that. David's immediate answer was to increase his wage to three pounds and five shillings a week. A couple of glasses of good Spanish wine followed.

CHAPTER 12.

'When all the World is Young'[5]

David Sutton opened the letter from Don Enrique Alguilo dated 17th March, 1872. Having read the formal salutations and good wishes his eyes moved to the second paragraph. Sergio and Francisco were anxious to know whether the invitation for them to come on a vacation still stood. They would have almost a three-week vacation from school during Easter. Their parents would let them go only if it suited the Suttons, and provided they would constitute no inconvenience. David was immediately in favour of it. "It will be a delight for my *estancia* to ring with the sound of boys' happy voices, and for us to witness their freshness, enthusiasm, and vitality."

David then pointed out that the boys' parents had requested that a few conditions be observed. If either or both of the boys misbehaved, they must both be sent home at once. Both boys were allowed to ride ponies, but asked that they please be careful with Francisco. Still dreaming of becoming a *gaucho*, he might want to try jumping fences or hedges. Malcolm would assure the parents that, there being virtually no hedges on the *estancia*, that danger would not exist. "Then it is decided," declared David. "I will write to Don Enrique and Doña Alejandra tonight, saying the boys are most welcome and that all of us, especially I myself, are looking forward to their arrival."

---

5   (Charles Kingsley)

On the Monday of Holy Week, in mid-April, Malcolm and Richard headed for Lujan in the gig. At nine am the next day, the two groups would meet up in a pre-arranged restaurant in the city centre. Catalina and Isabella would arrive with the two boys, their own chaperone, and the coachman.

Both young men stepped out of the restaurant to greet the Alguilo coach. Formal handshakes and slight bows to the two young ladies, handshakes to chaperone and coachman, and embraces to the boys. Francisco could not hide his excitement. "After coffee, Malcolm, can we start our drive?"

"Francisco," reprimanded Isabella, "we have not seen Malcolm and Richard for some months. We want to talk to them."

Malcolm explained. "We will commence our journey at ten am. It Is sixty-four kilometres, and we hope to cover between eight and ten kilometres each hour. How long will that take, Sergio?"

"Six and a half to eight hours." Catalina spoke. "I would love to visit the shrine of Our Lady of Lujan."

Malcolm beamed. "I can drive you there, Catalina. We can be back here in thirty minutes. Maybe, Sergio, you would like to come too." Richard stayed behind to converse with Isabella and Francisco. On Malcolm's return, Richard could detect a real bounce in his friend's step.

The gig was loaded with the two boys' luggage, plus a few purchases made for the *estancia*. Richard had purchased three boy *gaucho* things to represent prizes for the stages of Francisco becoming a young *gaucho*, a boy's ornate belt, a small whip, and a small gourd for *maté*. With Francisco beside him, he assumed his place as driver on the box seat. Each boy would take turns there every hour. The terrain of the pampas was similar to that of the route which Malcolm and Richard had experienced on their first journey, so Richard could point out some features to the ever-excited Francisco, especially the pampas animals and birds.

Sergio, on seeing the two rifles under the seats, nervously asked. "We are carrying guns, Malcolm. Are we fearing an *Indio* attack?"

"Calm your fears, Sergio. This is a busy road and such an encounter is highly unlikely. Besides, *Indio*s might still steal cattle or sheep from an *estancia*, but murders are now rare."

"So, Malcolm, there is no danger of them attacking the *estancia* and kidnapping Francisco."

"I'm afraid you're right, Sergio. You will have to put up with him for your vacation."

"That is alright, Malcolm. He is a good boy most of the time. But, when I go home, we might leave him behind to ride the pampas as a young *gaucho*."

Malcolm laughed, and then told Sergio about what to expect on the *estancia*, and the importance of safety. The courtesies included respect for the *Indio*s, kitchen staff and *peon*s, and not taking the Irish workers too seriously.

The arrival of the travelling party at the Sutton *estancia* was met by another welcoming party similar to the one which had greeted Malcolm and Richard. Malcolm escorted the two boys to their bedroom, followed by a short tour of the *estancia* buildings. At dinner both boys seemed a little awed by the persona of David Sutton. Malcolm helped them to feel more relaxed by asking them to tell David about their first meeting on the ship and their experience at *Il Trovatore*. Francisco's impression of the bizarre plot resulted in some genial laughter from his listeners. As Richard noted that both young boys' eyes were beginning to droop, he suggested that they should both go to bed after dinner.

Next morning Malcolm gave Sergio and Francisco the tour of the outbuildings. He explained some features of the various pieces of equipment. Both boys were fascinated with their tour of the shearing shed, up to now largely unaware of the journey of the wool from the sheep's back to its culmination as a blanket on their bed. Sergio expressed great interest in the story of the *meitheal* and the celebration, especially of the concert and dancing sections. Francisco for his part almost refused to believe that *Indio* boys had played instruments and that two *Indio* women had sung. Malcolm replied that he might be able to provide proof. At the end of the tour, he led them both to the horse corral, and to their two ponies prepared by an *Indio peon*. Richard suddenly realised that this was probably the first *Indio* man both boys had ever met. Nonetheless, both young boys displayed courtesy to him. Richard and Malcolm, mounted on their own horses, led the two boys and their ponies to a large stretch of pampa.

Neither boy displayed any hesitation about mounting ponies for the first time. Richard gave the boys some basic instructions. "A flick of the reins will get the pony moving; a slight pull on the reins will halt it. Bend your torsos slightly forward in the saddle. This morning you are being taken on a tour of part of the *estancia* to view large flocks of sheep, cows and cattle, some of our new innovations, and to hold some newly born lambs."

As the party of four rode through the vast expanses of the Sutton *estancia*, Richard perceived the awe in the boys' faces. He was especially pleased to see that Sergio was revelling in his new environment. While Francisco's excitement at every aspect of the ride was constant, Sergio broke into smiles at every new vista or innovation – the shepherd's hut, the fences, the corrals, the sheep dip.

When they stopped under the shade of a tree for their morning tea, Malcolm broached his question. "Would you two boys like to help us with some tail cutting and branding? We use the Spanish word *señalled* to describe the branding. We cut the lambs' tails to prevent flyblow infecting them. My uncle has introduced this in the region, and is currently doing it only to a small number of his sheep as an experiment. I will be doing the tail cutting, known as docking, and Richard the branding on a total of about one hundred sheep already corralled."

Francisco immediately offered. "I will help with the docking as that sounds like a real *gaucho* task, and a *gaucho* has to get used to the sight of blood."

Sergio eagerly said. "I will help Richard with the branding. I love to participate in scientific experiments."

Malcolm handled the actual cutting of the tail while Francisco held the frightened little animal, both while it was being cut and while Malcolm rubbed a substance on the wound to prevent infection and to ease the pain. Francisco's next task was to lead the lamb to the branding area. Branding was a painless procedure, simply marking its ear with a dye, bestowing on it the Sutton distinctive mark. Sergio held the lamb, and then led it out of the corral where the group of mother sheep awaited their young. He was intrigued by how the lamb could find its mother with apparent ease.

Richard explained, "It is the work of nature, Sergio. Sheep and lamb find each other by instinct. It is rather like what Jesus said, *I am the good shepherd. I know my flock and they know me.*"

The procedures took up about three hours of the afternoon. On their return to the *estancia* house, David Sutton was met by sheer youthful exuberance. The boys' exhilaration rubbed off on him for the rest of the day.

The next day, Holy Thursday, the working hours were shorter. The task was to move some flocks of sheep to new pastures on the *estancia*, assisted by two sheep dogs. Richard informed the two boys that they were now ready to try cantering.

"Dig your heels slightly on the pony's sides a couple of times. As the pony begins to trot, let your bottom jog up and down with the rhythm of the trot. When you wish to stop, pull lightly on the reins as normal. Malcolm will lead us."

Sergio and Francisco were exultant. "You can both be *gaucho*s," called Malcolm. "But don't *gaucho*s have to gallop their horses?" asked Sergio.

"Actually, no," answered Malcolm. "The *gaucho* is more like the Arab riding his horse or camel through the desert. He loves to breathe the air, to savour the magic, to hear the sounds of the pampas. For the *gaucho* is their uncrowned king."

Doña Alejandra Alguilo had stipulated that her sons had to attend all three Easter ceremonies. Accordingly, the family drove the gig to the Mass being held at its local 'Irish' church early evening on Holy Thursday. David took the box seat beside Richard, leaving more room in the gig for Malcolm, the boys, Rosa and Marita. This was the first close encounter of Sergio and Francisco with *Indios*. On seeing the relaxed manner in which Malcolm chatted with Marita, the boys summoned up the courage to chat to fourteen-year-old Rosa. She told them new things about the pampas. The Sutton party took the same journey on Good Friday, the rapport between the Creole boys and the *Indio* girl developing.

For the Mass on Easter Sunday the party attended the Basilica of San Antonio de Areco. The church resounded with the triumphant singing of celebratory hymns in Latin, Spanish, and English. After Mass, many of the Irish came forward to welcome the two Creole boys to the pampas, regarding them almost like celebrities. Word had travelled about Francisco's skill and bravery on his pony the previous day.

That day, the party of four had been continuing its work of moving some flocks of sheep. They had moved one flock and were slowly cantering through a stretch of long grass. A large bird shot out of the grass right in front of Francisco's pony. Totally frightened, it lunged forward and changed from canter to gallop. Francisco felt himself moving to one side of the saddle, unable to readjust his position. Adhering to Richard's advice, he withdrew his feet from the stirrups, for fear of falling on the ground and being dragged by the pony. Just as well, for he fell to the ground, the pony continuing to gallop forward. Richard drew up alongside him, jumping from his mount, and bidding Malcolm to catch the runaway pony.

Richard, his face revealing terror, gazed at the boy, motionless on the grass. What had they done? What if Francisco had suffered a severe head injury? He noted, however, that the boy's thick woollen cap was still in its place. By this time a white-faced Sergio had reached him and dismounted. Richard shook Francisco gently. No response. Ashen faced, Richard shook him again, more strongly. "Francisco, can you hear me?" The flicker of the boy's eyes. Slowly they opened, albeit with a somewhat dazed look.

"Richard, where am I?" Richard had never been so pleased to hear his name called.

"You are on the pampas floor, Francisco. You fell off your galloping pony."

"Ah yes, now I remember. The bird. My pony got frightened. Is he alright?" Sheer relief flooded the faces of Richard and Sergio, but the former wished to be sure that the boy had not suffered any injury to his brain.

"What is your name?" he asked.

"Richard, you know my name. It is Francisco Alguilo."

"Who is that boy?"

"That is my brother Sergio who thinks he can push me around."

"Where are you now, Francisco? No, don't try to sit up yet."

"Why, I am at Malcolm and his uncle David's *estancia*."

"Where is your home?"

"My home is in Buenos Aires. I live there with my parents, my sister Catalina, whom you like, and my other sister Isabella. Why are you asking me all these questions?"

"I am just making sure that you have not had an injury to your brain. *Gracias a dios* (Thanks to God), I do not think that you have."

Francisco reassured him. "I don't think I have either, because my head is not hurting much, although my back is somewhat."

By this time Malcolm had returned with the pony. "Francisco," he said, "can you lift up your knees?"

"Of course, I can, Malcolm, and there is no pain in my legs or any extra pain in my back when I do it."

Relief all round.

"Great. If you had injured your back, I do not think that you would be able to lift up your knees without feeling extra pain. I think it is now safe, Richard, for him to sit up. Bring him to sit up slowly and gently. Then, see if he can stand up slowly."

This movement presented no real problem.

"You see, I can stand up. I am like a new born lamb," said Francisco proudly. By this time the two boys were hugging each other. "*Gracias a dios, Hermano,* (brother), you are alive and well."

Malcolm declared, "We will have our lunch right here. Tell us if the pain in your back gets worse. Richard will take you back to the *estancia* on his horse."

Francisco's face fell. "Can't I ride my own pony back? I am sure that even *gaucho*s sometimes fall off their horses. I won't let one little fall stop me getting up on my pony again."

"You are a brave boy," Richard said. "Alright, you can ride your pony, but no cantering. I will attach a rope between your pony and my horse. However, I am first going to calm your pony to prevent him galloping again. But, Francisco, I have one condition. If *Señor* Sutton decides that you must go to his own doctor, you will travel with me in the gig, and no arguments. Sergio, you can go with Malcolm and the two dogs and help him to move the flock."

Richard moved to the uneasy pony. He smoothed its head and its neck with his hands, whispering some soothing words and sounds into its ear. Sergio and Francisco watched in amazement as the animal became calmer. Richard must have some secret, magic power with horses.

Doctor San Martin spoke, "A fall from a pony. Not unusual with children. You say, Richard, that you asked him some questions. In English or in Spanish?"

"In English, doctor. Should I have asked them in Spanish?"

"No, Richard, it is even better that you used English, and that, even hearing a strange language, he gave you correct answers. That is an excellent sign that there is no injury to the brain, but I will check for any internal bleeding in the head."

He carried out a thorough examination of the boy's head, shoulders, neck, back, buttocks, hips, legs. Although Francisco stated that the pain in his back had almost disappeared, the doctor still prescribed some tablets.

"The one thing I strongly advise is that he should rest on his return to your *estancia*, because he may suffer from some delayed shock. Put him to bed, and make sure he remains there until this evening. There is no need to wire his parents. Let them enjoy Easter Sunday in peace. I can look at him again quickly after Mass in the basilica. I suggest you take him now and buy him an ice cream. You probably both need one."

"He can have a double ice cream," stated an overjoyed Richard.

"*Muchas gracias, Señor medico*," Francisco said. "I think it was worth my falling off the pony for that treat."

A special late lunch on Easter Sunday turned out to be an occasion for a celebration. The two school teachers were invited. Rosa and Marita had prepared a number of appetising courses. Following the dessert, David Sutton rose to his feet.

"It is my singular honour to make a presentation. I am most pleased to announce the successful passing of master Francisco Alguilo in his first stage of becoming a young *gaucho*. He has proved that he can handle a galloping mount, sustaining no personal injury,

245

and, most importantly not letting it prevent him from immediately taking to the saddle again. Francisco, please come forward to receive your *gaucho* belt."

Francisco proudly accepted the token, attaching it around his waist. Returning to his seat, it was hand shakes of congratulation all round. Sergio bestowed on his brother another deep hug.

It would be the highlight of the Alguilo boys' stay on the Sutton *estancia*, two days and two nights as shepherd boys out on the pampas with Richard. The boys would sleep in the cabin, while Richard would sleep near the fire. They would bring implements for work and sufficient food for two days.

It was perhaps the beauty of that morning which inspired some poetic writing. The trio set off just before dawn broke, accompanied by Juglar the sheep dog. Both boys could barely hide their excitement, Francisco sporting his *gaucho* belt. A declining full moon lit their way. The bleating of the occasional sheep, and the call of the first bird in the chorus which welcomed the dawn raised the boys' expectations. Other birds entered the chorus rather in the manner of musical polyphony, interrupted by Francisco's excited chatter and questions. An entrancing yellow light slowly spread over the pampas, a band of red on the far horizon displaying a reluctance to disappear.

As the morning light increased, so did the trio become aware of the carpet of fresh autumn flowers, endowing the green of the landscape with varied colours of scarlet, yellow gold, blue and white. The aroma of fresh rain merged with the scent of these flowers, while the plumage of birds darting and flying about added another layer of colour to nature's welcoming canopy. Richard noticed that Sergio was unusually quiet. Was he concerned about what lay ahead? No, the boy assured him. He was just absorbing the beauty before him, but how, he wondered, could he store that same beauty in his memory forever?

The boys adapted easily to the task of watering the sheep. Richard explained that they would use both ponies to initially heave half a container of water from the well, increasing the amount gradually to three quarters. The boys attached a rope to each of their saddles, then led their respective ponies away from the well. Richard followed behind them with his horse, filling another container. As more water was now being poured into the channels, many sheep could be watered. The result was that the trio succeeded in watering sheep at two wells in the morning, followed by another two in the afternoon, preceded by a *siesta*. On their return to the cabin that evening both boys rested by the campfire while Richard cooked the dinner on the camp oven.

"Is everything all right, Sergio? You seem rather quiet. I expect you are hungry, but don't fret. Dinner will be ready soon. I know that all this must be strange to you, but are you lonely or homesick?" The boy was seated in front of the campfire while Francisco was caressing Juglar. "Oh no, I am perfectly fine, Richard. I am just absorbing the beauty of this moment."

"You mean the peace of the pampas at night, Sergio?"

"Yes, Richard, the peace and the quiet, but not just that."

"Tell me more, Sergio, *por favor* (please). "

Sergio opened up. "The whole experience today has been magical." Sergio elaborated about the beauty of nature at the emergence of dawn. "I wish I could capture it and keep it forever."

"Sergio, I want you to write down all the thoughts you have expressed to me about the pampas. Together we will try writing a poem. I have in the past written some poems in English, but not good ones. With your help maybe we can create a nice poem in Spanish."

Francisco had just joined them. Richard requested, "Francisco, can you please go to the camp oven and look after the chops. Make sure they don't burn and don't let Juglar eat them. Sergio, remember the glorious sunset this evening. Now look at the clouds as they sail across the vast ocean of the sky, with the vivid stars like the beams of lighthouses. Put all this too in your thoughts. Would you like to start writing your ideas after dinner?"

"And who is going to play with me, Richard?" called Francisco. "You can play with Juglar. He really likes you."

Sergio emerged from the cabin. "I have written down all my thoughts."

"Can I please read them?" Hesitatingly the boy handed them over. Richard studied it.

"I think that they are lovely. Now, please remember that my Spanish is not very good, but I think I understand what you are describing. Now, can I suggest that your poem has a refrain. In Ireland we regard the land as our mother. That could be the subject of your refrain. Tomorrow morning you and I can get up a little earlier. We will breathe in the morning air, listen to the sounds, and begin writing.

Tomorrow we will be going on a night ride, so maybe leave a verse to describe that. Truly I am excited by what you are achieving."

Francisco sat up. "Where are we riding to?"

"It is a secret, Francisco," Richard replied.

The boy probed further. "We have eaten all the chops today. What are we going to have for dinner tomorrow?"

"That is part of the secret. We will probably have to kill a sheep," Richard replied.

Sergio arose early next morning. Seated by the remnants of the fire he absorbed the sights and sounds of the dawn. Richard joined him. Within half an hour they had written two verses of the poem and a refrain. Their work today consisted of examining the wire and repairing any breaches. They carried some basic tools for cutting wire, and some smaller coils of wire for the breaches. Richard demonstrated the simple process of twisting the wire and fashioning it into loops.

"Run a section of the new wire along the existing wire. Cut off a strip of the new wire at both ends. Attach it by means of twisting it with the implement and with your fingers to two parts of the existing wire to cover the breakage point. Then pull the new wire at each end to strengthen the knots."

After some initial trial and error, both boys proved able for the task. This enabled Richard to move forward a few hundred metres to repair other breakages, always within vision of the two young initiates. He would check their repairs every so often. On completion of the task, Francisco now asked whether he had passed his second stage of becoming a young *gaucho*.

"Almost," Richard replied, "but the day has not finished yet."

"So, *chicos* (boys), are we all set for our night ride of two miles? I am bringing my fiddle. Sergio, have you brought the football? Good boy."

"But Richard," Francisco said, "we have not brought any knives to kill the sheep."

"Don't worry," answered Richard, "we will probably find a dead sheep on the way."

"What! A smelly sheep with swarms of flies around it. I am not eating that."

"O hush, boy," Sergio retorted, "Richard has it all planned. Look, the three-quarter moon has become a full moon to light our way. It is almost as bright as day."

Francisco relaxed on his pony. This was exciting but very mysterious. Where was Richard taking them? Maybe to meet a real *gaucho*. Richard had instructed them to ride slowly in order to listen out for the sounds of the pampas at night.

The moon assumed the persona of a beacon, as the pampas too took on a different character. A sheep bleated. The sound of a bird or an animal assumed a new prominence against the background of the silence. The trudge of their mounts and the changing position of the moon made Francisco feel that he was like one of the Magi following the heavenly star guiding them to the infant saviour in Bethlehem. Richard had told him that the *gaucho*s followed certain stars by night. Francisco decided that when riding the pampas as a real *gaucho*, he would not feel lonely or afraid. The stars would be his compass as he sailed his ship over the vast desert of the pampas.

"Smoke and a fire." Sergio called.

"It could be some *Indios*," suggested Richard. "Maybe they are sending smoke signals to other tribe members. But don't worry. They should realise that we are friendly, I hope."

"I do not believe you," Francisco countered, unconvinced, "You are only trying to scare me."

The moon sailed from behind a cloud, revealing a small cabin with trees in the background, a campfire near it. The vista became clearer as the trio approached, revealing two small figures tending a fire. One of them turned to look at the approaching party. He had long black hair, a dark but handsome complexion.

"It is a strange looking small boy. Surely an *Indio*," declared Sergio.

"Yes, it is my friend Xiemen and his brother Taquia." Richard confirmed. "Boys, take a deep breath? Isn't that a delicious smell? It is not a sheep, but delicious steaks. These boys have prepared an *asado* (barbecue) for us, steaks with succulent vegetables."

"Who is that standing by the door of the cabin?" Francisco asked.

Richard laughed. "That must be their father, a brave chieftain." The figure emerged from the doorway to the light of the moon.

"It is not a chieftain," called out Francisco jubilantly, "It is Malcolm." Both boys jumped from their ponies, running to embrace Malcolm with cries of delight.

"Enough, boys," laughed Malcolm, "Come and meet our young friends." He led them to the *asado*, where the two *Indio* boys stood up. Each pair of boys displayed a slight nervousness on meeting the other.

Sergio shook their hands confidently, Francisco more hesitatingly. Xiemen led them to stools around the fire. After a minute Taquia emerged from the cabin with glasses of lemonade for the boys and wine for the two young men.

"Come, boys, and look at the *asado*," Xiemen invited. "This is the way the *gaucho*s cooked their meat. They lit a fire in a pit, then placed their steaks on the grill over it. See, the fire has now become a load of embers. On it I have placed potatoes in their skins, and other vegetables, which cook slowly. Your steaks will have a charred flavour on the outside and be rather crunchy, but really juicy on the inside. They are going to be the best steaks which you boys will eat during your holiday."

Conversation between the Aguilo boys and Taquia began to flow while Xiemen continued to tend the repast. They discussed their work on the *estancia*, their ponies, the sheep. Francisco was amazed to hear that both *Indio* boys rode their ponies bareback. Sergio warned him not to even consider it. As the conversation progressed, Sergio especially began to realise that these two boys were not really much different to himself and his brother, and indeed to many of their friends. After about fifteen minutes Xiemen announced that the food was ready, asking Taquia to serve more drinks.

Following the meal, Xiemen stoked up the cinders to relight the fire, for the cool autumn night air was settling in. Filled with the delicious food, rather tired from the day's work, they all might fall asleep in the balm of the firelight. Francisco announced, "We brought a football. Who wants to play?" Francisco described the new game of soccer introduced to Argentina by the British railway constructors. Taquia added that the *Indio*s had played a similar game but with a more oval shaped ball.

Between them the sextet worked out some rules which incorporated a mixture of both styles of play, Richard, Xiemen, and Francisco against the other three. Although they tried to abide by the rules initially, as the game progressed things became more relaxed. Francisco and Taquia commuted between their positions as goal keepers to those of defenders and even mid fielders. A good deal of body contact became a feature, a positive development in Richard's opinion, as the Creole boys became used to touching the *Indio* boys, further breaking down barriers. Was not sport a great leveller of racial fear and mistrust, of antagonism and suspicion?

A scene around a campfire on the verdant plains of some of the lushest lands on planet Earth to a full moon. Six people, two young men and four boys. Four races, if you include the Yola race, are represented. The young Irishman plays some hauntingly beautiful Irish and Scottish melodies on his fiddle. He and the two *Indio* boys play some indigenous melodies. The young Yola man sings a couple of songs from his native county of Wexford. The two Creole boys follow with two Argentine songs. Easy conversation, a few funny stories and adventure stories. Both *Indio* boys invite the Creole boys to visit their native settlement on their next vacation. Three hours have passed since the start of the night ride, but it is now time for them to return to their cabin. Demonstrative and sincere farewells are made between both pairs of boys. They represent the future of this great land.

Xiemen gazed into the fire. He ruminated about the evening. He lifted his head towards the heavens, addressing the god of the pampas, as if in prayer. "Oh God, Taquia and I really like those two Creole boys. We are all the young generation of Argentines. Will such good relations continue between our races as we move to becoming adults? Recent years on the pampas, oh God, have been years of peace. But below the pampas floor the tensions still exist. Tensions which just a spark can ignite. Terrible consequences for my Indian race. Oh God of the pampas, preserve and protect our peoples. We like Malcolm. But one day he will become a large *estancia* owner. He will surely be pulled two ways. Taquia and I both love and trust Richard. He has witnessed it all in Ireland, famine, dispossession, persecution of the Irish poor. Richard is our brother. He visits our *Indio* settlements, meets our elders, learns our language, plays our music. O God of the pampas, guard, protect and preserve our good and valiant brother Richard Barron."

Only a few days of the boys' vacation remained. Their exuberance, energy, motivation had inspired all the *estancia* workers whom they had met. Evening dinners were the highlight of the day, when they recounted their experiences of that day to David Sutton. David had informed them all that he would drive the boys back to Lujan, where he would meet their father and Catalina. Richard detected a shine in Malcolm's eyes.

Francisco had passed his second stage, as a shepherd, as well as for his growing appreciation of *Indio* culture, earning his prize of the riding whip. Meanwhile they were unsure as to what might comprise his third stage, as he would not be taught any further skills. However, an unexpected and rather funny incident solved their dilemma.

Sergio displayed a particular interest in scientific investigation. He had conversed with David Sutton about the science behind the sheep dip. Receiving permission from David to bring some dip samples back to his school laboratory, he arranged that Malcolm, Richard, Francisco, and he himself should head for the sheep dip on the Friday, three days before their journey home. Both young men went to inspect some fences about two hundred yards from the sheep dip, while the boys collected their samples. The water in the sheep dip reached a height of about two feet.

Sergio called out, "Richard, come quickly! Francisco has fallen into the sheep dip. He may be drowning."

"Let him drown! It will teach him not to do it again," Malcolm called jokingly. But Richard was already on his horse and galloping across. Rather than drowning, Francisco was actually floating on the surface. Jumping down, Richard grabbed hold of the boy and pulled him out of the water. By this time Malcolm had joined them.

"So, how is Tom the water baby? He looks fine. Francisco, did you swallow any water?"

"No, I kept my head above the water and kept my mouth shut. I am sorry that I have frightened you all again. I was walking on the wall of the sheep dip and fell in."

"I apologise too," Sergio added. "I should have kept an eye on him."

"No harm has been done." Malcolm assured. "In fact, Sergio, you might have found out more information for your studies. Who knows, perhaps ingredients in the water can keep adventurous boys afloat. Meanwhile we must get the water baby dry. We do not want him developing pneumonia."

Francisco, out of sheer relief, began to laugh. All three of the others joined in.

"Right," Richard commanded, "Francisco, strip yourself to your underclothes. Lie in the warm sun for twenty minutes. That should almost dry them. We will wrap you in a couple of ponchos. Then I will bring you back to the house for a hot bath."

Malcolm was looking at Francisco rather intently. "Richard, won't he have to be scrubbed in the bath to get rid of all the sheep dip mixture? You will have to get Rosa and Marita, or, if he prefers, some of the *peon*s, to do that."

Francisco coloured seven rainbow colours. "I am not having women, *Indio* women, or even any of the *peon*s scrubbing me. No, I am not going back."

Richard patted him lightly. "Francisco, you should know by now that Malcolm cannot resist pulling someone's leg. He calls it *clammin.* Why, the second day I met him, in that taverna in Wexford, he was doing it to me. Pay him no attention. You can wait in your bed. I will get the bath water heated, and you can scrub yourself clean."

"Richard," said Malcolm, "Francisco did not panic when he fell in. A *gaucho* often has to wade across a stream or even a river. He has passed his third stage."

The Sunday following was a day of farewells. Following Mass in the 'Irish church' the two boys were surrounded by some people bidding them farewell, best wishes for their next school term, and expectations of their next visit to the pampas. Two well-wishers bestowed on them woven handmade Saint Brigid's crosses. The Sunday late dinner included some specially invited guests. Rosa and Marita excelled in their cooking. This was followed by a short soiree, featuring Richard on the violin, songs by a couple of the attendees, and the presentation to Francisco of his gourd. But the highlight of this occasion was the recitation by Sergio of his and Richard's poem. Richard had coached him in some skills of delivery and oratory, learnt years ago from Master Ford.

Sergio strode out confidently to face his audience. He raised his parchment, scripted in calligraphy in his own hand. Sergio's eyes invited his audience in. Proudly he announced the title, *Una Oda a las Pampas, Mi Madre.* The boy's mellifluous treble vocal tones at once arrested their attention. The young orator rose to the occasion, entrancing his audience with his delivery. During his stay on the pampas Sergio had ably identified their uniqueness, their beauty, their magic. A couple of seconds of silence followed his bow at the end. To the delight of Richard, loud clapping ensued, all of the attendees standing and moving to shake Sergio's hand. Sergio had won his own spurs.

Poema: 'Una Oda a Las Pampas Mi Madre.

By Sergio Alguilo & Richard Barron

1.   *Un lustre de oro del este anuncia al avenimiento del amanecer.*
Cintas minúsculas de nubes mas oscuras
Se someten en homenaje al sol que aparece.
Otros grupos de nubes blancos como la nieve
Intercalan el horizonte de todos lados.

2.   *El lustre de oro se renuncia a una prenda de tono azul tenue.*
El sol le confere a nuestra madre la pampa su color, su alimento.
Los cantos de naturaleza dan la bienvenida al amanecer.

CORO. Porque la pampa es mi madre. Miro a su belleza incomparable.
Me abraza, me acaricia, me envolve, me sustenta, me protégé, me guia.
Si, los humores de la pampa cambian, pero nuestro amor mutuo es para siempre.

3.   *La Lluvia de otoño durante la noche ha reponido los pastos sedientes.*
Las flores de la pampa hacen alardes de sus colores,
escarlatas, amarillas, doradas, azules, blancas'

Mi madre me ha conferido sus regalos de la lluvia.
Su aroma, su fragancia me enriquecen.

4.   *Cuando las estrellas se apagan de la corona de mi madre,*
Naturaleza se pone a cantar en un coro incomparable.
Un pájaro solitario canta, un conjunto responde.
Un oveja lejana bala, una vaca muge de bajo.
Pájaros aparecen del pasto de la pampa
Sus colores realzan el dosel de las flores.

5.   *Todavia mi madre esta sitiado por sus enemigos,*
El viento pamplono propaga del sur.
Las lluvias torrenciales la sumerge en sus mares.
Las sequías despiadadas buscan poner fin a su vida.
Todavia ella surge triunfadora, lista para preservarme,
Su resurrección me imbue con vida nueva.

6.   *La pampa yace dormienda. El sol ha descendido*
Las nubes navegan por el cielo, guidado por las
constelaciones.
Viajo en mi poni, por los gauchos de antigüedad.
La luna esta mi faro en el cerro del cielo.
Mañana mi madre se despertará de nuevo.
Su vida es eterna, mi pampa amada.

CORO

TRANSLATION:

AN ODE TO THE PAMPAS, MY MOTHER

*Verse 1. A sheen of gold from the east heralds the advent of
dawn.*

*Tiny ribbons of darker clouds bow in homage to the emerging
sun.*

*Other clusters of snow-white cloud intersperse the horizon on
all sides.*

*Verse 2. The sheen of gold yields itself up to a garment of light
blue hue.*

*The sun bestows on our mother, the pampa, its life-giving
warmth, its nourishment.*

The sounds of nature welcome the dawn.

*Chorus. For the pampa is my mother. I gaze at her beauty
unrivalled.*

*She embraces me, caresses me, enfolds me, sustains me,
protects me, guides me.*

*Yes, the moods of the pampa do alter, but our mutual love is
forever.*

*Verse 3. The autumn rain during the night has replenished the
thirsty grasslands.*

*The flowers of the pampas flaunt their colours, scarlet,
yellow, gold, blue, white.*

Our mother has bestowed on us her gifts of the rain. Her scent, her fragrance enriches me.

Verse 4. When the stars fade away from my mother's crown,
Nature sings in a chorus unrivalled.
A lone bird sings, an ensemble responds. A distant sheep bleats. A cow moos the bass.
Birds emerge from the pampas grass. Their colours enhance the canopy of flowers.

Verse 5. Still my mother is besieged by her enemies.
The Pamplona wind sweeps up from the south.
The torrential rains submerge her in their seas.
The unmerciful droughts seek to end her life.
Yet she emerges triumphant, ready to sustain me.
Her resurrection imbues me with new life.

Verse 6. The pampa lies sleeping. The sun has declined.
The clouds sail through the sky, guided by the constellations.
I ride on my pony, like the gaucho of old.
The moon is my beacon on the hill of the sky.
Tomorrow my mother will awaken again. Her life is eternal, my pampa beloved.

Chorus.

David Sutton and Michael Roche shared the driving to Lujan, the two boys alternating in the box seat. The farewells at the *estancia* had been sincere, affectionate, even emotional, accompanied by invitations to return in the spring. Sergio had been entrusted by Malcolm with a letter for Catalina, the former promising to keep it a secret from David Sutton and from Sergio's own parents. Malcolm assured the young boy that there was nothing irregular in the letter, that he and Catalina just shared certain interests. All this was beyond Sergio, for he had thought that Richard liked Catalina and she liked him. Young adults were impossible to understand.

On meeting Don Enrique and his daughter Catalina now aged nineteen, David Sutton was struck by her emerging beauty and her feminine charm. If Malcolm was falling in love with her, he could not blame him. Nonetheless, one had to be practical. An eight-year age gap existed between them, as well as a cultural difference. She was a refined and well educated young Argentine lady, and he only a national school educated Irish-Argentine farmer on the pampas. David and Don Enrique struck up an immediate accord, David assuring him that everyone had really enjoyed the boys' visit and that they must come again. He mentioned Francisco's two little mishaps, but the boy was as hale and hearty and amusing as ever. Driving back home David and Michael realised that the Sutton home and *estancia* would be a less lively place for the immediate future.

CHAPTER 13.

'All, All the Valliant Chiefs of Old are Gone,

One by One Fallen on the Pampas Wild'[6]

The rest of 1872, 1873, and the earlier part of 1874 passed in a manner similar to Malcolm's and Richard's first eighteen months on the *estancia*. Overall, its prosperity increased, mainly thanks to its owner's farming innovations. New immigration from Ireland had almost ceased, with immigration from Italy markedly increasing. David Sutton had purchased an additional five hundred acres of good land adjoining his property. This he leased to Richard Barron at a nominal rent, the latter also accepting a few hundred lambs as part payment for that year. David did not bind Richard to the conditions traditionally imposed under the system of 'halves' or 'thirds.' He hoped that the young man would purchase more land of his own, build his own house, marry, and produce some children. He envisaged a future where Malcolm's and Richard's children would become great friends, and bring joy to his own old age. Both lads courted local girls, mainly ones of Irish parentage, but neither did so in what could be described as a serious manner, and David suspected that Malcolm was still smitten by the lovely dark-haired Catalina.

---

6 (Juan Zorrilla de San Martin, Trans. Walter Owen)

The Sutton family's links with the Alguilo family continued to grow. Sergio and Francisco came for other vacations during the autumns of '73, '74, and '75. The letter entrusted by Malcolm to Catalina did produce results, for communications between both young people continued. Malcolm and Richard, on their trips to Buenos Aires were always welcomed almost as family by the Alguilos. On some occasions they took Catalina and Isabella to dinner, to concerts, or to the opera, the young ladies' parents having decided that a chaperone was unnecessary. Richard detected that Malcolm and Catalina were developing a mutual attraction. For her part, Isabella was assuming a certain nobility of countenance. Sergio was becoming more serious about his studies, and Francisco was gradually moving away from exciting boyhood to adolescence.

Meanwhile, Richard was also developing a friendship with Xiemen, the *Indio* youth. The boy had reached sixteen years of age, and had been taken on as a *peon* on the *estancia*. Richard had in a manner become his mentor, united as they were by a love of horses, music, football, and an appreciation of their respective cultures. The mentor had taught the youth how to read in Spanish, while the latter continued to instruct the former with tales of his tribe's lore.

As Xiemen moved further into adolescence, his striking features were revealing a real handsomeness. This surprised Richard for, even though he had got to like the *Indio*s of the pampas, he could not describe them as a particularly handsome people. He decided to discuss this with Xiemen's father, Pueno.

Pueno commenced his story, "I am glad that you have asked me this question. Ricardo, I can now tell you that I am not by my birth of this tribe. I was not born in Argentina, but in Uruguay, known then as the Banda Oriental. I will now tell you the story of the fate of my people, of my tribe, the Charrúa tribe, once lords of the pampas of the Banda. Have you got any whiskey? Good, please pour me one and one for yourself. For I think we will need it.

"Look at me, Ricardo, and at my sons Xiemen and Taquia. We are taller than your usual Creole man or boy, and even than the other *Indio*s here. Our bodies are well built, not fat, our muscles are strong. Yes, our features are proud and, as you have noted with Xiemen, often handsome. When the Spanish brought the horses to the Banda, we mastered the horses. We were a brave, hardy, and unconquerable race. We let the Spanish have the coastal regions, while we moved up north. Let them live in the cities; we were a nomadic people. They never enslaved us. Nor could they force us to live in missions."

"But what happened to your people?" Richard asked.

The Charrúa took a draught of *maté*. "Today the Creole child in Uruguay is taught that my people died out, due to disease. That is not true. As a nomadic people we did not fall victims to such diseases. It was only by despicable treachery that the Creoles defeated us."

"Ricardo, please fill my glass with one more whiskey. The next part of my story is the hardest to tell, but tell it I must. Ah, here is Taquia. Can you sit beside me, *Hijo,* although you have heard this story before."

"It was April of 1831, three years after the Banda became the independent country of Uruguay. Even the new Uruguayan government and army could not conquer us. In their eyes we were savages, pagans, degraded hordes, the wild children of the pampas. Yes, I admit that at times we did steal their property, animals, and crops, and at times murdered Creoles, but had they not invaded our land? There was more than plenty land for us all."

"Our two chiefs Venado and Polidoro told us that the new Uruguayan government had summoned us to a great peace conference which would offer us favourable terms. The government had stated that they needed us to be on their side in the event of a war between Uruguay and Brazil. We would be well rewarded. Most of our chiefs were in favour of the conference. After all, the Creoles wished to be our friends. Some of our old chiefs remained suspicious, but they were outvoted. I was only eleven years of age at the time. My brother Vacuna was nine. It was so exciting. There must have been about a thousand or twelve hundred Charrúa who went, warriors, women, old men, and children."

"Our Charrúa army and the Creole army camped facing each other, some distance apart, at a place called Salsipuedes, on the banks of a river. The Charrúas in good faith tied their horses. Most of our warriors left their weapons in their tents. The Creoles supplied us with the gift of plenty of alcohol. Mine and Vacuna's parents would not let us drink any alcohol. However, I stole two bottles of wine for both of us, and for our friend Joona. We three boys headed into the forest, choosing an elevation from which we could still observe the activity in the Charrúa camp. Twilight descended, while we were enjoying our wine."

"The Creole army began to parade around the Charrúa encampment. What were they doing? Some of the Charrúa men went to get their spears and to untie their horses. We saw the leader of the Creole army move towards our chief Venudo, now mounted on his horse. We witnessed Venudo hand him his knife, or maybe it was his sword. The Creole leader raised his pistol and fired it over Venudo's head. This must have been the signal, because in an instant, following the command of 'Charge', the Creole army had almost surrounded the Charrúas. About a thousand soldiers headed straight for their mostly unarmed prey, many of whom were drunk. Those of our warriors who were armed put up a valiant fight, but they were hopelessly outnumbered. The Creoles drew their sabres, their bayonets. I can still see the flash of the silver blades. I can still hear the screams of terror and agony from our warriors, and indeed from some of the women and children. Their unarmed bodies were cut to pieces, hacked, butchered, as if they were merely animals. The rivers of blood ran down to the river of water, Charrúa blood. I would guess that about five or six hundred Charrúa men and youths fell to the cold earth, bodies that were. The devil walked alone. I cannot describe it anymore. The memory haunted my dreams at night during my youth. Even now, some nights I wake up to the screams of the slaughtered."

Pueno's head and shoulders sank to his chest. His narration had exhausted him.

After two minutes, he raised his head slowly and embraced his son Taquia.

Richard found the courage to ask, "What happened to the remaining women and children, Pueno?"

"We were told later that they had been bound in groups like herds of cattle and marched away. We are sure that they were marched three hundred kilometres to Montevideo. The women were sent to the military barracks, and you can imagine what they were used for there. The children were enslaved in the homes of the wealthy. Did my mother and my two sisters survive the massacre? To this day I do not know."

"But, Pueno," Richard asked, "How did you three boys survive?"

"Ricardo, while we watched the butchery, we were transfixed. We could not move. Then, Joona roused us with, 'Boys, we must escape.' We followed him, terrified, running at our utmost speed into the forest, still hearing the screams. We must have run for about twenty minutes like young deer. We had to pause in a clearing for a short rest. Suddenly, we heard from behind us the sound of rapid footsteps. Even more terrified, Vacuna and I jumped to our feet. But Joona held up his hand with, 'I am sure that they are Charrúa men.'"

"He was right. Four such men crashed into our clearing. Silently, two of them slung Vacuna and me and on their shoulders. All seven of us ran for a long distance through the deepest forest until we felt relatively safe. Those four good men led us north towards Bella Union in the northwest of Uruguay. Later on, some of the forty or so men who had survived the slaughter joined us. We lived there in an isolated region for some years. When I reached fifteen years of age, Vacuna, I, and a girl named Aduna, now my wife, crossed into Argentina. We have lived here ever since. For me, Uruguay is a body that was, for the invincible Charrúa tribe is no more. Do not cry, Taquia, or you too, Ricardo. Always remember, my son, that you are a Charrúa, one of the last of a proud and unconquerable race."

Richard sat immobile, totally overcome by the harrowing story. Some tears flowed. Was Salsipuedes a battle, an ambush, or a massacre? He was sure that some people would describe it as a battle. But, he was convinced that it had all been planned by the Uruguayan government. The Charrúas had been totally outwitted, outnumbered, and outgunned. There and then he resolved to do all in his power to help and protect Xiemen and Taquia, two of the last remnants of a proud, unique, and invincible tribe of Indians.

CHAPTER 14.

'The Course of True Love Never Did Run Smooth.'[7]

In March 1874 Malcolm had commenced his formal courtship of Catalina. David Sutton raised no objection to his nephew's monthly trips to Buenos Aires. The Alguilo family welcomed the young suitor. Very handsome looks and manly bearing, a future large *estancia* owner, of excellent character, a good Catholic, he was eminently suitable. Sergio especially was most enthusiastic about it. On some occasions he, rather than a chaperone, would accompany the young couple. Malcolm would give him a present of an absorbing book, so he he would barely hear the endearments which they would express to each other. Besides, he was not interested. Malcolm would return to the *estancia* with increased buoyancy. On a few occasions Catalina and Isabella, visited the *estancia*. She seemed to fit in well to its environment, although Isabella was the one who felt more at home when mounted on a horse.

July of 1875.

Needing to talk in private, Malcolm had invited Richard to lunch with him in San Antonio de Areco. After the main course, Malcolm spoke. "Richard, our bonds of friendship, formed in the Selskar Arms, are as strong as ever, are they not?"

"Of course, they are Malcolm. Why would anyone think otherwise?"

---

7   (William Shakespeare).

"So, Richard, I can trust you with a plan I have."

Richard hesitated for a moment. "You have my word on that. However, I cannot promise that I will be part of it, especially if it involves causing harm or suffering to anyone."

"You know that I would never harm, cheat, or dishonour anyone, especially my uncle. Alright, my plan might meet with his disapproval to begin with, but I know that he will come around. So, I can tell you my plan in complete confidence?"

A nod.

"My plan has to do with Catalina. I love her so deeply. She is my light, my soul, my inspiration, the main reason for my living. She has told me on so many occasions that she loves me deeply too. This mutual love can only end in one way – marriage."

"I too can see that you are both meant for each other, and that your uncle and Catalina's parents see it also."

"Richard, my uncle would not raise any objection. The problem is Catalina's mother, Doña Alejandra. She feels that Catalina is too young, and that she needs more time."

"Possibly," Richard stated. "She is only twenty-two, and you are nearly thirty. Maybe some more time would be the best thing for you both."

"Richard, we cannot wait. Why should we when we are meant for each other? I have been most faithful. During the past eighteen months I have barely looked at another woman."

"So, what *is* your plan?" Richard was beginning to dread the answer.

Malcolm elaborated, "Doña Alejandra has come up with this idea of Catalina going to Europe for a year. Travel, do some educational studies, learn another language, maybe French, broaden her horizon, that kind of nonsense."

"What does Catalina think of that idea?"

"Richard, she seems quite keen on it, although only for a year. But I am sure that I can talk her out of it. To prevent it, I think-that we are going to have to elope."

"Elope! Have you gone completely *loco*? Think of what that means. The scandal, the disgrace, the effect it might have on Don Enrique's business, the likely loss of their friendship with all of us. Why, Don Enrique might even have you arrested for the abduction of his daughter. Wake up, man!"

Malcolm glared at him. "Richard, can you not understand? Catalina and I love each other. Nobody, not even you, is going to stand in our way." A pause. "You are not going to warn the Alguilos, are you?"

"Malcolm, how can you for one moment think I would? But listen to me, please. Let Catalina go to Europe. If she feels the same about you when she returns, you will be rewarded with such a memorable wedding. A splendid occasion, Catalina's beauty unsurpassed, her parents overjoyed, flowers, music, speeches, a wedding feast, maybe even photographs, a lovely honeymoon, one of the great weddings of the year in Buenos Aires, and your mutual love stronger than ever. The blessings of Catalina's parents. You both remain on excellent terms with them. How can you both even think of turning your back on all this?"

Desperation was showing in Malcolm's eyes. "But Catalina might fall in love with someone else in Europe. I could not continue living if that happened, knowing that I had lost her."

Somewhat resigned, Richard asked. "Well then, please tell me your plan for an elopement."

"It is really simple. Catalina takes a train from Buenos Aires to Pilar unchaperoned. I will meet her at Pilar. We will lodge in separate rooms in an hotel. I will arrange with a priest for him to marry us next morning. The wedding will be witnessed. Catalina will send a wire to her parents informing them of it. We will have a brief honeymoon of a few days, and then return to the *estancia*. Simple."

"And how do you think your uncle will receive the two of you?"

"Oh, he will probably be annoyed to begin with, but Catalina's beauty and charm will win him over. He likes her a great deal already."

Flabbergasted, Richard asked, "Malcolm, you mentioned witnesses at the wedding. Who will they be? They have to be reliable and respectable people, so that the wedding cannot be disputed."

"Richard, that is where you come into my plan. I want you to be the chief witness, the best man. After all, you will be the godfather of our first child."

"And the female witness, Malcolm. Who will she be? Not Isabella?"

"No, Richard. We will probably have to use the priest's housekeeper."

Fury invading Richard's face, he sprang back in his chair. "Malcolm Sutton, I will have no part in this plan of yours. I will not betray your good uncle who has treated you like a son, and me almost the same. And do not ask me either to betray the Alguilo family. From the first day when we met them on the ship, they have treated us like family. How can you even ask me to be part of your wild insane plan? I will walk home. You can drive the gig."

Richard Barron stood up to leave, but Malcolm restrained him. "Please sit down, *Mi Amigo*, *Mi Hermano*, and stay calm. You will be betraying none of us. You did not know anything about my plan, because there never was a plan. This will be your version. You and I just decided to go to Pilar on a Sunday. While there, Catalina arrived at the hotel. I had informed her two weeks prior that you and I would be making a trip to Pilar. She had had a row with her mother over the planned trip to Europe. So, she was weeping, terribly upset, and had travelled alone on the train. Now, my friend, remember that you had always liked her, so you hated seeing her in such a terrible state. So, I proposed to her that we get married next morning, to which she agreed. No force or persuasion from us. Nothing immoral. You and I had our own room at the hotel, and Catalina had hers. You, my true friend, offered to be the best man, the chief witness at our wedding, to make it all legal. The priest's housekeeper would be the other witness."

Richard, almost exhausted, queried, "And what happens after the wedding? Do I return home and tell your uncle? Surely not."

"Richard, that is the only other thing I will ask you to do, please. That will prepare him for our arrival. You will do this for me, won't you?"

Richard's memory flew back many years. Daniel Cody's seemingly harmless plan to break into the school. Kevin O'Meara's wild scheme to intimidate a landlord's agent. What had it all led to? Trouble, consequences, fiascoes, and ultimately his exile from Ireland. How would David Sutton take all this? Richard's flock of sheep now numbered nearly seven hundred, but David owned the land. Would David order him to leave the house, to lose his position as a virtual member of the family? Maybe he would become an exile again, to Australia. Ashen faced, he looked at Malcolm, "Malcolm, I have to tell you that I cannot do this. I cannot be part of your plan, and that is the end of it. I am leaving now."

Malcolm Sutton's hand shot out, roughly grasping Richard Barron's chin, and forcing him to look at him, just as he had done at the Selskar Arms. On that occasion Malcolm's touch had been soft, even affectionate. This time it was more like the grip of a vice, matched by the sudden rare, hard expression on Malcolm's face. His voice assumed a steeliness, a threatening tone, dropping in pitch.

"Richard Barron, who brought you to Argentina? Who paid your passage? Who gave you work, a new family, and, as you have admitted, almost a new father? Who gave you a lovely home, new friends, a good life, your own flock of sheep, great prospects? Richard

Barron, who has been your constant, loyal, and true friend in good times and bad, and will continue to be so as long as you live? You owe it to him to do this one favour for him. You have his word that this will be the only time when he will ask of such a thing."

A minute's silence passed. Accepting the inevitable, Richard slowly spoke. "Malcolm I will on this one occasion do what you want. However, when I tell your uncle of your marriage, because I doubt that he will believe the story of my innocence, I will also inform him that I am leaving his house."

"But why, Richard? Where will you go? Surely you are not going to leave the *estancia*."

"No, Malcolm, I will continue to work on the *estancia*. I will continue to graze my sheep on your uncle's land, if he will allow me to do both. I will rent one or two rooms in San Antonio de Areco, and will ride to and from the *estancia* each day."

Malcolm felt compelled to ask, "Is it because you still like Catalina, and cannot bear to be in the same house as us?"

"It is partly that, Malcolm. Yes, a young married couple needs their space, their privacy. My room will be perfect as your lounge room, a room for your children which I hope and pray that God will send you both. I would feel like an intruder in the Sutton household. However, I would point out that if you were to wait until Catalina returns from Europe and married her then, that would give me some time to build my own small house on the land I lease from your uncle. So, in a way, I leave the choice to you."

Richard did feel that this was putting the onus on Malcolm to change his plans, but then, had not Malcolm pressured him?

"Richard, I have decided that I am going to marry Catalina Alguilo in four weeks' time. Do I have your word that you will come to Pilar?"

"Yes, Malcolm. You have my word that I will come to Pilar with you and be the best man at your wedding." A handshake sealed the compact, firmer on Malcolm's part. For his part Richard's heart was pierced as if by a lance. He would forever grieve for the loss of his Argentine home, his adopted uncle, his close friends the Alguilos. But most of all, relations between him and Malcolm could never be the same again. That would be a loss which he knew at times would be almost unbearable, and for more reasons than he cared to admit, even to himself.

A journey to the town of Pilar early in August. Two young men are seated on the box seat of a gig, a prospective bridegroom and his prospective best man. Part of this route was identical to the happy route they travelled on their first journey to the *estancia* almost five years prior. But this journey is marked by sombre periods of silence, concerns about the future both immediate and long term. The prospective bridegroom is concerned with the possibility that his bride may get cold feet and fail to arrive. His companion is stricken by worry about losing his home, his employment, his livelihood, the trust and friendship of his employer. But most important of all, the bond of friendship between both young men has been frayed. The prospective best man cannot help but feel that a form of emotional blackmail has been used against him.

Malcolm spoke, "Ricardo, we are like Manrico and Ruiz in *Il Trovatore* rescuing Leonora from taking the veil as a nun."

"And look what happened to Manrico, Malcolm. Captured, imprisoned and beheaded. We could end up in prison too."

A long silence followed. Richard contemplated that his whole life in Argentina could be upended. Recently he had been thinking that he might well mount his horse, ride across the pampas, cross the Andes by well-trodden routes, descend to Santiago de Chile, and board a ship for Australia. The sun slid from behind the clouds, illuminating the pampas with a slightly red midday glow. They would reach Pilar within an hour, well in time to attend midday Sunday Mass, and then to meet the train.

1.30 pm. Malcolm excitedly announces. "The train will arrive in fifteen minutes." Malcolm and Richard sit together on a bench in Pilar Railway Station. Malcolm's rather sweaty hands move in nervous gestures to his head, his face, his throat, torso, legs. The slightest sound makes him move. God, Richard thinks, let this train be on time. Let this torture end, whatever the outcome. At times Malcolm paces up and down like a caged lion. They have pre-arranged that, as the train had four carriages, Richard will inspect the first two and Malcolm the rear two.

The toot of the train whistle. Malcolm jumps up. "It's coming. She is here. Richard, to your post." Five minutes later the train pulls in. Richard watches the passengers alighting, people of varying ages, social classes, styles of dress. No young woman travelling alone, wearing a light blue overcoat. Malcolm too watches intently. A young woman dressed in a blue coat alights from the fourth carriage and halts. Well, this is it, Richard thinks. From this moment the lives of the Alguilos, the Suttons, and your own life, Richard Barron, will change forever. Richard sees Malcolm running towards her, opening his arms wider. The young woman by this time is joined by an older woman. Malcolm stops running, his arms sagging by his side. Both women turn to look at the crazed young man, positioned now about five metres to their left. They march out of the railway station. Malcolm turns around, runs back to the back of the fourth carriage, inspecting all four carriages of the train from the outside. Nobody has remained inside. His head stooped, his shoulders sagging, his knees bent, he stumbles to the bench with the gait of an old man.

A couple of minutes later, Richard joins him. "She has not come." Malcolm repeats this phrase six times, his voice starting in a low pitch, almost a sob, then ascending in pitch and increasing in volume and in anger.

"Calm yourself, Malcolm. She probably missed the train. There is a later train. I will go and find out when it arrives."

Malcolm buries his head in his hands. On returning, Richard touches his friend's arm and gently says. "The next train arrives in two hours time. She will be on that for sure." To his consternation his friend shies away from him. Malcolm slowly raises his head from his hands, looking at Richard as if he were a stranger. The latter notes the suspicious, even accusing look, in the former's normally mesmerising eyes. How can he believe that I am an informer? Hesitatingly he summons the courage to speak gently. "Come with me, Malcolm."

"Where are we going? We cannot leave here."

"We are going for a walk and then for some lunch. I know that I, for one, am starving. We will return here half an hour before the next train arrives."

Malcolm stands up slowly, and walks like a sleep walker.

The two young men return. They sit on the bench. The station master approaches them. "You are waiting for someone, *Jovenes*?"

Richard replies. *"Si, Señor,* a young lady."

The station master declares. "There will be no young ladies arriving by train today. In fact, there will be no trains nor people travelling from Buenos Aires today."

Terror encompasses Malcolm's face, "Why not, *Señor*? Has there been an accident?"

"Not an accident, *Joven*. But I have received a wire which states that there has been an outbreak of cholera in Buenos Aires. Nobody is allowed to enter or leave the city. No trains will run to or from there while the outbreak lasts."

"How long might that be, *Señor*?" Malcolm pleads.

The station master is nonchalant. "I hope not for long. Days, weeks, months. Who knows?"

Richard consoles Malcolm, "Malcolm, let us go to our hotel. We can enquire here again tomorrow."

"And if there is no train tomorrow, Richard, what will we do?"

"We will go home, *Amigo*. Catalina will write you a letter. Come with me, and remember that I will always be your truest friend." Partly reassured, Malcolm allows Richard to take his arm. He has not shied away this time.

During the following days Malcolm, while still somewhat on edge, was more relaxed. On their return to the *estancia*, they informed David Sutton about the cholera in Buenos Aires. David tried to reassure them, pointing out that from their relative safety in Palermo the Alguilos might escape it. But Malcolm needed convincing. He would visit the post and telegraph office in San Antonio early every second morning.

While Richard was also worried about the Alguilos and the residents of Buenos Aires, he felt consoled. This outbreak had undoubtedly prevented Catalina from making the journey to Pilar. To Richard's delight all this resulted in the partial restoration of the close bonds of friendship between both men. On their return journey their conversation had been friendly. On the final stage Richard suddenly realised that he would not have to leave the Sutton household, at least for now. His eyes gazed upon a dark cloud, on which he was sure he detected a silver lining. Hopefully Malcolm would now view his own situation in a more rational manner. Meanwhile neither of them would drop even a hint to David Sutton of the aborted elopement.

The following Tuesday morning at their breakfast Malcolm rushed in bearing a telegram, his face a mixture of relief and concern. Handing it to Richard, he collapsed onto a chair. *To Señor David*

Sutton from Doña Alejandra Alguilo. Cholera has broken out in Buenos Aires. Francisco is very ill. Please send your prayers to God that it will not take our beautiful son. A nurse is tending him in his room well separated from us. Tell Malcolm that Catalina is safe and well.

David Sutton calmed Malcolm, "Richard has told you how he survived cholera with the ministrations of a skilled nurse. Doña Alejandra has requested our prayers. We will say the rosary each evening. We will also ask members of our Irish community who have met and love Francisco to do the same."

Nevertheless, Malcolm still insisted on visiting the telegraph office. Thursday, nothing. Saturday, same. Richard assured him, "Malcolm, from my own experience, cholera runs its main course within five days. Francisco must have been struck down by it on Monday, so by now he must be over the worst. If he had died, we would have been informed."

On Monday morning Malcolm walked into breakfast, overjoyed. Another telegram.

To Malcolm Sutton from Catalina Alguilo. Gracias a dios, Francisco is recovering. The worst is past. We are all safe and well, although still in quarantine. I will write you a letter soon. Your beloved, Catalina.

Expressions of thanks to God in the Sutton household and throughout the *estancia* and the neighbourhood. Malcolm almost his normal self again.

Three weeks later, Malcolm walked into Richard's room, handing him a letter.

Dear Richard, I hope that you, Señor Sutton, and Malcolm have kept safe and well and that the cholera did not reach your district. I am the only person in our house who got it. But then, am I not the only person to whom death approaches, whether it be falling from a pony, falling into a sheep dip, or getting struck by cholera? My father says that since I met you and Malcolm, the luck of the Irish is with me. He wonders when it will run out.

This is how I got cholera. I am a member of my school's junior soccer team. On the Saturday we went to play a game against another school in the middle of Buenos Aires. A boy in the other team must have been getting cholera, for I and two other boys in my team got it. On Monday morning I felt very sick. The doctor came later that day and told my mother he thought it was cholera. I had to stay in my room, while all my family moved to another part of our house. The doctor sent a nurse to look after me and, gracias a dios, she cured me.

Sergio told her the story of how a nurse cured you many years ago, and she said, "If a nurse can cure a five-year-old boy in a small cabin in Ireland, I, con ayuda de dios (with God's help), can cure a boy of fifteen in a big house in Palermo." And cure me she and God did. My two friends also got well. I am still rather weak, and will not return to school for a few weeks yet. Maybe I can come to the estancia again and be with you and Malcolm. I have asked my parents, but they say, "We will have to see how matters work out." I do not know

*what they mean. I must finish now as I am getting tired. Tu Amigo
Amado, Francisco."*

Meanwhle, Malcolm read his letter from Catalina three times,
then passing it to Richard.

Dearest Malcolm,

*"We are so grateful to God for sparing our brother Francisco.
We would have been devastated to lose him. During the short cholera
outbreak, some children did die. Their families are stricken by grief,
and asking why it had to be them. The authorities believe that the
outbreak has passed and, con ayuda de dios, will not return.*

*Malcolm you will realise that it was the cholera outbreak which
prevented me from meeting you that Sunday in Pilar. I had still hoped
to travel to Pilar, but my father on that Sunday morning ordered all of
us to remain in the house. Then, when I heard that all travel in and
out of the city had been forbidden, I knew that it was the hand of God.
When Francisco was struck down the next day, I thanked God that I
had not travelled. How would all of us – you, I, Richard, my parents,
Isabella, Sergio, your uncle – have felt if I had got married on the
very day when her brother was at death's door? If Francisco had died
a day or two later, it could well have killed my parents. I do believe
that the hand of God was at work in preventing me from travelling.
For that reason, I have decided that I can never be part of such a plan
again. I will certainly marry you, but only when both my parents
agree that the time is right for us to marry and give us their
blessing."*

"My dearest beloved Malcolm, I have decided to go to Europe for a year. My sister Isabella will travel with me, as well as Señora Lopez, my father's first cousin. We will leave for Portugal in about a month's time, after which our travel plans will become clearer. Believe me, my heart is your and yours alone. Having experienced Europe, I am sure that I shall be more prepared to settle down as your wife on your estancia. *Like Sergio has done, I know that I shall grow to love the beauty and magic of the pampas, and the friendship between our two families will grow. My father also promises that he will buy us a small townhouse in Buenos Aires as a wedding present.*

I will speak to my parents about whether you should come and visit us here before our departure. Maybe Richard can come too, as I am sure he would like to see Francisco again. However, they may feel that such a visit might unsettle me. My dearest Malcolm, you are the sun of my world and will always be el rey de mi corazón (the king of my heart).

Siempre para ti (yours always), Catalina.

Richard waited for Malcolm to speak, "Yes, I do agree with her. Suppose she had travelled and we had got married next day, with Francisco possibly on the verge of death. If he had died, how would we have felt? I would have felt that in a way I had killed him. Yes, the hand of God works in mysterious ways. What kind of a marriage or life would we have had after that, probably eternal outcasts? Her parents, Isabella, Sergio, would have never forgiven nor accepted us, nor accepted our children."

"And her going now to Europe, Malcolm, can you accept that?"

"Well, Richard, I have no choice. I have to. I accept it as my purgatory."

"Don't be so hard on yourself, Malcolm. Her letter radiates with love for you."

"Yes, Richard. I trust her and believe her. My Catalina will return. She will be mine and I hers, forever."

"Richard, the coming year will be hard for me. Will you be here during that time?"

"Of course I will, Malcolm. That time when I talked about leaving your house it was-"

"That was my fault, Richard. I should not have forced you into that corner. I used a form of blackmail on you, and most of the things I said in that restaurant were not true. It was my uncle David who brought you here and who has rewarded you for your great work and loyal service. You are welcome to remain in our house for as long as you like. Now, you will stay with us at least until Catalina returns, won't you?"

Richard sealed his promise with a clasp of his hand. Malcolm smiled, with the words. "Catalina will return in the spring next year. *Mi á ngel vendrá sobre el mar con la aurora.* (My angel will return over the sea with the dawn)."

Malcolm did not get to see Catalina before her departure. The Alguilo family were too involved with preparations for her journey. Besides, the shearing season on the Sutton *estancia* was due to start at the end of September. Malcolm would have liked for him and Catalina to become engaged before she left Buenos Aires. She consoled him in a letter declaring that, as far as she was concerned, they were engaged, and that her parents had consented. Furthermore, Doña Alejandra had written to Malcolm stating that he, either alone or with Richard, was welcome to visit their home anytime during the coming year. Sergio and Francisco were anxious for that too. Between Catalina's correspondence to both her family and to Malcolm, each family would be kept informed of the travelling party's fortunes and whereabouts. Both Malcolm and Richard rested assured, neither suspecting that a severe trauma awaited them around the corner.

It struck Malcolm on the Sunday after the termination of the shearing. During the final week he had sometimes complained about strange sensations in his head. As he had not come into dinner, Richard checked on him. Malcolm was sitting on his chair, a dazed look on his face, his eyes betraying fear. Shaking him gently Richard asked, "Are you alright?"

Malcolm's hands shook. "I am not sure. Something strange has happened to me. I was sitting here resting. Then it seemed as if a cloud descended. It spread through my head and I was overcome by a feeling of deep depression, a *macht* (depression). I felt that I was sinking into a great black hole, and a voice within me said, 'Your joy of life, your happiness, is finished. You will never get out of this black hole.' What can it be?"

"I do not know. You are probably overtired after the shearing season."

"Please do not tell my uncle. Just say I have a headache. I am going to bed now. Richard, can you stay in my room. Maybe you can play some music to soothe me. I should be alright in the morning."

Next morning some of the workers observed that Malcolm had a flushed look on his face. As Richard observed him more closely it became obvious that his friend was sinking into a melancholy state. Gone were his smiles, his witty comments, his laughter, his *joie de vivre*, (joy of life). His eyes conveyed a frightened look.

Matters came to a head on the following Thursday. Both young men were working on reinforcing parts of the wire fences, Malcolm selecting a spot about half a mile ahead of Richard. Having worked his section, Richard rode up to join him. Malcolm was sitting on the grass, none of the work done. On riding closer he could see that Malcolm's head was bent low, with tears gushing down his face. Richard jumped from his horse. Strong action was required.

Richard sat down beside the invalid. Placing his arms around the shoulders, he drew Malcolm towards him, cradling his head against his breast. With his fingertips he gently massaged the sick man's face, forehead, head, even running his fingers through his hair. Richard proceeded to massage the shoulders, the upper arms, the chest.

His actions and words stemmed the gushing of tears, for the invalid finally spoke, "You must think me a right idiot to be sitting on this grass, weeping like a child. But I could not help it. The cloud came down again, but more severe this time. Richard, I am sinking further and deeper into that black hole."

"Don't speak any further about it. I am here for you. Are you able to stand up and climb on to your horse? We are going home. Then I am taking you straight to doctor San Martin."

A look of sheer terror. "What can he do for me? My sickness is not physical. He will tell my uncle. They will lock me away in one of those institutes for mad people. People yelling, screaming, banging their heads against walls. Fighting for food thrown before them on the floor. Richard, I am not going there or to any doctor."

"Malcolm, listen to me. Doctor San Martin is no ordinary doctor. He is a physician. Your uncle himself has told us that in the early days of shepherding some of the Irish shepherds suffered from deep depression and melancholy, after months isolated in their huts. Your uncle brought them to Doctor San Martin. Most of them he cured, except for those already slaves to the demon drink. You do not have that problem. With the doctor's and my help, you will overcome this *macht*, and become a better and stronger person. When we arrive home, I will harness the gig. We are driving into San Antonio de Areco."

The doctor spoke, "The first thing I have established, Malcolm, is that you are not mad or insane, so you are not going to be locked up. From what you both have told me, this sudden depression struck you unexpectedly, although you had some tensions and strange feelings beforehand. What caused all this? Your worries about Catalina especially during the cholera outbreak; the fact that you did not see her before she departed for Europe; your concerns for her safety during the sea voyage; whether she might break off your engagement during your year of separation. Added to this were your increased responsibilities during the shearing season. I am convinced that all those worries came together and brought about that first cloud of depression."

They listened to his assuring words with some relief.

"Richard, can you now please leave the room for a while. I will call you in after my examination. Malcolm, you will need to remove all your clothes."

After about fifteen minutes Richard was asked to re-enter the surgery. "Richard, Malcolm does not show any signs of insanity, of the type I have found over the years with especially some Irish shepherds. His eyes betray no signs of such illness, and you lads may have heard the expression *The eyes are the mirror of the soul.* However, Malcolm, I have found some tremors occurring in your body. Have you felt them?"

"Yes, I have, doctor."

"Well, they are really nothing to worry about."

Richard now spoke. "*Gracias*, doctor San Martin. But what if another cloud descends on him? These attacks terrify both him and me. What can you give him to help him?"

"Over the years I have found that a special liquid mixture can help to decrease the intensity of such attacks. The *Indio*s use this mixture, containing herbs, juices of plants. My nurse will prepare a gallon for you. Drink a half pint immediately. Drink a quarter pint of it each morning and another at night. If you have another cloud attack, drink half a pint immediately. The gallon should last for two weeks. See me again in two weeks' time. Lads, you do need to tell David Sutton about the illness."

"Now, Richard," the doctor continued, "I want you to do one more thing for Malcolm. In a week's time bring him to the *Indio* settlement four miles away. Ask for the woman named Shoana. She will massage most of his body. Please remain with Malcolm during this."

Handshakes followed, accompanied by the physician's parting words, "Malcolm, you have nothing to fear but fear itself. Believe me, you will come through this."

A stop at the telegraph office followed. Richard emerged with a telegram, praying to heaven for good news. It read, *Dearest Malcolm, we have arrived safe and well in Lisbon after a pleasant voyage. I think of you every moment of every day. I will write a letter in two days' time. Your own, your beloved, Catalina.* A light punch from Richard followed, "See, *Amigo,* she did not fall for the ship's first officer. What did I tell you?"

The *Indio* tent. A sheet is spread across a pallet of soft grass and hay. On it lies a handsome young man face down, his arms dropping to his sides. He is naked except for a loin cloth Seated on a chair is his friend. He has advised the young man to imagine that he is a young *Indio* warrior being prepared for battle. The woman enters. Middle aged, striking features, relaxed manner. She places her hands just below the young man's neck. She moves them up to his head, massaging, using finger tips, palms, sides and back of hands, moving them down to his back and sides, embracing every part of his torso. Sometimes, on encountering an area of tension she chops it gently with the sides of her hands. The young man yields himself to her hands, to their solace, their warmth, their healing properties. She applies the same tender touch to his arms, stretching them a little.

The woman whispers, "Now turn over, *Joven.*"

His eyes are closed, his body now completely relaxed. His friend gazes in wonder at the peace and calm of the young man's features, at his almost Grecian body. The woman repeats the process. Her hands move down to the bottom rim of the loin cloth. They progress down to his knees, to his well-formed and sturdy calves, and eventually to his feet. She stretches each toe a little. When the massage is completed, she departs.

The woman returns with a bowl of warm liquid, its scent permeating the tent. She rubs it into all the young man's exposed flesh. Her action is accompanied by wordless chants in modal tonality. She has advised him to breathe deeply in and out. The ascending contour of her melody has its counterpart in the expansion of his chest and abdomen, the descending contour in their contraction. On the completion of the application of the liquid, the young man is at peace.

The woman departs, instructing him to remain in this position until he feels ready to leave. A young *Indio* youth enters bearing a wooden wind instrument, meeting a smile from the friend. Again, modal melodies fill the tent. After about ten minutes the young man slowly rises from the pallet. He removes the loin cloth. His friend gazes for a moment at his body, scented with the fragrant oils. He hands him his clothes. How can such a perfect body harbour a deep and troubled mind and soul? The invalid's face breaks into a smile. The friend leaves the tent, beckoning to the instrumentalist to follow him. The former whispers, "What do you think, Xiemen? Is he on the way to being healed?"

"Ricardo, his smile reveals it all. He is definitely on the way to recovery. I have seen it before with men wounded in spirit, *Indio*, Irish, Creole. But I am now certain that our young warrior inside the tent is conquering the dark spirit within him."

Malcolm had suffered one further cloud attack, a few days after the first visit to the doctor. Not as severe as the second attack had been, he coped with it better, aided by immediately drinking the liquid. Following the massage treatment, he had shown further signs of healing. His features were less clouded by fear. His smiles began to return, and some semblances of his former happy persona began to manifest themselves. Nonetheless, Richard was aware that the road to full recovery could still be fairly long.

An early morning in late November 1875. Richard and Malcolm were on their way to Gualeguaychue. Doctor San Martin had advised them and David Sutton that both lads needed to take a few weeks vacation in northern Uruguay. They spent their first night in a *posada* halfway, the second night at their destination. The drivers of the gig, Michael Roche and young Xiemen, bade them farewell next morning when they boarded the river boat for Paysandu. This steam boat was foreign made, carrying mostly passengers but some freight. It contained sixteen private cabins, but most of the economy passengers opted to sleep on the deck or in hammocks. Malcolm and Richard had their own private cabin and dined at the Italian captain's table.

The journey to Paysandu involved only one night on board. Malcolm's recovery was progressing well, abetted by the boat's slow motion. He and Richard spent their hours reading, socialising, observing river scenery and wildlife, and partaking of the occasional glass of wine. All in all, a most enjoyable river voyage. The boat docked next morning at seven, the passengers disembarking an hour later after breakfast.

A gig and driver were procured by the two friends for the journey to Guichon and the cuchillas. At their destination the driver obtained the services of a sixteen-year-old Creole named Santiago as their hill-walking guide. He was friendly, intelligent, and knowledgeable about the terrain, flora and fauna.

Malcolm, Richard, and Santago commenced their ten-day walk. These walks were not strenuous, the altitudes rarely exceeding three hundred metres. The rhythm of walking, the vistas of the plains from the heights, the peace and serenity of the hills, the scent of the trees especially the eucalyptus, all would between them aid Malcolm's full recovery. The presence and expertise of Santiago relieved them of any concerns about accommodation, encounters with strangers, or becoming lost. Their scaling of a hill rewarded them with vistas of the canvas of lower landscape, colours of green and yellow. The deeper streams provided the trio with the chance to clean and refresh their bodies.

Richard would later make an entry in his journal about one particular incident. 'We had reached a pool which formed the junction of two streams, one rather wide and the other narrow. Santiago and I had decided to have a refreshing swim.'

"Santiago, would you know the names of these streams?"

"The larger one is called the Salsipuedes Grande, the smaller one *Arroyo* (stream) Salsipuedes."

'Sheer horror engulfed me. I had to get out of the water immediately to sit down. Somehow I managed to ask. "I think I have heard of them. Are they famous for any reason?"

"I do not know of any reason why they should be."

'Was Santiago hiding the truth? Was he too ashamed to admit the massacre? More than likely he had never heard of it. Had some of the Charrúa blood somehow flown into one or both of these streams? I felt that I had contaminated myself. I consoled myself with, "Richard, how were you to know? God will find a way for you to cleanse yourself."'

The evenings presented a variety of experiences. On two nights the trio lodged in *posada*s in two hamlets. There they joined some working travellers for *maté*. On Santiago's informing each group that these two hill walkers were neither Argentinians nor English, but Irish, an effusive welcome was offered. Both Malcolm and Richard were warming to the Uruguayans. On two occasions Santiago brought them to two *estancia*s owned by English people. The owners insisted that the trio sleep in their spare bedrooms and join them for meals, all offers of payment being refused.

But what amazed Malcolm and Richard most of all was the kindness and generosity of the Uruguayan peasants. Although poor, and some living in miserable mud huts, almost reminiscent of such dwellings in Ireland, they represented hospitality personified. A meal was always offered, a bed for one of them, and space near the cabin to pitch their tent. The two Irishmen were often regarded as celebrities, and a few neighbours would on occasions be invited to join the family in the evening. The *maté* gourd would be passed around; some Uruguayan peasant songs sung; Irish songs sung by Malcolm and Richard, and some tunes by the latter on his tin whistle. Legends of the Banda Oriental, some involving the Charrúas, would on occasions be told, mostly about their feats against the Spaniards.

On one night Richard and Santiago were alone in the tent, Malcolm asleep in the cabin. Richard summoned up the courage to ask Santiago.

"Santiago, what happened to the Charrúas in Uruguay? Are they still here?"

"No, Ricardo, they all died out."

"Died out, Santiago. How?"

"Oh, their numbers began to become smaller about eighty years ago. Many of the men fought with Artigas and died fighting or from their wounds. Most of them refused to go into the missions, so they died of misery, hunger, disease."

Richard ploughed further. "Did the Uruguayan government not try to save them?"

"Oh, it probably did, Ricardo. But you know what *Indio*s are like. They were very likely suspicious and refused help."

"Did you learn all this from your parents, Santiago?"

"Part of it, but we learned most of it at school. I must go to sleep now. *Buenos noches.*"

"*A te, También, Amigo.*" (To you also, friend).

Richard pondered. Not only had the proud and unvanquished Charrúa race been slaughtered or enslaved. The memory of their heroism and exploits was slowly being obliterated from the pages of the history of Uruguay.

By the end of the vacation, Malcolm had virtually recovered. He and Richard had made a compact that after his safe return from his planned expedition to the southern pampas and Patagonia, and whether he was married or not, they would take a similar walking holiday in Uruguay, a country they had grown to love. This trip to the hills had bonded them even more closely together.

Chapter 15.

'All Will be Revealed.'

The three European travellers returned in mid-September of 1876. An overcast day in Buenos Aires, it was debatable as to whether Catalina brought the radiance of spring. The trio were in perfect health. Both sisters had developed a further level of sophistication, although preserving their previous charm. They had visited and toured Portugal, Spain, Italy, Greece, Austria, Switzerland, Germany, Holland, and England. A break from their travels had been provided by a sojourn in Paris, where they had attended a language school to study French language and culture for a month. The travellers expressed immense delight at finally returning home.

Malcolm visited the Alguilo family a week after their return, heading back to the *estancia* in an exuberant mood. Catalina's love for him had grown in intensity. He had formally asked her parents for her hand, immediately and readily given, followed by him finally placing an engagement ring on her finger. A date for the wedding was fixed, to be held on the fifteenth of January 1877 in Buenos Aires. Their engagement was announced shortly afterwards in a leading Buenos Aires newspaper. Malcolm had been advised by Doctor San Martin not to mention his serious illness. There had been no re-occurrences.

By the end of October, the shearing having finished, Richard felt it was now expedient to raise with David Sutton the question of his own future. Having decided on his plans to travel and explore Argentina, he wished to return to this region of San Antonio de Areco.

However, as he was still renting his five hundred acres from David, he saw little point in even beginning to build a house on it.

David queried, "Richard, when do you intend to commence your journey?"

"Shortly after the birth of Malcolm and Catalina's first child. As you know, they want me to be the godfather."

"Have you decided who will accompany you on your long journey?"

"*Señor,* I feel Xiemen might make the best companion. I hope to travel as far south as Patagonia, where there are still large *Indio* populations. Xiemen would provide a valuable and natural link to them. He is now nineteen, mature, intelligent, and adapts well to different social situations."

David briefly considered. "Yes, I agree. Xiemen will make an ideal travel companion for you. And when you return, Richard, where do you intend to live?"

"I am sure, *Señor,* that I want to return to this region, to be near the Sutton family, my Irish, Creole, and *Indio* friends. I would like to start building a small house next year, but the problem is its location. I have not bought any land yet, although I am most grateful for the low rent you charge me for the land where I keep my sheep."

David Sutton walked to the drinks' cabinet, pouring two glasses of wine. "I think, Richard, that now is a good time for me to reveal my plans to you for next year. Shortly after the wedding I myself intend to make a long trip overseas. Firstly, to Ireland, to visit my family, and to see more of that beautiful but tragic land. Then to

England. I would also like to visit Italy, especially Rome, the eternal city. My journey may also take me to Vienna, city of my dreams. I would also like to visit Spain and maybe Portugal. From there I can take a ship back to Buenos Aires."

"For how long will you be gone, *Señor*?"

"Including the voyage, which takes about a month each way, I think I will be gone for six months. I must make this journey now while my health remains good. None of us know what the Almighty has in store for us." He continued, "now, Richard, this is my plan for this property. While I am away, Malcolm and Catalina will move into this building. You can remain in your room, and Malcolm's present room can become a guest room. Would you be happy with that?"

"Yes, *Señor*, of course."

"Meanwhile, Richard, why not start building your own house next year on your land?"

"But, *Señor*, it is not my land. I-"

"Richard, before I start my big trip I need to make my will. I am going to finalise this at the office of my solicitor in San Antonio next week. A will is best witnessed by a non-relative and a non-beneficiary. Will you be that witness?"

"Of course I will."

A rather austere solicitor's office. Solicitor Guiraldes handed a document to David Sutton who, having perused it, handed it to a surprised Richard. "But, *Señor*, you said that all I have to do is witness your signature."

"Read it, please, *Hijo.*" Richard's eyes gazed in disbelief at the wording of the document. "*Señor* David, you cannot do this. You cannot give me that *morcal* (amount) of land. It belongs to Malcolm. Five hundred acres. No, I will not accept it, never."

"Richard, Malcolm and Catalina know and approve of my giving you this land. I bought that land only a few years ago. So, I do with it what I like. You want to build your own house. All of us want you to return here, to your home after your travels."

"But I have done nothing to deserve this. People will say that I cultivated your friendship, took advantage of your good nature, that-"

The solicitor coughed gently, "*Señores*, it is time for my elevenses. I suggest that you both go to that nice café across the road to discuss this. I will expect you both back here in about half an hour."

"Richard, we all agree that you have earned this land. Malcolm's illness was very serious, potentially deadly. Think of the horror for all of us if Malcolm's illness had led to suicide. Malcolm. I cannot even bring myself to do so. Because of your support, he is restored to his full health, has become a better person, and is about to marry a beautiful and eminently suitable bride. You saved him from the horrors."

"Alright, But I did not do that expecting any reward."

Half a minute's silence.

"Richard Barron, please give me your hand. Vow to God and to me that you will never reveal to anyone in Argentina, and especially to Malcolm, Catalina, and their children, what I am about to tell you."

Richard offered a shaking right hand, and spoke the vow. David did not release his hand. "Richard Barron, you did not save my nephew. You saved-my son. My one and only beloved son."

Totally bewildered, Richard spoke. "*Señor* David, I know that you treat him like a son and me almost the same, but-"

David poured a small amount of brandy into their coffees, and proceeded to tell his story.

"I was born in 1820 in Kilrane, one of four children, another boy and two girls. My older brother Edward would inherit the tenancy of our small farm, so at age fourteen I became a labourer on the farm of our landlord Steven de Lacy, a good landlord, and a good employer. So, my prospects for life even as a landless labourer looked good. At twenty-one years of age I fell in love with a lovely Yola girl named Cecilia Sinnott, aged nineteen. We married two years later. For the first year of marriage there was no sign of a child. Then at the beginning of the second year the doctor confirmed that a child was due in about seven months time. Our joy and happiness were complete. Cecilia did not have a difficult pregnancy and, thanks to a couple of skilled midwives, the child, a beautiful boy, was born in August of 1845."

Richard's bewilderment had now altered to puzzlement.

David continued, "However, a few days after the birth, some infections or complications set into Cecilia's body, and after three days the Almighty took her to his own. It is impossible for me to describe in words how grief stricken, how utterly devastated I was. My parents, my brother, my two sisters, my friends, the priest, gave me some *soh-hoe,* sympathy, help, counsel, advice, but it was not enough. At times I felt like ending my life. I did not have a friend like Richard Barron to help me during this terrible time."

David took a large sip of his coffee, his eyes now glistening with tears.

"And the boy?" Richard tentatively asked. "What name did ye give him?"

David Sutton sat up, his sad countenance was replaced by a great smile. "We named him Malcolm. Malcolm Sutton."

A radiant glow gradually encompassed Richard's countenance.

David Sutton continued. "My brother Edward and his good wife Anna took immediate care of him, adopting him as their own, together with their own children, James and Caroline. They realised that I was in no fit state to take care of a baby. Edward and Anna, especially Anna, treated him even better than they did their own children, and Malcolm formed a special bond with her."

Hearing these words, Richard could not help but reflect on the at times rather torrid relationship he had had with his own foster mother.

The atmosphere now more relaxed, Richard queried. "Was that, *Señor* David, what caused you to emigrate?"

"Yes, Richard, it really was. Kilrane and its surrounds had too many sorrows for me. Besides, the first indications of potato blight had appeared in Wexford that same summer. It was the de Lacy family who suggested Argentina as a good destination. They were friends with the Browne family, Catholic gentry from Forth and Bargy.

Patrick Browne was really the person who initiated emigration from Forth and Bargy region to Argentina. Mr. de Lacy wrote to him, informing him of my loss, and recommending me. He also advised me that, once I had made a success of sheep farming, I could bring out Malcolm. I sent money back to Edward and Anna for his upkeep. I had meant to bring him out earlier, but delayed it. Just as well, for if I had, he would never have met you or Catalina."

"Do you ever intend, *Señor,* to inform Malcolm of who his real father is?"

"Maybe some day, Richard, before I die. I will wait and see how many children they will have, my own grandchildren. Alternatively, I might wait until my brother Edward, his foster father, dies. Meanwhile, as a secret between you and me, I declare Malcolm to be my true son, so I declare you, Richard, to be my unofficial nephew."

A pause.

David Sutton concluded his confession with. "So maybe now, *Sobrino,* you will understand why I found it so difficult to help my son in his severe illness. It brought back to me the terrible memories of my own suffering thirty years ago. But let us look on the bright side of things. Did I ever believe that one day my son, son of a landless Yola labourer, would be marrying the beautiful daughter of one of Buenos Aires' leading mercantile families? It was you, Richard, who brought them together in the first place, with your music, on that ship that bore him to me. So, Ricardo, will you accept this grant of five hundred acres as the token of the eternal gratitude of a father who almost lost his son, not once, but twice in his life?"

"Yes, *Señor* David Sutton, I will accept it from you and your son Malcolm."

"Good, Richard. Let us now return to the solicitor's office to sign the deed of transfer and my will. And remember, my story does not leave these four walls in San Antonio de Areco."

The Wedding. January 1877.

A great event in the Buenos Aires social calendar. The wedding of the twenty-four-year-old daughter of a leading city merchant and the thirty-two-year-old nephew and heir of a large and highly successful *estancia* owner. It took place in the church of Santo Domingo, Buenos Aires, the bride's choice of venue. She loved the architecture and the atmosphere of this eighteenth century Catholic Dominican church.

The bride alighted from a carriage, accompanied by her father and her two young train bearers. She was attired in the customary long, white silk flowing bridal dress which widened below her knees, her white veil extended into a short train. Her neck revealed a pearl necklace, an heirloom from her grandmother. The bride took her father's left arm as they entered the church to the glorious strains on pipe organ of the bridal chorus from Wagner's *Lohengrin*. They walked, flanked by the large carved pillars rising up to the high ceiling. Overshadowing the splendour of her attire was the bride's own resplendent beauty.

The bridesmaid, her sister, clad in a light blue satin dress, led the bridal party up through the forty paces of the aisle to the chancery area, where groom and best man awaited them. Both were clad in cream white dress suits, similar colour waist coats, white high collar shirts and bow ties, colours enhancing the very handsome features of the groom. Seated in the left pews were the bride's immediate family, other relatives, family and personal friends, business colleagues of her father. Seated in the right pews were the groom's uncle, closest friends, business colleagues, and young friends of the groom and best man. All eyes were focused on the quartet at the front of the altar.

Malcolm and Catalina were sealed in holy matrimony. Attendees were effusive in their congratulations and good wishes, all agreeing that they make a perfect and beautiful couple. The wedding feast at one of the city's most exclusive restaurants was underway. Bride and groom sat in the centre of the head table, flanked on each side by their respective close families. The feast was followed by Viennese waltzes, some songs from Viennese operetta performed by a soprano, a few solos by Richard Barron including *Home to our Mountains*. Argentine dances, and even a couple of Irish dances were the order of the day. Following the celebrations, the young couple departed on their honeymoon to Brazil.

Malcolm and Catalina returned from their honeymoon in mid-February. Apart from a few small hiccups in their travels, most things had gone to plan. Two weeks afterwards, Malcolm entered Richard's room, his face gleaming. Catalina had been to doctor San Martin, who had confirmed that she was pregnant. The child was due in mid

November, and Malcolm was convinced that it would be a boy. Would Richard remain until then? Richard, delighted with this happy news, assured him that he would. "However, I will shortly begin constructing my small house on my land."

"I will help you," was Malcolm's immediate reply.

Richard's plan for his house was not grandiose. He really just wished to have his own bachelor abode at least partly built by the time of David Sutton's return. It consisted of a lounge with a small kitchen, one bedroom, a small bathroom, a verandah. Richard employed a reputable builder and the villa style small house was virtually completed by the end of July. Accordingly, on David's return, Richard was established in his new home. He and Xiemen would commence their journey a few days after the baptism. No amount of persuasion would convince them to remain further.

November the ninth, 1877.

Catalina Alguilo Sutton gave birth to a baby boy. Her mother, sister, and a skilled midwife assisted the birth, with Doctor San Martin also in attendance. The labour had taken a couple of hours, but thankfully had not involved any complications. Malcolm was ecstatic, as was David Sutton. Straight after the birth, Richard rode fast to the telegraph office to wire the news to Don Enrique. The baptism date was set for the twelfth of November, which Don Enrique and his two sons would also attend.

The Alguilos had requested that the baptism of their first grandchild should take place in the basilica in San Antonio de Areco.

The name chosen for the baby was David Edward Sutton. Richard was the godfather and Isabella the godmother. When Malcolm and Catalina had discussed the possible Christian names with Richard, he had had to use all his circumspection and diplomatic skill to suggest the name David. The boy would be given the second name Edward, after Malcolm's father in Ireland. Malcolm agreed to all this immediately. For Richard, it represented his final act of gratitude to David Sutton.

Their horses were packed, ready for the marathon ride. The two adventurers had been provided with a fine pair of horses, a mixture of Spanish, Arab, and Berber blood. Richard's horse, which he named Pooka, was of the piebald colour, Xiemen's steed of the buckskin colour. Both friends were also bringing two pack horses to carry their gear, as well as two dogs. Their saddles, also serving as pillows at night, were of a light framework, about two feet in length, overlaid with a covering of hide. A further covering of sheepskin would double as their blankets. Their ponchos could also be used as an extra blanket in colder climes. A tent, changes of clothes, a rifle each, and Richard's Irish fiddle comprised most of their remaining gear.

Early morning. It was time to leave. Malcolm had sworn their eternal friendship, and had assured his friend that he would personally look after his land, house, and sheep. Richard received warm and affectionate hugs from David Sutton, Malcolm, Malachy Curnow and his wife, Rosa and Marita and to crown it all, two kisses from Catlalina. Xiemen was farewelled in almost the same affectionate manner. Both lads were reminded that this was always their home. They were most welcome back at any time and under any circumstances, even if their fortunes might change. Both adventurers jumped on their horses. Yes, it was a sad moment, but before them lay the beauty and uniqueness of this great land and of Patagonia. They were both young, adventurous, enterprising, and thirsty for what life could offer.

They scaled the small hill. Looking back for one last vista, Richard saw that the tableau of his friends was still present, still unbroken. His final, lingering wave was returned. He experienced some pangs of nostalgia, but was consoled by the thought that he had as his great friend and companion a handsome and very able twenty-year-old Charrúa. His years in Ireland had been dominated by his friendship with his Norman-Irish brother Patrick, convinced now that they were actually first cousins. The pampas had witnessed the growth of his depth of friendship with the young Yole, Malcolm Sutton. His journey to the south of Argentina and Patagonia would be marked by his mateship with one of the last of that proud, noble, and unconquerable race, the Charrúas of the Banda Oriental.

A figure at the bottom of the hill to their right, mounted on his horse, called out. "*Joven Irlandés y joven* Charrúa. May the god of the pampas guide you and protect you both always. *Joven Irlandés*, you ride to meet and fulfil your destiny."

It was none other than Don Sacando.

PART III.

THE ODYSSEY TO PATAGONIA

Chapter 16.

The Pampas Enfold Us.

July 1874. The Great Hall of the National Military Academy of Argentina, Buenos Aires.

On hearing his name, this young cadet stood to attention. His visage and body language revealed a mixture of emotions – nervousness, relief, pride, and awe at his surroundings. While the cadet in front of him was being conferred, the young cadet's eyes focused on the audience, which consisted of family members, friends, and business colleagues of himself and the twenty-one other cadets on the stage. He had achieved his ultimate goal. Two years of tough intensive training had realised his dream of an army career with male camaraderie under the pampas' skies. He would play a vital role in forging the relatively new republic of Argentina.

This same young cadet moved to the podium. Sporting his multiple decorations, the Head of the Military Academy exuded power, self-importance, and inspiration. His sparkling white uniform fitted him to perfection, gold braid on cuffs and collar. The young cadet felt a twinge of nervousness in his stomach. He hoped that the Head did not notice the slight twitch in his jaw when the former handed him the beautifully printed declaration. He did not think that his right hand shook as he raised it and declaimed the words in resonant voice and confident manner, "I swear to uphold the constitution of the Republic of Argentina, to defend the nation from its enemies internal and external, and to honour and respect my country's values and unique heritage."

The eyes of awarder and awardee met. The former pinned the epaulette on the cadet's right sleeve, signifying his new and exalted rank as a sub-lieutenant. Smiling effusively, he handed him his ultimate prize, the coveted Diploma as a graduate of the National Military Academy. Meritorious applause from the Great Hall. The click of a camera. Still overwhelmed, the new sub-lieutenant returned to his chair on the stage. He took a deep breath, then relaxed.

The conferring ceremony had concluded. A young notable military figure took to the podium. His bearing and stride exuded charisma and confidence. He raised his head, his eyes taking in the whole of his assembled audience. His voice possessed a resonance sweeping the whole building. The Head of the Military Academy introduced him as Colonel Julio Roca, quite recently elevated to the vital position of commander of the Southern Front. Roca briefly outlined his earlier career, interrupted at times by bursts of applause.

Coronel Roca indicated that the applause should end. He must now make the greatest impact. "My final words will focus on the future. As commander of the Southern Front, I am becoming aware of the potential of the lands to the south in the region known as Patagonia. God has there created infinite vast tracts for farming and ranching, ideal for Creole and European settlement. Furthermore, he has bequeathed those lands abundant minerals which our great country needs. But a neighbour is casting an envious eye. Which neighbour? Argentina's unfriendly rival Chile. Should Argentina turn a blind eye to this?"

Cries of *"nunca"* (never) emanated from the assembled audience.

Roca, inspired even further, continued, "Oh yes, a species of humanity dwells in those vast lands of Patagonia, has by some accounts lived there for thousands of years. But what have they done with this abundance?" Roca waited.

Some cries of *"nada"* (nothing) were heard.

Roca seized the moment. "It is the mission of Argentine Creoles and European immigrants to tame and cultivate this God-given promised land and to bring it to its true potential." Roca's voice rose in pitch and increased in volume, speaking like one possessed by a grandiose vision. "Argentina, under its government and with military commanders like the twenty-two young heroes on the stage will march towards its proud, noble, and God given destiny as one of the world's great nations."

The audience rose as one body with cries of *Argentina por siempre,* their cry and tumultuous applause lasting for a full minute.

The young sub-lieutenant's father whispered to his wife, "That colonel is going to go far. His ambitions do not end with the military."

The Provinces of Buenos Aires and La Pampa. Richard Barron and his young Charrúa friend Xiemen intended that their odyssey, commencing in November 1877, would last around two years. Richard could not deny that his years on the Sutton *estancia* had been mainly happy and fulfilling. The generous grant of land gave him a security which many would envy. But he wished to broaden his horizon. This odyssey would deepen the bonds of friendship between himself and Xiemen. Meanwhile the vast lands of central Argentina and Patagonia awaited them.

Xiemen too, as one of the few surviving Charrúas living in Argentina or Uruguay, had his own reasons for joining Richard. He sensed that the fate of Indian tribes in Argentina was, to say the least, uncertain. Rumours had reached him of the difficulties arising between the government, the military, and the Indians in the province of Rio Negro. Xiemen was adamant that where at all possible he would use his knowledge of the fate of the Charrúas to prevent future massacres. Both he and Richard agreed that they would keep their ears open for any hints emanating from *estancia* owners or their workers.

Richard and Xiemen would spend their first couple of weeks simply riding south at a leisurely pace, feeling the vastness of the pampas, and not deliberately seeking work. The locations of their sleep varied. The options of accommodation were rather similar to those of which Richard and Malcolm had availed in the hills of Uruguay, as well as camping on the open pampa.

They had been riding through Buenos Aires province for about ten days. A dark night. No moon. Both were asleep in their tent. Xiemen woke with a start. A rustle outside. Probably an animal. But no. He heard a slight cough. A human. A whinny from a horse. With his native silence and stealth, Xiemen got out of bed, opened the flap of the tent a little. An Indian youth was beside one of the horses. Xiemen reached for his rifle. He silently emerged from the tent. The youth's hands were on the ropes tethering the horse. Xiemen commanded, "Put your hands up now, or you will lose your head." The would-be horse thief froze. "Now."

The youth did as bidden. "Face me." The youth turned slowly. The horse whinnied again. The youth turned and ran past the horse into the dark.

"What is happening, Xiemen?" called Richard, emerging from the tent.

"A young *aguara,* (indigenous) an Indian has attempted to steal one of our horses. He has run away. I will keep guard for the rest of the night."

Richard protested, "No, *Amigo*, let me."

"You go back to sleep, Ricardo. But from now on we will take it in turns to keep guard at night. If we lose our horses, it can mean terrible death for us on these deserted pampas. Bring me a few bullets."

"Was your gun not loaded?"

"No, Ricardo. But our guns will be loaded at night from now on. It must have been the luck of the Irish again which caused him to believe me."

They had agreed to travel the roads and occasional tracks which led them south from their starting point of San Antonio de Areco to Lujan and then to Chivilcoy. From December 1877 they were ready to recommence work on *estancia*s. On more than one occasion an *estancia* owner entreated the two young men to extend their stay longer than a month, with the incentive of higher wages and better accommodation. But Richard and Xiemen were adamant. Their eventual destination was the province of Chubut, and their ultimate goal was to return to their homes on the Sutton *estancia*.

It was shortly after they had commenced their journey that Richard Barron began the writing of a journal. He wrote a synopsis of his boyhood and early manhood in Ireland. Richard touched on the abortive plot against the land agent Fraser, but wrote in detail about the life-changing meeting with Malcolm in Wexford, his decision to change his destination, and how this decision had resulted in a good life on the Sutton *estancia*. One night by their campfire, Xiemen asked. "What are you writing in your journal, Ricardo?"

"My main goal is to try and capture the spirit, the magic, and the uniqueness of the lands we are exploring. I might even try to poetise my impressions."

Xiemen's reply was to pat Richard on the back. "Ricardo, I can help bring the pampas to life. Remember that we Charrúas rode over the Banda Oriental for three hundred years. So you, Ricardo Barron, may become a bard on the pampas."

"I do not feel I have the talent to be a poet, Xiemen. With your help maybe I can match what Sergio and I did."

On an early December night in 1877 Richard and Xieman had been riding during a hot day, and were in need of a cooling drink. The *pulperia* looked rather unprepossessing, but their thirst overcame their reservations. They walked inside, causing four Creoles seated around a table to halt their card game and stare at them. They averted their eyes, and carried their drinks to a table some distance away.

After five minutes, a middle-aged Creole came up to them. "We would like you two *jovenes* to join us for *maté*." They felt a little apprehensive, but the Creole persisted. "We insist that you join us, both of you." Best to accept in accordance with Argentine custom. They made room for Richard and Xiemen, displaying more curiosity than hostility. Richard gave them some information about their planned route. The oldest Creole then looked at him with steely eyes.

"You are an *Inglés* (English), are you not? I do not like the *Ingléses*. My grandfather bravely fought them at the siege of Buenos Aires in 1806, and paid for it with his life. Why do you *Ingléses* have to always interfere with other countries? I want your answer, *Inglés*."

Richard's stomach felt a knot. "*Bueno Señor,* I am certainly not an *Inglés*."

"Don't try to fool me," he declared, "What are you then if not *Inglés*?"

"I am an *Irlandés*," Richard replied.

"Isn't that the same thing as *Inglés*?"

Their original host spoke. "No, Arturo, it is not. *Irlanda* is a separate country, a separate island, but is it not ruled by the *Ingléses, Joven*?"

Relieved, Richard replied. "Sadly it is, *Señor*es. My country has fought the *Ingléses* in battles, wars, and sieges for the past seven hundred years. My Barron forebears bravely fought them in two battles and a terrible siege in 1690. We do not like the *Ingléses* either, *Señor*es."

A low cheer resulted, followed by the youngest Creole declaring, "*Irlanda, la tierra del Admirante Guillermo Brown. Bienvenidos a nuestra compañia.* (Ireland, the land of Admiral William Brown. Welcome to our company)." Handshakes to Richard, but none to Xiemen.

Richard still felt uncomfortable. The youngest Creole, possibly more out of curiosity, asked, "But why do you travel with a *buck* (young Indian), Ricardo?"

Richard answered. "I have to tell you that I am something of a scholar and a musician. I am interested in the Indian languages, their music, their customs and religion. Also, I value Xiemen's knowledge of the soils and sources of water. He is an excellent guide. If we were to meet hostile Indians, I would feel safe in his hands."

The young Creole asked. "You feel safe. Do you not know about all the Creole settler families who were slaughtered by the Indians of the desert for decades?"

Xiemen was quick to respond. "Buenos *Señor*es, I am not an Indian of the desert. I am a Charrúa, an *aguara,* from the Banda Oriental. We were a peaceful people. We shared our lands with the Creoles. We traded with them. Most of us moved into the missions and became Christians." Xiemen realised that he was taking a gamble. However, these four Creoles were most likely unaware of the terrible fate of his people.

The young Creole spoke, "Well as the friend and protector of our *Irlandés* companion, we welcome you as well." But again, no handshakes to Xiemen.. Ten minutes later Richard and Xiemen excused themselves and continued on their journey. Another valuable lesson learned. Keep the fate of the Charrúas a secret. It might be repeated here in Argentina.

Richard and Xiemen had left the province of Buenos Aires, crossing now to the province of La Pampa. There was no real difference in the terrain. However, Xiemen seemed to come more into his own as he identified differences in the flora and fauna. His remarkable eyesight proved a real boon for Richard's journalistic endeavours. The sparser the surrounds of the pampas, the more at home Xiemen seemed to be.

Travelling through the eastern ends of La Pampa on an exceptionally warm day in March 1878, Xiemen had removed his shirt, causing Richard to gaze in awe at his profile. Xiemen's naked torso was proportioned like a young Greek god, displaying few body hairs, the muscles of his upper arms vibrant and powerful. The young Charrúa's slightly haughty but noble countenance was heightened by the manner in which he carried himself, completely at home in the saddle. Truly Xiemen did justice to Richard's regarding him as the Last of the Charrúas. On telling Xiemen this, he responded, "Ricardo, my Charrúa forebears rode almost naked over the Banda. Get ready to gallop. *Yapug-janie,* that means hold on fast. I am the lord of these pampas."

January 2nd, 1878.

'We had spent Christmas and New Year as guests at the *estancia* of the Heywood family, hospitable and cultured English people. Shortly after our departure the pampas seem to open in all their majesty. Xiemen decides to canter ahead of me, spurred on by an aromatic breeze from the east in tandem with the rising sun now asserting its dominance over a belt of morning cloud. From our slightly elevated viewpoint the tapestry of the lighter green pampas is interspersed with the buildings of a few farms, islands in this vast ocean. I spur on my horse in order to a canter in order to ride abreast with my friend. We revel in the clouds of dust we create on this wide track.'

'Our movements produce different responses from the animals and birds of the plains. The domesticated animals are safely behind the farmers' wires. Yet that does not prevent the flocks of sheep and their lambs running towards the safety of the interior of the large field. Some horses with glistening skin stand to attention and neigh in greeting to our steeds, the latter returning the compliment. Our passing seems to make little impression on the cows and cattle, which, apart from a few curious glances, continue to graze in peace. The *teros* screech into the air, as if protesting at our unexpected and uninvited visitation, while myriads of small birds from time to time encircle us, a form of royal escort.'

'"See, Ricardo. Nature also recognises me as a lord of the pampas. *Chaja,* Ricardo." I took that to mean, "Let's go, Richard." I look at his profile in admiration. There he gallops ahead of me. The last of the Charrúas.'

Summer of 1878.

Xiemen called to Richard, "Ricardo, I have to show you the hidden pampas. Not just the vast plains of grass, their greenness weakening during the time of the long suns. Life giving to the flocks, yes. Abundant, yes. But you and I will search for the hidden treasures."

'I began to see the pampas as a panorama of life, animal and vegetable. On some evenings I thanked God that the implacable sun was descending from its relentless campaign of baking the earth, withering the trees, paralysing the progress of life. Yet at the same time I might observe squadrons of birds flying to the west, maybe to greet the tyrant on the horizon. The humidity of the night assumed the post of a sentinel, as if to remind us that tomorrow the tyrant would return with at least equal vehemence. Yet the beauty and clarity of the stars served as a consolation. Sometimes at night the breeze, warm like a breath, glided over the high and parched grasses, unable, however, to bestow any moisture upon them. Yet, the grasses and plants, animals and humans welcomed it.

The sun, the sun, this demon fire, it burns and bakes in field
*   and home,*
Though mother nature scorns to yield, and in resistance, finds a
*   way.*
The dampened night, the cooling breeze, the icy stars of
*   heaven's dome Afford the living short respite, survival for*
*   another day.*

'While many of the streams and small lakes had virtually dried up, one afternoon I found a water hole. On joining me Xiemen took one look at it and shook his head. "No, Ricardo, that is a *cuaro,* a bitter hole or well. We must not drink it. We could become bodies that were."

"Are you sure, Xiemen? We need water."

He raised his finger to his lips, pressed his ear to the ground, got up, and smiled. "We are near what I think will be good water. Follow me, *Amigo.* "

We rode for about another kilometre. To my delight the vista of a lake opened before us. Two swans glided along its surface, arching with pride their elegant necks. Suddenly there arose from the foliage a group of marine birds. Forming a convoy behind both swans, they followed them for some distance, their red, blue, and yellow wings vividly illuminating with a sea of colour the sun-baked atmosphere. We pitched our tent by that lake. Next morning I woke to find Xiemen shaking my arm, "Ricardo, *chaja* and look at this." We observed four flamingos rising from the lake. The flap of wings and the explosion of vivid colours. What a perfect way to greet the emerging day.'

May 1878.

Once again Richard and Xiemen were suffering from thirst after a hard day of riding. They entered yet another unprepossessing *pulperia,* this time occupied by only one drinker, a soldier at the bar. Richard ordered two drinks. They sat quietly opposite each other for ten minutes. The soldier got off his stool, and stumbled over to them.

It seemed as if he were about to collapse on top of Richard, when Richard righted his posture.

"*Gracias, Amigo*. You are a true gentleman. May I join you for a moment. I prefer to drink in company. My name is Gregorio. I am a gregarious soldier."

Not waiting for a reply, he sat down uncomfortably close to Richard. He did not appear to have noticed Xiemen. His conversation was incoherent, difficult to follow. "Yes, *Amigo*, it will be a hard campaign but worth it, when we have cleared all those savage Indians to beyond the Rio Negro. And good enough for them. Do you know, *Joven*, that we now have a new Minister for War? None other than General Julio Roca." He kept touching Richard's torso with his dirty hands. If Richard moved away, he moved closer.

The drunken soldier continued his tirade. "They have slaughtered our menfolk, despoiled our women, taken our children captives. Even shoving the tame ones into reservations will be too good for them. I say, wipe them from the face of the Earth, the lot of them. I bet that that is what General Roca thinks too. Don't you agree, *Amigo*, don't you agree? I am sure you do."

He brought his eyes full of hatred up close to Richard's. "And do you know, *Amigo*, some so-called good people say that we should show mercy to *Indio* women, children, and old people. That we should not drive away their cattle and livestock. Should not burn their camps. I say, fuck them all. Let them starve to death."

"Excuse me, *Señor,*" Richard said, "could you please not crowd against me." His stench was becoming unbearable, especially his breath.

"My apologies, *Joven*. Where was I? Yes, we are going to solve the Indian problem once and for all. More land is needed for our great country to expand. I am proud to say that I am serving my country. Are you?"

He turned his head quickly round and, for the first time, seemed to take in Xiemen. He staggered up. Taking a slight lunge in Xiemen's direction, he collapsed on to the table. Xiemen and Richard immediately stood up, left the *pulperi*a, and let the owner deal with him.

By contrast, a hospitable priest informed Richard and Xiemen that the Indians were fighting back. More frequent and larger raids against settlements had become common, sometimes with thousands of cattle taken, and, true, some of the settlers captured. The priest did not condone such actions.

"War," he proclaimed," leads to atrocities on both sides, but human greed lies as the root of these evils."

The scar-faced man and his mate entered the *pulperia*. Having ordered their drinks, they sat down on two chairs adjoining a small table. Conversation between them was limited, indicating a certain level of boredom. After about twenty minutes a lone soldier entered the *pulperia*. He looked somewhat dishevelled, wearing his uniform carelessly. The scar-faced man beckoned him to join them. He told the soldier how he and his mate had recently left their employment on an *estancia,* and were now seeking work elsewhere. "Do you know of any good *estancia*s where we might find work?"

"What are you two *desperados* like with your guns?" asked the solider.

"We are both excellent shots, especially when using them to kill those savage Indians."

"Magnificent," replied the soldier. "The *estancia* owner, *Señor* Batista, desperately needs a couple of men who can do just that. He has lost too many cattle to them. His *estancia* is five miles in that direction. Tell him the soldier Gregorio sent you."

"What do you think, Jorge?" the scar-faced man's mate asked.

Jorge replied. "What do you expect I think? Where there are savages, there will I be. To avenge my father, and rid our land of that plague."

"That is what I like to hear" added the soldier.

The soldier paused for about twenty seconds. "You know, about two weeks ago, I had a strange experience. I was in another *pulperia* drinking. I admit I drank too much. I got talking to a young white man who was travelling with an Indian buck. It must have been a dream. No respectable white man would do such a thing."

Jorge sat upright. "Did you get his name? Maybe he was an American."

"No," the soldier answered, "I did not get his name. I think he could have been English."

"That is enough. Me and my mate Alfonso will keep an eye out for them. They will enjoy a bullet from both of us."

Chapter 17.

'Heroes Without Redemption.

No History Records nor Tear Laments.'[8]

Richard decided not to show this newspaper article to Xiemen. Similar vitriolic articles had appeared in the Uruguayan press during the months leading up to Salsipuedes. This particular article talked about Argentina's long standing "Indian problem." The Indians were depicted as a doomed race fated to disappear, having rejected the saving power of civilisation, progress, and Christianity. In almost Old Testament rhetoric it expounded how God in his infinite wisdom had led the Spaniards, the Creoles, and now other European peoples to this promised land of Argentina, and that their eventual destination was to bring their enlightened civilisation even to the southern reaches of Tierra del Fuego. The climax of the article painted a vivid picture of mass murder, looting, rape, and unimaginable destruction perpetrated by the savages of the desert. The author even claimed that such atrocities were even now being perpetrated against border settler communities, a real and direct threat to the survival of the nation. All efforts at negotiation – trading agreements, the payment of tribute to the Indians, treaties – had failed dismally. A final solution was needed.

By July 1878 Roca was sending initial forces south against the Indians, a prelude of what was to come. They focused upon the region between the existing military frontier and the Rio Negro. By

---

8   (Juan Zorilla de San Martin, Trans. Walter Owen)

December of 1878 over five thousand Indians, and not all of them warriors, were dead, with negligible deaths on the government side.

Roca's initial campaigns were directed against the Indian community at large. Hundreds of captives were taken. Horses and cattle, the lifeblood of the indigenous people for sustenance and transportation, were destroyed. But Roca did not delight in such measures. Those Indians who would surrender their weapons to the military and bow to the authority of the State would be offered a new life. They would live in places ordained by the government, where they would be granted herds of sheep, horses and cattle. This was Roca's and gradually the government's solution to the perennial "Indian problem."

Winter 1878.

By June 1878 Richard and Xiemen had reached the southernmost part of The Pampas province, and winter had arrived. Richard had finished his two-hour night shift. He had felt the breeze intensifying; had seen the blue-black border of cloud covering the horizon to the east. Xiemen assured him that if a storm arose, he would soothe the horses, and would call on Richard, if needed.

The clap of thunder woke Richard. A flash or lightning and more thunder. Richard rushed to the front entrance, "Xiemen, are you there? Are you alright? The horses?"

"I am safe, Ricardo, as are the horses. I am calming them. All is well. Go back to bed."

"Xiemen. This storm. It looks and sounds as if the heavens are tearing themselves apart."

Xiemen was reassuring, "It is alright. I can sense that it has reached its peak. The god of the storm will soon quieten."

Richard was unconvinced. The black storm clouds were moving across rapidly, as if goaded by the regular and vivid flashes of lightning. "Xiemen, you must be frozen. The cold of that wind. The icy rain will start in a moment."

"Ricardo, I am a Charrúa. Storms do not frighten us. Bring me a blanket. I am not leaving the horses while that wind howls."

As Richard wrapped the blanket around Xiemen, he felt his bitterly cold body. "Ricardo, the wind will drop soon, and I will come into the tent. Stay awake."

The rain did arrive within a few minutes. As it increased in intensity, the wind, lightning, and thunder decreased. But the temperature dropped markedly. Although the horses were safely tethered under the trees, Xiemen was still exposed. He called, "The horses are just about calmed now. Give me a couple more minutes."

"Alright, then I will take over from you."

"There is no need for you to take over, Ricardo. No bandits or horse thieves will be out tonight. And even if they are, our dogs will wake us. Stay in the tent."

Reluctantly Richard did as bidden. When his friend entered the tent, he was handed a glass of whiskey. Xiemen drank it, restoring some colour to his cheeks, but his whole body was shaking.

"Xiemen, get out of those clothes immediately. Put on fresh undergarments, fresh trousers, and then straight to your bed. Here, put on my jumper as well. Take my blanket too."

Within a minute Xiemen was in his bed. But his teeth were still chattering, his body still half frozen. His voice rose in desperation,

"Ricardo, the heat is not entering my body. The cold and the rain possess it."

Terror encompassed Richard's face. What if the young lad was overcome by pneumonia way out here with possible fatal consequences. "Xiemen, there is only one solution, the oldest known to mankind. My body is warm. Let me move it to yours, *Amigo*."

Richard wrapped a blanket around himself. Then without hesitation crept under Xiemen's bedclothes. He put his left arm around his friend, moving it up and down to increase circulation. Even through the lad's undershirt he felt the ice-cold body. God, what else could he do? Instinctively he knew. Richard moved his left leg over Xiemen's legs, working a similar motion. Xiemen moved closer to him, nestling in his friend's body warmth. The treatment slowly had a positive effect, and any inhibitions or taboos had gone out the tent. Richard felt his own warmth encompassing Xiemen's body. The shivering had virtually ceased. But Richard kept his arm and leg moving in the same positions. By now Xiemen's chattering teeth and shivering had given way to deep breathing. Xiemen was asleep. Nonetheless Richard decided that he must remain with him. The cold of the night was intensifying, even though the rain had eased. Xiemen's body was by now warming Richard's own. He experienced a great feeling of calm, security, and affection for his young Charrúa friend. Was this an aspect of that mysterious thing called mateship which helped two friends to survive in exceptional circumstances?

Richard awoke suddenly, to find his arm still around Xiemen. The temperature was still very cold. Gradually he remembered what had occurred the night before. To his relief the lad's body temperature and breathing seemed normal. Richard moved back to his own space in the tent. "Xiemen, are you awake? How do you feel?"

"I am fine and rather warm, Ricardo. Your warm body saved me. How did you know it would work?"

"Xiemen, I had seen animals, especially sheep doing it. Although we are not animals, we can learn a few things from them."

"Ricardo Barron, you make the greatest friend. I am so lucky." Another pause. "You know, we Charrúas say that there should be no secrets between friends. Do you agree?"

Richard hesitated. "As long as revealing a secret does not end the friendship."

A longer pause.

"Ricardo, there is one question I would like to ask you, but you do not have to answer. Whatever you answer, you have my word that it will not end our friendship."

Well, let the question come. He might as well give Xiemen the full truth.

"My question is, Ricardo, have you ever lain with a woman? You are not offended, are you?"

Richard, although somewhat taken aback, replied. "Not in the least. But why do you need to know? What makes you think I have or haven't?"

"Ricardo, you are quite a religious young man, a very moral person, a good example to me. But you are around thirty years of age, and some people say that to lay with a woman is a rite of passage. I have never done so, but I am only twenty-one. I do not think there is anything wrong with me for that."

Richard felt that he should be honest. "Father Antonio Fahy expected high moral standards from the Irish on the pampas. If I had got a girl with child, I would have felt forced to marry her, possibly leading to an unhappy and even hateful marriage. But I would not have abandoned her, like I think my natural father abandoned my real mother. Yes, my religion did partly come into it."

"But, Ricardo, could you not have used other women, women known as comfort women, maybe in Buenos Aires?"

"Xiemen, I did at times consider that. But I had heard that one could catch diseases, terrible, incurable, even fatal. That was enough to prevent me doing so."

Richard continued. "However, there was an occasion a couple of years ago. I was very friendly with a girl. It was a scorching hot day. We had been riding our horses and decided to have a swim in the river."

Xiemen smiled. "Did you swim naked, like we men sometimes do, Ricardo?"

"Of course not, Xiemen, but we did shed some clothes. When we got out of the water, passionate feelings took hold of both of us. I will not go into details. Suffice to say that we could have had intercourse, but we both held back. My main reason again was that I might have put her with child. Still, I did experience a certain relief, if you know what I mean. So, *Amigo*, in answer to your question, yes, I have lain with a woman, but not to the full extent."

A short pause followed. "Then, Ricardo, *Amigo*, I am glad that you kept to your code. You have used your healing and soothing hands to calm horses, and the warmth of your body to restore health and warmth to your best friend. You may be Irish by birth, but at heart you are becoming a Charrúa. Now, stay where you are. I am getting up to light the fire and to brew some tea."

That evening Richard wrote, 'He lay at my feet, looking up at the star-studded sky. I played the main theme of the fifth movement of Beethoven's pastoral symphony to his instrumental harmony. Our horses were tethered, grazing peacefully and contentedly on the rich pampas grass. Our music seemed to blend even better than heretofore. It was as if the experience of the previous stormy night, and our mutual revelations, had bound us even closer together. On occasions I looked down at his handsome young face, a picture of peace and calm. For our final tune we played *Home to our Mountains*. Xiemen sat up, "Ricardo, that melody is so special to you. For me it will always be Richard Barron's own special melody, and not just Verdi's. I want you to teach me how to play it and to sing it in Italian."

"Excellent, Xiemen. We can start now."'

The sub-lieutenant was not really happy. He had led his platoon for a month now on General Roca's preliminary campaigns. His men had fought admirably, with no losses. Although the Indians had some guns, they mainly resorted to spears, lances, and swords. The Remington repeater rifle gave the Argentine army a significant advantage over them. This platoon was part of the first division, which moved southward under the command of Colonel Villegas.

The preliminary campaign could not be regarded as full-scale war. The Argentine military attacked Indian communities, killing warriors and taking captives. The policy of the Indians had been to flee when warned of an impending raid. Their knowledge of their own environment and terrain initially served them to advantage. But Roca was not to be thwarted.

Attached to the sub-lieutenant's platoon was a scientist. His tasks included making maps of the pampas, studying soil composition, waterways, and other natural resources, and terrain. Yet, the sub-lieutenant was not happy with Roca's policy of his soldiers driving off the Indians' horses, livestock, and cattle. In an interview with Colonel Vilegas he achieved the latter's permission to discourage his soldiers from doing this and of instead encouraging the soldiers to accompany both himself and the scientist on the latter's work.

The sub-lieutenant had cited to Colonel Villegas the horrors of the Irish Famine, as related to him by his mother, when British soldiers had driven cattle and other animals to ships bound for England, to support his argument. The interview had concluded with

Villegas stipulating, "But be aware, Sub-Lieutenant, that I never authorised this permission."

The next phase of Richard Barron's journal would reveal the horrors which he and Xiemen would witness during the terrible summer of 1878 and early '79.

He wrote. 'The summer of 1878 to '79 arrived early, and was unlike any other summer I had experienced. I had become accustomed to the hot and, at times, scorching summer weather. Yet even then the infrequent long and heavy showers of summer rain and the odd storm allowed a temporary respite. However, this summer fell upon us like a Biblical plague. It was as if a perverse magician had cast an evil spell over the vast extent of the pampas. Nothing was spared its destructive hand, and it sealed forever the fate of the Indians.'

'At the height of this summer, the days could be suffocatingly hot. At times the implacable sun assumed the persona of a crystal ball of fire, spreading its tyrannical grip over the Earth. It withered the trees, baked the earth, paralysed much of life. The immense pampa became overwhelmingly sad, pleading for refreshing water, dying under the unrelenting grip of drought. The once verdant and abundant grass lay dead and burnt before our very eyes. Some days on our journey we were attacked by spells of scorching hot winds, winds which seemed to originate in Hell itself, bringing us to exhaustion. They blew ahead of them clouds of dust. Our only protection was to cover ours and our horses' mouths, noses, and most of our faces with masks and scarfs. The trees which had always served as our refuges could no longer shade us. Stripped of their foliage, black, gnarled, and twisted, dying from thirst, they assumed the personas of old and decrepit hospitality providers who, at one time welcoming and comforting, now slammed the door in our faces.'

'And what effect did this terrible change in the weather have on the animals of the pampas? Some of the richer *estancia* owners were able to purchase animal feed from farmers in Patagonia. But such supplies were limited, and prices increased rapidly as the conditions worsened. The poorer farmers were less fortunate. As we travelled, we heard heart-rending stories of farmers having to slaughter their herds. At one *pulperia* we were informed that a certain Creole farmer needed some workers urgently. On arriving there we surmised the reason, seeing the sheep with their faces turned towards the sides of the corral. Their eyes were closed or half closed, overcome by tiredness, heat exhaustion, thirst, and sheer pain. Partly suffocated by the heat, they panted, but no fresh oxygen relieved their suffering. Rather did the cruel scorching wind invade their mouths with the smell of burnt grass.'

'Xiemen and I were engaged by the farmer to dig large pits. He explained. "I have hoped against hope for this cruel weather to change, holding out as long as I could. We will dig the pits, and then I will give ourselves one more week. I will need your help when the inevitable moment comes." We agreed to this, as he needed moral as well as physical support.'

'During the early morning light, we drove the sheep towards the large pit. They followed each other, slowly, listlessly, too exhausted to even bleat. What did it matter to them where they were going? It was fortunate that most of their lambs had died, for I would have found the spectacle of the lambs with their mothers too much. The leading sheep had reached the edge of the pit. We drove them into it, they running to the bottom possibly in the expectation of water. The rest followed, probably about five hundred in all.'

'We placed ourselves around the large pit, our rifles loaded, the farmer, his son, Xiemen, I myself, and two *peon*s. For the next ten minutes the devastated pampas resounded to the crackle of our rifles. Before this day, we had carted loads of lime to the periphery of the pit. This we spread with large shovels over the dead carcasses. It sealed our act of destruction, albeit a cruel necessity. Our final action was to cover the pit with the clay which we had dug out. We all walked back to the farmer's house in silence.'

'Xiemen was in tears, and I suspected the reason. "Xiemen, has our killing the sheep this morning, although necessary, struck some hidden chord in you?"

'"It has, Ricardo. Sheep herded into a pit to end their suffering. But think of my Charrúa people, men, women, children. The men and youths cut to pieces with sabres and bayonets. The women and children look on. The cold dream. The bodies that were. My father, his brother, their friend, gaze down from high above at the horror. At least today we were civilised. One shot, one sheep dead. They felt hardly a thing. We spread a blanket of lime over the sheep that were. Covered it with earth. Was any blanket or earth spread over my people that were? Who knows?"

'I let him weep for a while, spreading my arms around him. "Xiemen, I will fetch two glasses of whiskey. Then we will play some music together."

'At the conclusion of our music, I broached my thoughts. "Xiemen, I think that we should leave this farm. The *Señor* says that, now that he has only his cattle and horses to feed, he may get through the summer. If he cannot, the cattle will be the next to be shot. I do not wish to be here for that."'

"Nor me either, Ricardo. But where shall we go?"

"Xiemen, we have earned enough money to last us a while. Let us find some Indian communities. Their stock may be dying too, and maybe we can help them. We cannot bring back your Charrúa dead, but we perhaps can help the Indians of this region to survive."

'He jumped up and embraced me with, "Ricardo, spoken like a true Charrúa. I feel that the spirit of my murdered grandfather has entered you."

'As we rode further south in La Pampa province it became obvious that the extreme weather was devastating more than crops and cattle. We were hearing stories of the outbreak of an epidemic called smallpox. I knew from my own experience in Ireland that famine could bring with it fevers and diseases. Xiemen and I, having visited some *tolderias* to find them deserted, decided to obtain some medical information.'

'We gained an interview with a doctor. He outlined the symptoms of smallpox to us, advised us to wear protective masks, and praised us for our planned mission of mercy.'

'We always approached a *tolderia* (Indian camp) with Xiemen blowing the *chifle*, the Charrúa horn. About two hundred yards from the *tolderia*, he would call out. "Do not be afraid. We are not the military. My name is Xiemen, and I am an Indian like you. Do you need food? My friend Ricardo and I have brought you some sheep"

'Sometimes some men, would emerge from a couple of tents, accepting the gifts. We would then release the sheep in their direction, driven by our dogs. While I could not really see the Indians' faces from a distance, their gait revealed their suffering. Indeed, it reminded me of groups of the dispossessed walking the roads outside our house in Ireland.'

'Our approach to one particular *tolderia* was greeted by a deathly silence. No signs of life human or animal, apart from a couple of mangy dogs that slunk around the outside of the tents. After the *chifle* call, we always waited fifteen minutes, keeping our distance.'

'Two humans slowly emerged from tents. Xiemen called out. "Are many of you living here?"

'An Indian woman, almost naked, replied faintly. "Only a few of us now. We are all suffering from the *viruela*, the small pox. Most of our children have died. Only some women and a few old men have stayed here. All the other men, some women, and a few children have fled, because they are afraid of catching it.'

'"What food do you have?" called Xiemen.'

'The Indian woman moaned."'We are eating roots. That is all we have now."

'"My friend Ricardo and I have brought you some sheep. Our dogs will drive them to your tents. Or we can kill them for you."

"Young *Indio*, please do that."

'Xiemen and I cut the throats of the sheep and dissected them into parts. Xiemen then sounded the bugle again. There now emerged from tents an old man, and two children. Xiemen called out, "Come immediately, before the birds eat them."

'We waited until they were about a hundred yards from us. Then we had no choice but to turn our horses and ride away. Xiemen was very moved by it all. "Ricardo, I wish that we could have done more for them. How they must be suffering from that terrible smallpox."

"Xiemen, we have done all we can for them. We ourselves must not fall to the plague."

'He looked back, but swiftly turned his head, "You are right, but do not look back. They are eating the meat raw."

'We were yet to encounter the most harrowing case of human suffering. A sound. Moaning. Crying. Wailing. Could it be animals, or maybe the *pamplona* wind rising?'

'Xiemen called, "Look, Ricardo." A blur on the pampas landscape, assuming shape. People moving slowly, aimlessly. A broken group, disunited. Sometimes they stopped to rest, then resumed their walk. One member of the group lay still, did not arise.

The rest of them moved on towards us, ignoring the fallen one. We halted and waited. Through my field glasses I observed on their faces and their half naked bodies the terrible signs, the skin rashes, the flat spots, the blisters giving forth foul-looking liquid, the scabs. I handed the field glasses to Xiemen.'

"What will we do, Xiemen? Will we turn around? Can we do anything for them?"

'He answered. "We can still leave them food. We can kill the sheep. Let me go ahead."'

'Xiemen rode about two hundred yards ahead, and sounded the *chifle*. Some of the group halted, but more kept walking, unhearing. Xiemen called out,"Why are you Indians walking when the smallpox has possessed you? Where are you going?" No reply. He asked again, at which point most of them halted.'

'An old man called out. "We have been driven out of our *tolderia* because we got the smallpox."

'"Who drove you out? The Military?" Xiemen called.'

"No, our own menfolk drove us out. They fear the smallpox more than they fear the military. They said that they must keep well in order to fight the military."

"Stay where you are," Xiemen ordered, "We have food for you. Sheep. We will kill them and cut them up. Make sure you cook them. Do not eat them raw."

'The group of Indians collapsed. Another sound from them. Whether a wail of forlornness or a communal cry of thanks, I will never know. Xiemen and I did as promised. Then we turned our mounts and followed another route. Who or what was the real enemy of the Indians – the strange weather, the plagues, the Argentine military, or even maybe themselves? Xiemen and I did not look back.'

'An Irish Famine victim falling to his or her death on the road or in the ditch; fever ridden victims shunned and deserted by their own communities; people possibly driven out by their own families, not to mention those evicted by their landlords and their agents. Wasn't I seeing it all played out again before my very eyes? Did the same fate of the Irish await the *Indio*s of the pampas and Patagonia? My anger mounted. Races perceived as inferior, the Irish, the *Indio*s of Argentina, Uruguay, North America, the indigenous people of Australia. So many wiped out by wars of conquest, massacres, famine, plague, disease brought by conquerors. Would it remain the same for time immemorial?'

The young sub lieutenant could not understand the Indians. General Roca, Minister for War, favoured capturing the Indians but not killing them, and of not applying more force than was necessary. Rather than allowing them to wander over the pampas as they had done for centuries, the Argentine government wished them to submit to State authority. Provided they surrendered their weapons, the government would provide them with herds of cattle, sheep, and horses. Their women could weave products which they could sell to the wider population. But, the sub lieutenant reflected, the pampas Indians were stubborn, unnatural, unable to change. Why could they not see that their nomadic way of life had to change?

The sub lieutenant and six of his soldiers cautiously entered the military camp. It harboured Indian men captured in battle, women, and even children who had resisted their *tolderias* being 'cleaned' by the military. General Roca had decreed that such Indians had to be kept as effective prisoners in these camps, known as concentration camps. The visiting soldiers had donned protective masks and scarves. On entering the office of the military superintendent, the latter laid the mortality figures in front of them.

"A high percentage of the Indian inmates have died of smallpox, admittedly caused by the close living in the camp. But, gentlemen, some of our military guard, brave, patriotic soldiers, have sadly succumbed to the same fate. Some of the Indian warriors have died from their wounds in battle, and a few, I admit, have died at the hands of their military guards. But remember, the second cause of Indian deaths has been the oppressive heat this summer, the resulting famine, and of course malnutrition. These were enemies from which they were suffering in their own *tolderia*s even before they stupidly resisted the military. So, in many respects they have brought death and suffering upon themselves."

The sub-lieutenant reflected. This argument had a certain logic to it. "*Señor* superintendent, you blame famine as the cause of many deaths. Do you have sufficient food in the camp?"

"Sub-lieutenant. our food stocks are limited. The military outside the camp try to bring us stocks of food. But they are subject to attacks by savage warriors as yet unsubdued. My policy is that the military guards here receive priority for food and nutrition. The Indian prisoners take second place, but none of them are allowed to starve. Indeed, were it not for the smallpox, I would say that they are better off in these camps than in their *tolderias*. Indians have suffered poverty, illness, starvation for generations. Thankfully, when General Roca has finally solved the Indian problem, all that will be history."

Superintendent and sub-lieutenant each nursed a glass of whiskey. The latter had sent four of his soldiers to inspect the camp, knowing that Pedro and Vincento, would give him a true and undiluted report. Fifteen minutes after the end of his formal meeting, they returned. On removal of their face coverings, Pedro's and Vincento's faces and eyes revealed horror and even fear. The superintendent passed them a glass of whiskey each.

Pedro described some of the scenes witnessed: bodies covered with skin rash; blisters emitting a foul-smelling liquid; ugly scabs. Worse still was their sight of Indians lying in their own vomit and excrement; other bodies writhing with intolerable backache; children wailing, struck down by devastating headaches and fever. Hardened soldiers even as they were, it had all been too much for the men, "No people, even savage, uncivilised, pagan Indians, should be left to suffer like that," Vincento declared.

The superintendent spoke, "*Señor*es, I know that you are severely shocked by what you have witnessed. But I have already explained to your able and heroic sub-lieutenant what the real cause and the only solution are."

He recounted the interview. Fifteen minutes later the seven military men left the concentration camp. The sub-lieutenant would dispatch his report to Colonel Villegas. Pedro's and Vincento's report had shook him profoundly. He did not know the answer to the human suffering. In war there were no easy solutions.

The sub-lieutenant looked up from his desk. His eyes took in a young Creole, probably in his late twenties, scar-faced, unkempt hair, a mean and even cruel countenance.

"Yes, *Joven*, what is it?"

The Creole replied. "Colonel Villegas has assigned me to your platoon. My name is Jorge."

"Where are you from?" asked the sub-lieutenant.

"I was born in the region around San Antonio de Areco. I have lived and worked on the pampas for the past seven years."

"Can you handle weaponry?"

"Indeed I can. I had to learn how to shoot a rifle at eight years of age, shortly after those savage *Indio*s murdered my father. I also learned how to fight with a *punal* (dagger) and to use a pistol, because myself and my older brother became the defenders of my family. Two years after murdering my father, those savages returned. We defeated them, killing half of them. You can be sure we never saw them again."

The second lieutenant wondered how much of this was true, and, if true, was that the motivation for this scowling *joven*'s reason for joining his platoon. He might well become a loose cannon.

The sub-lieutenant looked at the young recruit. "Why do you want to join the army?"

"I have been inspired by the words, the aims, and the leadership of General Roca. He wishes to extend our national territory into the great plains of Patagonia. The *Indios* there have done nothing with the land. All they do is attack and slaughter peaceful citizens. Why, they now even pose a threat to the citizens of Buenos Aires."

The sub-lieutenant spoke. "*Joven*, firstly you will please address me as Sub-Lieutenant. Secondly, I must tell you that my platoon fights Indian warriors only. Of course, we kill in war but we kill warriors, not women, children and old people."

"So, Sub-Lieutenant, you forbid them to kill other degenerates?"

Angered by his insolence, the sub-lieutenant spoke loudly, "I do not forbid them. I lead by example during and after the battle. After a successful battle both my men and I myself, together with our scientist, go to inspect and examine the land we have captured. So, do our actions not fit in with your intention to join my platoon?"

Jorge cast his eyes downward, mumbling. "Yes, Sub Lieutenant."

"Can you repeat that, please, and louder."

The young man raised his head in the air, almost declaiming. "Yes, Sub Lieutenant, but, does Colonel Villegas know about this?"

"Yes, private Jorge, I am sure he does. After each successful engagement our scientist reports to him, and he may well report to General Roca. Any further questions?"

"No, Sub-Lieutenant."

"Then I welcome you into my platoon." The recruit's handshake was limp.

"Damn it. Not another Indian lover!" Jorge thought. He had met some in Buenos Aires, do-gooders, evangelists, even some clergy who maintained that the Indians could be civilised and Christianised. Where was their evidence? As a race the *Indio*s of the pampas were utterly doomed. Yet, he mused, Colonel Villegas had lauded this sub-lieutenant. However, he would find a way of giving those savages their just deserts, be they young *Indio* bastards and bitches, women *putas*, or degenerate old people. *Mi padre*, you will be avenged a hundred-fold.

Jorge's memory swung back to that *Indio* lover on the Sutton plantation. What was his name? B... b... b... Barron. Richard Barron. That was it. He had no idea where that bloody bastard was now. Probably enjoying the high life as owner of an *estancia* on land 'stolen from the Indians.' Stolen my arse! Brave Argentine soldiers had fairly and justly won that same land, many paying with their lives. Jorge was certain that the last place you'd find that bastard Barron would be in the army. Fucking pet boy.

CHAPTER 18.

Viva Patagonia!

'We had completed our mission of mercy. It was time for us to to travel on over into Patagonia. Accordingly, on 1ˢᵗ February 1879, we crossed the Rio Negro in the town of Cipoletti, leaving behind the province of La Pampa, and entering the province of Rio Negro. Our journey along the north side of the Rio Negro had presented us with a pleasant vista of groves, orchards, and even some vineyards. However, we were under no illusions as to the landscape which awaited us.'

'We had decided to initially follow the course of the Rio Limay, aided by a map given to us by a government surveyor. Rivers offered a good supply of food, fish, fowl, geese, and some edible plants which Xiemen had identified. To these we added fruits, and birds' eggs, providing us with a healthy diet. Our map gave us the confidence to, at times, divert from the river and to ride into the less lush and bleaker Patagonian landscape. Two days after leaving the Rio Limay, our food supply had almost run out.'

"What do we do now, Xiemen?"

"Why are you worried, Ricardo? You are in the safe hands of a Charrúa, who knows how to live off the land. I will show you tomorrow morning early. We are not going to starve."

'Just as day was breaking, Xiemen woke me. We rode for about a quarter of a mile. Then he stopped, silently pointing ahead. My eyes took in a flock of about twenty beautiful animals. "*Llamas*?" I quietly asked.'

"No, Ricardo, *Guanacos*, but related to the llama."

"Are you saying that we should kill such exquisite animals, Xiemen?"

"Not today, Ricardo, but maybe once a week we can kill one. Most of the time we can live on Patagonian hares."

"I prefer that, Xiemen. I would hate to have to kill a creature of beauty."

"You can live on hares if you wish to, Ricardo. The Indians of Patagonia and the Andes kill the *guanaco* only when necessary for a variety of food. To survive here, we have to become like Indians. Also, our dogs need some different food. We will go and find some hares."

'This difference of opinion was one of the few that we encountered. On reflection, I became more convinced that my Indian friend was right. Survival in this bleak landscape was our preeminent aim.'

'Later that morning we came across a couple of hares sun bathing. Xiemen silently removed a *boleadora* (ball) from his bag. He brought his hand back. Then he threw the ball with great force, striking one dead, followed by the other with a second *boleadora*.'

"Ricardo, they did not feel a thing. Meat tonight for dinner."

'Three days later, "Ricardo, this morning I am going to try and kill a *guanaco*. Do you wish to come with me?"

'I replied, "Yes. I will. Apart from a change of meat, I am curious to see how you will do it."

"It could be difficult, Ricardo, as it is an extremely fast animal. Still, it is a skill I must learn."

'We rode for about thirty minutes. Again, we spied a flock. We slowed down as we approached them, gazing at their beauty. Xiemen moved his horse, quickening his pace. He reached for a *boleadora*. He cast his eye on a *guanaco* at the back. Turning his head and spurring his horse, he built up momentum. Then, from a distance of about sixty yards, he threw the ball with all the strength of his arm. The impact intertwined the animal's back legs. It fell, tangled. "Ricardo, jump down. Bring your knife to cut its throat."

"Why cannot you do it, Xiemen?"

"You know how to kill animals humanely, Ricardo. We survive in Patagonia together."

'I did so, closing my eyes. But, I reflected, how could I have hoped to survive there without the companionship and the native skills of this invaluable Charrúa. That night we feasted on its juicy, tender and lean meat.'

'Keeping ourselves supplied with water was our greatest challenge. On our departure from the Rio Limay, we had attached some full drums of water to our own mounts and to our pack horses. We were adamant that we must economise on this precious substance. As the heat of summer moved towards the warmth of autumn, this became easier. Streams of water in Patagonia proved to be less abundant than on the pampas. Yet again Xiemen's innate knowledge of the properties of the soil proved invaluable for locating water. What a godsend this young Charrúa had proved to be.'

March 1879.

'A chance encounter with some government surveyors and six soldiers near the border of the province of Chubut had occurred. They had told us about a Franciscan mission, which we had now reached. I had succeeded in calming Xiemen's apprehension about visiting and working there. "The Charrúas refused to live in missions, and look at how they were punished," he warned.'

"Xiemen, we are going there as workers. If they try to convert you, we will depart secretly and silently during the night. But I do not think they will. According to Carlos, they do not even try to convert the local Indians. They leave that to the voice and hand of God."'

"Good, Ricardo, for no Catholic priest or friar is going to convert me. Remember that I am going to meet my murdered grandparents and my forebears in our Charrúa afterlife, in the land of the just where my grandparents wander."'

'Wooden buildings set in a beautiful valley. We could see the lake in the distance, nestled beneath the towering mountain slopes. As we approached a few bearded, brown-robed figures emerged from the buildings, sandals on their feet. One of them, Father Boniface, welcomed us effusively.'

"Brother Damian, show these two lads to their room. Allow them a *siesta*. Then give them the tour of our mission."

'On our tour, Brother Damian showed us the small chapel, kitchen, refectory, dormitory, some workshops and outbuildings.'

'On the evening of our second day there, Father Boniface outlined his community's aims and dreams for this sublime valley. "We are patiently forging a new land, which someday may well blossom and bloom into agricultural land, pastoral land, olive groves and maybe even vineyards. Yes, Patagonia is barren, arid, featureless. Yet God in his bounty has placed therein oases like this valley, awaiting only the hand of man to cultivate it and bring it to some degree of perfection. My community and I represent a new breed of men who, with the help of the local Indians, may well lay the seed of a larger secular community consisting of Indians, Creoles, immigrants. Together we will live in harmony, peace, and prosperity."

'My earlier worries about Xiemen's fears were groundless. He exulted in this new experience. Our accommodation in the guest room consisted of two beds and a few pieces of furniture. After our months in the saddle and camping out, this was heaven. The three hot meals a day saw our features reassuming a healthy and even youthful glow, and our weight increasing. Our diet consisted of bread, porridge, fruit, vegetables, cream, eggs, cheese. Meat was served three days a week, with wine served on Sundays. We had arrived in mid March, and within a few days informed Father Boniface that we would remain and work until Easter, which was on 20th April.'

'The rhythm of work was more novel and varied than that on the Sutton *estancia*. Brother Augustine had asked me to help with the grape harvesting. With a team of six Indians, after a week of tiring

353

labour, we had almost completed it. Our other work consisted of tending the sheep and cattle, milking the cows, picking and storing the fruit and vegetables. The drought which had devastated parts of the pampas had not cast its fearsome hand to any extent down here. Clouds from the Pacific ocean had brought almost sufficient rain over the Andes and into our valley. We also helped the brothers to construct some new outbuildings.'

'And so, our weeks slid by. Meals at regular times with the friars; the morning work period, the afternoon two-hour *siesta*, the late afternoon and early evening work period, the later evenings for rest and recreation. Brother Rodrigo was building up the community library, in which I immersed myself. As for Xiemen, he spent most of his evenings with the local Mapuche Indians. I would sometimes join him, for I loved to listen to their lore, hear their songs, play our instruments with them, and join in the children's games. And thus, we played our part in the construction of an oasis within the arid steppes of Patagonia.'

'So, did the Franciscans try to enlist me to their ranks or to convert Xiemen to Catholicism? I can honestly say that they did neither. Both of us were invited to join them for their twice daily chants of the Divine Office. The first was the office of prime at six in the morning, the second the office of Compline before they retired at night. I usually joined them for the latter, for it bestowed on me that peace of spirit. I would attend Mass usually twice a week, as well as Sundays, at which I accompanied the hymn singing on my fiddle. What impressed me most about the Franciscans was the joy they expressed in the beauty of God's creation, their care of the Indians, and their emphasis on justice to all people. Their simplicity and humble way of life presented an uplifting counterpoint to the sublime setting.'

'Xiemen too was most impressed by the friars' philosophy. Gradually he was drawn towards some of their religious practices. On the third Sunday after our arrival, he joined me for Compline. As the chant progressed, he appeared to become more immersed in the soothing rhythm of the psalm, the rise and fall of the predictable melody, and the beauty of the Latin. By the end of the third psalm, he was singing the Gloria Patri.'

'On our leaving the chapel, I stated, "Xiemen, you seem quite at home with the melodies of those chants."

"Why would I not be, Ricardo? Did they not write some of them them in the pentatonic scale, the scale of some *Indio* chants. My father said that some Charrúa chants also used that same scale. So, you see, *Amigo*, we were not uncivilised as the Uruguayan government made us out to be."

"They say that he has swept all before him. A young thirty-five-year-old general. Many Argentines regard him as a south American Napoleon, the saviour of civilisation in Argentina."

Richard listened to Mark the young Englishman in silence, during their special Easter Sunday dinner. But the news from those two pleasant and personable young English men had placed a damper on his happy feelings. *Gracias a dios*, Xiemen had dined with his

Indian friends, but Richard would tell him all this later. He tentatively asked Mark. "At what stage is Roca's campaign now?"

"His campaigns in La Pampa province are virtually over. His army marches towards the Rio Negro. Roca regards that as the natural frontier line of civilised Argentina. There will be no place for savage Indians north of that line."

Matthew, Mark's friend, now gave his opinion, "Part of the reason for the veneration of Roca is because his army has suffered so few losses. In January the military reported only about twenty soldiers dead or wounded, while it is estimated that the Indians have lost over five thousand, killed, wounded, or captured. Don't you think that that is a great achievement, Richard?"

He countered, "Roca's army uses Remington rifles against the Indians' slow loading guns and their traditional weapons. I cannot regard that as being fair in war."

Mark spoke, "Spoken like a true Irishman. But there is no fairness in war, Richard. To some extent I sympathise with you. But who can halt the march of civilisation against barbarism? Still, why do we discuss such matters on this joyful day? Yes, thank you, brother Damian, you can fill our glasses with your excellent Scotch whiskey. Will you not join us for one, or does your rule forbid you?"

"Normally it does, *Jovenes*, but today I am allowed."

Richard had one final question, "Do you think Roca will stop at the Rio Negro, or will he move south into this province?"

Brother Damian pondered, "I hope he will not. What benefit would it have for him or for Argentina to invade these barren wastes?

The Indians of Patagonia are generally peaceful. People like us, including you *Jovenes*, can transform this land with the ploughshare, as God intended. Let us hope and pray that General Roca will realise this and put the sword back in its sheathe."

Xiemen listened in silence. Matthew and Mark had not spoken of any massacres, but that did not mean that they had not taken place.

"What do you think, Xiemen? What should we do?"

"Ricardo, I think we should continue our journey. We both like Matthew and Mark, but Mark supports Roca. Sooner or later things could turn ugly between us and them, which could affect the peace of this mission. We did say that we would stay here for about a month. We can give father Boniface our notice, obtain our pay, and leave next week around the first of May."

Richard nodded. "I agree. Let us cross over into the Chubut province. Relations between the Welsh colonists and the Indians are reported to be good. Maybe we can work at an *estancia* down there for a couple of months. The Welsh in Chubut are semi-independent of the Argentine government. I doubt that Roca would bring his war down there."

"And if he does, Ricardo, what will we do?"

He was looking at Richard intensely. "I think that I will feel duty bound to join with my fellow Celts and to resist the invader."

Xiemen clasped Richard's hand with, "And I too will feel duty bound to join with my Mapuche Indian brothers and resist the invader, the tyrant, the murderer."

Another farewell to an assembled gathering. The whole community of friars, Matthew, Mark, and some Indians assembled at the mission gates to wish Richard and Xiemen *adios* and Godspeed. Father Boniface gave them Saint Christopher medals. They were also given a rough map, and advice to follow the river, which would lead them to the Chubut border. The estimated distance was around one hundred kilometres. Rested and refreshed, they made the border in three days. Richard felt elated at the prospect of meeting some fellow Celts again.

They move stealthily. No moon shines. A perfect night for the task ahead. Before them lie ten tents. The tents of 'peaceful Indians.' Bullshit. Such a thing does not exist. Their menfolk are away from this encampment, still futilely resisting the military. Only women, children, and some old people will be found here. The scar-faced soldier signals to his six soldier mates, his partners in crime. Hand picked men, experts with their daggers. Two men allocated to each tent.

Their leader orders, "Cut all their throats. I know that is too lenient for them. But they won't make a sound."

Within ten minutes the whole operation has been accomplished. But wait. Two soldiers are dragging an adolescent Indian girl from her tent, alive, another soldier covering her mouth. The girl could be described as comely and nubile, probably still a virgin. The soldiers' leers indicate their intentions. One soldier unbuckles his belt. But the scar-faced soldier strides up to him. A soldier addresses him.

"Do you want to go first, Jorge? You can break her in."

Fury pervades Jorge's face. "No, I do not, and neither will you. Do you want to mix your seed with that of a savage? Would you fuck a dog, or a pig, or a sheep? These savages are little more than animals."

The scar-faced soldier draws his knife, plunges it into the unfortunate girl's heart. He slowly withdraws the knife. Cleans it with some grass. Then orders. "Now, all of you. Back to our revered sub-lieutenant's camp."

'Another campfire. Another group of men who welcomed us into their midst, ten Welshmen and two Tehuelche Indians. As advised by the friars and aided by their maps, we had followed the course of the river, and had halted at a point where it was joined by two tributaries. Henry Jones, their surveyor, embraced me. "Welcome to our company, *Irlandés*, fellow Celt."'

'Other words of welcome included, "We welcome you as a brother. How fortunate we are to meet you and your friend."'

'"You will enjoy our full Welsh hospitality."'

"We call the Indians 'our brothers of the desert.' That is what Xiemen is now."'

'More handshakes, back slaps, and some more embraces. Two young Indians emerged from their tent and greeted Xiemen like a blood brother. No alcohol was forthcoming. These were temperate Welshmen from their colony in Rawson, all of them devout Congregationalists.'

'Over dinner Henry explained what they were doing so far from Rawson. "Our mission is two-fold. Our Tehuelche friends have told us of the existence of a few beautiful valleys in the north west of Chubut province, well watered and abundant in vegetation. These might prove suitable for a new Welsh settlement. However, our ultimate aim is the Andes themselves. Our party consists of myself, two soil specialists, five farmers, one carpenter with knowledge of medicine, and an orchardist. The two young Indians serve as our guides. We have followed the course of the Chubut river for most of our journey, about four hundred miles."'

'Our hunting next day proved successful and beneficial, Xiemen capturing and killing one *guanaco* and four hares. During dinner that night he was treated like an honoured guest. William Roberts, the orchardist, had brewed a special non-alcoholic mead using juices of fruits, berries and honey. He handed me a cup.

"Now, men, it is time for some music and singing. Richard, get your fiddle; Xiemen, your wind instrument; Omanda, your instrument."

'To my amazement, Omanda, the young Indian, emerged from his tent with an accordion. William enlightened me, "He learned to play it from Edward Richards. Did he not take to it like a duck to water? Second nature to him."

'The scene which followed would be repeated on many a night over the weeks which followed. Fourteen men around a campfire or an *asado*.'

'Well-fed from the spoils of the hunt and from the abundance of natural vegetation. Drinking tea, coffee, and at times mead. Three instrumentalists. Welsh and Irish airs, some Argentine songs, some Indian melodies and chants. But it was the sounds of those ten male Welsh singers which produced an upsurge in my spirits and brought me to a higher plane of aesthetics. Their voices blended in a natural and seemingly effortless harmony. Their ancient Celtic Welsh language touched a dormant chord within me. The deep sincerity of their singing, whether a depiction of their longing, their yearning, their *hiryath* (deep nostalgia) for their homeland, or in praise of the God who had bequeathed to them this new Wales, was to me unrivalled. The beauty of the valley seemed to imbue their singing with an added vein of glory and richness. And all beneath the silver moon in a Patagonian sky.'

'We were now following the course of a lesser river, travelling in a south west direction. Surprisingly, there were no trees on its sides as it wound its way through that valley. But the two soil specialists and the surveyors were pleased to see black soil there. On examination, they concluded that it could be as good as if not better than the soil in Rawson. Nonetheless, Omanda proclaimed, "Men of *Gales* (Wales), this is not the valley of our dreams. That is three days away. But this river will provide multitudes of ducks and fish, a welcome change to our diet."'

'We had reached the promised valley, and what an exquisite sight. Above it towered the mountains, now displaying first falls of snow.

The base of the valley was quite shallow, sprouting long lush grass, strawberry plants, flowers, and soil of rich black loam. As a bonus, the slopes of this valley possessed a multitude of trees. Henry Jones pronounced his verdict, "These slopes could feed at least fifteen thousand sheep. The valley is watered by a couple of streams. Our Indian friends confirm that most of the plants are edible, the wild black and red currant trees, watercress, rhubarb, raspberry and cherry trees. I estimate that the area of the valley is six miles by six miles. I am becoming convinced that we have found a potential new home."'

'It did not come as any real surprise. Albert Evans, a farmer, and the leader of the expedition, had asked us both to consider joining them to the Andes. "Both of you have skills which will be so useful to us. You, Richard, have a real understanding of horses, their sense, moods, ailments, treatment and cures. Xiemen, you understand weather, plants, animals, safer routes. You both are good living, decent, temperate lads, and all the men already have a great liking for ye. We will spend a few weeks exploring and working in the Andes. Following that we will return to this valley, and then head south to the Rio Senguer. From there north to *Paso de Indios* and finally home to Rawson. You can leave us at *Paso de Indio*s or accompany us on to Rawson. You have plenty of time to decide."'

'I did not intend to write in any detail about our expedition to the Andes. One of the Welshmen, Abraham Wynne, had been commissioned by the council in Rawson to write up a daily journal. Nonetheless, the new knowledge which Xiemen and I gained in such areas as soil, vegetation, weather patterns, searching for minerals could prove invaluable for us.'

'Our initial path was unclear. Stones which had rolled down from the mountains proved a hindrance. Boggy and springy soil, together with late autumn snow, proved hazardous for the horses. Indeed, at one time my own horse fell, trapping my legs beneath him. However, the soil turned out to be an advantage, as my friends quickly released me unhurt.'

'Our three *Indio* guides led us up a steep hill with firmer soil underfoot. The ground on the summit was rich, demonstrated by an abundance of vegetation and trees. Albert Evans addressed us, "We will camp here for a day in order to conduct some investigations. The farmers think that cereals can be grown on such soil. Hares are less abundant in this terrain, but *guanaco*s abound. Omandu has led a few of us to flocks of wild cattle which he reckons can be corralled and tamed."'

'The most challenging task for our team was finding the right path and keeping to it. Our leader had informed us that one of our aims was to arrive reasonably close to the Chilean border. Our guides favoured scaling the mountains covered with trees, for the latter offered protection from the cold and the wind. On some occasions, however, such forests proved impenetrable, causing us to retrace our steps. Omandu, Poyana, and Xiemen usually proved themselves competent in differentiating between *Indio* hunting paths and more permanent *Indio* paths. Our path on occasions took the form of a narrow track, sometimes with sheer drops into the abyss on our left side.'

'This led to the one tragic day on this expedition. We had reached a narrow path where Albert Evans advised us all to dismount. Robert Morgan, a likeable young lad, had an over-confident streak, and continued to ride ahead.'

"Come on, Albert. This path will be no problem to my champion, Tristan. I have ridden narrower paths by the Welsh coast when I was a boy."

'Albert called out, "Robert, the track is wet after last night's fall of snow. Can you not see the danger?"

"Albert, Tristan can see the danger, can't you, boy? We lo-."

'Tristan's rear legs were over the edge, the horse clawing desperately.'

"Robert, jump off," shouted Omandu.'

'He landed dangerously close to the edge. In an instant Omandu and two of the men were dragging him to safety.'

"Let me go to Tristan," he screamed.

"Tristan is gone, over the edge."

'By now the three men had him pinned to the ground. Robert continued to plead.'

"Robert," Omandu said, "He has fallen hundreds of feet. He will not have felt a thing."

'Robert struggled to break the men's hold. "But let me look over the edge and see him."

"No, Robert, you are coming with us."

'Gently but firmly the three men heaved him to his feet. The two Welshmen held him tightly until our track was clear of the abyss. On a patch of open ground, Robert sat down and wept bitterly. Tristan had been his closest companion. For now, we could only leave him to his tears.'

'For the rest of that day's journey, about ten kilometres, Robert insisted on walking alone. On arrival at our destination, he was still inconsolable. "How could I have done what I did? Why did I not walk, like the other men? No, I had to be the brave one, the adventurous one, the stupid one. I sentenced Tristan to a terrible death on those crags. I have lost my closest friend. It was all my stupid fault."'

'Xiemen and I sat on each side of him, gently massaging his arms and shoulders. Words were useless. That night we insisted that he sleep in our tent, our bodies placed between him and the tent's entrance, for we dreaded to think what he might do.'

'Robert Morgan did accept another mount next day, a mare which he named Isolde. During the ensuing days either Xiemen or I rode beside him. Remembering the incident of Malcolm's depression, I watched for any tell-tale signs. Robert's spirits seemed to rally somewhat. Most of the other men were in their thirties or forties, so initially Robert had appeared to be something of a loner. Xiemen and I took him under our wing. By the third night Robert was more at ease. I told him about my own life in Ireland and on the pampas, he listening mainly in silence. Before retiring, he came up with a profound statement, "You know, *Amigos*, it could have been me who accidentally went over the edge too. God must have had a purpose in watching over me and saving me. One good result is that I have found two new friends, the Irish lad and the young Charrúa."'

'Xiemen came up with another bright idea. "Ricardo, why don't you write about the Andes like you wrote about our journey through the pampas and Rio Negro. You composed some lovely descriptions of those regions."'

"That was fairly easy, Xiemen. Because the landscapes were so flat, I could focus on their other aspects. The Andes are towering, majestic, with streams and lakes intermingled, clouds descending and embracing the peaks. How could a mere mortal like me capture in words such ultimate beauty and magic? It needs a real poet to do it justice."'

"Richard, you have just convinced me with your initial description," Robert interjected.'

'I gave in. "Alright, I will try my hand, but please do not expect wonders."'

'It was as if the peak desired some recognition and comfort when a cloud descended to enfold it in its caress. A white cloud denoting sunshine; a dark cloud foreshadowing rain; a grey cloud threatening to clad us and our surroundings in a canopy of drizzle, and a crimson cloud promising a glorious day ahead.

> *The towering peak accepts the cloak of cloud*
> *As a monarch accepts his mantle.*
> *Last night the cloud was crimson-lay,*
> *The promise of a glorious day.'*

'And yet it was during our struggles through mist and fog that I felt we were not alone. A rustle of the vegetation, a whisper, a bird-like call, all convinced me that the ancient people of the Andes were there, concealing themselves, observing our progress, our difficulties, our successes. Our two *Indio* guides were reassuring.'

"If there are *Indio*s there, they are just curious. They see that we are not military. We are well dressed, clean-shaven. Our guns are for hunting only. The good Welsh reputation has gone before us."'

'The bright Andean blue sky shielded us like a benevolent canopy, giving me the sensation of being only footsteps from Heaven itself. The morning dew manifested itself with sparkles on the grass, as if Heaven had sent down emeralds and rubies to enrich our odyssey. As we rode through valleys and plains, we were welcomed by a rich tapestry of green grass and green undergrowth, interspersed with the bloom of Andean flowers which formed multicoloured veins. When I looked upwards, I observed the perfect harmony of the pure white snow on the peaks against the exquisite blue sky.'

The blue Andean sky, a bright benevolent shield,
In harmony with the snowy peaks.
Sparkling dew-drops like precious jewels in valley and plain,
Wildflowers on a tapestry of green in veins of multi-colour.

'Lakes of emerald blue, smaller lakes of emerald green; some mountain peaks irregular and rugged, others shaped like symmetrical cones. Stretches of rocky paths testing the endurance of our mounts, and boulders for them to circumvent. Our horses wade through cold rivers, interspersed with cascades. They circumvent lakes. We wend our way through the sanctuaries of warm forests, reassured by the calls of animals and birds. Our hopes rise that the forests will not yield to impenetrable barriers.'

We rode our mounts on rocky paths past lakes of blues and
  greens.
Crossed icy rivers, tall cascades. We skirted deep ravines.
In warm tree-lined sanctuary we heard the wild birds call,
In hope that forest pathways might not lead us to the wall.

'On the advice of our two guides, by mid June we had returned to the enchanted valley, albeit by a different route. The expedition had largely fulfilled its aim. There had been no serious accidents or illnesses since the tragic death of Tristan, but all of us were now tired.

Albert Evans addressed us, "We will camp here for three days, our only task being to hunt for food. We will then travel south east to reach what is known as the curve in the Rio Senguer, about two hundred miles away, an estimated ten to fifteen days journey. The terrain, although initially hilly, will gradually give way to flatter land. A further one hundred and sixty kilometres should see us arriving at Paso de *Indio*s. Richard, are you and Xiemen willing to travel that distance with us?"'

'We needed little convincing. Our growing friendship with Robert and his need for our support was the deciding factor.'

'Robert had read my descriptions and reflections on the Andes. He now requested that I show him what I had written on our journey through the pampas, as well as my observations as a shepherd. Eventually he pronounced his verdict. "I like your descriptions of the

Andes, *amigo*. However, you do not capture their true spirit and magic quite as well as you do when describing your journey through the pampas. But you excel in your descriptions and impressions of your solitary life as a shepherd. There you were one with your surroundings. Richard Barron, you are the Irish shepherd poet. Indeed, you are a true bard on the pampas.'"

Paso de Indios, Late June 1879.

Richard, Xiemen and Robert were conversing with four farmers from Lancashire, inspecting land viable for settlement. Having ridden through La Pampa province, they were familiar with General Roca's campaign. He had marched as far as the Rio Negro in May 1879, and had established that same river as the present boundary of the Argentine state. Inside this boundary the Creole population would be forever free from "the barbarians of the desert."

Allan, one of the men, spoke. "I hope the war has now ended. Roca intends to move all the pampas Indians to the concentration camps."

"Where will the *Indio*s who disobey obey that order go to, Allan," Xiemen asked. "They will flee across the Rio Negro to Rio Negro province," Allan replied.

Martin, another Lancashire man, joked, "Who would want Patagonia anyway except some mad Welsh people?"

"So the *Indio*s in Rio Negro and Chubut will be safe down here?" Robert asked.

"I would think and hope so," Allan assured them. "I do not really approve of Roca's methods, but he is a brilliant general. He regards the Rio Negro as the natural frontier line. With the *Indio* problem solved, the Argentine state will need only three or four forts along it. The width and depth of the river will deter any *Indio*s from the south from attacking the Creoles to the north."

Next day, Edward, another Lancashire lad, spoke privately to the three lads. "On our way down here, in Rio Negro province, we met a group of military and surveyors. They had concluded a favourable examination of the soils. Patagonia, they declared, is rich in mineral resources, possibly oil. Certain newspapers are declaring that all the lands south of the Rio Negro belong to the Argentine Republic, and one surveyor hinted that Roca is of the same mind."

"And the *Indio*s, what is to be their fate?" Xiemen asked.

Edward replied. "The impression we got from those Creoles was that the *Indio*s of Rio Negro province are more civilised than those in La Pampa, and that Creole and *Indio* can live in peace there."

Richard replied, "I am not so sure. Xiemen and I have witnessed some terrible things done to the *Indio*s north of the Rio Negro. Greed and avarice can drive even good men to barbarous acts."

Edward departed. Xiemen seemed determined. "Ricardo, I feel that we must go back now. We can warn the *Indio*s of Rio Negro, advise them, even help them."

"And fight for them, if necessary, Xiemen?"

"I, Ricardo, am prepared to fight for them. You, *Amigo*, do not have to."

"Xiemen, wherever you go, I will follow. Now will be my chance to prove that I am indeed an adopted Charrúa."

'Another farewell. This one the most sincere and poignant since our leaving the Sutton *estancia*. A special dinner the previous night, copious draughts of mead, and the songs. Those beautiful and glorious Welsh songs and hymns emanating from the very souls of their vocalists. Even when we both rode back through the steppes of Chubut and Rio Negro provinces, I cast my mind back to that night. The memory of their evocative singing raised my spirits, the occasional tear in my eye. I felt blessed that that on this odyssey we had become part of two groups of good, God-fearing, and Christian men, the Franciscan friars, and those Welsh colonists of Chubut. Our journey to Patagonia had more than served all our intended purposes.'

'Furthermore, we had helped to save our new friend Robert from severe melancholia or even worse. We both had bade him an emotional farewell. We now looked forward to eventually arriving at our Sutton home, even though for the moment it could have been on another continent.'

'Our journey to the Andes had revealed to me parallels with my own inner being. I could see how Andean physical features had similarities with my own private fears, inclinations, and longings. The Andean fog always eventually cleared, fully restoring my sight. But my own fog of self doubt never cleared. Would it at times rear its ugly head to torment me, to interrupt my normal feeling of happiness?'

'I longed to climb that snow-capped mountain, to gaze at the exquisite beauty from its summit. Yet, I knew that this vista would be permanently withheld from me. I might enjoy the sanctuary of the warm and welcoming forest. However, it would always lead to the impenetrable barrier, impossible to break through. The emerald blue lake tempted me to swim and explore its hidden waters. But that could lead to a fate worse than death, and the loss of all that I held dear. I must remain content with the life, the faith, and the deep friendships which sustained me. My feelings of love must remain my dark secret.'

Chapter 19.

"Your Destiny Must be Fulfilled."

Richard felt strangely at peace. He had completed a three-day retreat at the Franciscan mission. A time of prayer, contemplation, meditation, attending Prime, Mass, and Compline each day. Richard had had private uplifting conferences with Father Augustine.

Xiemen chided him a little. "Why have you made this retreat? Are you thinking of joining? Please be honest."

A moment's hesitation, Richard looked him in the face. "I am determined to fight with the *Indio*s of Rio Negro, if they are attacked. Who knows what the result will be. I hope and pray that conflict will not occur. But I have a foreboding. My soul is now clean. Please make sure, *Amigo Amado*, as my guardian angel, that I do not fall by the wayside between now and the *Indio* region."

Xiemen laughed. "You do not need me for that task, *Amigo*. What opportunities will there be for you to fall in the deserts of Patagonia?"

July 1879.

An impressive conference held about one hundred kilometres south of the Rio Negro, by the confederation of Mapuche and Tehuelche *Indio* people. Eight major *caciques*, led by Valentine Saygueque. Each *cacique* commanded around one hundred warriors, smaller divisions within these being led by lesser chiefs. Word had reached them from their spies that Roca was not going to halt at the Rio Negro. Should they fight as a united front, in divided units, or should they negotiate? Richard and Xiemen had been invited to attend the conference.

Sayqueque addressed the assembled company: "For many years I have sought peace and conciliation with the Argentine government in the interests of my people. I have forged the great alliance between the Mapuche and the Tehuelche peoples, for our mutual protection. Witness this great gathering as proof. Yes, I know that terrible things have been done to the *Indio*s of the pampas. But General Roca holds the *Indio*s of Patagonia in high regard. The numbers of our tribes are decreasing due to, among other reasons, many of them fleeing across to Chile. By choosing peace and security, our numbers will increase."

A chief raised his hand, "What about the delegation of our men whom you sent to represent our cause to Barros, the governor of Patagonia? What has been their fate?"

Saygueque hesitated, stumbling his words. "I regret to say that they have been detained by Governor Barros."

A murmur arose. "Detained, and how have they been treated?" the chief queried.

"I must admit that they have been tortured."

"Tortured! That is how the Creoles treat our delegates."

The cries of rage had risen to a swell. "This is war. Let us show Barros our mettle. Death to the Christian."

Saygueque called for calm. "I have sent another letter to Governor Barros requesting that he free the delegates and let them negotiate with the government in Buenos Aires."

The same chief stood up. "And his reply?"

Saygueque's face fell. "I have not received a reply yet."

"He used your stupid letters to wipe his arse. We have heard enough from this useless *cacique*. To arms, brothers."

A lesser chief spoke. "What about that letter you received last week from Colonel Villegas?"

Xiemen gasped, "Villegas, that Uruguayan!"

Richard signalled him to hush.

Saygueque spoke confidently. "He addressed me as *Governor of Las Manzinas, chief don Valentin Saygueque*. He wrote about our true friendship. All he asked was that I try and persuade you *caciques*, especially *cacique* Purran, to respect and welcome his column when it crosses the border to our province. I tell you on my honour that Colonel Villegas does not want any bloodshed, only peace and friendship."

The assembled company responded, "Peace and friendship, my arse! What else did he say?"

A young chief spoke, "We have our own spies north of the river. Four of our spies captured an *Indio* spy working for Villegas. We threatened to flay him alive, and, I admit, tortured him a little, obtaining from him the advice he gave Villegas. Villegas told the traitor *Indio* that he would write to you, warning you that by now he knew all about the *Indio* methods of fighting, that he had thousands of men and horses, and that he would defeat and destroy us even if we were joined by all the *Indio*s from Chile."

An absolute uproar.

"Is that true, *cacique*? Why did you not tell us?"

Visibly shaken, Saygueque' face had turned ashen. "I have to admit it is. That is why I so much want peace and reconciliation. What hope do we have?"

A young *Indio* called out. "And, comrades, what did you do with the traitor afterwards?"

The young chief replied. "We slit his throat. He hardly felt a thing." Laughter and cheers followed.

With some difficulty, *Cacique* Saygueque assumed control of the meeting.

"Colonel Villegas has invited all the *caciques*, and a hundred of our best warriors to a formal peace conference. This will take place on the plain of La Serena near the Canyon de Las Pumas, about a day and a half's ride from here. The colonel says that the excellent terms of the treaty will be revealed there. He and I, two renowned leaders, will meet face to face."

Another voice. "How many soldiers will he have?"

"Because he wants us to feel safe, he will bring only twenty soldiers."

A chief stood up. Striking features. Captivating eyes.

"That is *cacique* Purran," Xiemen whispered.

Purran addressed the assembly. "I do not like the idea of a meeting near a canyon. Xiemen, our young guest, has told me the story of the treacherous betrayal and resultant deaths of his people, the Charrúas of Uruguay, who had been invited to a peace conference."

Saygueque queried, "So, what do you suggest, *Cacique* Purran?"

"I propose that both you and I, *Cacique* Saygueque, write to Colonel Villegas. We shall say that this province of Rio Negro, and indeed all of Patagonia, is our land. Yes, we will tell him that we too desire friendship and peace, mentioning the strength of our warriors. We are willing to negotiate a lasting peace, but in a place of our choosing. We will invite his delegation, each of us bringing a similar number of warriors and representatives or soldiers, to an *asado*. Our chosen place for the treaty and the *asado* will be on a great plain. *Cacique* Saygueque will welcome Colonel Villegas as the leader of the Argentine delegation. Will you not, *cacique*?"

All eyes moved to *cacique* Saygueque, who announced, "You are right, *Cacique* Purran. That is what we will do." A rousing unanimous cheer. Richard beamed at Xiemen. "Well done, *Amigo*. Fate has guided us here."

Colonel Villegas addressed the captains, majors, lieutenants, and sub-lieutenants. "Gentlemen, it is decided. General Roca has ordered me to send six platoons, three hundred soldiers across the river into Rio Negro province. You must note that this is not a military operation, but simply a military expedition. Let me explain."

Villegas recounted what Richard, Xiemen, and the assembled Indians had already heard about the conference and the invitation to the *asado*.

"And his reply?" queried a sub-lieutenant.

"*Cacique* Saygueque and *cacique* Purran rejected the invitation."

"Why, Colonel?"

"They said that they would be happy to meet us, but in a place of their choosing. They named a different plain in Rio Negro where we would conduct negotiations and they would host us to an *asado* on that plain. They will supply the cattle, other food, and all the drink. I feel that it is Purran who is behind this idea. Furthermore, they had the effrontery to imply that they are lords of the Patagonian plains and that we, while welcome, are intruders. Our President and General Roca are adamant that the Argentine State should extend down to Tierra del Fuego. We can do this in co-operation with the Indians."

The military expedition was about to depart. Colonel Villegas emphasised that its main objective was to sound out the general situation in Rio Negro, to ascertain the military strength of the *Indio* confederation, and to investigate the mountain passes into Chile. In answer to Sub-Lieutenant Ramirez's question whether the army should prevent the *Indio*s crossing over into Chile, the answer was a firm "Yes," from Villegas. "As long as such escape routes are available, the less likely are the *Indio*s willing to negotiate."

Ramirez persisted. "And, Colonel, if non-combatant *Indio*s are fleeing, should we kill them?"

"Only if deemed necessary by platoon leaders, Sub-Lieutenant."

"And, Colonel, what if their warriors fight back?"

Villegas laid down the law. "Violence must be met with violence. Our brave soldiers must defend themselves."

The young lieutenant, recently promoted from the rank of sub-lieutenant, looked up at the full Patagonian moon. Its light beamed down, calming, benevolent, serene. Both his platoon and that of lieutenant Enrique Lopez were camped about one hundred kilometres south of the Rio Negro. To date they had not encountered any opposition. However, their *Indio* spies had advised them that those low hills twenty kilometres away contained tracks leading to the lower slopes of the Andes, perfect escape routes to Chile. The passes had to be taken and blocked. Early next morning both platoons would make their move.

Richard Barron and his great friend Xiemen sat in the *Indio* warrior camp on the hills, the location named *Sitio de Guanacos*. Chief Zolastan had watched for two days the two Argentine platoons camped below. He had that night ordered that tomorrow his forty warriors should take up positions on the highest points on the range of hills. Should the enemy move towards the hills, the old men, the women and the children must immediately escape through the passes. Zolastan's warriors would defend the hills at all cost.

Zolastan spoke. "Xiemen and Ricardo, I want you both to defend this peak, together with four other warriors. Two men take up positions behind each of the three rocks. You two sons of the fine moon are champions with your rifles, perfect for this high point. Remember that many Argentine officers admire the bravery of us *Indio*s. So, if one of you is running to help another warrior, make sure to hold up a white flag. The enemy usually respects that and will not fire. Also, if both men behind one rock are killed or wounded, one man from an adjoining rock should run to take their place."

Richard and Xiemen too gazed up at the Patagonian moon. They sat in silence, for each knew what tomorrow might bring. Xiemen could not hold back any longer. "Ricardo, you do not have to do this. This is our fight, not yours. You are free to leave, to return to the *estancia*, to David, Malcolm, Catalina, and their little boy."

"No, Xiemen. It is my fight. I fight for the rights and freedom of persecuted and dispossessed peoples worldwide. I fight to try and prevent massacres, to defend the down-trodden. I fight to avenge the Charrúas, the *Indio*s of the pampas, the Scottish, the Irish. Those Creoles camped down there are the invader of the *Indio* homeland. The invader cannot be content with what he has taken by force and by murder. He must always strive to take more. I am not trying to be a hero, but at times we must fight for those we love and what we love."

A pause, in which both lads fought to hold back their tears. Richard regained his composure. "Xiemen, I have had a good life. A good home in Ireland, surrounded by so much love and affection from my family, close neighbours, and teachers. My love of and my skill with horses. The gift of music. The affection of the Sutton family. But most of all I count myself so lucky for the deep and everlasting bonds of friendship between myself and three other people – my foster brother Patrick, my great friend Malcolm Sutton, and finally with you, Xiemen, last of the proud and indomitable Charrúa race. I think of destiny which brought me to this great land of Argentina, to the pampas which enfolded me in their embrace and in effect became my spouse, and to your *Indio* tribe which welcomed me as a son and a brother. Most important of all, my peace is made with God. I am ready to flee to his forgiveness and his embrace, if that should be my final destiny tomorrow.

"One more thing I must say. Even though I never knew my mother, I do not for one moment feel that she abandoned me. It was really she who bestowed on me the gift of life and music. If she had kept me in Ireland, what terrors of famine and fever might we both have faced. The hand of fate brought me to bounteous Argentina, to the pampas which I have loved beyond measure, which inspired me to write some reasonable poetry. It brought me to the towering and majestic Andes mountains. To my mother, wherever she is, I send to her my deepest love and devotion. If, by the minutest chance, she ever gets to read my words, let her be consoled by my beautiful life, and, if God ordains it, by my heroic death. And I know that we shall meet up in the furthest Heaven, the Christian Heaven or the Charrúa after life."

"Therefore, Xiemen, if you survive me. I ask you to do one thing for me, if it is possible. I entrust you to bring back my pocket watch, my horse, especially my journal, and my fiddle to the Sutton *estancia*. No, please, I do not wish to see any tears from you. We will face this battle together, as my forebears did at the Boyne and at Aughrim."

"Ricardo, your heart is as brave and valiant as that of a Charrúa warrior. Wait a few minutes." Xiemen returned with some blue paint-like substance in a bowl and some cloth. He removed his own shirt, advising Richard to do the same. "Some of my Charrúa forebears painted their skin, Ricardo, as they prepared for battle. Would you like me to do the same thing on your chest?"

Richard nodded. Xiemen dipped the cloth in the substance, applied it to his own chest, and daubed some diagrams thereon. He repeated the action on his friend's chest. Finally, Xiemen held up his knife.

"See this knife. With it I will mix and mingle our bloods together, two Charrúa brothers and warriors to the end. I will cut my own hand first, then yours, and join them together at the wound. Thus, our blood, Charrúa and Irish, will unite. Your blood will imbue me with the bravery and resistance of your Barron forebears. My blood will imbue you with the indomitability of the noble and always undefeated Charrúas. *Somos hermanos hasta el final.*" (We are brothers to the end).

After a moment, Xiemen broke the silence. "Ricardo, those thoughts you have expressed are beautiful. You must write them in your journal immediately. If anything happens to you, either here or on our journey home, they will be there for others to read. Richard Barron, friend and champion of the down-trodden and the dispossessed."

"Well, my friend Xiemen, I do have to admit that that is how I would like to be remembered."

Both Argentine platoons make their way unhindered across the plain towards the foothills of the Andes. On approaching them, paths come into view. The paths skirt three large rocks, about five metres apart, on the summit of a hill. The two young lieutenants consult each other. They must take those three rocks and set up camp on the summit.

The platoons begin their ascent. Cautiously. Quietly. No sign of any enemy.

Four hundred metres from summit.

Three hundred.

Approaching two hundred.

A rifle shot from behind a large rock. A soldier lying wounded beside his horse. Both lieutenants give the command. "Sabremen. Draw your sabres. Shoot directly at the rocks."

Heads emerge from behind rocks. A volley of rifle shots, spears, *boleadoras* aimed at the sabremen. Another soldier lies wounded on the ground.

The young lieutenant commands, "*Rifleros*, right flank move to right of rocks, left flank to left. Centre flank, retain your position."

The *Indio* defenders become confused. One defender of the large middle rock is struck by a rifle shot from the left flank. The second defender falls to a bullet from the right-attacking flank. What is this? The young lieutenant, part of the central flank, sees a defender of the rock to the left running to the middle large rock to take their places. A shot. The running man drops his rifle, grasping his side. He staggers towards the front of the middle rock and collapses. The young lieutenant gasps. He is a white man. What on Earth is he doing here?

A young *Indio* holding a white flag aloft bravely runs from the right rock to a position in front of the wounded white man. The young lieutenant calls, "Cease all firing, *rifleros*. Sabremen, halt your advance. We must respect the flag of truce." The young lieutenant himself has by now almost reached the middle rock. All firing from both sides ceases.

"A white man fighting with and for those savages!"

The young lieutenant turns to see, four metres to his right, a scar-faced soldier, pistol in hand, who shouts, "Fuck me, it is that Barron bastard. No surprise there. That fucking Barron bastard. Let me have the honour of finishing him off. But first I will put a bullet in that *Indio*." He raises the pistol.

The lieutenant commands. "Put down that pistol. Our military code forbids us to shoot a wounded enemy soldier or an *Indio* carrying a white flag. I command you."

But the scar-faced man primes the pistol. "Fuck what our military code says, and fuck you as well, Álvarez." He pulls the trigger. But no shot erupts. By a miracle the pistol has jammed. By now the lieutenant is wresting the pistol from his hands. It drops to the ground. It explodes. His furious fist smashes into the face of the scar-faced man, who falls on the ground.

He calls. "Juan, Santiago, this soldier, Jorge, is under arrest for insubordination. Take two other soldiers with you and place him under constant guard at the bottom of this hill. I will deal with him later. You are all witnesses to his actions."

The lieutenant speaks, "Young *Indio*, you are safe now. Rarely have I seen such bravery and courage on the battle field, when you shielded your friend. But that Jorge called the wounded man Barron. Is that his name? Is he English or American?"

"Neither, lieutenant. My great friend is Irish. And his name is Richard Barron. My name is Xiemen."

The lieutenant queries. "Irish. Is he a Catholic?"

"Yes, lieutenant, and a very good Catholic."

The lieutenant commands. "Leo, go and get Father Alonso immediately. Miguel, fetch one of the doctors. He may be bleeding to death. Xiemen, pass me your shirt. We can try bandaging his wounds, but I think they are fatal. Hold up his head to prevent him choking in his own blood."

The lieutenant questions, "Xiemen, do you know which part of Ireland he came from?"

"Yes, *Señor,* From a region called county Kilkenny."

The lieutenant gives a start. "My mother's maiden name was Barron. She too was from county Kilkenny. This man is possibly a very distant kinsman of mine. He will be given every help and respect."

Father Alonso has arrived. He whispers the act of contrition into the ear of the wounded man. There follows the recitation of the prayers of extreme unction, the laying of his hands on the man's head, the anointing with the oils, the final blessing. The priest turns to Xiemen, "Whatever happens to his body now, his soul is cleansed of any sin. If he dies, he will go straight to God. I do not agree with the cause for which he fought, but I respect him as a brave and noble young man. Ah, the doctor has arrived. Maybe he can work the miracle."

The agonising groans of the dying man. More bandages. Some potions applied to the wound. The doctor declares, "The bullet wound is too deep. Even if I could extract it, I cannot stem the flow of blood. But continue to hold his head, Xiemen."

The wounded man gives some convulsions. The doctor speaks. "He is slipping away from us. He cannot have long now. Xiemen, whisper to him. He may be able to hear you."

"Ricardo, my ever-true friend, can you hear me? I am here beside you, here to the end. I do not want you to die. Please, Ricardo, try with all your might to live. You are too beautiful to die. Yet know that the priest has given you the last Christian rituals. A distant kinsman of your is here with us. Your soul will speed to your God in your Heaven. It will voyage to the land of the just. Your death is only a journey to the afterlife, to *Igua*. There the great and good Charrúa god Tupa will welcome you to the green and broken plains where my Charrúa forebears wander. Brave Ricardo, you will chase the deer and the feathery ostriches, and enjoy the peace of the hunt."

A gentle hand from Lieutenant Marcelo Álvarez touches Xiemen's arm. "I am not sure whether he heard you. I saw no flicker in his eyes."

"Then," I will sing to him." As he sings, he holds his beloved friend's head. *Al nostril monti ritorneremo. L'antica pace ivi godremo. Tu canterai sul tuo liuto, In sonno placido io dormiro.* The eyes of the dying man flicker slightly. This continues at intervals.

Riposa, Ricardo, io prono muto. Lamente al cielo rivolgero. Tu canterai, sul tuo liuto in sonno placido io dormiro. A beatific smile crosses the dying man's lips. The young *Indio* struggles to continue.

Marcelo places his hand on his shoulder. "Continue to the end, Xiemen. He hears you."

La mente al cielo rivolgero. Riposa, Ricardo, riposa, Ricardo. Xiemen feels the hand tightening slightly on his hand. *Riposa, Ricardo. La mente al cielo, rivolgero. La mente al cielo rivolgero.* Xiemen sobs. "He has gone. I am sure he has gone. I felt his hand tighten on mine as I neared the end. Then I felt it relax."

The doctor checks the heart, the pulse, some other locations. He nods to the small group. Standing around the dead man are his distant relative, doctor, priest, the young *Indio*, and six soldiers. The *Indio* has requested a couple of minutes alone to mourn. They respectfully withdraw a few metres away. He goes into a form of trance, as he sends his friend's soul to the abode of the Charrúas across the great plains. He intones phrases in the Charrúa language, both spoken and at times in a chant. Yet he does not weep. Ricardo has died fighting like a fearless Charrúa, and in keeping with the valour of his Barron forebears. It will be up to the young *Indio* to ensure that the story of the hero will live on. The skirmish had ended. The *Indio* fighters have retreated further into the foothills. All is peaceful and tranquil.

Lieutenant Marcelo Barron Álvarez takes hold of the situation. "Xiemen, we will bury Ricardo in a suitable piece of ground close by. He will sleep under the Patagonian sky and resplendent moon. His grave will be marked with a cross. Our surveyor will make a map of its location. This is in case any of his friends and you yourself ever wish to erect a headstone. Do you agree with all this?"

Xiemen through his tears replies. "Of course, Lieutenant Marcelo. We could not have asked for more. You are a very noble person. Father Alonso, will you conduct the burial service?"

"Indeed I will. I will be honoured."

Xiemen speaks. "Lieutenant Marcelo, it is important that I tell you that Ricardo wrote a journal. In it he wrote about his early life in Ireland."

Marcelo quickly asks. "Where is it?"

"It is with his belongings on his horse, tied to a tree about two hundred metres in that direction. I can go and fetch it."

The soldier Alejandro interrupts, "Lieutenant, this young *Indio* could be trying to escape. You cannot let him go there."

Marcelo quietly answers. "I did not realise that he is our prisoner. I never arrested him or ordered such."

"Alright, but can four of us accompany him? He could be leading us into a trap. We should tie his hands."

Xiemen proudly stands up, "Lieutenant Marcelo, I must here and now declare that I am not an *Indio* of the pampas or of Patagonia. I am a Charrúa of the Banda Oriental, as are both my parents, one of the few remaining Charrúas, for reasons which I will not tell now. I give you my word that I as a Charrúa would never stoop to such treachery. Two soldiers can walk before me, two behind me, but they will not tie my hands. I will carry the white flag. I am sealed by my promise to Ricardo that I will retrieve his journal, his fiddle, and his great-grand father's pocket watch."

Marcelo commands. "You four soldiers escort our young Charrúa to their horses. You other two soldiers, I ask you to locate a suitable site for the grave."

The body, wrapped in a shroud, is lowered into the deep grave. The priest reads the burial service. The dead will rise again on the resurrection of the last day. The dead Irish soldier wears the crucifix which has been blessed by Pope Pius IX. Rosary beads are interlaced among his hands. At the young *Indio's* request, his gun and a few of his personal effects will accompany him across the great plains. His head faces the Andes mountains. Some other soldiers, mostly of Irish-Argentine parentage, have joined the service. They recite a decade of the rosary, followed by Marcelo Álvarez leading them in the haunting Irish ballad, *Shule Aroon*, a lament for the Irish Wild Geese. Marcelo places his arm around the shoulders of young Xiemen, as the body is covered with the soil of Patagonia. Then the latter places over the grave the wooden cross, on which he has carved the words, *Richard Barron, born in County Kilkenny Ireland, in 1847. Died, a hero in battle on 30th August 1879. RIP.*

Marcelo Álvarez gazes intently at the year of birth. The year his mother Catherine Barron migrated to Buenos Aires.

As the group walks back to the rocks, Marcelo asks, "Xiemen, you sang *Home to our Mountains* from the Verdi opera *Il Trovatore*. Where did you learn that?"

"Lieutenant, I learned it from Ricardo. He used to play it beautifully on his violin. He loved especially the arias of Verdi, Bellini, and Donizetti."

"Xiemen, so did my mother. She used to play them on the piano. There must have been a musical gene in the wide Barron clan. Xiemen, I know that no one else can ever replace Ricardo for you. Can I, as his distant kinsman, offer my services and my protection to you on your journey back to Buenos Aires?"

The young Charrúa Xiemen was a guest in the tent adjoining that of Lieutenant Marcelo Álvarez. He shared the tent with six of the soldiers, his protectors, who had helped bury his friend. Few of their platoon disagreed with or condemned this. Many of them had witnessed Xiemen's outstanding acts of bravery, and empathised with his irretrievable loss. The renegade Jorge remained under guard, due to be escorted to Neuquen next day. In a letter to Colonel Villegas Marcelo made it clear that he no longer wished him to be part of his platoon. It would be up to Villegas to handle the matter.

By candlelight, Marcelo immersed himself in Richard's diary. Until the death of her beloved husband two years prior, Catherine Álvarez had revealed little of her childhood or early years in Ireland to her own children. It had been sufficient for her to state that the Great Famine had left an horrendous imprint on her memory, recollections which she tried to block from her mind. Having read Father Fahy's glowing accounts about Argentina in Catholic newspapers, that great land had beckoned. And look at how her decision had been rewarded. She could not have asked for a better life anywhere.

Ironically it had been Marcelo's expressed wish to pursue a military career which had caused Catherine Álvarez to reveal some of the Barron family's illustrious lineage: their arrival in Ireland as English Normans, Burnchurch castle, the dispossession, the Boyne, Aughrim and Limerick, and a little about her own branch This information motivated Marcelo even further, and caused his father to cease any opposition to his son's military career. Marcelo ruminated on how he himself and his distant Barron kinsman, Richard, had fought on different sides in this conflict.

Following her husband's death, Catherine Alzvarez had opened up more to Marcelo about her early years in Ireland. "My reasons are that far in the future, when I am dead and gone, a couple of my children or grandchildren might wish to make a journey back to their ancestral homeplace, where they would be made most welcome."

She told Marcelo about the location of her home, their small farm. More importantly Catherine imparted to Marcelo the names of her ancestors and immediate family. At the end of her revelations, Catherine made Marcelo solemnly promise one thing: he would never write to or contact any member of his family in Castledown without her expressed permission. He did wonder at times, however, whether there was more than the Great Famine which led to her decision to emigrate. After all, disputes between family members were common.

The lines in Richard's diary slowly increased Marcelo's suspicions. Born in Castledown in July 1847 to Andrew and Mairead

Barron, Richard had then written that his aunt Catherine had emigrated to New York in September of that year, that she was a governess and an accomplished pianist. Was this aunt Catherine a cousin of Marcelo's mother? Sometimes cousins shared Christian names. But why had his mother not told Marcelo of Richard's existence, and of her cousin Catherine? Amazingly, both Catherines had been governesses and accomplished pianists. Anyway, could this mean that Richard was his cousin?

Marcelo continued to read. Richard began to voice his own suspicions that Andrew and Mairead were not his actual parents. But it was the appearance of the mysterious dark brown-haired man which arrested Marcelo's attention. The visit to Richard's bedside when he lay on point of death; the memorable St. Stephen's Day at the Heffernans in 1858; the unexpected presents on occasions, and the anonymous parting gift of five pounds. And finally, Richard had described his final farewell to his father at the Club House Hotel, and his father's nervous answer to Richard's question about his true parentage, reassuring him that he was a true Barron. Why, he had even cited Richard's aunt Catherine's prowess with music as being bequeathed to Richard. Was all this an indication of Richard's true parentage? Was Richard's 'aunt Catherine' and Marcelo's mother one and the same person?

Marcelo could not bring himself to think about what all this implied. His own mother, a paragon of virtue. Could it mean that Richard had been his half-brother. And, if so, his platoon had killed him. But calm yourself, Marcelo. It was war, a form of civil war. In civil wars brothers, cousins, fathers, sons, had found themselves fighting on opposing sides. Marcelo had had no inkling that a man fighting for the Indians might be a cousin, let alone a half brother. He needed a glass of whiskey, and he persuaded Xiemen to join him.

Why did Richard state and believe that his aunt Catherine had migrated to New York? Maybe her family had chosen that as her destination, but she had decided differently. Immediately the possible reason struck Marcelo. They needed to hide from Richard his mother's true destination. But why had Richard not been offered America as a destination? An obvious answer: to whom would he have migrated but to his aunt Catherine, who did not exist there? Instead, they had offered him the furthest shore of Australia, where he had no relatives or family members. But that did not explain Richard's migration to Argentina.

"Xiemen, do you know how and why Richard ended up in Argentina?"

"Marcelo, he was meant to go to Australia. But by complete chance he met Malcolm Sutton in a public house in Wexford, and that changed everything. I suggest that you continue reading."

Richard had glossed over any events which led up to his departure from Ireland, but had continued his fairly detailed account of the change of destination and his journey to the Argentine.

Three days after the skirmish Marcelo and Xiemen departed for Neuquen. By prior agreement Marcelo left the rest of his platoon under the command of his sub-lieutenant. He himself would commence his well earned and long overdue leave of service.

Marcelo, Xiemen, and their military escort would travel to Buenos Aires, initially by horse, and later by train. Marcelo felt a certain euphoria at the prospect of his long leave. Far less attractive, however, was the prospect of the questions which he knew he would need to ask his mother.

Marcelo Álvarez would always be surprised by the ease with which Colonel Vilegas granted him Xiemen's release. The former described the battle, Richard's death, and the honourable Catholic funeral. Marcelo's trump card was Xiemen's friendship with the Alguilo family. Villegas was well aware that Don Enrique Alguilo had publicly opposed extending the campaigns into Patagonia. After some consideration he had pronounced his verdict.

"When you reach Buenos Aires, send young Xiemen to his friends the Alguilos. After an interval, he can slip back to his *estancia*."

Late September 1879.

Marcelo Álvarez braced himself for the inevitable conversation with his mother. He had been home a week, been welcomed as a hero, and been feted by family, friends, and relatives. Xiemen had gone straight to the Alguilo family. They had embraced him as a virtual family member, and had comforted each other at their mutual loss. Marcelo mused that, during all his campaigns, battles, and skirmishes, he had often drawn on untapped reserves of courage. Hopefully these would not desert him now. Marcelo had agonised over Richard's death. This conversation might to some extent salve his conscience.

Marcelo chose the servants' free afternoon. Mother and son sat in chairs in the parlour. Having informed her about the humane way his platoon had treated the *Indio* non-combatants, she bestowed upon him one of her sincere and loving smiles. "But you seem to be on edge, *Hijo*. Is there something you wish to tell me?"

"On our last expedition, mother, the one into Rio Negro, I had an extremely strange experience. I am not even sure if I should tell you of it."

"Marcelo, you know that you have always been my favourite child. There have never been any secrets between us."

Marcelo proceeded to tell her about the skirmish, the running white man being hit, the bravery of Xiemen, the actions of the despicable Jorge, the struggle.

"So, *Hijo*, you risked your own life to prevent the death of a wounded enemy. You could have been killed by that evil Jorge. You behaved like a true Barron. How proud I am to have such a brave and fearless son. Did the wounded white man die?"

Marcelo continued with his full story, up to the singing of *Ad Nostri Monti* and *Shule Aroon*. This caused her to sit up straight with. "Why, *Hijo*, did ye sing that song?"

"Mother, Xiemen told me the wounded man's surname, the name of a proud family of the Wild Geese. Were not the Wild Geese Irish soldiers who went into exile in Europe to fight for the Catholic monarchs?"

"Indeed they were, my son. And tell me, where did the young Indian learn *Ad Nostri Monti*, Marcelo?"

"*Mi Madre*, he learned it from that same white man, his friend and travel companion, the man who played the violin."

"Was the white man American or English or European, *Hijo*?"

"No, *Madre*. He was Irish, originally from County Kilkenny."

"And his name?"

"His name was Richard Barron."

Catherine Álvarez's hand flew to her throat. But just as quickly she steadied her nerves. "Marcelo, Barron is a prominent name in my county. The names Richard and indeed Catherine are common Christian name within my clan. Many Norman-Irish families kept the same names between generation. I am even more proud now that you respected and honoured a distant clan member with a proper funeral."

The moment had arrived. Would Marcelo baulk now and regret it for the rest of his life? He felt a voice within him calling, "Do it. Do not lose courage now." He spoke quietly. "*Mi Madre*, do you forgive me for my platoon taking his life?"

His mother smiled nervously, "Of course, I forgive you. How were you to know who he was? You acted like a chivalrous officer, and unknowingly like a loyal kinsman."

Marcelo paused, then his courage rose again. "Then, *Mi Madre Amada*, (my dear mother) I too will forgive you for anything you choose to reveal to me. But it must be completely your choice."

Now, the look of fear from the mother.

Marcelo spoke. "*Madre*, this Richard Barron, aged thirty-two years of age, had written up a journal. In it he described his early life in county Kilkenny. Xiemen handed it to me, together with this." Marcelo handed her a pocket watch. "Turn it over."

Engraved on its back was the name "Andrew Barron, 1793."

In sheer amazement, Catherine looked from the watch to Marcelo, and then back to the watch. "He had this?" she whispered. "Yes, *Mi Madre*, Xiemen told me that it belonged to Richard's great grandfather, Andrew Barron. Richard's father, also Andrew Barron, gave it to him during their final farewell in Kilkenny before he took the train bound for Wexford, where he would take ship to Australia. He did this to help convince him that he was a true Barron."

Another whispered question. 'Was Richard doubting that he was that?"

"For some reasons, he must have been."

Marcelo's mother sunk deeper into her chair. Once again, her hand moved to her throat. She seemed shrunken, crushed by what she feared he might reveal.

Marcelo sprang to her aid. "*Mi Madre*, are you alright? Should I call a doctor? Can I get you a glass of water."

"No, *Hijo*. Do not call a doctor. But yes, a glass of water. And a glass of whiskey, a large one. And one for yourself. We may well need them."

Catherine had taken a few sips. Marcelo placed his hand on her shoulder. "*Mi Madre Amada*, please only tell me what you wish, and nothing that you may regret later. You have my word that I will never reveal it to a living soul, not to my brother or sister, nor to Xiemen, nor to the Sutton family, to no one. You have given me your word that you will not breathe to a living soul my platoon's part in Richard's death, and that you have forgiven me."

Catherine Álvarez, now ashen faced replied. "Marcelo, *Mi Hijo Amado*, I want to tell you all. I just do not know how to begin."

"*Madre*, read the early part of the journal, written in Richard's own hand. During our long journey homeward, I copied it out in case this original might get lost. It makes for great, although at times, sad reading."

"Let me read it, *Hijo*. You can take a walk in the garden."

With trepidation, and with tears in her eyes, Catherine Álvarez opened the diary. Could she bear to read what most likely was the handwriting of her lost and beloved son? Summoning her own courage, she began. Everything matched her recollections: the small farmhouse behind the pond, the lane, the orchard, the long garden, the fields, Richard's parents, Andrew and Mairead Barron, the neighbours, Castledown chapel, Kilcolman. Her attention was arrested by the description of Richard's near death from cholera; the nurse, and to Catherine's surprise and relief, the dark brown-haired man in the sick room.

"So, Walter had saved our beloved son." Catherine paused. She cried for a little while. Then bravely she continued. Burrane National School. The lessons on the fiddle. Patrick, their school friends, the childhood adventures. It was all there. What came through especially was that Richard had been loved by his foster father and been treated fairly well by his foster mother. What a relief it was to read that.

Catherine found the next section easier to read. Richard's youth, leaving school at fourteen; his good progress on the fiddle; his continued education with Mr. Ford; his growing concern for the poor, the down-trodden, the oppressed, the dispossessed. A son whom any woman could regard with pride. But Catherine also read about Richard's doubts regarding his true parentage; the odd slip by good neighbours, the anonymous gifts, the occasional heartless and vicious comments.

Catherine stopped. The words leaped out at her like a dagger. *'As time progressed, and as I heard more about my aunt Catherine, I became more convinced that she might be my real mother.'*

"So, he virtually knew, and all the time he thought I was in New York. Oh, my poor, beautiful boy. How you must have suffered. What anguish you must have endured. Will you ever forgive me?" Her tears flowed.

But wait. How had her son ended up in Argentina? Catherine had reached the point of the preparations for Richard to emigrate to Australia. Could he have somehow found out that his mother was in Argentina? Virtually impossible. The whole neighbourhood believed that she had gone to New York. The secret was known only to six people. She must read on.

The hand of fate. The force of destiny. The chance meeting with Malcolm Sutton had changed everything. A new life, land, home, family. How fortunate Richard had been. She read of the deep and undying friendship with Malcolm; the almost paternal affection and care of David Sutton; the virtual fraternal bonds with the Alguilos, and with Xiemen and Taquia. Richard had obviously grown to be a beautiful young man whom destiny had treated so kindly. Could she have offered him anything even approaching that in Ireland? Impossible.

She read about his musical talents, his skill with horses. Talents derived from the Barrons. But what shone out most of all was his love of Argentina. That same land had blessed both of them with its bounty, its beauty, its benevolence. Catherine Álvarez put down the diary. She wept profusely.

Marcelo Álvarez entered the parlour. Silently he placed his arms around the shoulders of his mother. Marcelo held her tightly in his embrace. After about two minutes, she managed to speak.

"Marcelo, I cannot at this moment express all my feelings after reading Richard's diary. The one feeling which I can express is one of relief. For over thirty years I have had to keep all this a secret. I feel that a gigantic weight has been lifted from my heart and my soul. Now I finally have discovered what happened to Richard. You, *Mi Hijo Amado,* have been the instrument of the release of my dark and troubling secret and the revelation of his beautiful life and heroic death."

Early October 1879.

The travelling party left their hotel in Pilar early morning. The woman's son drove the gig. By his side sat the young Indian whom he had befriended. Seated in the gig were the driver's mother and her young personal Italian maid.

The young Indian turned round, "Doña Álvarez, I felt that early morning, when the sun begins to emerge from the horizon, is the best hour for you to witness the emerging beauty and glory of the pampas. It, together with sunset, were the hours which Richard and I most enjoyed. Your witnessing of what he loved may help you come to terms with his happy and fulfilling life and his glorious death."

Catherine answered. "Xiemen, you know that I still have not come to terms with it. Maybe I never will. After all, did I not abandon him as a child?"

Marcelo had to speak. "The pampas inspired Richard to write his poetry."

"His poetry, Marcelo. What do you mean? You never told me this."

"*Mi Madre,* I decided to leave it until now. I will explain about it later. But remember, did I too not have a hand in his death? After all, he died fighting against my platoon."

Xiemen felt compelled to speak. "Doña Álvarez, I suggested that we make this journey so that I could show you both not what Richard lost, but what he gained in my ancestral lands of the pampas. We will reach that small hill in about fifteen minutes. I suggest that we pray to our gods. You, Doña Álvarez, Marcelo, and Anina, to your Christian God. I will pray to the god of the pampas."

The four sat down on the hillock. Xiemen spoke. "Breathe in deeply. Feel the gentle spring breeze through all your body. It is the breath of the god of the pampas. Breathe in through your nose to smell the scent of the spring flowers, his perfume. See the beginning of the sun's orb, as it slowly emerges from that far away hill. The sun is the messenger of that same god. Look up at the stars, what we Charrúas called the fine moons. They are the eyes of the god of the pampas. Sometimes when he weeps, be it for joy or for sorrow, they replenish the pampas with life saving rains.

"Yes, we all weep for Richard. I weep with sorrow for his death, but I also weep with joy for his beautiful life. You must learn to do the same. The pampas sun bestows life. It refreshes, inspires, adds radiance. Look at the fading full moon. It will energise your spirit. The fine moons, the sun, the full moon, the tears of the gods, his breath blowing lightly over the pampas grass, these are part too of Charrúa spiritual life. They inspired Richard to write his poetry."

A pause of about five minutes. Marcelo broke the silence. "Have you chosen the two poems to read to us, Xiemen?"

"Indeed I have"

Xiemen paused for a minute. He let his listeners take in the unrivalled beauty of the emerging dawn. "I will read for you the poem which Richard composed with young Sergio Alguilo."

Xiemen stood up, and declaimed the full poem to the pampas. On occasions, he glanced at the countenance of Doña Álvarez. Her tenseness had relaxed, albeit so little. Xiemen could detect a few tears in her eyes, but he sensed that they were not solely tears of sorrow. "Now, Marcelo, I hand over to you."

Marcelo stood up. He showed Catherine a small booklet titled, *The Poetry of Richard Barron, 1847 to 1879.* He explained, "Richard wrote his poems in a special notebook. They were with his journal.

Two weeks ago, I arranged for a publisher to publish them. I took the liberty of writing the declaration. *Dedicated to Richard's good parents, and to his ever-true friend, the Charrúa Xiemen.* I will read to you my favourite one."

"The rise and fall of the sun, the metronome of my days.
The sacred hour of evening drapes the sky
With ribbons of gold and the red and orange of sunlight.
The sinking orb darkens the clouds,
Tracing shapes of rocks and trees and angels' wings across the
heavens.
And the stars like a shy child come faintly at first.
Then crowd the sky in a rich palette of twinkling light."
"I stood to watch the rising sun, a sheen of gold in eastern
skies,
With scattering trails of darkened clouds, and cotton puffs in
snowy white,
And then his majesty the sun, with gilded beams for bugle call
Ascended to the lightening sky, and spread benevolence over
all."

Xiemen walked across to Catherine. "You are now smiling a little, Doña Álvarez."

"Yes, Xiemen. I feel more at peace than I have felt for some weeks, since Marcelo rightly broke the story to me. But is it right for me to feel this way?"

Xiemen replied, "*Señora*, if you and Richard had remained in Ireland during the Great Famine, I dread to think what your fate would have been. Richard and I witnessed deadly famine and fever.

We saw how they can change even good people, divide families, have members cast out. Destiny brought you both to our land, you to recover your life and be rewarded with the happy life you have lived here; Richard to find his own *Igua,* his own heaven, under the skies of the pampas. I hand you the collection of his poems, inspired by the resplendent vista which is now opening before us. In time you should read them. But for now, maybe you should read here his thoughts written down the night before the battle. It is truly an ode to a life well lived. Then read his final message to you."

"To me?"

"Yes, *Señor*a. Like his premonition of death, he must have foreseen that some day destiny might bring you to read it."

Catherine read Richard's final written words. Lifting her head from the page, the three people observed her face breaking into a smile.

Xiemen ventured with, "You see, *Señor*a, we Charrúas always felt that death is a phase natural and worthy. The death of a good person nourishes other living human beings in the constant cycle of life. Richard will be immortalised in the stories and in the memories of the Mapuche and the Tehuelche tribes, although sadly not among my Charrúa people. The young Irish hero who gladly gave his life in their cause. He will live forever."

Marcelo pointed to the heavens. "Xiemen, do you see that strange formation of a cloud over there?"

"Marcelo. maybe to you, it is just a cloud. A horizontal cloud attached to a smaller vertical one. We Charrúas believe that even the clouds send us messages. I sense that it represents Richard, riding his horse across the pampas of *Igua*. He is sending his message of love and peace to all of us."

The party had reached the outskirts of Buenos Aires. Catherine spoke. "Xiemen, thank you for what you have done today. Truly I feel more at peace now. Like your god of the pampas, I will weep for Richard. But they will be a mixture of tears of sorrow and of joy. Tears of sorrow for the son I lost, not once, but twice. A noble, brave, and beautiful son, who died so young. But he died fighting for a cause dear to his heart, a martyr. My tears of joy will flow for the bountiful life God gave him. A life of beauty, fulfilment, surrounded by love from people who welcomed him into their homes and hearts. And I will weep with pride for the care which you and he bestowed to the starving and fevered Indians.

"Richard was the child of Walter's and my love at that time. We could not have asked for a better son. Walter saved him to live his beautiful life. You, Marcelo, by bravely disarming that hideous Jorge, saved him to enter unblemished into his eternal reward. But what did I give him?"

Xiemen summoned up his courage. '*Señora* Álvarez, You were the first to give him the gift of life. And by handing him to the care of Andrew and Mairead, you gave him the gift of immortality."

Xiemen and Francisco were nearing the end of their journey to the *estancia*. The final stage comprised the route taken by Malcolm and

Richard when they had first brought the two boys there. Francisco, now twenty, had been granted leave from Don Enrique's office. Both of their hearts were heavy, but time would be the great healer. A glorious mid-October day.

They paused on the summit of the hillock. Xiemen spoke, "Look, Francisco. The house and the five hundred acres which Ricardo had left to me and my family in his will."

"Yes, Xiemen. It will be a haven for your family, and, we hope, for your own children when they arrive. A haven for the last of the Charrúas. Richard wanted to give back to the Indians a tiny part of what was taken from them. Xiemen, destiny brought your father and mother to these pampas. Even if you represent only one family of the survivors, your farm will signify that the proud, noble, and unvanquished Charrúa tribe perpetuates itself. And there too we will perpetuate the memory of that generous, and brave son of Ireland, Richard Barron."

Francisco spoke, "There it is, scene of so many wonderful holidays. With you, with Taquia, with David, Malcolm, and Richard. I remember the first time we arrived on this hill. I was only twelve and was so excited."

Francisco could not continue, unable to contain his tears. Xiemen moved astride him. "What an idiot I am, Xiemen. A grown man, crying like a child. I am sorry."

"There is no need, *Amigo* Francisco. Let your tears flow. My own have flowed on many a night. It helps us to heal." Francisco felt his friend's arm on his shoulder. "Look, Francisco, someone is riding up the hill."

"Xiemen, is it Malcolm?"

"I do not think so. He looks much older. Dark skin, stocky build, long tangled hair, old clothes. Francisco, I cannot believe it. It is Don Sacando."

Francisco was mystified. "Xiemen, did he know we were arriving? How could he have?"

"Maybe he did, Francisco. Maybe he did."

The *gaucho* halted about five yards from them, gazing intently into Francisco's misty eyes. "You are crying, *Joven*. You are crying for Ricardo."

Francisco wiped his eyes. "Yes, I am, Don Sacando, but how do you know what happened to him?"

Don Sacando took time to reply, and spoke slowly. "The first time I met him, *Joven*, here on this *estancia*, I foresaw that a tragic fate awaited him. I did not know how, where, or when. As I got to know him more over the years, I became certain that his fate, Xiemen, *Indio Joven*, was linked to the fate of your people. During the last full moon, one night I lay on the pampas floor, halfway between sleep and waking. I saw Ricardo lying and bleeding profusely in front of a large rock. You and a young officer were tending him. When you sang to him, I saw his beatific smile, as his soul was leaving his body. I think that he smiled at me, for I always felt that I was his *padrino*."

Xiemen asked, "And where, Don Sacando, did his spirit go to?"

"Where do you think it has gone, *Joven*?"

"I like to think that the great Charrúa spirit Tupa will welcome him to the green and open plains of my own people. There Richard will enjoy the peace of the hunt of the deer and the ostrich. Francisco, only Richard's body has departed. His Irish soul, his Charrúa spirit, are still with us."

Don Sacando declared, "You are right, *Indio Joven.* Ricardo's soul will look down upon Ireland, his land of birth. But it will anchor over the pampas with their unique beauty, their rivers, their streams, their trees, their grasses, animals and birds. His beloved pampas, nurtured by the constellations of stars, the paternal moon, the rain bearing clouds, the radiant sun. His spirit is now riding on his celestial steed in yonder heavens. Dry your eyes, *Joven* Creole. Would you like to add anything?"

"Yes, I would, Don Sacando. I would like to recite the chorus from the poem which Ricardo, a bard on the pampas, and my brother Sergio composed."

Francisco sat straight on his horse, and declaimed

"Porque la pampa es mi madre. Miro a su belleza
incomparable.
Me abraza, me acaricia, me envolve. Me sustenta, me protégé,
me guia.
Si, los humores de la pampa cambian, pero nuestro amor
mutuo es para siempre. "

Don Sacando was silent. Xiemen and Francisco took this as the sign for them to ride down the hill. On reaching the bottom, they turned round to observe the *gaucho* still on the summit. Slowly he raised his hands to the heavens. "Is he raising his hands in farewell to us, Xiemen?"

"I do not think so, Francisco. Rather do I think that he is raising them to acknowledge Ricardo Barron."

Epilogue.

Late August 1918.

The young soldier tied his hired horse and trap to the sycamore tree, having driven them the seven miles from Kilkenny. After the final turn, he had been greeted two hundred metres ahead by the spectacle of a fine white two storey farmhouse. A number of well-crafted outbuildings, built of quarried stone, formed an L shape. Was he in the correct place? His grandmother had told him that she was brought up in a mud cabin behind a pond. The soldier had driven into a lane. Yes, she had mentioned a lane. And yes, there was was the pond, but no mud cabin behind it.

The soldier knocked on the door once, twice. A voice replied with what sounded like a "Come in." Facing him in the hallway was a tastefully crafted wooden staircase. He turned left into the kitchen. To the right of the fire were wooden shelves holding crockery. Below them was a cupboard. To the left of the fire was a large cupboard, probably for food. Large pieces of cured bacon hung from a beam suspended from the ceiling. In front of the fire was a rocking chair.

Dozing on the chair was an old man. The soldier coughed gently, waking him. "Pardon me, Sir, but is this the Barron home?" On turning round, the old man beheld a rather tall young man of somewhat brown complexion, clad in a light raincoat. Drowsiness, puzzlement, even fear lit the former's countenance.

"What did you ask?"

"I asked is this the Barron home?" The visitor sounded as if he was unused to English.

"Who are you? If it be money you are looking for, take what little there is in that drawer. Then get to hell out of here."

The soldier replied. "Sir, I am not looking for money. I will not harm you. But, am I speaking to Mr. Patrick Barron?"

"Yes, you are, young man. Who the devil are you? Where are you from, and what the hell do you want?"

"My name is Vincento Álvarez, from Buenos Aires, Argentina. My grandmother was Catherine Barron, who I believe was your aunt."

"My aunt Catherine Barron? She went to New York. No, that was all lies. A dark family secret for years. She went to Argentina. Is that where you are from. Sorry, I am all confused."

The soldier spoke. "Sir, I left a few valuable things and some drink in my trap. I need to get them."

The old man shook his finger. "You left things in your trap. That is bad. We get thieving tinkers around here. They might even steal your horse. Go and get them. Give your horse some hay from the haggard and some water. That is if you know what hay is. Hurry. My aunt Catherine. Young Richard's mother."

Vincento did as bidden. Maybe now the door would be barred to him. But no. A smiling Patrick Barron was leaning on the half door, and extended his hand. "Vincento Álvarez, please excuse my early rudeness. I was confused. Welcome to the home of your grandmother. She left here in the black '47. Take off your coat and hang it on that wall hook." A nervous pause. "You are a soldier. In the British army?"

"No, Mr. Barron, in the Italian army. My mother Anabella is Italian. She encouraged me to go and fight for her homeland against the invading Germans. I was wounded at the battle of Piave, but only a slight limp now. I am on four weeks leave. My grandmother Catherine and my father Marcelo told me years ago, that if ever I got the chance, I must visit my ancestral home in Ireland."

The old man smiled. "Well, son, a wounded man should not be standing. Come and sit down in the kitchen."

Now relaxed, the soldier spoke, "Mr Barron, I am so happy to be here. But the old home is gone. What happened?"

"Let me explain, son. We became owners of our original farm in 1890. Captain Saunders decided to move to England in 1912, so his estate was divided up. My son Andrew got twenty acres of his land. I myself married in 1875. My wife Joanna passed on five years ago."

"Around 1900, Andrew felt we needed a new house. So, he helped the builder build this one. He is getting married in October. Maybe you can come to the wedding. His sister Margaret will get married on Saint Stephen's Day. Thank God for that. It means I won't have to put up with two women in this house. My other daughter Catherine is in New York."

Patrick Barron continued. "Vincento, you can call me Uncle Patrick, by the way. Tell me about your grandmother. Do you know her full story, why she really left Ireland?"

"I think I do, Uncle Patrick."

Patrick sighed. "A terribly sad story. She wasn't good enough for the Drummonds. I think that Walter Drummond would have deserted her and their son completely, only for my father Andrew Barron. He, shall we say, persuaded young Drummond to provide for the boy until he reached fourteen, and pay for Catherine's passage to a new life in your country. Vincento, did your grandmother tell you this story?"

"No, Uncle Patrick, she never mentioned it to me. I was only ten when she died. My father Marcelo told me about it some years later. He had also found out more about her son, Richard."

Vincento related all he knew about his mother's good life in Buenos Aires. He added that of her three children, one son had become a lawyer, her daughter had married a doctor, and that his own father Marcelo had earlier pursued a military career, but he did not agree with the campaigns against the Indians of Patagonia, so he had resigned his army commission and had later become a university lecturer. Marcelo had died in 1912.

Patrick reminisced, "Yes, Catherine wrote to my parents saying that she had married well, to a man called Álvarez. You see, son, only my family, the Drummonds, the parish priest and Mr. Townsend knew that she had gone to Buenos Aires. Everyone else believed she had gone to New York."

Vincento was puzzled. "But what about her letters. Wouldn't the stamp and postmark have shown where she was?"

"Ah, Catherine got around that one. She always sent her letters to an old nun in the Presentation Convent in Waterford. The nun sent them to us in a new envelope with an Irish stamp. The letters stopped after the old nun died."

Vincento trod warily. "And the boy, Richard. What happened to him? Where did he go?"

Patrick replied. "He went to Australia. Wasn't it the best place for him. He kept in touch with us for a few years, but then we lost touch. You see, son, he wrote that he was always moving around and could not give us an address. His last letter arrived in 1875, but I have kept most of his letters. Sadly, I will go to my grave not knowing what happened to Richard, my cousin and foster brother."

Vincento agonised. Should he shatter the old man's illusions with the truth? Vincento would need all his courage for the task ahead. "Uncle Patrick, I can tell you what happened to Richard. It is a proud and noble story which his family should know and celebrate."

"But how would you know. Did Richard find out about his real mother and write to her?"

"Uncle Patrick, rest assured. Richard never found that out. Where are Andrew and Margaret now?"

"Vincento, they are up in the fields, stacking the corn."

"Can I call them, please?"

"Certainly, son. Go out to the barn. Pick up the big stick. Bang the tin roof three times. That is their summons."

Andrew and Margaret Barron entered the kitchen. The former was quite handsome, well built, and with the Barron light brown hair. Margaret possessed a forehead and nose similar to those of Vincento's grandmother, light brown hair, and pretty features. Following effusive greetings, Margaret led them all to the parlour. Vincento noted the lovely black Kilkeny marble fireplace. A sofa, two armchairs, a piano, and a glass press were the main furnishings. Vincento produced a bottle of whiskey and a bottle of sherry.

Patrick instructed Andrew, "*A Mhic*, pour us men a glass of whiskey each and a sherry for herself."

Margaret protested. "Father, you know I seldom drink."

"Daughter, You will today. Our cousin has come all the way from Argentina. Accept his generosity."

Margaret handed him Richard's letters, still in their original envelopes. Vincento was suspicious, "Uncle Patrick, why were all these letters posted in London or Liverpool, and not in Australia?"

"Vincento, Richard did not really trust the Australian postal service. He used to give his letters to a friend, or an acquaintance, or anyone travelling to England, especially when sending money home. After two years he had sent back the money which my father had given him for his fare, with extra money. A very honest lad."

Vincento trod warily. "You know, there could be another reason."

"What reason, son?"

Vincento took the plunge. "Maybe Richard never went to Australia, and did the same things with his letters in another country."

Patrick held up his hand. "But where would he have gone? He would not have deceived my parents."

"Uncle Patrick, do you recognise this watch?"

Patrick accepted it. "My father had one like it, his grandfather's watch. A family heirloom. He gave it to Richard the morning he left home."

"Turn it over, please." Patrick looked at the watch, amazed. *Andrew Barron, 1793.* Father, son, and daughter sat upright.

Patrick queried. "Young man, where did you get this. Did Richard go to Argentina after Australia? Did he find out about his mother and go looking for her?"

Andrew added. "Did he go from Australia to Argentina as a shearer?"

Margaret asked. "Did he go there looking for a lovely Argentine wife?"

Vincento slowly moved his eyes to each adult in turn. "My answer to all your questions is No. The truth is, Richard Barron never went to Australia He went straight to Argentina from Wexford."

Flabergasted, Patrick persisted, "But that cannot be true. I remember clearly the morning he left. My father drove him to Kilkenny. He put Richard on the train to New Ross. Richard had his ticket for Australia."

Vincento quietly asked. "Did he, sir?" A silence one could cut with a knife. Patrick grappled to remember. "Now that I think of it, he did not. He was to buy his ticket in Wexford."

Andrew Barron grabbed Vincento's arm. "Did Richard meet his mother in Argentina, even by accident? My father needs to know."

Vincento calmed them. "Uncle Patrick, Andrew, Margaret, such a meeting could not have happened. Richard all his life thought that his so-called aunt Catherine Barron, whom he suspected to be his natural mother, was in New York."

Patrick Barron grabbed his cane, rising a little from his chair. "I cannot believe a word of this. Richard would not have tricked my parents and Father Aylward. He bought his ticket to Australia in Wexford. That is where he went. Is it wanting to fill us with lies that you wish?"

Margaret intervened. "Then, father, how do you explain Vincento having your great grandfather's watch?"

"Easily, Margaret. Just because it has the same name and date on it does not mean that it is the same watch." Patrick brandished his cane threateningly, "Young man, whoever you are, I demand that you leave this house immediately."

Vincento Álvarez persisted, "Mr. Barron, Richard tricked no one. When he made his decision to migrate to the Argentine, he handed Father Rossiter, a priest in Wexford, the eight pounds donated by the diocese of Ossary towards his fare. He instructed the priest to send it to them after a year."

Andrew and Margaret stood up, the latter speaking. "Father, you have just told us that he paid back to your own father the money he owed him. He did not trick anyone."

Andrew added. "And let us hear no more about our cousin leaving this house immediately. He has not even seen the ancestral farm or shared a meal with us. As owner of this house, I insist on that."

Vincento handed Patrick a bag, instructing him to open it. "A fiddle. God be praised! Is this Richard's fiddle, given to him by Colum O'Leary, the one I sang to?"

"Look at its back, sir." A signature. *Richard Barron.*

"Where did you get this, son?"

Vincento looked at all three of them. "That is what I want to tell you all, if you will let me tell Richard Barron's true story."

Patrick Barron stood up, stretching out his hand. "Cousin Vincento Álvarez, can you please forgive me. Like the apostle Thomas, I doubted you. You have brought back to life the foster brother whom I loved. How can I thank you?"

Tea and scones were served by Margaret. Vincento began his story, as told to him by his father. The chance meeting in the Selskar Arms, Malcolm Sutton's charming and friendly personality, his offer to Richard of a new life. "It was almost as if Malcolm wove a spell on Richard, but one which gave Richard a good and happy life."

"Was Richard attracted to the idea of Argentina, then?" asked Andrew. "No, Andrew. I do not think it was so much Argentina. If Malcolm had offered a life in the USA, New Zealand, South Africa, or especially Australia, Richard would have accepted it. Father Rossiter's advice helped him to make the final decision."

A description of Richard's life on the pampas followed. Vincento now described the strong friendship with the Alguilo family, especially with young Francisco and Catalina. On his recounting of Malcolm's courting of and especially winning Catalina, adding that this did not cause any friction between both young lads. He moved on to describing Malcolm's serious illness, Richard's unflinching support of his friend. Vincento progressed to describing Richard's growing friendship with Xiemen, his steeping himself in Indian and Charrúa lore. His three listeners were appalled to hear the harrowing story of the fate of the Charrúa people.

Margaret was curious. "Were there any women in Richard's life?"

Vincento reflected. "I believe there were, but nothing really serious. He always enjoyed the dances, had a few dalliances. Uncle Patrick, does that sound like the Richard you knew?"

Patrick laughed, "Indeed it does, lad. He always treated girls with great respect. They felt safe with him. You see, Richard was quite religious."

"Yes, I am sure that Xiemen said the same thing too."

Margaret was ruminating. "You know, Vincento, Richard's story might make a good novel. Did he leave any writing?"

"Margaret, he certainly did. When he and Xiemen reached Patagonia, he began writing a journal. That is where I found much of my information."

Patrick sat up "Where is that journal now. Do you have it with you?"

"Indeed I do, uncle Patrick. I will show it to you after my story. The next part will be the most difficult for me."

Patrick declared. "Then we all need a top up of whiskey. Andrew, do your duty."

The whiskey was poured. Vincento sensed that his audience had already surmised that Richard's story would end in tragedy. His narration moved from the marriage of Malcolm and Catalina to Richard and Xiemen hearing about the planned campaigns against the

Indians. "It is at this point that the fortunes of Richard and my father Marcelo begin to meet. Do you want me to continue?"

Andrew answered. "Yes, please, cousin. We must hear the whole story."

"Uncle Patrick, did Richard have a sympathy for the hungry, the down-trodden, the dispossessed?"

"Indeed he did, lad, right from his early boyhood."

Patrick related some incidents. "I have reason to believe that he may have become involved in a plot to at least frighten a landlord." He concluded with the story of the pikes, and the words, "A brave lad was our Richard, always ready to help the dispossessed. I was the cautious and careful one."

Vincento now moved to the story of his own father, Marcelo. His example to his soldiers about not killing Indian civilians, but his limited sympathy for them. Vincento contrasted this with Richard's and Xiemen's mission of mercy during the plague-like summer of 1878 and '79. Vincento concluded with, "Of all Catherine Barron's children, Richard is my absolute hero. You should all be proud that this small farm in Ireland produced such a man."

Vincento continued his narration. "You can read in his diary all about Richard's and Xiemen's journey into Patagonia, their time on the Franciscan mission, and their expedition to the Andes. By early 1879, General Roca had virtually defeated the Indians. My father expressed his wish to Colonel Villegas that they would stop at the Rio Negro, but Villegas ordered them to cross the river. On their return from the Andes expedition, Richard made a short retreat at the mission. He might have had a premonition, so he made his peace with God. Andrew, can I please have a small drop more. I am near the end."

Vincento's voice faltered somewhat. The Indians' conference, the opposing forces preparing for an encounter; Richard's decision to fight.

Andrew interjected with, "So, you had two brothers, well, half-brothers, fighting on opposite sides."

"I am afraid so, Andrew. But you must read Richard's final thoughts written the night before the battle. It is a beautiful piece of writing." Vincento's account of the battle had become part of the Álvarez's family lore.

Andrew stated, "This kind of thing often happened in the American Civil War. But in this case, neither brother even knew of the other's existence."

"But," added Margaret, "Your father too proved himself a hero. At risk to his own life, he tackled that cruel and evil Jorge. This enabled Richard to receive the sacrament of extreme unction. He saved Xiemen's life. He gave Richard a Christian burial, took care of and protected Xiemen."

Patrick Barron concluded with "Both men proved to be true Barrons. They lived up to their proud military heritage. I feel so proud of my foster brother and of your own good father, Vincento."

Vincento reached into his bag. "Uncle Patrick, the time has come for me to hand you the part of Richard which will live forever, his journal. Here it is. I have brought it home."

Patrick Barron was almost in tears. "I cannot believe it. It is in Richard's own lovely copperplate handwriting. We will keep it in the glass press, with a lock. It will never leave this house."

Margaret placed her hand on his shoulder, looking down at the diary. "So, if I, or one of my children or grandchildren want to write a novel about Richard's life, we will have to come here. Will we always be welcome, Andrew?"

"Of course you will, unless one of my own decide to write it first." Andrew looked upwards, "Richard Barron, born of our land, fine horseman, musician, master of languages, South American hero, defender of the dispossessed, the infirm, and the starving, pray for us all as you smile down upon us."

A cup of tea after supper. Patrick took the initiative, "Cousin Vincento, you will stay with us for a couple of days, won't you. You will get to meet some of the old neighbours who remember Richard."

"Indeed I will, uncle. I have one question. What happened to the Drummonds?"

"Ah, the Drummonds. Walter and his wife had no children. Stephen went to Australia, bought a farm, married, and had some children. He always felt that Walter should have married Catherine. Over the years, he and Walter lost touch. Sadly, their line died out. Poetic justice, one might say. The Drummond farm is now owned by strangers."

Andrew spoke. "I am reading in the journal that Richard did not have a farewell wake."

"No wake, son? He must have had one." A pause. "Ah, I remember. He did not. What was the reason? I think it was because he was leaving a few weeks after the murder of the landlord's agent, Mr. O'Keefe. The whole district was in quiet down."

Patrick sat up, as if inspired, "We will give him a wake."

Andrew stared at him. "Is it madness has come upon you?"

Patrick held up both hands. "No, son, I am not mad. We will wake our family hero. We will invite the neighbours who remember Richard. Vincento, you will tell them the story of his life and death in Argentina. We will have music, songs, story-telling, barn dancing. You two men can clear it out. Vincento, you will play the fiddle for the dancing. Margaret, you will play the piano and sing. Brush up on those songs from *Maritana* and *The Bohemian Girl.* I might sing a couple of Thomas Moore's ballads. Margaret, you and young Mrs. Mahony will prepare some food."

Vincento offered. "I will buy some drink, uncle Patrick."

"Aren't you the generous lad. Sure, it will be a great night. Richard, my foster brother, we will do you proud almost fifty years late."

Andrew had the final word. "I will support this wake provided the next day or the day after we will visit the family cemetery. Ireland and Argentina will meet there. Is that alright with you, my father?"

Patrick grasped his upper arm. "Of course it is, *A Mhic.* Doesn't a burial usually follow the day or two after the wake?"

The small group entered the cemetery, sited about two hundred yards from the road. As they gathered around the family headstone, a car drew up outside the gate. An old man, well dressed, walked through the gate, accompanied by a young man in British military uniform.

Patrick Barron recognised them. "It is Mr. Arthur Poe and his son Major Henry. Arthur and Richard were friends. Richard taught him how to ride a pony. Mr. Poe, a sincere welcome. Can I introduce our cousin, Vincento Álvarez, all the way from Argentina."

Arthur Poe replied, "Patrick, and please call me Arthur, I do hope we are not intruding. I heard from one of our workmen that all of you neighbours were gathering here. I want to pay my respects to the memory of my old friend Richard Barron. I hear he was a real hero in Argentina."

Patrick was honoured. "Delighted that you both have come. As you can see, Vincento is also in the army, fighting for the Italians."

Arthur Poe shook his hand. "And Patrick, after the ceremony you and your family are invited to our house, Culloney House, for drinks and Sunday dinner. My son Major Henry, has been fighting on the Western Front. He and Vincento may wish to exchange stories. Thank God, it looks as if this terrible war might soon reach its end."

By now, Andrew had joined them. "We are about to begin. Are you ready, Vincento?"

Father James Gorman read the prayers, followed by a brief and moving eulogy about the Richard he had known. Having devoted forty years of his life as a priest in darkest Africa, he had retired on his brother Gerard's farm. Andrew read the final paragraphs from

Richard's journal. Vincento played on his fiddle *Scenes that are Brightest* and *Home to our Mountains.*

Vincento delivered the final words. "Some of you have asked me where Richard now lies. For about twenty years he lay where my father Marcelo and Xiemen had buried him, under the Patagonian sky. However, in 1903 my father achieved his long-held dream and wish, as promised to his mother. The British had by now built us an excellent railway system. My father Marcelo, I myself, Xiemen, an undertaker and his assistant travelled to Richard's grave to exhume his bones. We placed them in a coffin, loaded it onto our train, and brought it back to the Sutton *estancia.*"

Vincento concluded with, "We knew that Richard would have wanted to lie under his beloved pampas, those lands whose beauty, serenity, and timeless magical spell he captured so eloquently in his writings. We buried him in a corner of one of the fields of his farm, which he had left to Xiemen. Xiemen is still alive, surrounded now by, I think, eight grandchildren. Every year I try to make a kind of pilgrimage there. I also meet Malcolm and Catalina's son David, his wife, and their children."

"Finally, to conclude this short ceremony, as a soldier I felt it right to quote a text from that great English war poet Rupert Brooke. Rupert will forgive me for changing two words." Vincento raised his voice, *"There is one corner of a foreign field that is forever ... Castledown.* Richard Barron, brother, cousin, friend, and hero, you lie today *in hearts at peace, under an Argentine heaven."*

A lone blackbird sang from a tree. A few cows in a field nearby moved a few paces. A couple of sheep bleated to attract their young. The sun emerged from behind a cloud. The landscape of Castledown, County Kilkenny, Ireland, lay bathed in its early autumn radiance…

Sources.

'The Yola Sub-Culture of south County Wexford, Ireland.' Unpublished paper by John A. Clancy, MLS. Presented at the ISAANZ biennial conference of Irish Studies, held at the Australian Catholic University, Melbourne. December 2023.

'Nineteenth Century Irish Emigration to Argentina.' Text of lecture given by Professor David Barnwell, Department of Spanish, National University of Ireland, Maynooth. Ireland. Lecture presented at the Department of Spanish and Portuguese, Columbia University, New York.

'Nineteenth century Irish Emigration to, and Settlement in, Argentina.' MA Geography Thesis by Patrick McKenna, Saint Patrick's College, Maynooth, Ireland. 1994

'Father Fahy: A Biography of Anthony Dominic Fahy, O.P, Irish Missionary in Argentina (1805 -1871).' Author - Monsignor James M. Usher. Publisher: Talleres Graficos de Guillermo Kraft Ltda. 1951.

'Priests and People in pre-Famine Ireland, 1780 – 1845.' Author: S. J. Connolly. Publisher: Pelgrave Macmillan. 1982.

'The Irish in the Argentine Republic: John Cullen's 1888 Report.' Author: Edward Walsh. Source: Collectanea Hibernica, 2001. No. 43 (2001), pp. 239-246. Publisher: Franciscan Province of Ireland.

'Ireland and Latin America: A Cultural History.' Author: Edmundo Murray. 2010. Appendix C: Letters of the Murphy Family of Wexford and Argentina. Letters to Martin Murphy, 1844 to 1881.

'Mirrors: Stories of Almost Everything.' Author: Edwardo Galeano. Translator: Mark Fried. Publisher in the USA: Nation Books. 2009.

'Mitos, Leyendas, y Tradiciones de la Banda Oriental.' Author: Gonzalo Abella. Publisher: Betum San Ediciones, Almirón 5081. 2001.

'Los *Indios* de Uruguay'. Author: Renzo Pi Hugarte. Publisher: Editorial Mapfre, S.A. 1993.

'Diario de Viaje de la Expedicion de los Rifleros'. Author: John Murray Thomas. Publisher: Museo Histórico Regional de Gaiman, Chubut, Argentina in 'Camwy, No. 10. Noviembre 1985.

'The Conquest of the Desert: Argentina's Indigenous Peoples and the Battle for History.' Editor: Carolyn Larson. Publisher: University of New Mexico Press. 2020.

Full text of ' A Glossary, with some pieces of poetry, of the old dialect of the English colony in the baronies of Forth and Bargy, county of Wexford, Ireland". Compiler: Jacob Poole. Publisher: William Barnes. 1867.

'Gauchos and the Vanishing Frontier' by Richard W. Slata. 1983. University of Nebraska Press.

'El Pais Charrúa' by Eduardo F. Acosta Y Lara, 2002. Fundacion Bank-Boston. Libreria Linardi Y Risso.